OUT OF THE ASHES

THE ENDING SERIES BOOK THREE

LINDSEY POGUE
LINDSEY FAIRLEIGH

Editing by Sarah Kolb-Williams
www.kolbwilliams.com

Book cover design by Molly Phipps
We Got You Covered Book Design

L2 Books
101 W American Canyon Rd. Ste. 508 – 262
American Canyon, CA 94503

978-1-723815-06-5

OTHER NOVELS BY THE LINDSEYS

THE ENDING SERIES

The Ending Beginnings: Omnibus Edition

After The Ending

Into The Fire

Out Of The Ashes

Before The Dawn

World Before: A Collection of Stories

NOVELS BY LINDSEY POGUE

A SARATOGA FALLS LOVE STORY

Whatever It Takes

Nothing But Trouble

Told You So

FORGOTTEN LANDS

Dust And Shadow

Borne of Sand and Scorn

Wither and Ruin (TBR)

Borne of Earth and Ember (TBR)

NOVELS BY LINDSEY FAIRLEIGH

ECHO TRILOGY

Echo in time

Resonance

Time Anomaly

Dissonance

Ricochet Through Time

KAT DUBOIS CHRONICLES

Ink Witch

Outcast

Underground

Soul Eater

Judgement

Afterlife

ATLANTIS LEGACY

Sacrifice of the Sinners

Legacy of the Lost

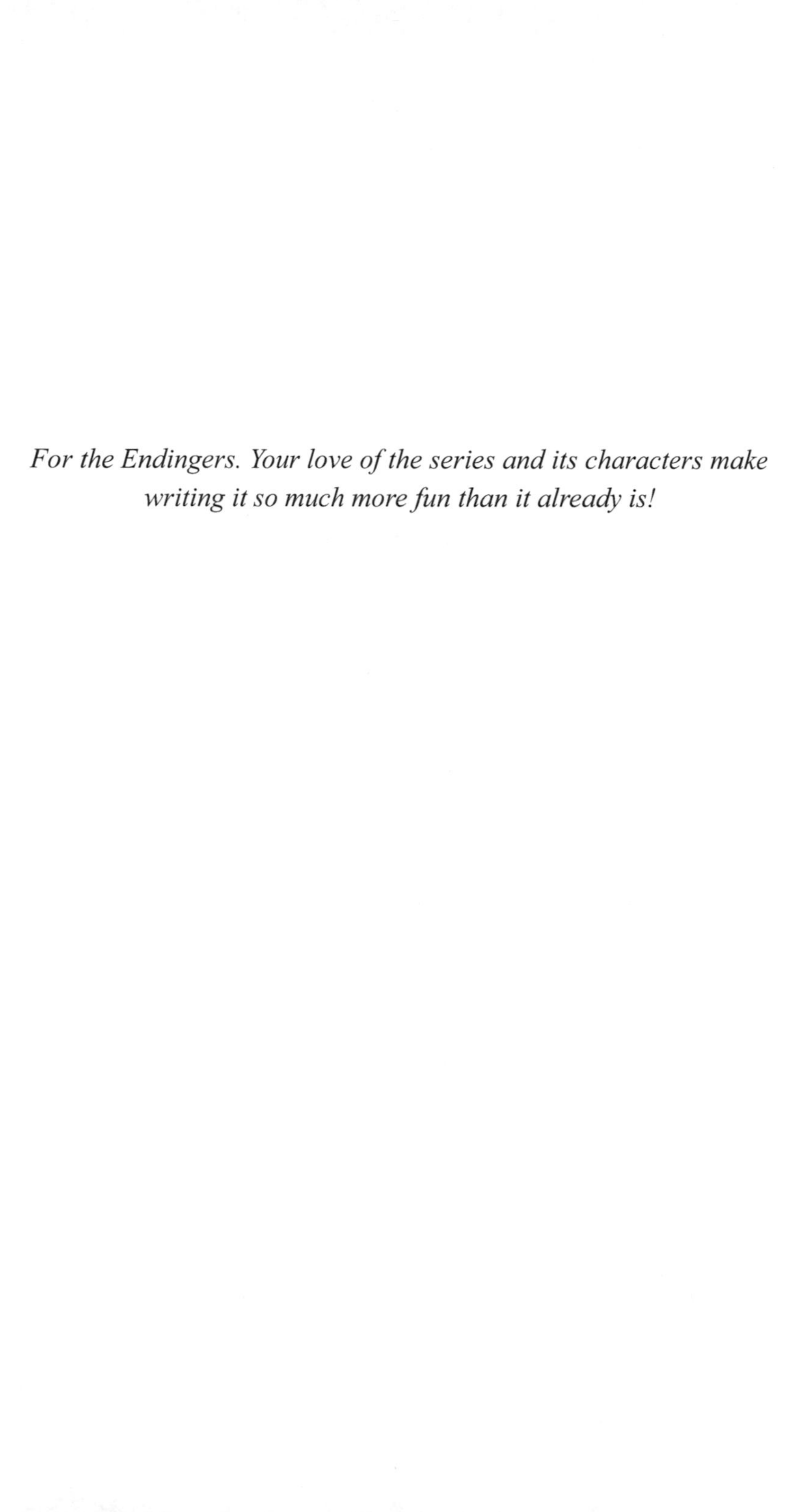

For the Endingers. Your love of the series and its characters make writing it so much more fun than it already is!

MAPS

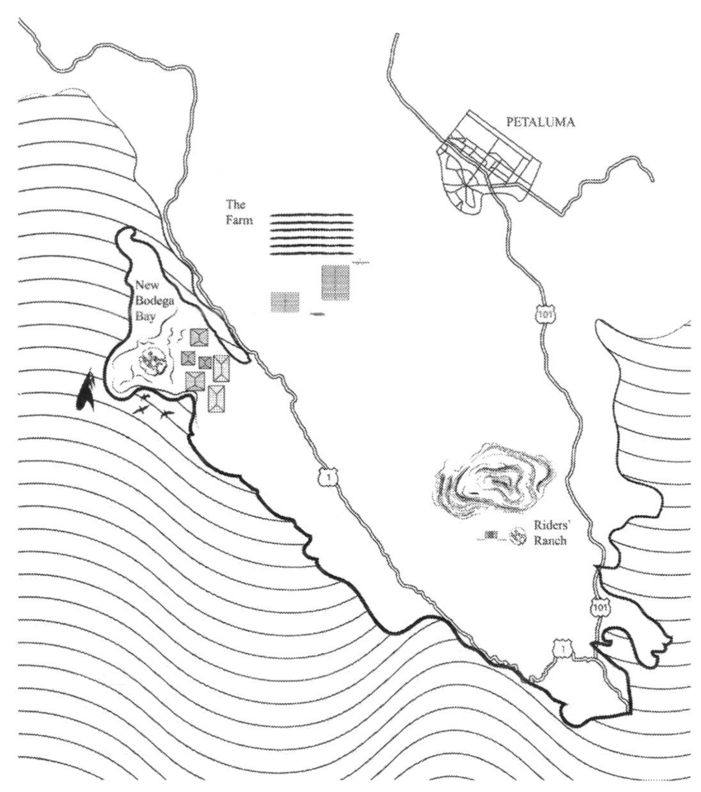

NORTHERN CALIFORNIA COAST MAP

MARCH 1 AE

1

JAKE

MARCH 23, 1AE

Colorado Springs, Colorado

Body tense and heart racing, Jake scoured Zoe's face for *any* inkling of recognition. He couldn't allow himself to believe she had no memory of him or all they'd been through together. She'd admitted she loved him only hours earlier. Now, she was scared, casting furtive glances around the room at friends and family she clearly didn't remember—including him.

In the dying moonlight seeping through the undressed windows, Jake watched her, desperation making it hard for him to breathe. Her eyes…he couldn't tear his gaze away from her teal eyes.

Zoe studied the two women in front of her, taking in Chris and Dani before settling her gaze on her brother, Jason. Her wide, appraising eyes narrowed and her chest heaved, like she was frantically trying to remember him. Her gaze lingered a moment longer without a hint of recognition, and then landed on Jake. He could see the confusion and fear warring within their depths, making his heart ache and his conscience cloud with an undeniable guilt.

He shouldn't have left her alone on the golf course.

Her head tilted slightly as she considered him, and he prayed there was even the slightest nagging familiarity. *Remember,* he silently pleaded. But seeing no recognition of him—of *them*—reflected in her eyes, he knew the Zoe standing in the room, looking at him like he was a complete stranger, was only a shadow of the woman he'd fallen in love with.

His grip on the doorframe tightened so hard he thought the wood might detach from the wall. Zoe was terrified, and for the first time since he'd met her, there was nothing he could do to help her. He fought the instinct to go to her, knowing that if he did, he would frighten her more, and then he might risk losing her completely.

Unable to stand the tension any longer, unable to bear the feeling of loss and his encroaching devastation, Jake turned and strode out of the suffocating room. Each step provided distance, and the more distance he put between them, the easier it became to breathe. He couldn't get away fast enough.

Cooper, his loyal-friend-through-it-all husky, trailed behind him, panting and trotting to keep up as Jake made his way down the hall. He needed space…needed air. Continuing toward the kitchen, he hoped the fresh air beyond the sliding glass door would give him a clearer head. But regardless of how quickly he strode through the house, the image of Zoe's fearful eyes remained, permanently projected in his mind, a constant reminder of his failure to protect her.

His hands fisted at his sides. He'd known something wasn't right when she said she felt strange outside the Colony, and if he'd have just stayed with her instead of leaving her side to help Harper, she might not have run off…she might still be *her*.

With a roar, Jake spun toward the wall. His fist met the hard, textured surface in unbridled anger. His knuckles cracked beneath his skin as they barreled through a layer of drywall, but he barely noticed. Bracing his hands against the wall, he tried to catch his breath, to stop his mind from spinning out of control. They'd already been through so much…why was this happening?

Hearing Dani and Zoe's muted voices in the bedroom down the hall, Jake turned away from the hole his fist had made and continued into the small kitchen, then stopped. With a heavy sigh, he leaned against the Formica countertop, not ready to go outside with the others. Not ready to answer questions.

Almost immediately, Jason came through the doorway behind him. In two steps he was at the counter, gripping the ledge, and in the dim light pouring through the sliding glass door, Jake could see the hard set of his features.

"I can't blame the Colony this time," Jake said. "I knew something was wrong." Zoe was infuriating and stubborn, but she wasn't stupid; she wouldn't have just run off for no reason. But without her memory, there was no way to know why she'd done it.

With a yawn, Cooper lay down on the linoleum floor, his eyes angling up to Jake and then to Jason, ensuring that, even in their silence, they were still standing there.

After what felt like a few minutes, Jason grunted and shook his head. His shoulders were tense, and Jake could almost feel the apprehension rolling off him in waves.

Jake couldn't help but wonder if Gabe—his best friend turned traitor—was to blame for all of this. Despite their friendship as children, Gabe had brought soldiers into Jake's home, ready to take his sister, Becca, away from him, and then he'd lured Dani into the Colony for the General. Had he been involved in what had happened to Zoe, too?

"What a fucking mess," Jason said, shaking his head. "I guess I'll just keep nulling her, at least until—"

The sound of footsteps approaching brought both men's attention to the hall doorway. Chris spoke softly, Zoe's hand resting in hers as they entered the kitchen, Dani and Jack, her German shepherd, close behind them. Though Chris and Zoe were both grown women, the image of them walking hand in hand resembled that of a mother and child.

Jake's eyes met Zoe's as she was led past him; hers were shrewd and penetrating. They were the same eyes that had affected him so intensely the first moment he saw her, their brilliance and expressiveness capturing his attention—his soul—in a way no other woman ever had. Regret and anger gnawed at him; he'd never told her any of that, and now she might never know how he felt.

Her eyes fixed on him. He could tell from the way Zoe walked —with less fortitude and more uncertainty—that she was a poorly made replica of *his* Zoe. But she was a version of her, nonetheless, and like always, the bottomless depths of her eyes housed her every emotion: embarrassment—curiosity—confusion. Jake was grateful she didn't seem to be afraid, and he knew he had Chris's Ability to curb Zoe's unease with a single touch to thank for that.

Chris whispered something inaudible, and Zoe's gaze shifted to the sliding glass door. They stepped through and outside, heading toward the rest of the group and the horses waiting in the early morning shadows, Dani's dog traipsing after them.

Dani, however, hung back in the kitchen. She moved closer to Jason, her gaze darting between him and Jake. With her broken arm, swollen and bruised face, and hunched shoulders, she looked like she'd been the General's punching bag while held captive in the Colony. She gave him a sidelong glance.

Jake's blood ran cold. "What is it?" he asked.

"There was a letter," she said tentatively, fingering the edge of the sling holding her left arm. "It's from one of my Colony contacts. She brought Zo here after finding her in the golf course…with Clara."

Jake stopped breathing. His anger drained from him, his stomach knotting with fear.

Clara.

He exhaled slowly and rubbed his hand over his face harsher

than was necessary, fighting to maintain what semblance of composure he had left. Clara'd had it out for Zoe from the first moment they'd met. Back at Fort Knox, she'd poisoned Zoe in a desperate attempt to get rid of her, then attempted to kill them *all* in the barracks fire that had claimed several lives. And now she was here, in Colorado, trying to hurt Zoe *again*.

White-hot rage and self-loathing scorched through Jake, and he clenched his shaking hands into fists. He should've left Clara in the hospital where he'd found her, pleading and scared.

"She's dead now," Dani said, but Jake's anger lessened only slightly.

"Dead," he repeated hollowly. Clara might've been dead, but not before managing to strike one final blow.

Dani's eyes met his for a brief moment before settling back onto Jason's. "Did you tell them about the T-Rs and the memory wiping?"

Jason nodded.

"It looks like that's what happened to Zo…sort of. Clara started the process, got interrupted…at least now she's gone for good."

Jake studied Dani. "How do you know for sure?" he asked.

Dani smiled weakly and shook her head, wisps of her curly red hair escaping the braid it was gathered into. "My contact said so," she said. "I trust her…at least with this." She glanced between them once more, like she wasn't quite sure of something. "There's more, but we should probably get going."

Jason reached for her, lacing his fingers with those of her good hand, and nodded. "We'll figure the rest out on the way to Colorado Trails," he said. "We've got to get moving or Ky and the others will think something's happened to us."

The sliding glass door opened, and Becca stepped into the doorway. She glanced between Jason and Dani, and even though she still didn't seem to believe that Jake was her brother, her eyes found and locked with his. "We should go," she said, her voice raspy, as it had been since she was young. "I have had a vision. If we do not leave soon, the General will find us."

"Shit," Jason muttered, and Becca turned slowly and exited the kitchen, leaving the door open behind her.

Dani led Jason toward the sliding glass door, his imposing form dwarfing her petite, battered one. Part of Jake wished Zoe's wounds were as straightforward as bruises and broken bones; *those* wounds would heal. What Clara had done to her might not.

Feeling deflated, Jake followed after them. Once again, Zoe was right in front of him, but as unreachable as though she were miles away; it infuriated him. While Clara's first attempt to kill the only woman he'd ever loved had inevitably brought Zoe closer to him, Clara's *final* attempt might have succeeded in tearing her away completely.

2

ZOE

MARCH 24, 1AE

Rocky Mountains, Colorado

"Potty break," Dani said, halting her paint horse, Wings, in the middle of the highway just ahead of me.

I'd been riding a brown mare named Mocha since leaving the house in Colorado Springs, the others taking turns staying close to me, since I had no clue what I was doing. Tavis was my current companion, riding on my right. I liked him; he was a funny Australian man who didn't talk much, but when he did it was playful and put me at ease. Becca, the woman sharing his saddle, seemed nice, though she hadn't said much to *anyone* during the five-plus hours we'd been on the road. She seemed almost as lost as I felt.

Dani struggled to dismount Wings using only her right arm, since her left arm was cradled in a sling. She was obviously in a lot of pain, despite the medicine the doctor, Harper, had given her.

I glanced up ahead at Jason, assuming he'd be charging toward us to help Dani in her flailing attempt to dismount and chastising her for attempting it on her own. But he was at the head of our parade line, talking to Chris and completely oblivious to Dani's self-dismount.

When Dani's boots hit the ground, she glanced toward Jason, then looked up at me, a sheepish grin on her face as she brought her index finger to her lips. "Don't tell him…"

I smiled and shook my head. I liked Dani, a lot. She was fiery and peppy, and the ease with which she spoke to me made it easier to cope with what was going on, like I had a friend who would stay by my side no matter what. When she'd tried to explain to me what had happened to the world, that we'd grown up together and had spent the last three months trying to get to one another only to be separated by the Colony again, I'd begun to freak out. The weight of reality and my lack of memories and sense of self were all too much to bear at once.

But Chris had been quick to wrap her arms around my shoulders, telling me that it would be alright, I just needed time to readjust, and for some reason, that had made me feel better. Dani had later explained that it was because Chris had the innate ability to comfort people. Although I got the distinct impression there was more to Chris than that—a nagging suspicion in the back of my mind—I liked the way I felt in her presence and savored the reprieve of unwanted emotions when she was around me.

"Come on, Zo," Dani said, holding her good hand up to help me climb out of Mocha's saddle. "Let's go pee. You never know…" She scanned the tall aspens on either side of the road. "We might not find another woodsy spot before we stop for the night. Might as well take advantage of the privacy while we have it."

I considered the image of the two of us standing side by side, best friends who, I'd been told, were so completely altered from the last time we'd seen each other. Tiny little Dani, with her bruised pixie face framed by wild, red curls, and me, tall, with an unmarred exterior but hollow interior. *I wish I could remember...*

But having been found inside the bedroom closet of an abandoned house the night before was as far back as my memory went.

"Zo? You okay?" Dani's brow furrowed. "Do you need me to get Harper?"

I shook my head. I had a million and one questions, but a pee break wasn't the time to ask them. Instead, I offered her what I hoped was a reassuring smile. "No, I was just thinking." I waved her proffered hand away. "I got it, Dani, but thanks." I didn't want to hurt her by jerking her body around as I dismounted. "It's only a couple feet." I'd decided it was much easier getting up into the saddle than it was getting down, an art I was determined to master if this was going to be my *spot* during our several-day journey.

While the others seemed all too excited to meet up with the rest of our group, it meant that *I* had even more people to "reacquaint" myself with. Dani had spent part of the morning filling me in on my relationships with them. Now I just needed to remember all that she'd told me: Sarah, apparently a friend I'd traveled with from the East Coast, was pregnant; her boyfriend, Biggs, was a military man we'd met up with along the way; Mr. Grayson was my high school history teacher and had been traveling with Dani for months; and Jason's best friend, Ky, and Ky's older brother, Ben, were waiting for us deeper in the mountains.

I stood up in the stirrups, prepared to fling my leg over for an awkward dismount.

"Here," Tavis offered kindly as he strode up beside Mocha. I hadn't even noticed him dismount his own horse. He wore an easy smile, and his blue eyes crinkled in the corners where his smile touched them. His dirty-blond hair was a little long and mussed from running his fingers through it so frequently.

Caught off guard, I felt my heart flutter a bit.

"Fling your leg over, and I'll help ease you down…"

Flashing him a brief smile, I did as Tavis instructed. With one hand gripping the saddle horn and the other gripping the edge of the saddle seat for leverage, I swung my leg over Mocha's rump, just like Dani had shown me. As I was about to lower myself to the ground, Tavis's hands grasped my waist, firmly but gently, and he helped lower me the rest of the way down.

"It's not mountain climbing, so you'll be a pro in no time," he said as I pivoted around to face him.

"Thanks," I chirped, and he answered with a nod before he turned and headed back for his horse.

Turning around, I found Dani eyeing me carefully. Jake, a man who hadn't uttered a single word to me since they'd found me but had taken to watching me with unnerving intensity, sat upon his horse behind her, his gaze equally assessing.

"Jason," Dani called ahead, startling me. I looked up toward the front of the caravan as Jason turned around in his saddle, his gaze questioning as it shifted between us. "We're gonna pee," she said. "It might be difficult for you to keep nulling for a minute, but we'll be right back."

Jason's eyes hardened. "Be careful."

"Come on, Zo," Dani said, biting her lip. There was a hint of uncertainty in her voice. "There's some stuff you should know." She hooked her arm in mine, and we headed toward the tangle of bushes a dozen yards away.

"Dani," Jake said, swinging his leg over his saddle, clearly intending to come with us.

Dani shook her head at him and patted the handgun in her shoulder holster. "We'll be fine, Jake. I need to talk to Zo for a sec."

Although Jake didn't seem pleased with the decision, he remained in his saddle, his gaze shifting between us as we turned away.

"Wait, Zoe—" Sam, a forward little boy I'd spoken to only a few times, called from behind us.

"We'll be right back, Sam," I said over my shoulder as Dani pulled me forward; I was practically stumbling as I tried to keep up with her. "What's—"

"Zo, I know you're probably exhausted and more than a little confused about everything that's going on, but you're super close to getting yourself into a mess that you'll regret later."

Trying to stay at least partially aware of where my feet were landing, I gave Dani a sidelong glance. Her bright green eyes were a bit glazed over in the sunlight. I could tell the pain meds were starting to kick in.

"What do you mean by 'a mess'?" I asked, near panting as we clumsily hurried through the underbrush and over uneven ground.

"You're with Jake," she said.

I blanched and stopped, the abrupt movement making Dani wince. "What?" A faint thrill wriggled down my spine.

"Yeah, for a few months now, I think…" She shook her head. "What's important is that you remember that, especially when you're chatting it up with Tavis." She urged me toward the berry bushes a few feet away.

Falling into step behind her, I frowned. "But Jake hasn't even talked to me."

She snorted. "That *might* have something to do with the fact that you don't even know him anymore." Pulling a wad of tissues from her pocket, Dani handed me a couple, and then looked down at her broken arm. "This is gonna be fun," she muttered, and I tried not to laugh, though I didn't do a very good job

I found that preoccupying my mind with observing Dani, her little quirks that I was still trying to understand, was a good distraction from all the things I was *supposed* to already know, the things that threatened to overwhelm me and bring me to tears.

As we each squatted behind our own cluster of bushes to do our business, I allowed my mind to wander, if only a little. I considered what Dani had told me about Jake and me being together, and I found it impossible to picture. He seemed so quiet and capable, it was a little intimidating. I couldn't even imagine having a conversation with him, let alone *being* with him. But in spite of my reservations, there was also a mysterious air about him that was intriguing, and I was curious to discover what the old me already had. The number of questions ticking through my head increased exponentially.

Hearing leaves crunch beneath footsteps on the other side of the shrubbery, I sighed and finished up. "Geez, you're fast." I assumed I'd have to *help* Dani, not that she would leave me in the dust. Jumping up to my feet, I zipped up my jeans and stepped out from behind the tangle of leaves and branches. I froze.

Sam was standing a few yards away, his bow drawn and an arrow aimed at the figure of a small girl standing between us. Her back was to me, her blonde hair hanging in a knotted mess.

Sam's expression was one of pure horror—his pale eyes wide and his nostrils flaring—but his stance and aim were unwavering.

"What the hell are you doing, Sam?" I screeched.

"What's wrong, Zo?" Dani called from behind the bushes. But I was too focused on Sam and the little girl he was prepared to shoot an arrow through to answer.

"Sam," I said again. "She's just a little girl. Put your bow down."

Dark brown hair hung in his eyes, but he stared at her, unblinking, and I could see his uncertainty.

"Sam…"

As if hearing the scolding tone of my voice had brought the little girl to life, she slowly turned around. At the sight of her, my heart nearly stopped. The front of her nightgown was *covered* in dried blood, as were her arms and neck. Her face was doll-like, with crystal-blue eyes wide and gleaming in the sunlight, and her porcelain skin was hidden beneath what looked like weeks' worth of layers of dirt and blood.

"Mommy?" The haunting pitch of her voice sent chills up my spine.

"Jesus," I breathed. "Are you alright?" Although I had the innate urge to run away from the little girl, I took a hesitant step toward her, wondering what the poor child had been through.

"Zoe, get away from her!" Dani said from behind me.

The little girl took a step closer to me, her eyes narrowing and her lip curling into a snarl. Her body was suddenly trembling, like her muscles were coiling to strike. Gritting her teeth, she growled, "Mommy?"

As she lunged toward me, an ear-piercing crack resounded through the air, and before she could take another step, the little girl fell to a crumpled heap on the ground. A crimson patch blossomed on her nightgown, spreading across her chest.

My hands flew to my mouth and I screamed, tears trickling down my face. "Oh my God." Turning around, I found Dani, handgun drawn and still pointed where the little girl lay. Dani's eyes were wide, her face ashen, and her mouth hung open. "What have you done?"

Dani blinked several times, and her gaze slowly shifted from the small body to me. Her eyes were filled with shock and horror. "She was a Crazy," she said, lowering her gun. "She was a Crazy." I wasn't sure if she was trying to convince me, or herself. "I—I had to…she was a Crazy…"

"A *what?*" I turned back to the little girl and stared down at her. I was suddenly shaking uncontrollably. "What the hell just happened?" I asked no one in particular. "She's just a little girl."

I heard a rush of footsteps and calling voices, but I couldn't focus on anyone but the dead child lying horrifyingly still on the ground. Her eyes were open and staring directly at me. *She thought I was her mother…*

"I've never seen a kid one before," Sam said, and I looked at him. "I tried to warn you."

"This is gonna be bright," Harper said as he sat me down on a log beside the fire and clicked on a small, near-blinding pen light. He shone it directly into my eyes. On instinct, I tried to blink, but Harper wouldn't let me; his fingertips were warm and firm as he held my eyelids open.

"Sorry, Baby Girl, but I just want to check one more time…"

Still trying to understand the whole Ability thing Sam had explained during the last stretch of our journey, I decided now was as good a time as any to start asking more questions, especially since Sam was probably getting tired of being the one having to answer them all. "Harper?"

"Hmmm."

"Were you a doctor before, or is this, you know, just part of your Ability?" I had no idea what counted as an "Ability," only that Sam had said everyone who survived the Virus had one—at least those who weren't "Crazies."

Harper He smiled. "This doctor stuff is all training, Baby Girl. I was a medic in the Army. My Ability has to do with visions and seeing things that haven't happened yet."

I snorted, determined not to cry out in confusion and disbelief.

"I know it's a lot to take in, especially all in one day, but we can't risk another incident like earlier today."

I shrugged, figuring the more answers I had the easier it would be for me to fit in. "Yeah, Sam said he has heightened senses, that he can hear, smell, and see things that others can't." I shook my head.

"Try not to move, Baby Girl."

"Sorry."

Harper shifted his hand down to my chin, gently gripping it while he moved my head from side to side in tandem with the flashlight he waved in front of my face.

"What are some of the others' Abilities?"

"Well," he began, "let's see—I'm not sure what Tavis or Daniel can do, but Carlos can control electricity, Dani can communicate with animals, Sanchez is telepathic, Jake can regenerate…Chris and your brother, well, they're the reason you're dealing with things as well as you are; Chris is keeping you calm, and you're brother is keeping your Ability hidden. He can actually nullify *or* amplify other people's Abilities."

Regeneration? Communicating with animals? Telepathy? Controlling electricity? I was almost afraid to ask… "What's my Ability?" I placed my hand on Harper's, gently pushing the pen light down so I could look him in the eyes. "What's Jason protecting me from?"

Harper gave me a sympathetic smile. "You can see people's memories. You can feel what they're feeling. On top of everything that's happened today, we didn't think it was a good idea to add your Ability into the mix, too."

Jason and Chris had been shadowing me pretty closely all day. Part of me wondered if I should be offended that they hadn't told me about this sooner. But then again, the idea of having an Ability, especially one that was so intrusive, didn't seem like something I could handle on top of everything else.

Harper clicked the light on, blinding me once more.

"Is there something *wrong* with my eyes?" I asked a bit tersely. The more he wanted to check them, the more concerned I became.

"No. Sorry to scare you. There's nothing wrong, I just—" He gave me another sympathetic smile as he clicked the light off. "I was just making sure there's no brain damage, or…I just want to make sure I'm not missing anything that might help us figure out exactly what she did to you, or how bad it is." He sighed. "But I don't see anything, and I doubt I will without doing an MRI or—"

"It's only been a day," Dani chimed in as she walked by. It was the first time I'd heard her speak since the incident with the little girl…the Crazy. Dani stopped in the narrow clearing where everyone was setting up their tents for the night. "You might be back to your old self by tomorrow, Zo. Could be all you need is a good night's sleep."

Dani fought to keep a nylon sleeping bag from slipping out

from under her good arm. Although she flashed me a smile over her shoulder, I could tell it was weak and forced. I could picture a real Dani smile brightening her face to glowing, nothing like the halfhearted smile she gave me now, which had quickly faded.

I watched as she struggled to open a tent bag. "I'm sure you're right," I said and glanced up at Harper. "Tomorrow will be better. Can I be done?" I felt like I needed to be doing *something* to help Dani, since I was otherwise useless and she was having such a hard time after such a crappy day.

Harper nodded absently, not really staring *at* me so much as staring *through* me. He rubbed his jaw and took another deep breath.

I stepped toward Dani but hesitated the moment Jason appeared beside her, crouching to help. He muttered something I couldn't hear.

"Yeah…I just want to go to sleep," Dani said.

"This isn't even our tent, and you shouldn't be doing this on your own, Red. You'll just make your arm worse. Please…just ask me for help next time." Jason, a man of words that were few and to the point, continued to grumble as he pulled the tent out of its bag and unrolled it like doing so was second nature.

"I didn't want to bother you." Dani rested her hand on his shoulder, his body tensed and stilled. "I was thinking Zo and I could share a tent tonight. You know, since it would be weird for her…" Dani's gaze drifted to Jake.

Hurt flashed in Jason's eyes.

"It's alright," I rushed to say. The last thing I wanted to be was more of an inconvenience than I already was.

Jason and Dani both looked at me.

"I don't mind having my own tent. You guys share, really."

"I don't think you should be alone tonight, Zo. What if something happens?" I noticed Dani's eyes skirt to Jake again; he'd just dropped his own tent on the ground on the other side of the fire.

"What if your memory comes back and you're all alone?" Dani

said, bringing my attention back to her. "I should be with you… unless…" Again, her eyes drifted to Jake.

What does it mean that he can "regenerate"? A rush of anxiety filled me as I thought about sleeping in the same tent as him. Dani might've told me that Jake and I were *together*, but she hadn't given me any of the details, and I wasn't quite ready for that yet.

Becca walked past, startling me. Her face was soft and glowing in the building flames. "We can share a tent tonight, if you would like," she said. I hadn't talked to her much since we'd left Colorado Springs, so I was surprised she'd even offered.

I flashed her a grateful smile. "Thanks, Becca." Looking at Dani, I asked, "Do you mind?"

Dani shrugged and shook her head. "Only if you're sure, Zo."

"Yes, I'm sure."

"You can use this tent," Jason offered, prepared to pull the tent poles out of the pack.

"That's okay, Jason. I can finish. You guys can set up your stuff. Can you just point me to my things?" I hadn't needed them for anything yet, since we'd been riding all day. "I do have *things*, right?"

Jason nodded to Dani, and with a willing smile she picked up the flashlight he'd set on the ground and walked with me over to Mocha.

As I trudged along behind her, I noticed how many people were bustling around, chatting while they set up for the night. Our cramped little camp was in a wooded area off the highway, out of sight but not so far away from the road that I couldn't hear one of the horses clip-clopping lazily on the asphalt.

Stepping up to Mocha, Dani started untying the two long stuff sacks secured behind the saddle with one hand, tossing me each as she freed them. Both were black with a purple Celtic knot painted on the side.

"That's your sleeping bag and sleeping pad," she said, pointing to each before she peeked into one of the saddlebags, which were still on the horse. "Yep, your clothes and whatnot are in here. Give me a sec and I'll have these down for you."

"Don't worry, I'll get them," I said, not wanting her to struggle needlessly. As I fumbled to loosen the saddlebag, I stared at the knot painted on it. I had no idea what the heck it meant. "Apparently I really like this symbol," I said. "It's all over my stuff."

Finally unfastening the bag, I turned around. Dani eyed me a moment, her face cast in shadows; obviously it meant something important to her, too. I glanced back down at the bag, the knot glaring at me.

Assuming it was my confusion that made her expel a tiny sigh of sadness, I released a sigh of my own. "I'm sorry, Dani. I wish I could remember…"

She stepped closer and nudged my arm with her good shoulder, offering me a reassuring smile that didn't touch her eyes. "It's okay, Zo. We'll figure it out tomorrow. It's been a long day, and we all need our rest."

I nodded and turned to tug the leather bags off of Mocha's back, but grunted when they were heavier than I'd expected. "What the hell did I put in he—"

"Here." A deep rumble came from behind me, and an arm reached over my shoulder and grabbed the cross strap of the saddlebags. Jake pulled them effortlessly off the horse and asked me where I wanted them.

"Over by Becca," I said, pointing dumbly. I'd decided Jake was intimidating—alluring but intimidating—and it prevented me from putting on a show of calmness around him, like I could around everyone else.

A pained expression pinched his features, but without another word, he headed to the other side of camp, toward Becca.

Dani was watching me, idly patting Jack, his tongue hanging out of his mouth. She gave me a reassuring nod—the nod that I'd grown used to over the past twelve hours—before I followed quickly after Jake.

Feeling inadequate in our silence, I occupied my mind with observations of the rest of the campers, busy in their various stages of getting situated.

Chris, just finished setting up a tent for Camille and Mase, was pulling her blonde hair up into a ponytail, while Mase, huge, dark, and imposing, stood in front of the tent with Camille in his arms, her head resting on his shoulder. They'd been inseparable since she'd awoken right before we stopped for the day, and despite being unconscious since before they'd found me, she still looked exhausted. Mase stared at the nylon dome like it was from another dimension. He seemed constantly confused—even more than me, which I thought a little strange—but after a brief moment of hesitation, he ducked inside the tent with Camille.

Gabe, the tall, blond man who seemed to keep to himself, was setting up another tent beside theirs.

"What's his Ability?" I asked Jake. When he peered back at me, I pointed to Gabe.

Jake's jaw clenched, and I immediately regretted asking him. "He can manipulate people's dreams," he said. I didn't need to know the history between them to know it wasn't a good one.

"Oh."

Sanchez, who seemed to be leading the group with Jason, was stacking wood next to the campfire, while Sam and easygoing Tavis hauled over bunches of kindling. I enjoyed watching Sam and Tavis interact; they acted more like brothers than father and son—though I'd been told they were neither—and they laughed more than the others, which I found comforting.

But as much as everyone *seemed* to coexist easily enough, a cloud of tension hung over the group. I wasn't sure I wanted to learn the cause yet. Trying to remember everyone's names, their Abilities, and my relationship with each of them was chore enough.

Jake stopped short in front of me, and I ran into his back.

"Sorry," I said, unable to stop a nervous laugh from bubbling out of me. "I got distracted." I dropped the load in my arms on the ground near Becca.

Jake set my saddlebags down as well. "I'll be right back," he said and headed back toward the horses.

I watched him for a moment—watched the way he rubbed the back of his neck and the way his shoulders relaxed the further he was from me.

I turned to Becca, who was attempting to finish setting up our tent. "Thank you, Becca. I appreciate you offering to stay with me tonight."

When I realized she was practically wrestling with the tent poles, I crouched beside her to show her how they worked. "It's pretty easy once you get the hang of it," I said. I was surprised I remembered silly things like that—how to set up a tent, how to excuse myself when I sneezed and cover my mouth when I coughed. *Why can I remember those things but not others?*

"You have done this before," Becca said quietly, watching the way my fingers moved and how I maneuvered the fabric of the tent as I pushed the poles through the red nylon loops.

"Yeah, I guess I have. You've never been camping?" Slowly, I forced one end of the pole into the corner of the tent, and watched as Becca mimicked what I was doing.

"Not that I remember, no." Her voice was distant, as if her mind was somewhere else.

"Yeah, me neither…at least, not that I can remember."

Jake returned, dropping two more stuff sacks on the ground, what appeared to be another sleeping bag and pad. He looked at Becca. "Those are mine, but you use them tonight. We'll stop somewhere tomorrow to get you your own gear." Becca watched Jake, her mouth pulling into a barely-there smile. "Thank you, Jake." The way she spoke to him seemed deliberate, like she meant more than what she said.

He watched her for a moment, his head tilting slightly to the side before he nodded. When his stare shifted to me, he appeared uncertain and regretful. There was a long, awkward silence before he said, "Will you please let me know if you need anything else?" His tone was soft, beseeching, even. There was something warm and inviting about his deep, velvety voice. "*Anything*," he repeated, his eyes filled with a sadness I didn't understand.

"Yes, I promise. Thank you," I said. With a final nod, I watched him walk back toward his tent, which he had yet to finish setting up.

Becca unzipped the tent door behind me and I turned around, ready to follow her inside. But she just stood there.

"What's wrong?" I asked, stepping up beside her. The light from the fire danced around inside, illuminating the tent enough to see there was nothing wrong with it.

"I guess I will sleep in my clothes," she said so quietly I almost didn't hear her.

"Is that all?" I asked and snatched up my saddlebags before sidestepping her and heading inside. "I'm sure I have something you can borrow."

Becca followed me in, bringing the sleeping bags and pads in with her.

Fiddling with the ends of my hair, which were draped over my shoulder, I watched Becca as she just stood there. "Have a seat," I said and opened my bag. I rummaged through the haphazardly folded clothes tucked inside, trying to find something for each of us to sleep in. "Here," I finally said, handing her a long-sleeved thermal shirt and a pair of sweatpants. "These look comfy, and it looks like I packed…yep, two of each."

Becca smiled, or at least I thought it was a smile; it was the first time I'd seen her be very expressive at all. "Thank you, Zoe."

"Why don't you have any clothes?" I asked, zipping up the tent to change.

Slowly, Becca peeled her clothes off one by one, until her ensemble was piled on the floor of the tent. "I have only just joined the group, along with Dr. McLaugh—I mean Gabe, Mase, and

Camille. We were unexpected, so we are relying on your friends' kindness to take us in. Dani and the clothes on our backs were all we brought with us."

"Dani was with *you*?"

Becca made a noncommittal noise and pulled the sweatpants on. They were too long and very baggy on her, but I figured that meant they were perfect for sleeping. "Yes," she said. "Dani was with Gabe and Dr. Wesley…in the Colony." Becca's voice was distant, her demeanor instantly shifting from open to hesitant.

I tugged my long-sleeved V-neck on over my head. "Did you not want to leave the Colony with Dani?" I couldn't stop myself from asking. The more complicated things became, the more my curiosity amplified. "You don't seem happy to be here…" I glanced over at Becca in time to see the bruises on the side of her body before she pulled her borrowed shirt down.

"I am happy to be away from there. It is just that things are not simple for me." She looked at me. "Or for you."

I shrugged. "Hopefully my memory will come back tomorrow."

The look Becca gave me made me feel nauseous.

"You don't think it will?" I asked.

"I do not know everything," she said, offering me the slightest of smiles.

"Only some things?" I asked wryly.

Without hesitation, she said, "I have the gift of prophecy."

Still unable to fully process the whole "Abilities" thing, I paused.

Becca bent down and began folding her clothes so meticulously that I thought she might be in the military. I looked over at my saddlebags and almost laughed. The clothes I'd changed out of were tossed on top, no rhyme or reason or organization. Feeling self-conscious, I gathered up my dirty socks, jeans, and shirt, and after unwadding them, I folded them as neatly as I could. My attempt was pathetic compared to Becca's, but it sufficed.

Becca must've been watching me, because when I looked up at her, her smile turned genuine. "You are very different from the last time I saw you."

My eyes widened. "How so?" I unrolled my sleeping pad, then pulled my sleeping bag out of its stuff sack and laid it out on top. Unzipping it, I crawled inside to keep my feet warm.

Becca studied me and did the same with Jake's sleeping gear. "You and Jake were fighting."

"Really?" I hadn't been expecting that. "We were fighting?"

She nodded, her eyes fixed on mine like she was gauging my reaction. "He was going to leave you and your people and take me away; he said it was not safe. But Father sent a team to retrieve me, and I escaped during the gunfire." Becca looked down at her fingers, which were laced on her knees. "I had to return to the Colony…Jake did not understand."

"Did Father do that to you?" I asked, pointing to the bruised side of her body.

After contemplating my question for a moment, Becca nodded. "I had to get them out of there," she said to herself, and I assumed she was talking about Dani and the others she'd escaped with.

My mind filled with images of a distraught Mase and newly-conscious Camille. "The others are like you, too," I said, suddenly feeling an intense desire to know what had happened in the hours I'd lost my memory. "Mase and Camille, they're…different, like you. The way you speak, and how you see things like it's for the first time…they're the same."

Becca nodded. "Yes. We are called Re-gens at the Colony, though Jake says I am his sister as well."

My brow furrowed at yet another surprising truth. Jake didn't treat her like a sister—but then Jason didn't treat me like one either, at least not how *I* thought a brother should treat a sister. I was beginning to think that whatever remaining perception of reality I had was both misleading and impractical.

"I saw things," Becca continued, her voice a panicked whisper.

"Horrible things. Things that I could not let come to pass. I had to tell them. I had to get away from there." Becca continued to stare down at her hands. "I am not sure what to think anymore."

"No?"

After a depleted sigh, she said, "No."

Pulling the rubber band from my hair and letting it fall around my shoulders, I ran my fingers through the dark strands, wading through my limited memories, trying to determine how *I* felt… what I *thought*.

All I remembered were strange voices and surprised faces staring down at me as I huddled inside the closet. *Did I really forget* all *that Becca just described?* It seemed impossible, and a ravenous emptiness drained any optimism and hope I had left. A sick feeling settled in my stomach as it dawned on me: every single moment that shaped me into Zoe was gone.

I am no one.

"You are not 'no one,'" Becca said, and I stirred, not realizing I'd been thinking aloud. She rested her hand on my shoulder. "You are important."

"You've seen this?" My sudden curiosity to know more of what she'd *seen* was making me antsy; I twirled a strand of hair.

Becca shook her head. "No, I haven't seen your future, nor do I know your purpose, but your mother is Dr. Wesley, I know that much. If you are her daughter, you are important." She paused in thought. "Jake loves you, and he is important…I know that as well. So, you must be, too."

Jake loves *me?* I wasn't sure why I was surprised; Dani had told me much the same earlier. "He's barely talked to me all day," I said.

"All day, I have thought about two things," Becca began, her voice a bit softer than before. "I considered what I might do now that I no longer have a home, a place I belong. And I thought about Jake. If what he says is true, if I *am* his sister, then he has lost both his sister and the woman he loves. Now, here we are again, and neither of us remembers him. I cannot imagine how he might feel." Becca frowned. "I generally am not so…reflective, I think is the word, but much is changing…" She stretched out in her sleeping bag, staring up at the bouncing shadows on the nylon overhead.

We were quiet for a while, and I nearly allowed the crackling fire outside and the sound of crickets in the woods beyond our tent to lull me to sleep. But before I was out completely, I heard low voices by the fire.

"We've got to figure out a way to fix her," Harper said, his voice low and thoughtful.

"It's not like there are rules to any of this shit," Jason grumbled.

The sound of wood being tossed in the fire filled the momentary silence.

"There has to be a way." It was Jake's baritone, followed by retreating footsteps.

I glanced over at Becca to see if she was awake, but her back was to me, and all I could see was the outline of her torso rising and falling with each breath. I lay there, listening to my "friends" discuss my condition like it was simply an infection needing proper treatment. My mind reeled with questions and mounting fear until their voices fell silent, and I eventually drifted to sleep.

A slight breeze caressed my skin as I sat on a dock, gazing out at a lake—its glassy surface was illuminated with pinks and oranges, like it was set aflame by the sun sinking behind the rolling hills.

My chest grew heavier, and I was nearly suffocating under the weight of too many emotions.

"I know what I want," said a deep, rumbling voice.

I spun around to find Jake standing beside me, his luminous, amber eyes peering into the depths of my soul. He knew me; I could see it in the way he looked at me, those eyes filled with longing and uncertainty and need.

Like his emotions sparked my own, I felt the need to weep from the inexplicable love I felt for him.

"Jake, I—" I didn't have time to think, to say anything.

In seconds his lips were pressed against mine, his kiss fierce and blazing. My hands moved of their own accord, grabbing a handful of his jacket and pulling him closer to me as his fingers tightened in my hair. An overwhelming, frenzied greed consumed us both as my arms snaked around his neck and his hands explored my body.

We were panting, and a low groan resonated deep inside his chest. My body throbbed with a pleasurable ache I wanted to both last forever and go away, ridding me of my torment.

Jake froze, sending an unnatural anger and despondency simmering through me. He stepped away, leaving me to stand there alone, the cool breeze turning icy against my exposed skin. Panic riddled my nerves, and I tried fervently to grasp hold of him.

He was pulling away from me…

He was leaving me…alone…

With a jolt, I opened my eyes. I was surrounded by darkness, only the starry sky overhead visible through the rectangles of netting on the roof of the tent. There was no more campfire, and there were no more voices. All I could hear was the wind whistling through the trees.

As I lay there, my heart still pounding from the dream, I felt completely lost and alone. I didn't like the dangerous intoxication that settled over me as I remembered Jake's hot breath…the thrill that sang through me as I recalled the feeling of his fingers pressing against my skin…

"Zoe? Are you alright?" Becca asked quietly.

"Yes," I said quickly, not feeling comfortable talking to her about it.

"Are you sure?"

"I just had a strange dream. I'll be fine."

Becca was quiet for a moment. "Was it a dream or a memory?"

Rolling over, I studied her darkened outline. "A dream. At least, I think it was…"

"Do not fight it," she said. "If it *is* your memory, you should not fight it."

Had it been a memory? It had been so vivid, so charged with emotions I couldn't remember ever feeling before, that part of me doubted it was even possible.

3

DANI

MARCH 28, 1AE

San Juan National Forest, Colorado

Carrying a small bin of grooming tools under my good arm, I led Wings toward a retention pond beside the field where we'd set up camp for the night. We passed between one of the three carts and the replica pioneer chuck wagon that we'd found in one of the barns back at Colorado Trails Ranch. We'd stayed at the ranch only one night, wanting to put as much distance between us and the Colony as possible, as *soon* as possible. That single night was just long enough for us to stock up on tack and another dozen horses from the area, redistribute our supplies among the packhorses and conveyances, and convene for a quick strategic meeting, and for Harper and Jake to attempt a regenerative blood transfusion on Zoe—which ended up being the most anti-climactic fail *ever*. She still remembered nothing of her life before the golf course.

Zoe's memory loss was proving to be as stubborn as my best friend was…or used to be. This new Zoe, this *not-Zoe* Zoe, was different; she was less closed off, less severe, and every time she said or did something that emphasized just how much Clara's violent mind-wiping had changed her, the thundercloud that had become my mood darkened. Just as it did every time I spoke to Jason—*lied* to Jason—avoided Gabe, or remembered my time in the General's concrete interrogation room, or the way the light had faded from the child Crazy's eyes as she bled out from the bullet wound I'd put in her chest.

Maybe if I hadn't burned out my telepathy *again*, and I could speak with Wings, Jack, and Ray, as I'd grown so accustomed to doing over the past few months, I would've been able to find comfort in their steadfast companionship and stave off the looming negativity. But my Ability *was* burned out, and missing my usually lighthearted, sometimes philosophical conversations with my animal friends only added to my doom-and-gloom mood.

I spotted Mase and Camille, sitting at the edge of the pond while they filtered water into large plastic jugs, and nodded a hello.

Camille's remarkable recovery was the only bright ray of hope keeping the thundercloud from overtaking me completely. She'd woken up five days ago, the night after we found Zoe and left Colorado Springs, her memory intact but her ability to speak apparently gone completely. Harper's best guess was that certain parts of her brain must've suffered permanent damage during her seizure and resulting coma, and he'd even proposed that she might have had a stroke, though he couldn't tell for sure without some pretty high-tech equipment. But she was awake, and more whole than she'd been since she'd died…the first time. Her recovery, at least, was something.

I sighed and shook my head.

Zoe was following Wings and me, Shadow trailing behind her. The other seventeen members of our group were moving among the tents clustered around the campfire or through the scattering of trees lining the field, searching for firewood. Except for Jason; he was absolutely committed to the task of nulling Zoe, of keeping her Ability from surfacing and pummeling her shattered mind with foreign memories and emotions, and therefore had become her ever-present second shadow…or third *shadow*, if you counted her horse.

I snorted at my lame silent pun, and blinked rapidly as my eyes started to sting. I would *not* start crying just because I found Jason's commitment to protecting my best friend—the sister he'd successfully estranged through emotional and physical distance—so sweet, so admirable. It was like this tragedy had jumpstarted his brotherly instincts, making him realize all he'd missed out on over the years. His renewed devotion to her made me feel like such a crap friend in comparison, because the more time I spent with this Zoe—this hauntingly familiar stranger, devoid of everything that had made her my best friend—the less I *wanted* to be around her.

Like I said—crap friend.

Reaching the edge of the pond, I set the small bin of grooming tools on the ground and waited for Wings to amble closer. She did and ducked her head down to slurp at the water.

Zoe and Shadow took up a position a few feet away, just on the other side of the bin, and Jason hoisted himself up and settled on the bench seat of the nearest cart. He pulled out a pocket knife and his latest whittling project—an as-yet-unrecognizable hunk of wood about the size of a baseball.

My eyes lingered on him for a moment longer, tracing the angry red scar crossing his face from hairline to jaw and the hunched set of his shoulders, before I bent over to grab a soft-bristled brush and turned my attention to Wings.

"Thanks for teaching me all this horse stuff," Zoe said from behind me.

I glanced over my shoulder to study her and frowned. I'd been doing that a lot lately, both studying Zoe and frowning. The setting sun gleamed a burnished purple off her and Shadow's onyx hair. I'd offered to walk Zoe through the basics of horse grooming, hoping that doing something *with* her, something *I* always found soothing, might alleviate some of my infuriating aversion *to* her.

Meeting her eyes, I forced a tight smile. "No problem. You

used to like helping me with grooming them, back when we were in high school, so I thought…" I shrugged. "I don't know." I returned my focus to Wings, running the brush over a coffee-brown patch on her shoulder. "I just thought you might still like it." I didn't tell Zoe that I was searching for some remnant of my best friend, some sliver of hope that she was still *her*.

There was a long moment of silence, and then Zoe exhaled heavily. "I've been thinking about that…about me before and me now. Do you think—" She paused. I could hear the sound of soft bristles running over Shadow's coat as Zoe started brushing him. The black gelding was still recovering from the neglect he'd suffered at the hands of a couple of Crazies, and the six-day trek through the southern Rockies with only a half-day and night's rest at Colorado Trails hadn't done him any favors. Although he was doing better than when Zoe's group had first found him, he was exhausted and hurting, much like the rest of us. I didn't need my Ability to know that.

When Zoe didn't resume her question, I looked at her. "Do I think…?"

She stopped brushing, turned to lean her shoulder against Shadow, and sighed. "It's just that, if I don't have any memories of what made me *me*, do you think I'm even still *me*?"

Do you think I'm even still me?

Zoe's question seemed to echo in my mind, burrowing deeply, mostly because it was pretty much the same thing I'd been wondering since we first found her. Was Zoe still *Zoe* if she had no memory of experiencing the things that had *made* her the loyal, guarded, and determined person I loved? A dull, incessant ache spread through my chest, a yawning void created by her mental disappearance.

My eyes stung—*again*—and I cleared my throat. "You know, Zo…I think knowing who you really are is hard for a lot of people."

Yes, I was avoiding answering her question completely, but I meant what I said. After all, I hardly recognized myself anymore. My frown reemerged. Anyone who cracked me open in an attempt to find out what made me *me* would discover a rancid, tangly wad of guilt. And self-loathing. And plain old misery.

My best friend—thanks to a psycho with the Ability to alter people's perception, even erase their memories—had no idea that she *was* my best friend. And the reason she'd fallen into Clara's manipulative little hands?

Me.

I'd been stupid enough to get ambushed and abducted, and thanks to my bad judgment, Zoe wasn't really Zoe anymore. My frown deepened into a scowl. I really hated myself sometimes.

After a few more strokes over the paint's sculpted shoulder, which I was pretty sure soothed me more than it soothed Wings, I glanced over at Jason. If he noticed me watching him, he didn't show it. It was like we'd traveled back in time ten years, to the days when I'd spend every possible moment stealing glances at him, and he'd spend just as much time ignoring me.

Before my stint in the Colony, I'd thought I had him figured out, but now he was even more of an enigma to me than he'd been during my teen years. He was still a classic Adonis, all lean muscle and chiseled features, but now his masculine perfection was marred by an angry red scar slashing across his face. It added a layer of menace to the confidence and sense of carefully honed power he usually exuded. He'd always been guarded, just like his sister, but since my abduction, he'd withdrawn further into himself. For the life of me, I couldn't figure out why, and I didn't know how to draw him back out. Even though he was never far from my side, emotionally, he was miles away. I missed him.

I turned around, facing Zoe, and leaned my head on Wings's shoulder. My need for girl talk, for Zoe to listen as I spilled out all of my gnawing worries and offer up her usual, no-nonsense advice, was becoming overwhelming. *Should I just talk to her like every-*

thing's normal? Can't I just pretend she's her*?* I really needed my Zo…

"You're staring at me," Zoe said. She lowered her brush hand and, using her opposite fingers, tucked a flyaway that had escaped from her ponytail behind her ear. "Are you okay?"

I blinked several times, noticing the excessive moisture in my eyes, and forced a smile. "I'm fine…I think."

Zoe shifted her feet and looked down at the dirt. She swiped ineffectively at a dark smudge staining her jeans. "You can cry…if you need to. I don't mind. In fact, you can consider me your official shoulder to cry on." She shrugged, meeting my eyes only briefly. "It's the least I can do, since I'm pretty much otherwise inept…at everything."

The thundercloud thinned, just a little, and I started chuckling. That was something Zoe would have said; she'd always looked out for me, always been the first to comfort me when I needed it and the first to defend me when I couldn't defend myself. Not that I didn't try to defend myself. It was just that I was so damn small nobody was *ever* intimidated by me. And when I *had* made a point to stand up for myself or shudder—lost my temper, I was pretty sure people saw me as the human version of a snarling Chihuahua. Not. Scary. At. All.

From the way Zoe was watching me, it was obvious that she was unsure how to respond to my abrupt shift from verge of tears to genuine, if gentle, laughter. Her eyebrows drew down, and the corners of her mouth twitched. She smiled weakly. It was like she was trying to figure out how *I* wanted her to react—how the old Zoe would have reacted. For a moment, the disquiet I felt around her melted, and the only thing that mattered to me was making her feel comfortable.

I pushed off Wings gently and stepped closer to Zoe, nudging her arm with my shoulder. "Don't try so hard, Zo. Just do what feels natural and stop worrying about the rest of us and what we expect from you." I flashed her a halfhearted grin. "We'll figure it out as we go." Empty platitudes for the most part, but from the way the tension around her eyes relaxed, I could tell the words meant something to Zoe. Apparently even crap friends could pull through every once in a while.

Just as I was turning back to Wings to resume brushing her, I heard a dog barking. I craned my neck to see around Zoe and Shadow and spotted Jack trotting through the overgrown field beside our camp. He barked several more times as I watched him draw nearer.

Without warning, something inside me snapped. A whoosh, like the most intense ear-popping imaginable, knocked the air out of me, and I doubled over. My Ability burnout wore off in an instant, and thousands upon thousands of sparks of awareness burst to life in my mind's eye, a glowing galaxy representing all of the life forms around me. It was glorious. And unexpected. And so far beyond too much that I thought I might be crushed under the enormity of what I was sensing.

Several things happened at once: Jack reached me, dancing a circle around me, his tail hanging low while he whined and chanted, *"Mother? Mother! Mother?"* in my mind; Zoe's hand wrapped around my upper arm, the support she offered the only thing keeping me from doubling over completely; and Jason appeared before me, crouching and placing his hands on either side of my head.

"Red?" Jason said. "Look at me, Dani. Open your eyes." His hold on my head tightened.

I hadn't realized I'd squeezed my eyes shut until he told me to open them. I obeyed, clenching my jaw. Jason's face, inches from mine, was carefully blank, but his eyes held a concern so wild and intense that it verged on panic.

"What's wrong?" His voice was low and even—too even. "What do you need?"

I swallowed, despite my mouth and throat feeling unbearably dry. "My…Ability…too much," I managed to say through gritted teeth. Something like this had happened once before; I'd overextended the reach of my telepathy and nearly lost myself to the collective pull of the minds around me. I should have been stronger now, especially after the painful but productive electrotherapy session I'd accidentally experienced back in the Colony. I should have been able to control my Ability, to pull back, to shut it off…to do *something*. But I couldn't.

As he'd done the last time, Jason acted as the grounding wire to my telepathic lightning rod. Using half of his Ability, he boosted mine, giving me back the control I so desperately needed. The magnetic lure of the minds around me waned, fading into the background.

I took a deep breath, then another. Smiling, I filled my eyes with as much warmth as I could and placed my hand over one of Jason's, giving it a gentle, grateful squeeze. "Thank—" My voice caught in my throat, and my chest clenched. Something was wrong.

I couldn't sense Jason.

I looked at Zoe, feeling my eyes widen. I couldn't sense either of them. I could sense the animals all around, but I couldn't sense any human minds at all.

"Red…?" Jason's voice was soft, cautious.

"You're gone," I whispered, feeling like I'd been kicked in the stomach. "You're all gone." I looked into Zoe's piercing blue eyes. "Gone." My voice sounded hollow.

Zoe's grip tightened on my arm. "Um…"

Jason swiped the pads of his thumbs under my eyes, wiping away the tears of strain streaming down my cheeks. "Do you have control of it?" The concern filling his eyes intensified, and his calm expression cracked. "I've got to stop boosting you. Zoe…"

Oh God. No. Reality slammed into me like a punch in the gut. Jason's Ability had two parts: he could amplify others' Abilities, like he was currently doing for me, or he could nullify them completely, but he couldn't do both at the same time. If Zoe's empathy kicked in as violently as my telepathy just had, and if she started feeling other people's emotions and seeing their memories without knowing how to control it…

I nodded vigorously. "I'm good. Help Z—"

Without warning, Zoe gasped, and her hand clenched. Her fingernails dug into my arm.

We were too late. The floodgates had opened.

4

ZOE

MARCH 28, 1AE

San Juan National Forest, Colorado

I gasped as an unused part of my mind sparked to life. It seemed to shift and realign, jump-starting my true consciousness as if I'd been running on autopilot, but was now finally in control. Everything changed in the blink of an eye…I felt *whole*. At least more "myself" than I had since the others found me.

For a brief moment, among the torrent of feelings and memories flooding my mind, I thought the old me might resurface, too. "I think I'm—" *Getting my memories back?* It was almost too much to hope for.

As my mind spun, so did the onslaught of conflicting emotions—too random and unrecognizable to have been my own.

"Dani," I breathed. My eyes met hers, and I used the comfort I found in them as my anchor amid the impressions of foreign lifetimes competing for space in my mind. "Something's…not right." Dizziness enveloped me, and I gripped Dani's arm more tightly, automatically reaching for Jason, too.

"It's your Ability, Zo," Dani said, composed and reassuring. "Don't fight it—you'll only make it worse."

Images of Jason and Dani flickered in my head, but instead of trying to push them away, I let them come, vivid and countless as they were.

With what felt like a breath of life, I inhaled, and everything in my mind's eye sharpened. As unsteady as I felt, the clarity brought a sense of relief I hadn't expected, and the dark recesses of my mind filled with colors and shapes and sounds—recollections of the past. Dani and Jason's pasts, but not mine.

"I'm so sorry, Zo," Dani said, her fingers brushing softly over the back of my hand. "This is all my fault. Stupid…so stupid…"

I could feel her guilt, and I shook my head, only vaguely aware of *why* she felt that way. Dani's concern replaced my confusion, her curiosity and hope quickly following. Although I didn't necessarily understand the onslaught, I welcomed it. Everything I saw—everything I felt—was new and unexplored; my mind, once an empty cave, suddenly housed echoes of the past, assembling them into an irrefutable truth that seemed to lighten the darkness and partially fill the lingering void inside me.

But as abruptly as the emotions assaulted me, they vanished, and I felt empty again—the images and feelings were nothing more than fading memories.

Disappointed, I turned to Jason. "You're taking it away?"

He exchanged a skeptical glance with Dani. "Yeah?" he said, sounding unsure.

No longer needing to steady myself, I loosened my grasp on his arm and looked at him beseechingly. "Please don't," I said, self-conscious but *needing* this other part of me. "It feels…right."

Jason frowned. "Well…it's your choice," he mumbled, and although he seemed baffled, he nodded.

In an instant, another flurry of guilt, frustration, and despair swirled around in my mind. I blinked, once again focusing on Dani as memories and feelings poured out of her. Like a camera shutter opening and closing, I *saw* Dani for the first time. Yes, she was a fiery, red-haired pixie with bright green eyes and a seemingly carefree nature, but she also felt lost and afraid and confused. I could feel everything—her undeniable love for Jason, and the relentless shadow of a not-too-long-ago broken heart. Inexplicably, I shared her longing to see the woman who'd raised her, her grandma who was gone, and her yearning to speak with her one last time. And then I saw an image of the dead little girl, haunting Dani and flooding her with guilt.

My best friend, who I only knew from her coalescing memories and our stilted conversations over the past week, stood in front of me, and now I understood why she seemed to cry at the drop of a hat. Her emotions were so raw, rampant, and fierce that they almost brought tears to *my* eyes.

Enthralled by the insight I felt bringing me closer to Dani, I vaguely registered Jason walking away.

I blinked again.

"Zo?" Dani's hand rested on my shoulder, sending acute waves of anxiety and eagerness rippling through me. "Are you alright?" Her voice teetered between panic and remorse, and I could *feel* the questions practically jumping off her tongue. She was hoping that my memories had returned, but felt guilty for thinking it, and she was worried she'd accidently and irrevocably hurt me.

Forcing myself, I smiled, if a little weakly, and refocused on her imploring eyes. "Yeah, I am. I'm fine. Better than fine, actually."

"Are you sure?"

Nodding, I tried to reassure her. "I can see and feel it all so clearly."

"Like you can feel what I'm feeling?" A burst of apprehension flared inside her.

I bit the inside of my cheek, trying to articulate it. "It's more than that," I said, my voice tinged with excitement. "There are images…like memories, too…"

Dani's eyes lit with hope. "You remember?"

Crap. I sighed and shook my head, feeling a tidal wave of

excitement recede between the two of us. "No, I don't remember," I admitted, watching the light in her eyes dim. "I still don't remember anything from before the golf course…but I *see* you, Dani. I see you and me…my dad and Jason." I shook my head. "It's the strangest, most horrifyingly amazing thing I've ever experienced."

Although I had no attachment to the memories themselves, Dani's profound intimacy with each impression made me feel like I'd found a small piece of myself within them. "It's like I was there…when you were sick and Jason found you…and then when you were alone and at Grams's house." I tried to shake away the overwhelming fog in my head. "There's so much…"

Dani eyed me curiously, her fingers stroking the sling cradling her injured arm.

"I can feel your pain," I said, studying her black removable cast. "I can see what happened at the Colony. I feel like I finally understand what's going on."

Dani's eyes widened as fear replaced her curiosity, and the jumble of images focused, a tumultuous memory flashing prominently through her mind.

Dani stood in a stark office, a perfectly organized desk separating her from Dr. Wesley, who was sitting behind it.

The doctor eyed Dani warily. "So you know?"

Dani felt a pulse of rage. "That Zoe and Jason are your kids? Yeah…"

Another more vivid memory immediately followed.

In the same office, Dr. Wesley still seated behind the desk and Dani standing opposite her, the doctor's features hardened into a frown. "If your actions kill my children, then everything I've done to keep them safe will have been for naught. That's *on you."*

Dani shook her head, so much hurt and anger filling her that she could barely speak. "Zo and Jason might blame themselves for everyone's deaths if they knew about you, but I don't. I blame you,*" she seethed and stormed to the door.*

"Would you rather I'd killed myself, thus killing the two people you love so dearly? Gregory would have found another geneticist to engineer his virus, and everyone would've died anyway."

The memory faded, leaving in its place violent emotions tangled in my gut, nearly bringing me to my knees.

Dr. Wesley is my mom… I'd completely forgotten that.

Dani took a step closer. "We *can't* tell him," she whispered as her eyes darted around us. "He can't know about your mom, Zo, not yet."

I hedged. "But she's our *mom*, Dani. He'll be furious if we don't tell him, won't he?" Lacking any tangible connection to Jason, I still wanted to do what was right, and I'd seen enough of his silent tantrums in her memories to know this instance would be no exception.

"She's your mom *and* she killed nearly everyone to keep you guys safe." Dani closed her eyes and took a deep breath, her eyes pleading when she reopened them. "Please, Zo. Don't say anything. He's not ready. Can't you see…can't you *feel* it?" Dani's acute panic and desperation were nearly overwhelming.

Rough laughter startled me, and I glanced over to the cart to see Jason and Carlos chatting as they sat on the bench, whittling. Although I had the impression that Jason wouldn't want me to pry around inside his head, I needed to; I needed to understand *why* Dani was so adamant to keep the truth from him.

Focusing beyond her swirling emotions, I searched for Jason's. While Dani's were easy to access, an invisible wall surrounded Jason's, cold and excruciatingly controlled. I focused harder. It was difficult with Dani so close, her emotions so intense, but I could see and feel just enough from Jason to understand. There had been too much heartache, and too many lies and surprises to unleash another tumultuous mess on him while he was already so distraught.

Like he could somehow sense my cerebral intrusion, Jason stopped whittling for a moment and glanced over at me. The instant his knowing eyes met mine, the invisible wall protecting his mind solidified, blocking me out completely.

Standing there, with only a brief impression of who he was fresh in my mind, I felt closer to him than I probably ever would have had my Ability remained dormant. And I understood; Dani was right. Learning that our mom was still alive, that she'd made the choice to leave when Jason was a young child, and that she'd been the cause of so much death would devastate him, especially while the real me wasn't around to help bear the weight of the discovery.

Dani clutched my hand, silently pleading with me to keep quiet as Jason glanced between us.

With a quick squeeze in return, I reassured her of my silence, at least for a while.

Harper and Chris emerged from the nearest cluster of trees, chatting amiably as they made their way back to camp with armfuls of firewood. When Harper's eyes found mine, his relaxed expression tensed, and he hurried over to us.

"You doing okay, Baby Girl?" His expression was pinched with worry—a look I'd grown weary of over the last few days. "You're pale."

"I'm fine," I said, waving his concern away. There was nothing like a resurgence of forgotten memories and pitying glances to make me feel like the most pathetic woman in the world.

As I took a few steps toward Harper and Chris, I stumbled, the bombardment of their worries, memories, and emotions throwing me off kilter. Dropping his armful of firewood, Harper jogged the final few steps between us to lend me a supporting hand.

I snickered. *Yep, I'm pathetic.*

"I'm okay," I said. "It's just my Ability…it's a little overwhelming, and my head's frazzled…I think."

"So, Jason's not…" Chris glanced over at my brother. "A little advanced notice would've been nice," she grumbled, though I didn't really understand her spike of irritation.

"It was an accident," Dani chimed in, sounding tired. She patted Wings's neck. "I'll send Wings and Shadow out to pasture with the other horses, then head over and warn"—Dani's gaze flicked to me, and her cheeks reddened as shame emanated from her—"tell the others." After a brief moment, the sound of lazy, clomping hooves retreated behind me.

Harper helped me over to lean against a lone tree trunk growing along the edge of the pond. His memories and feelings resonated within me, and I mentally waded through the streaming information, effortlessly absorbing pieces of who he was. He was so good and confident and calm; I couldn't help but admire him.

"You sure you're alright, Baby Girl?" he asked, scanning me as I gripped the trunk of the tree.

"Yeah. I'm okay, really." I blushed at being the center of unwanted attention.

With a pat on my shoulder, Chris excused herself and headed over to join Jason and Carlos. I hadn't missed her and Harper's silent, charged exchange before she walked away. Their growing connection was impossible to miss, especially when I could *feel* their mutual attraction.

Harper glanced over at Chris's retreating form, appraising her covertly, or so he thought. When he noticed me eyeing him, he smiled, a knowing glint in his peridot-colored eyes.

"Interesting," I said, eyebrows raised in amusement.

He nudged my shoulder with his. "You see too much," he said and waggled his eyebrows.

I knew *that* was true, so all I could do was shrug. "I'm still learning how to navigate this whole Ability thing," I said.

He winked at me. "You'll get the hang of it."

"And in the meantime, you'll all avoid me like I'm a leper?" I asked acerbically. Being bitter wouldn't help, but it was hard not to be when people were suddenly running as far away from me as possible, despite their smiles.

"Everyone just needs time, Baby Girl, including you. You'll get the hang of it, and if not, they'll warm up to it eventually."

"I sure hope so," I muttered.

Tavis's laughter rumbled on the faint breeze, and I could hear him and Sam bantering back and forth. After a quick glance around, I spotted them walking along the other side of the reservoir, water jugs in their hands. The still water began to ripple, and I realized I hadn't noticed the wind pick up.

"Whatever," Sam said.

I smiled as they drew closer. Their companionable chatter was familiar, the one feeling I yearned for the most. I welcomed the sense of comfort that came with the sounds of their voices.

"Not true," Tavis said with a laugh as they approached. "You'd never beat me if it weren't for your Ability, mate, and that's a fact."

Sam sighed, his annoyance making me smile. "You're just using that as an excuse."

"As if!" Tavis said with half a laugh.

"Even Zoe's a better shot than you," Sam said. "At least she *was*."

Tavis stopped mid-step, appalled by Sam's comment. "Not even true, and your Ability gives you an unfair advantage."

Sam laughed. "You're just mad because you don't know what your Ability is yet."

"What? Grayson doesn't know what his Ability is either." Narrowing his eyes to slits, Tavis tried not to smile. "Maybe we're Crazies…"

"That's what *I* was thinking," Sam said.

Looking to me and Harper, Tavis shook his head. "Can you

believe this kid? He has supersonic hearing and can see a mile away, and he thinks I'm using it as an excuse."

Unbidden, a soft chuckle escaped from my throat. "I just don't understand why you're not improving your archery skills, Tavis. I mean, Sam seems like a good teacher. Maybe it *is* you."

"I can't bloody believe it," Tavis said, peering up into the sky and spreading his arms like someone might actually care enough about his aiming issues to listen. "I taught the kid everything he knows, and suddenly *I'm* the one who needs to practice." He tsked and shook his head. "Cheeky little bugger." A wolfish grin spread across his face, and he and Sam sauntered closer, stopping beside Harper and me.

Harper rumpled my hair, messing up my ponytail. "If you're alright, Baby Girl, I'm gonna head back to camp." He glanced at Chris again, who was still standing with Jason and Carlos, before he turned to Tavis. "Her Ability's back online," he cautioned, and I sighed involuntarily. *My presence warrants a warning now—great.*

Taking a deep breath, I tried to remind myself that while others' memories helped me feel a little more like a member of the group, being so emotionally exposed wasn't something most people would appreciate.

"Do you remember us yet?" Sam asked as he crouched and picked at the burs in his shoestrings.

I bit at the inside of my cheek and felt my eyebrows draw together. "No," I admitted. "Not yet." I didn't bother telling him that I knew he'd won his first blue ribbon in a relay race in third grade, and that his sister, Anastasia, had been born a year and half ago, and that his father had died from the Virus right before his mother had been raped and killed by Crazies. I knew all of that, but had no recollection of him from *my* past. "But do you think you can work with me on my archery? From what Harper tells me, I used be a decent shot. I could use a skill or a pastime or…something, at least until my memories get sorted out."

Sam peered up at me. "Yeah, we might as well." He paused,

squinting one eye as he studied me. "Do you think you'll *really* get your memories back?"

Shrugging, I said, "I'm not really sure. I'm still trying to piece things together. It's weird to see myself with everyone…to watch their memories play out like a movie, but still not actually recall any of it."

Tavis crossed his arms over his chest and stared at me, contemplating. "Why not stop trying to figure out the past, and try embracing the way things are now? You can't change anything that's happened, and you have no idea how long this 'issue' might last. You might never be your old self again," he said matter-of-factly.

I looked into Tavis's inquisitive blue eyes. "I haven't thought about it like that."

"Well," Sam said, "I want you to get your memory back."

"Yeah? And why's that?" I asked.

Sam took a deep, thoughtful breath. "For starters, you can't hold up your part of our deal like this," he said somberly.

"Our deal?"

"Yeah." He shrugged. "You're supposed to teach me how to draw, and I'm supposed to help you with your archery." Sam seemed annoyed by the inconvenience of my memory loss, but I could tell he was more disappointed than upset with me.

"Well," I ventured, "I can try—"

Sam was shaking his head before I could even finish my train of thought.

"No?"

He looked at me, a yeah-right expression on his face. "Do you even know if you can still draw?"

I feigned offense. "Well, no, not exactly. I haven't thought to try. I can still do other things."

"Just trust me," Sam said.

"Well, you're an…honest kid, I'll give you that much. There's no beating around the bush with you."

Sam only shrugged again, and Tavis chuckled.

"Sam keeps things interesting," Tavis said, his tone more affectionate than I thought he realized, and a great big smile engulfed my face. Being around them made me happy; it was a welcome distraction from the awkwardness I felt around the others.

"A girl could get used to hanging out with the two of you," I said.

It was then that I noticed Jake and Cooper striding over from the other side of the pond. Jake's gaze shifted between Tavis and me.

The look in his eyes sobered me instantly. There was something about him, regardless of the fact that I couldn't remember him or the "us" I'd been told about, that made my insides flutter with anticipation. I took a step closer to him.

"Hi," I said a little breathily. We'd barely spoken, and I always seemed to struggle with what to say to him.

Being around him made me want more than ever to have my memories back, to be able to understand the feelings I thought I could almost feel somewhere deep inside me whenever he was nearby. *Or is it all just in my head?* It was impossible to say, but I wished, more than was probably healthy, that one day I might know.

If we were a couple, I should just talk to him. I didn't see any harm in that. He didn't bite…at least not that I was aware of.

Jake's eyes passed over Sam and Tavis to land on me, and a tight smile pulled at his lips. His dark gaze focused on me like he was trying to see inside me, trying to figure me out.

"Hey, Coop," Sam called and shuffled over to the husky, patting the dog's head and rumpling his scruffy neck. "Wanna play fetch?"

Jake smiled down at Sam as the boy fawned over Cooper, but I wondered what brewed beneath the surface of Jake's composed demeanor. His eyes were telling, I just hadn't figured out how to read them yet.

Just as I was about to push away from the tree I was leaning against, Sam jumped up to his feet, brushing his hands off on his pants. "Did you hear? Zoe's Ability's back."

Jake's smile faltered, and his gaze darted from Sam to me. "No," he said. "I didn't." His hands flexed at his sides.

"Not her memory yet, but the rest of her."

I thought I should probably talk to Jake about *us* before too much more time passed and the distance continued to grow between us. But just as I was about to ask him if we could go somewhere to talk, he turned and walked away, calling for Cooper over his shoulder.

Slouching back against the tree, I sighed. *Or not.*

5

JAKE

MARCH 28, 1AE

San Juan National Forest, Colorado

Lost in a tornado of thought, Jake swung an archaic, rusted axe, splintering the last of the firewood into stackable, burnable pieces—probably more pieces than were actually necessary. His palms were raw, but he welcomed the burn, the distraction.

The sun had just set behind the serrated mountaintops, and the brisk, evening air against his sweat-dampened skin helped take the edge off of a day filled with problematic surprises.

Jake crouched and gathered as much of the firewood into his arms as he could carry and headed over to the wood stacked on top of one of the carts. Cooper raised his head from snoozing, no doubt hopeful it was time to go lie by the campfire, where it was warm and there were plenty of people to pet him.

"Not yet, buddy," Jake said as he unloaded the armful of wood.

Watching Zoe, wondering what the hell she was thinking, had become almost unbearable over the past week. Simply talking to her about what had happened, about *them*, proved harder than he'd imagined. If she wasn't laughing with Tavis, she was with Dani learning the ropes in their new world, or Chris was prodding around in Zoe's brain, trying to figure out exactly how much damage Clara had done. And since the blood transfusion they'd tried a few nights ago hadn't done a damn thing to repair her shattered memory, he was beginning to lose hope that she would *ever* be the same.

The good things are worth fighting for, Joe, his guardian during the year after his mom died, had told him once. It was a motto Jake lived by, but now that Zoe's Ability was back, Jake wasn't sure fighting for her was the best thing for her. He was worried about what she might feel or see when she was around him, and he didn't want to scare the hell out of her before she even had time to get to know him—or herself—again.

But Zoe wasn't the only complication he was dealing with. Having Gabe *and* Becca suddenly back in his life was almost more than he could handle. His sister was still different, and looked at him like he was a complete stranger. And Gabe…Jake shook his head. He didn't want to think about Gabe, which was easy enough.

As usual, his thoughts returned to Zoe. Over the months he'd known the teal-eyed, raven-haired beauty, she'd become his home. But she didn't tease him anymore, and her maddening stubbornness and innate devotion to those she loved was nonexistent.

Resting the axe on its head, Jake let the handle fall to the ground. He exhaled and scrubbed both hands over his stubbled face.

A shadowed figure came toward him from the copse of trees a few dozen yards away. Cooper was up and running toward it before Jake even realized it was Gabe. He was carrying an armful of firewood that he let fall to the ground as he stopped in front of Jake.

Needing to put some distance between them, Jake decided it was time to call it a night, and he reached for his jacket draped over the cart.

"I need you to know something," Gabe said quietly. Jake

turned around to find Gabe crouched and leaning on the discarded axe.

Jake clenched his jaw, contemplating whether or not it would be best to simply walk away.

Gabe sighed and rested one elbow on his knee, letting his hand drape in front of him. "I know you won't forgive me," he said. "But I *am* sorry. I didn't want any of this to happen. If I'd known what Becca was going to do..." After a short pause, he shook his head. "I did everything I could to help her in the Colony."

"And Dani?"

Gabe let a despondent chuckle escape from his throat. "Like I had a choice? Don't you get it? I *had* to bring her in—to protect your sister." In an instant, Gabe was on his feet. "*Everything* I've done has been to protect Becca. The General—he would have *tortured* her. He *did* torture her. If I hadn't brought him a two-way telepath...you don't want to know..." Seeming to deflate, Gabe let out a humorless laugh. "And poor Dani was the one to pay for my loyalty to Becca...to you."

"Loyalty? Loyalty would have been telling us what the hell was going on in the first place, not bringing armed fucking soldiers into my house...not letting them knock me out, then disappearing and taking my sister's body with you." Jake gestured toward the campfire, where everyone was gathered. "What happened to Dani isn't on me and Becca—it's on you."

For a moment, Gabe said nothing. "I know."

His hopeless tone affected Jake more than he wanted it to. "How the hell did you get yourself in this mess to begin with?"

Gabe looked at Jake, his eyes silver in the moonlight. "I'd been researching Abilities for a while, but I didn't know about the General's plan until the Virus was already spreading. When you called and told me Becca was sick, it was right when I'd started putting the pieces together..." He looked away. "They wouldn't let me off base without an armed escort. I came—brought *them*—because I wanted to help her, and I didn't have much of a choice."

Jake pinned Gabe in place with an accusatory glare and allowed himself to ask the one question that outweighed all others. "Did you know they'd turn Becca into a Re-gen?"

Gabe returned his glare. "No, Jake, I didn't. I didn't know she'd kill herself, either, or that they'd knock you out or appropriate her body." He was breathing harder. "Do you know how I left your house that night?" He paused. "At gunpoint. I wasn't going to leave you, not passed out…I thought you were dying, but there was nothing I could do. I couldn't let them take Becca. I was barely able to write that goddamn note before I was *escorted* out."

Jake was speechless, more than stunned by Gabe's admission.

Gabe sighed, and his voice softened. "In case you lived…I needed to warn you, and I knew you would go to the gun cabinet." He was quiet for a moment, leaving Jake's thoughts to reel. Finally, he took a deep breath. "You're my brother in every way that matters, Jake—always have been, and always will be. Nothing could change that, not even you hating me for the rest of your life."

Jake leaned against the cart, crossed his arms over his chest, and sighed, expelling months' worth of anger and betrayal and hurt. Having no idea what to say, he stood there in awe, the orchestra of crickets the only thing filling the silence. He was surprised by how quickly things seemed to shift, and how grateful he suddenly felt to be standing only a few yards away from his friend again, despite all that had happened.

Jake shook his head. "What does Becca know?"

Gabe shook his head, and he ran his hand through his loose hair, a nervous habit he'd had since childhood. "Nothing. She has no idea who I am, or that I've been looking out for her. To her, I'm just Dr. McLaughlin." He lowered his hand. "And I swear I had nothing to do with what happened to Zoe. If I could do something, help somehow—"

"I know," Jake said. He knew Clara hadn't needed any incentive to hurt Zoe. "I know," he repeated. Not wanting to think about all the bad decisions *he'd* made and how they kept returning to bite him in the ass, Jake grabbed his jacket. "Thank you," he said and turned to head back to camp. "Come on, Coop."

Voices and laughter carried on the breeze as Jake drew closer to camp. Cooper rushed past him, heading straight for Becca and Carlos, who were chatting by the chuck wagon. Despite Jake's best efforts, his eyes automatically sought out Zoe. She was sitting by the fire, her hair wet and hanging around her shoulders. Sam was sitting beside her, and both had pencils in their hands and sketch-books on their laps.

Jake's heart ached at the sight of her smiling with the kid. And when he noticed Tavis leaning over Sam's shoulder, misery cemented in the pit of his stomach.

As if he'd voiced the thought, Zoe's gaze shifted up to his. Her smile vanished, making him feel like an intruder, and her eyes grew wide and questioning. Instinctively, he offered her a curt nod before he turned and strode for his tent.

"Hello," came a soft, raspy voice.

Jake turned around to find Becca standing directly behind him. He let out a shaky breath. He was still getting used to seeing his sister's gray eyes, no longer the violet color he'd been used to growing up.

Jake's hands found his pockets as he stood there, feeling an uneasy excitement.

"Are you hungry?" she asked, offering him a bowl of stew. "I noticed that you have not eaten much today, and you have been overworking yourself."

He eyed her curiously, wondering if it was concern that slightly changed the cadence of her voice. "Aren't *you* hungry?" He gestured to the bowl.

Becca smiled timidly and shook her head, her wavy brown hair brushing against her shoulders. "I've already eaten. This"—she took a step closer—"is for you." Her eyes shifted between Jake and the bowl. "Please, take it."

Realizing she might take his surprise as some sort of rejection of her kindness, Jake offered her a grateful smile. "I'm starving. Thanks." He wrapped his fingers around the warm bowl and walked back toward the fire, lowering himself into an empty chair and accepting a red- and white-checkered napkin from Becca as well.

"Sarah has been teaching me how to cook," Becca said as she pulled over a chair to sit beside him. A faint scent of herbs wafted off of her.

Becca had never been much of a cook; neither of them had, and Jake wondered if that happened to be the only thing about her that hadn't changed. He stared down into the bowl and then back up at her, hesitant.

When her eyes met his again, they were expectant.

Clearing his throat, Jake took a deep breath, leaned forward, and put a spoonful of stew into his mouth. The broth was warm and salty…and surprisingly delicious. He looked at his sister askance.

She was fidgeting beside him, worrying her bottom lip. "Well," she said, "what do you think?"

After chewing and swallowing a hunk of meat, Jake took another bite. "It's good," he said, proud of Becca's effort to become part of the group. He was comforted by the fact that she was going to the trouble to have a conversation with him, too. "It's really good."

Becca smiled. "I am glad."

"You like cooking, then?" he asked, taking another mouthful.

Her brow furrowed, and she looked at his bowl thoughtfully. "I think I do," she said. "At least, I do not *dislike* it."

"Good." He offered her a reassuring smile before taking another bite.

Becca sat beside him while he ate, watching him intently. Although he wondered what she was thinking, he didn't want to push her, so he sat with her in companionable silence.

"Jake," she finally said.

His gaze shifted to her as he swallowed another spoonful.

"I wanted you to know that I am sorry."

Nearly choking, he set his spoon down and wiped his mouth with his napkin. "You're sorry for what?" he asked.

Becca's eyes focused on his. "For not remembering."

Jake was the one who'd gotten her into this mess. He looked away from her and into the fire, frustration resurfacing as the events of the past couple months came crashing back down on him. "It's not your fault, Becca. None of this is. I should've—"

"Perhaps not," she interrupted and placed her hand on his arm. "But it still hurts you."

Jake was surprised she cared much about that; she'd been reticent to believe all he'd told her about her past in the first place.

"Although I do not have strong emotions like you and some of the others seem to have, I cannot imagine what it must be like to have me sitting beside you with no recollection of our past together. And now…" her eyes traveled over to Zoe.

Jake's chest tightened.

"I know it is not easy for you, and I am sorry there is nothing I can do to help."

Her final words to him the night she'd bled out in his arms coalesced in his mind, and he wanted so badly to know something. "You told me, that night—the last night I saw you—that I would save her, but that I would also kill her." He paused. "Do you have any idea why you said that or what it meant?" Every time Jake thought the moment Becca had warned him of had come and gone and that Zoe would finally be safe, something would happen that would make him doubt the danger had past.

Becca closed her eyes and shook her head. "No, I am sorry."

Appetite waning, Jake set the half-eaten bowl in his lap. "You don't have to be sorry, Becca. You—"

"The way you look at her," Becca interrupted him again. "You keep your distance when you should not."

Jake collected himself, a little stunned by Becca's adamancy, then his gaze darted to Zoe once again. Like before, her eyes drifted to his. "I don't want to scare her," he admitted.

"Why would she be scared?"

"She's not the same, I can see it in her eyes. She won't understand what she sees…what she feels."

When Becca said nothing, he met his sister's confused stare. "You mean, your feelings for her? Why should that scare her?"

"Wouldn't you be?"

"Scared?"

He nodded.

"I am scared right now. I know no one, just as she does not. But I am still curious. I still *want* to remember. I want to understand the truth…to understand who I am."

Jake closed his gaping mouth. "You do?"

Becca nearly smiled again. "It is hard to predict another person's feelings, is it not?" She frowned infinitesimally. "You cannot protect her from what is. You can only help her understand. If I said such a thing to you…before"—Becca glanced quickly to Zoe—"then there was a reason, I am certain of it, but it could very well already have come to pass."

Jake gave Becca a quizzical look. "Won't it be overwhelming for her to learn about *us* if she doesn't even remember *me*? I'm a complete stranger to her."

Becca's eyes brightened with understanding, and she smiled sympathetically. "You are assuming she will reject you."

"Hell yeah, I am."

His sister tilted her head. "And what if she doesn't? What if she accepts you instead?" she asked fluidly without her stilted, formal inflection. "Shouldn't she get to decide how she feels?"

Jake frowned this time. When he realized his sister's eyes were gleaming with an emotion he couldn't quite place, he couldn't help but think she knew something he didn't, and the hope that swelled inside him scared him shitless. Sighing, he leaned forward, knowing that allowing Zoe to see his memories could create an irreparable fissure between them.

"I should go," Becca said abruptly and rose, taking his bowl.

Surprised, Jake straightened and glanced up at her. He was about to ask her to stay when he noticed Zoe slowly approaching from the other side of the fire. Her hands tapped at her sides, and her gaze fixed on the ground. Her face was relaxed, unmarred by the worry lines he was so used to. She smiled at Becca as they passed one another. Jake watched her approach with bated breath.

"Hey," Zoe said, exactly as she had the day she'd walked into the auto shop at Fort Knox, the same uncertain, beautifully curious and awkward look on her face. But when she finally made eye contact with him, Jake couldn't help but notice that the usual, mischievous gleam was gone.

Jake smoothed his palms over his thighs and moved to stand.

Zoe held up her hand to stop him. "Please, don't get up." She shook her head, causing her hair to fall in front of her eyes. She let it hang around her face like it was a shield and stared down at the camping chair beside his. "This is so silly, isn't it?" she said and finally met his gaze. There was something about the look on her face that prevented him from speaking.

Automatically, she started to lower herself into the chair beside him, then froze. Eyebrows lifted and eyes filled with what Jake thought might be embarrassment, she cleared her throat. "Sorry," she said, and shook her head as she let out a nervous breath. "Do you mind if I sit?"

"Of course not," Jake said. He had to resist the urge to brush her hair away from her eyes, to pull her closer, to hold her hand, to do *something* that was *them.*

Finally, gathering the loose strands of her hair behind her head, Zoe twisted them away from her face before she let them fall and unfurl down her back. She dropped her hands into her lap, took a long, deep breath, and closed her eyes.

Jake wanted to reach out to her, to offer her some sort of reassurance. But then she tilted her head to the side and peered into his eyes, which surprised him.

"You're avoiding me—" she said as he began, "How are you feel—"

She smiled at him and licked her lips as she rested her elbows on her knees. "It's weird," she said, blushing.

"Which part?" Jake asked, knowing everything she'd learned about her life—about the world—was probably equally difficult to grasp.

Biting the inside of her cheek, she studied him for a moment. "You're more difficult to read than the others," she finally admitted.

Jake felt a sudden flood of relief.

"Well, except for Jason. But…" She waved the idea of her brother away. "Look, Jake…I know I'm not *her*, but I—" She gazed up at him thoughtfully. "I don't want you to have to feel like you can't be around me. I mean, if you still want to be. I don't want you to avoid me like the plague unless you…ya know…"

"I'm not avoiding you, not exactly," he finally said. "I want to give you your space…a chance to get used to things."

Zoe shook her head. "You're all so worried I'll see too much, so you avoid me. It just makes everything worse…harder." She bent her knee and pulled it up, hugging it against her chest. "I want to feel normal, but how can I when everyone acts differently around me, when everyone tries to censor themselves…their memories?" She stared into the fire, lost in thought.

Jake watched her as she bit the inside of her cheek. He'd never thought about it in that way.

When he didn't reply, Zoe peered at him, her eyes softening. "I know this must be hard for you, too, and I'm sorry I don't remember you or us. But maybe if you just give me some time…" Her eyebrows pinched together, and her voice sounded near pleading.

Jake studied her a moment. "I don't want to rush you," he said, and he forced himself to say the next words, wanting, more than anything, to comfort her. "You'll remember…soon."

Zoe offered him a weak smile. "Maybe." Her ambiguity was evident.

"You don't think so?"

Zoe shrugged. "I feel like it would've happened already, but…" She shook her head, her hair falling around her face again. "Anyway, I just wanted you to know that you don't have to avoid me…"

Abruptly, she rose, and without thought, Jake reached for her hand.

When she froze and glanced down at his fingers entwined with hers, a weak smile tugged at her lips. She cleared her throat. "Goodnight," she whispered.

"Goodnight," he said, and he thought he felt Zoe squeeze his fingers slightly before letting go and walking away. He tried not to let his heart swell with too much hope as she returned to her spot on the other side of the fire, Sam and Tavis laughing with one another and smiling at her as she plopped down between them.

6

DANI

MARCH 28, 1AE

San Juan National Forest, Colorado

I sat atop the bench of the chuck wagon, the highest spot in camp, keeping watch by staring out at the moonlit field of tall grasses and the wooded foothills beyond that. Not that the "keeping watch" part of keeping watch was strictly necessary now that my Ability had returned, even only partially; dozens of nocturnal creatures were linked into my telepathic network, ready to alert me of any incoming two-legs, and their senses were so much better than mine, even when I was paying super close attention. Which, I was a little ashamed to admit, I definitely *wasn't* doing at the moment.

Part of me was wondering what Jason was doing, since he'd originally been scheduled to be my watch partner tonight, and part of me couldn't get enough of basking in the gentle touch of the non-human minds all around me. It was one of those things I hadn't truly appreciated until I'd thought it was gone, maybe forever. I couldn't help but dwell on the possibility that my relationship with Jason might be headed in that same direction.

Apparently I was paying too much attention to those things,

and not nearly enough to my surroundings. Someone touched my knee—clearly not a "dangerous" someone, since the animals hadn't warned me, but that didn't stop me from being startled. My left elbow nicked the armrest, and just that small impact sent a shock of pain branching out along my forearm.

"Owww…" I scrunched up my face. Which also hurt, thanks to Clara getting a little too slap-happy with me during my time in one of the Colony's subterranean interrogation rooms.

"Careful," Carlos murmured as he hauled himself up onto the wagon's bench seat. He draped an arm over my shoulders and tucked me close against his side. Since my escape, he'd been hovering around me nearly as much as Jason had been, but unlike Jason, Carlos hadn't built an impenetrable fortress—with a moat and alligators—around his emotions. Having Carlos around was comforting rather than draining. In the several months since we'd freed him from the mind-controlling clutches of a madwoman, he'd become the little brother I never had.

I smiled up at him. He was a good half-foot taller than me, despite being only sixteen. But then, pretty much everyone was taller than me. Even Sam was taller than me, and he was only ten. I sighed my most damsel-in-distress sigh. "What would I ever do without you?"

"You *don't* want me to answer that." Carlos's tone was dry, but one corner of his mouth quirked upward.

My eyes narrowed. "Smart-ass." Inside, I grinned, just a little. At least Jason's sullenness wasn't rubbing off on his protégée like his general mess-with-me-and-I'll-rip-your-face-off attitude and absolutely filthy mouth were.

"So where *is* Jason, anyway? Not that I'm disappointed to have you join me, but he *was* supposed to be my partner for first watch…"

Carlos gave my shoulders a squeeze. "He fell asleep after dinner, when you were off with Zoe and Chris at the creek." He chuckled softly. "He was just sitting by the fire, his head hanging down like this." Carlos's arm slipped away, and he mimed nodding off with his chin lowered to his chest. "So I offered to take his place. He's passed out in your tent."

He scooted over, putting a few inches between us. "So, um…I haven't really been using my Ability since the breakout thing. I mean, I don't know if you noticed or anything…"

I *had* noticed, mostly because I'd been told about his Ability—that he had some sort of control over electricity—but other than knowing he'd knocked the power out during the escape from the Colony, I'd yet to see him use it up close. He'd overexerted it, resulting in Ability burnout just like me, but his had come back online days ago. He seemed reluctant to use it, and I assumed it was because he feared he would burn it out again.

"I noticed," I told him with a slow nod, continuing to scan the circle of colorful tents that made up our camp and the darkness surrounding them. "Sure, I'm totally curious to see you work your electricity mojo, but I've lost access to my Ability a couple times now, and I get it—losing it, even for just a little while…" I shook my head. "It's like going blind or deaf…or getting a hand chopped off, you know? You think about it—*miss* it—all the time, because it's not there." I sighed. *And sometimes, when it comes back, it's broken,* I didn't say.

Carlos crossed his arms over his chest and stared out at the horses, who were milling around in the overgrown grasses. "I guess, yeah, I was scared of losing it again. At first, I mean. I thought using it might burn it out again, and then I started thinking…what if something happens and, like, those people take you again—take any of us—and we have to do it all over again? What if that happened, and I couldn't send out an EMP blast?"

I studied his profile, thinking I should probably say something comforting or wise or Grams-like. Nothing. I couldn't think of a single thing to say. I touched my hand to the silver medallion hanging around my neck; it had belonged to Grams, and I was hoping to draw on some of her maternal wisdom through it. Nope; no such luck.

Carlos shrugged, still not looking at me. "But then I—" He met my eyes for the briefest moment and laughed a soft, humorless laugh. "It was like I could hear my sister yelling at me, telling me I was being stupid, that it was okay to be scared, but not to let it rule me, you know?"

It was the first time he'd ever mentioned a sister, but it wasn't a surprise that he'd never mentioned her before. Not many of my companions spent much time talking about the people they'd lost, myself included. Talking about it made it seem that much more real, that much fresher; it made us really acknowledge the fact that we would never see any of them again. *Because of Zo and Jason's mom...*

"So I started practicing again. Turning stuff on, sending out small EM pulses, and, well..." Carlos turned his moon-shadowed eyes on me, looking at me fully for the first time since joining me on the wagon's bench seat. "If I show you something, will you keep it a secret? I just—I don't want everyone to know yet." He smiled and shook his head and, for once, looked like the teen boy he was. "I'm not that good at it... *yet*."

I swallowed, searching his eyes for some clue of what he was about to share with me. Finally, I nodded.

"Hold out your hand."

I frowned, and hurt filled his eyes.

"You don't trust me?"

My heart felt like it dropped into my stomach. "No—I mean, yes, of course I trust you. I'd trust you with my life," I said in a rush. I held out my hand, palm up, and forced a smile that I hoped offered him some reassurance. "Please. Show me."

Relief filled Carlos's shadowed eyes, and he returned my smile with a tentative one of his own. "Don't move, okay?" When I nodded, he extended his hand, holding his palm directly over mine. "I found a physics textbook and have been reading up on electromagnetic fields and charges and Faraday's Law, and how—" He laughed and shook his head. "You don't care about that stuff."

But he was wrong. I *did* care about "that stuff." I cared that he was actively seeking out information that might help him explore his Ability. Electromagnetic fields, charges, and something called "Faraday's Law" sounded like fairly ambitious research topics, especially for a sixteen-year-old. *He should talk to Gabe...*

"That stuff I read got me thinking," Carlos continued. "And I tried some different things, and...well, I came up with this." He paused, and when he spoke again, his voice was nearly a whisper. "Ready?"

Again, I nodded.

He took a deep breath, and a gentle tingling sensation spread over my palm. It felt odd—a little itchy, but not unpleasant. Gradually, almost like I was dipping my hand into hot water slowly enough to allow my skin to grow accustomed to the temperature, the tingling sensation spread, climbing around to the back of my hand and up to my wrist and higher. When it reached my shoulder and just started to extend onto my torso, I drew in a shaky breath. "What—what is this?"

"Does it feel okay?" he asked, his eyes searching my face. "It doesn't hurt, does it?"

"No, no," I said, laughing a little. "It's just, um, I don't even know. It's almost fuzzy...sort of. Does that sound right?"

The tightness around Carlos's eyes relaxed, and he nodded. The tingling sensation started spreading down my torso and up my neck much faster.

"I got the idea from you, actually." A quick smile flashed across his face before it retreated under his increasingly tense mask of concentration. "I thought, maybe if I could control it enough, we could do our own version of that electrotherapy stuff you mentioned, but without the torture part." His eyebrows drew together as the tingling reached my opposite arm and my thighs.

"You know, so like, a lot slower and with less electricity and stuff, but still enough to make our Abilities stronger…?"

I had to stifle my first instinct at hearing him mention electrotherapy, which was to shudder and pull away. "I—" I took a deep breath. "I think that's an excellent idea. I bet Gabe would love to hel—"

"No." Carlos retracted his hand, and the tingling sensation evaporated immediately. "Not him. We can't trust him, not after what he did to you."

That earned another frown. "Carlos…" I reached over and touched his wrist. "Ouch!" As soon as our skin made contact, electricity shocked my fingertips, numbing my hand almost instantly.

Carlos leapt off the wagon, stumbling as he landed on the ground. "I'm sorry!" He spun around and stared up at me, his eyes opened too wide. "Shit, Dani, I'm *so* sorry!"

"Carlos—"

"You can't touch me when I've been doing stuff like that. I forgot to tell you—Jesus fucking—I could've *killed* you!"

Shaking out my arm, I laughed, aiming for nonchalant, but hitting nervous perfectly. "No worries. Just killed the nerves in my hand for a few seconds." I held up my hand and wiggled my fingers. "It's already going away."

Carlos didn't look the least bit reassured. "I'm sorry. I should've warned you." He hit his forehead with the heel of his hand several times. "I wasn't thinking. It was stupid. I—"

"It's fine, really," I said as I moved to the end of the bench seat and hopped down. I took two steps toward him and offered a tight-lipped smile. "It's better than fine, really." Pausing, I looked into his haunted eyes. "This could be a game-changer down the road. If we can use this to increase our Abilities…" As I trailed off, I shook my head. I wasn't exactly looking forward to the undefined period of having a nonfunctioning Ability that resulted from electrotherapy while my invigorated synapses settled back down, but there was no denying how badly we needed to be as strong, as capable, and as dangerous as we could possibly be. *And,* a tiny voice said in the back of my mind, *maybe this could fix my broken Ability...*

Carlos's brow furrowed, uncertainty and hope clear on his face. "You think this could work the same as the electroshock stuff they did to you?"

I took a deep breath, exhaling slowly. "I do," I said with a nod. "But I really think you should talk to Gabe about—" I held up my hand, cutting off Carlos's protests as soon as he opened his mouth. "He knows more about this kind of thing than anyone else. He's experienced it—*firsthand*—just like me, *and* he's a freaking genius. If you want your non-torture version of electrotherapy to work, he's your best bet."

Carlos's gaze shifted to some point low and off to the side. "I'll think about it."

"Hey," I said, and without thinking, I reached for his arm. "Maybe—"

He backpedaled out of reach so quickly that I flinched.

"I'm sorry." I held my hand up. "That was stupid. My fault, okay?"

Carlos stared at me with wide, horrified eyes. "You can't do that shit around me, Dani. If you—if I—I could—"

"Kill me, I know." I sighed, frustrated with myself for upsetting him. He'd already been through so much—too much for most people to experience and be able to keep going. And now he had one more problem to deal with—worrying about whether or not he might accidentally electrocute the rest of us if we touched him at an inopportune time. There was only one person who could help him with his new problem. I placed my hand on my hip and straightened my spine. "Do you have any clue what his job was?"

Carlos raised his eyebrows. "Huh?"

"Gabe—back at the Colony. Do you know what his job was?" I repeated.

Carlos kicked a small rock. "No."

"He was in charge of Ability research."

"He was?" Carlos looked up, interest flitting over his features.

"Yep." I moved across the trampled grass to stand in front of him. "And if anyone can, he's the one who can help you figure out how to do the electrotherapy thing safely and effectively *and* learn how to control that whole zapping people thing." I looked up, met Carlos's eyes, and waited.

A second.

Three.

Twenty.

Carlos pressed his lips into a flat line, inhaled deeply, and nodded. "Fine. Okay. Yeah, I'll do it."

"You will?" I said, doing a really poor job of hiding my surprise. Jason's stubbornness had been rubbing off on Carlos in a really unfortunate way.

Carlos looked at the ground. "Yeah, but…not yet. I mean, I want to get a little better at all this first, and…can we *not* tell Jason?" He met my eyes briefly, then looked away. "It's just that he hates Gabe, and I don't want him to, like, think I'm betraying him or something."

My stomach flip-flopped, making me feel a little ill. "Uh… yeah. Sure. Why not?" *What's the harm in one more secret, anyway?*

I ignored the part of me that whispered, *You mean, what's the harm in one more* lie*?*

"We can help, too," Mase said as he stepped out from between two of the carts, little more than a hulking shadow.

I yelped and jumped at least a foot off the ground. "Jesus, Mase!"

"Sorry." Mase ducked his head as he moved closer. Camille followed close behind him, her own slender, shadowed form half his size. They stopped a yard or so away from Carlos and me. "I knew you had first watch tonight, and we wanted—"

Camille hit his arm with the back of her hand.

Scowling, Mase corrected himself. "*I* wanted to tell you something *Camille* told me earlier."

My eyebrows rose as my gaze slipped from Mase's hard, dark features to Camille's pale, elfin face. She wouldn't meet my eyes. I glanced down at the small dry-erase board she was clutching to her chest. It was another of the items we'd taken from Colorado Trails Lodge. Camille still wasn't "speaking" much, but it seemed that Mase had managed to get her writing during the hours they'd spent driving a cart together earlier today.

I returned my attention to Mase.

"Dr. Wesley is a liar."

I frowned and glanced at Carlos, who shrugged before pulling himself back up onto the wagon. I refocused on Mase. "About…?"

"She loves him."

I cocked my head to the side. "I'm sorry, Mase, I'm not following…"

"Father—General Herodson. She loves him."

My mouth fell open. "That's not…" I started to shake my head. "That's not possible." She'd gone out of her way to save me by making the neutralizer and attuning it to my blood—twice. And Zoe…Dr. Wesley had shown up before Clara—the General's shiny new toy—could do more harm to Zoe than simply wiping away her memories. Dr. Wesley had been leading the anti-Herodson rebellion by supplying neutralizer to a trusted few, including Gabe and, before he'd been killed and made into a Re-gen, Mase. She *hated* General Herodson.

Except…she hadn't really done anything to stop him, and she had an Ability that could tear the foundation of his power, his mind-control Ability, right out from under his feet. She was even stronger than Jason and could probably nullify every damn Ability in the Colony all at the same time. So why hadn't she? Why didn't she do it after the Virus—the gene therapy—destroyed the world as we knew it and the General could no longer keep tabs on Dr. Wesley's family, could no longer hold their well-being over her head as additional motivation to behave?

"Before Camille died," Mase said, "she overheard a conversation between Dr. Wesley and someone else." Mase's dark gray eyes were wide, imploring. He looked from me to Camille. "Show her what you showed me."

I, too, looked at Camille.

Slowly, she pulled the small whiteboard away from her chest and turned it around so I could see the words, bubbly and slanted to the left.

Mase pointed to the board. "That's what Camille heard the doctor say."

The board said: "*I won't leave…won't abandon him. I love him too much.*"

My mouth was filled with sand. With cotton. With bile. I closed my eyes, took deep breaths, and somehow managed to convince myself not to lash out at Camille. It wasn't her fault that Dr. Wesley was an even worse human being than I'd originally thought…though I *did* wish Camille had spoken up earlier, so to speak.

I was now certain of two things: I could never, ever tell Jason the truth about his mom, and I couldn't trust anything *that woman* had written in her letter to me, not to mention whatever else she'd included in the "care package" wrapped in a manila envelope she'd left with mind-wiped Zoe in Colorado Springs.

I opened my eyes, swallowing my rage.

Camille's pale gray eyes were locked on mine, and she reached out to take my hand in hers and give it a squeeze. She let go of my hand and wiped the words off the dry-erase board with the sleeve of her sweatshirt. Hastily, she scrawled, "*I trusted her, too.*" She met my eyes, then continued writing. "*And she betrayed me.*" Her gaze flicked to Mase, filling with an overabundance of pain. "*She promised me that everything would be okay. She promised to look out for him.*" Camille wiped her words away again. "*SHE LIED.*"

I inhaled and exhaled slowly, then sent a sidelong glance over my shoulder at Carlos. He was watching the woods beyond the field.

"Do you know who she is…I mean, who she *really* is?" I met both Re-gens' eyes.

Camille wrote on her board, and when she showed her words to me, my heart seemed to plummet into my stomach. "*Jason and Zoe's mom.*"

As I kept an eye on Carlos, I swiped my fingers over the words, doing a half-assed job of erasing them. At least they were no longer easily comprehensible. When I looked at Mase again, he nodded.

"*How* do you know?"

"*She told me before I died,*" Camille wrote. "*She said she was sorry for her part in my mom getting sick and dying*"—Camille snorted, and her letters became sharper—"*not that she told me <u>what</u> her part was.*" She met my eyes, and I could relate to the hatred shining in their silvery depths. "*And she told me she did it to keep her kids, Zoe and Jason, safe.*"

"And apparently because she's in fucking love with General Douchebag," I muttered.

Mase grunted.

I met both sets of eerily gray eyes again. "You can't tell anyone." I raised my eyebrows to emphasize how serious I was. "I mean it—*no one*."

They both nodded, no hint of reluctance.

Inhaling deeply, I sighed. "Thanks for telling me. I needed to hear this…it'll help me figure some stuff out."

Mase nodded, and Camille's lips curved into a humorless smile.

I rubbed my hands together and turned to Carlos. "Right, so… about electrotherapy…"

7

ZOE

MARCH 29, 1AE

San Juan National Forest, Colorado

"Whoops!" Sarah chirped.

Wringing out the last of the wet laundry I'd just scrubbed clean, I glanced over at her. With one hand braced on the slim trunk of a pine tree, Sarah began to slowly lower herself down to collect the t-shirt she'd dropped on the newly sprouted grass lining the retention pond's bank.

"Sarah!" I jumped up from my crouched position at the pond's shore, letting one of Harper's shirts fall back into the water, and rushed over to her. "I'll get it," I said. I wiped the water trickling down my bare arms onto my pants and helped Sarah straighten back up before bending down to pick up the shirt myself.

After shaking the loose debris off, I draped the shirt beside the rest of the freshly-washed clothing that hung over a nylon rope we'd strung between two sturdy pines. "The last thing I need is you toppling over on my watch," I said, only half joking.

Sarah flashed me a halfhearted smile. "Thanks, Zoe." One of her hands automatically found her belly, while the other went back to straightening the clothes hanging on the line to dry in the early morning sunshine.

Returning to Harper's water-soaked shirt, I wrung it out once more and shook the wrinkles loose. "Here ya go," I said, handing it up to Sarah with an insuppressible yawn. I'd been trying to ignore my encroaching sleepiness since I'd woken. "Sorry," I said, shaking thoughts of sleep from my brain.

"Not sleeping well, Zoe?" Sarah asked as she draped Harper's shirt over an exposed portion of the line.

I yawned again. "No, not really."

Sarah glanced down at me, her brow furrowed. It was an uncommon expression for her. She was always so…bubbly. "Why not? Is everything okay?" She turned—more like hobbled—to face me. Her expression was intent as she brushed her hands off on her ankle-length skirt.

"I'm fine," I said, waving her concern away. "I just had a… strange dream last night." Leaning down to avoid eye contact, I collected the liquid soap and scrub brush I'd been using for the last hour. "I had a hard time falling back asleep is all."

That wasn't all, actually. Thinking about the dream had more than kept me up, and it had been smoldering in the back of my mind since the sun had come up.

"What sort of dream?" Sarah asked, her head cocked to the side as she rubbed her hands over her belly. She looked like a bohemian princess, with her dark curls falling messily around her face.

One vivid image after another from my dream flashed before my mind's eye. I shrugged and rinsed my hands off in the creek, trying to avoid her seeing my beet-red face. "Just a random dream."

Gathering my cleaning supplies, I dropped them into a canvas bag and looked up, freezing immediately.

Sarah's hands were on her hips, her eyebrows raised as she waited for an explanation.

She obviously wasn't going to let it go, so I cleared my throat. "I'll tell you, but don't…"

"Don't what?" she asked skeptically.

"Just don't judge me, okay? And don't say anything to anyone. It's sort of embarrassing." I dropped the bag of supplies into the empty wheelbarrow we'd used to carry the bags of dirty laundry down to the pond. "I had a dream about Jake last night…an"—I swallowed—"*intimate* dream. It left me a little…distracted."

Sarah burst into laughter. "Is that all? Well, that doesn't seem so bad. I probably wouldn't have gotten any sleep either."

My body warmed and tingled as I remembered the sensation of Jake's lips trailing down my neck and the heat of his touch as his fingertips drew a line between my breasts. I couldn't help but look down at my chest, remembering…it was like I could still feel his hot breath against my skin.

"That good, huh?" I heard her say. "Zoe?" I glanced at Sarah to find a huge smile engulfing her face. "You're thinking about him right now, aren't you?"

"No," I said in exasperation. "Of course not."

"Liar!" She giggled, but when she saw my mortification, she took a few steps closer and placed her hands on my shoulders. "What's wrong with thinking about him? You're together… it's normal, don't you think?"

My head was shaking before I could stop it. "We *were* together, Sarah. It's different now. Besides, I don't remember any of it…it's like he was with someone else, you know?"

Sarah's mouth quirked at the corner, and she stared at me, sympathetic. "You don't want to be with Jake anymore?"

"It's not that, I just—we haven't been together, we haven't even held hands really. Thinking about us doing more than that is…daunting."

"But why? It's Ja—because you don't remember him. Sorry, I keep forgetting." She waved her ignorance away. "I blame it on the pregnancy. It's like my brain doesn't have room for any more information or something."

I picked a rogue leaf from one of her flyaway curls. "It's not that he scares me. I mean…I'm petrified around him, but that's only because I'm completely clueless about what to do…how to act. He thinks about *her* when he's around me. At least, from what I can feel. He's really difficult for me to read." Putting my hands on my hips, I let my head fall back and exhaled my frustration. "I feel so stupid."

Jake's uncertainty around me and his apparent fear of what I might rediscover made it clear enough that there were some intense, private moments to be seen, and a part of me was secretly grateful he'd been keeping his distance. The pressure to be *that* Zoe made it difficult to just go with the flow and let things happen.

"You're just curious and nervous, Zoe. That seems normal." A knowing smile filled her face, and her eyebrows lifted before she winked. "Just give it some more time."

I appreciated her attempt to lighten the mood, but her teasing wasn't helping. I buried my face in my hands, trying to gather my thoughts. "As it is, it's hard trying to be someone I don't remember ever being on a daily basis. I mean, I'm not complaining. I know worse could've happened, but…"

"But what?"

"It's like there are expectations…expectations I can't possibly live up to. What if being with me is like being with someone else? The last thing I want is to finally work up the nerve to kiss him, or let him kiss me, only to learn he wishes I was someone else. I might be a shit kisser now." I groaned, leaning against one of the trees. "I don't think I'm ready for that sort of rejection yet."

"But it's you, Zoe. It's not just some other woman; it's you. You have to remember that."

"Easier said than done," I grumbled. "I just feel bad for putting him through this…"

"It's *only* been a week. Do you know how long it took you

guys just to say a few cordial words to each other in the beginning?"

I shook my head.

She tapped her index finger on her lips. "I don't either, actually, but it was a while," she said. "Look, Jake cares about you…a lot. It's obvious. *You* can even *feel* it, can't you?" She nudged my shoulder. "He knows you're different; we all do. Neither Jake—nor anyone else, for that matter—expects you to be the same as you were before."

I knew that wasn't true—only moments ago, Sarah herself admitted to forgetting I wasn't the old me, to expecting me to *react* like the old me—but I kept my observations to myself.

"Maybe you just need to give it a little bit more time."

Knowing she was right, that regardless of the pressure I felt, at least some of it was only in my head, I smiled. "Yeah, you're probably right. Thanks, Sarah."

She nudged my shoulder again. "Alright, let's get back to camp. I'm ravenous."

As I bent down to collect the folding chair Sarah had been using for her frequent breaks, I noticed a full linen bag resting up against the side of the large rock we'd been using to place the folded stacks of clean clothes that had been drying overnight. "Um, Sarah?"

"Hmm?" I looked over to see her wiping water from her mouth, an empty plastic bottle in her hand. "God, I love this stuff," she breathed. "What's up?"

"How many bags of laundry did we have to do this morning?"

Sarah squinted, and I could tell she was mentally counting. "Three—oh, crap." She took a step toward me and peered over to the other side of the rock. "Crap. I knew that seemed to go by way too fast." As if it were trained to do so, her stomach rumbled.

"Go back to camp," I said on a heavy exhale. "I'll finish up here."

"Are you sure?"

I dumped the contents of the half-filled bag onto the ground. "It's fine. Go ahead. I wouldn't want you to starve or anything."

Sarah smiled gratefully. "Are you sure you won't be mad?"

I nodded and snagged my bag of gathered supplies out of the wheelbarrow. "I got this."

"Alright, Zoe. Thank you. I owe you big-time."

"Yeah you do," I muttered playfully, dropping the bag by the water's edge. "Just leave me one of those chocolate bars I saw stashed in your secret hiding place."

Sarah's mouth dropped open, and her eyes widened. "How did you…"

Resisting a grin, I pretended to zip my mouth shut. "Just leave me a bite, would ya?"

"Alright," she grumbled and headed back to camp.

I crouched down to separate the dirty shirts and socks. Although it wasn't the most luxurious job in the world, it was a necessary task and something I could do without feeling inadequate, so I happily washed the laundry with Sarah when needed. It felt good to contribute, even in the smallest way. Plus, it gave me time to think.

I diligently scrubbed one shirt and then another until I was finished and they were rinsed, then I moved on to the socks. Most of the time, I was around people and unable to block their invading memories and emotions; no matter how hard I tried, I'd yet to figure out how to stop sensing them.

Although I initially thought it was exciting and useful to gain insight into the minds of the people I was surrounded by, it quickly grew bothersome. Like Dani, now *I* had to hold onto the knowledge that my mom loved the General—the man we were practically running for our lives to get away from. It was just one more item to add to the list of things Jason didn't know. Plus none of my companions liked having to worry about what I was gleaning from their minds, and some even avoided me outright. Cleaning the laundry was somewhat therapeutic, and it enabled me to have time away from the others to collect my *own* thoughts.

Hearing muffled conversation through the sparse trees beyond the pond, I glanced over my shoulder just in time to see Sam and Tavis emerge through a small copse of trees.

"Zoe!" Sam waved at me. He held up a string of rabbits attached to a tether. "We caught dinner!"

"Nice!" I called back, submerging someone's socks into the water before squirting a blob of liquid laundry soap onto them and working the fabric clean. "You mean we won't starve?"

"Not today," Tavis answered as they sauntered over. "Oh, good, you're cleaning my socks. I'm running low."

I stopped mid-scrub. "Oh, they're yours? In that case…" I pretended to toss them into the center of the pond.

"Such a comedian," he said.

Sam started toward camp. "You coming, Tavis?"

Tavis shook his head. "I better stay here and protect my socks." He grinned at me.

"Alright," Sam said. With a sigh, he trudged away, rabbit tether in hand.

For a few moments, only the sound of the scrub brush against the cotton socks and the trickling of water as Tavis rinsed off his hands filled the morning.

As I wrung the water from the last sock, an unexpected ripple broke at the pond's edge, splashing me. "Jesus, Tavis. Do you have to wash your hands so enthusiastically?" I glared over to find him crouched and picking at something on the ground.

He looked at me. "What?"

"Nothing," I said, shaking my head. I needed a nap to rest my addled brain.

Eventually, Tavis wandered over to me and stared out at the cloudless sky. "The weather here is funny," he said. "I'm used to the seasons at home. It should be getting colder, not warmer. I like it, though. I'm not much of a winter kind of guy."

"Really?" I said. I hadn't thought much about it. "I think I like the cold. I especially like the mornings. Everything seems fresh and new. There's something about the crisp water, too; it's refreshing. Sort of awakens my senses a little."

Tavis made a noncommittal noise.

"Hang these up on the line for me, would you?" I waited until Tavis turned to face me and tossed each balled-up sock at him consecutively, laughing as he juggled to catch them all without dropping any.

"Careful, those last two socks are yours. I wouldn't want you to have to wear them dirty."

He flashed me an easy smile and winked. "I'm so sure."

I enjoyed teasing Tavis and liked that we had so little history together…that he had so few memories of me, and that there wasn't much I had to live up to. I liked that I didn't have to worry about disappointing him.

"I'm just looking out for you," I told him.

"Like you care," he quipped, draping the socks over the line. I heard him swear, and when I looked over, he was shaking off a sock he must've dropped. "Damn it."

"That's Jason's…you better make sure it's clean."

Tavis strolled closer, holding out the soiled sock.

Shaking my head, I refused to take it and handed him the scrub brush instead. "Be my guest." I grinned. "I'll check to see if anything on the line is dry yet, and we can head back up to camp."

Tavis looked at me askance, then crouched down to grab the soap and scrub brush. "I just caught us dinner," he grumbled.

"And," I countered, "you just dropped my brother's sock in the dirt. In fact, you should probably make sure it's extra clean…you might want to scrub it a second time, just in case."

"Again, such a comedian," Tavis chuckled.

I batted my eyelashes at him and felt a splash of cold water on my face as a result. I blinked rapidly in surprise, my mouth gaping. "Really?"

"Sorry, I guess my aim with water is as good as my bow…but you *did* say you like the *crisp* water," he said in a sing-song voice and flitted his own lashes.

Smiling despite my annoyance, I tsked and shook my head. "You're the one who *doesn't* like it…" I said, splashing him back. Once…twice.

"Alright, alright. I'm sorry!" Tavis took a few hurried steps backward, chuckling and holding his palms out defensively as he stumbled over the larger rocks scattered about. "I surrender. Just don't make me drop the bloody sock again." He held the sock up, still laughing.

I nearly snorted in amusement at Tavis's sudden change in tune. "You're pathetic. It's just water."

Hearing panting and the crunch of twigs behind me, I turned around to find Cooper running happily toward the water and Jake standing beside one of the pines, holding a piece of grass between his fingertips.

My face heated, and I suddenly felt like I'd been caught doing something wrong. "Hey."

Jake's gaze traveled from me to Tavis and back as he let the blade of grass fall to the ground. "Hey."

"Just finishing up with the laundry," I said, wiping my wet hands on the front of my t-shirt. His eyes fixed on mine as I closed the distance between us. I appreciated the fact that the bright morning sun provided me the opportunity to study Jake's features. His nose was a little crooked, and long, honey-colored lashes fanned around his amber eyes. And although I could hear Tavis moving around behind me, my attention remained on Jake's freshly shaven face.

"Your brother wants us to start packing so we're ready to go after breakfast," Jake said.

I smiled. "Okay. I should get all my crap together."

I glanced back at Tavis, who was already putting my canvas bag of wash stuff into the wheelbarrow, along with a stack of the clothes that were already dry and folded on the boulder. "I'll get it," Tavis offered. He exchanged a quick glance with Jake, then pushed the wheelbarrow toward camp.

Walking side by side, Jake and I followed behind him.

"Your shirts are clean," I said awkwardly.

"Shadow's fed," he offered in exchange, and treated me to a rare smile.

I grinned. "Thanks. Maybe I'll get to start riding him soon. He seems to be doing a little better."

"Yeah, I think so," Jake said. I could tell he was trying to figure out what to say.

"So, what do two people talk about when one knows nothing and the other knows everything?" I asked, wondering if my nervous babble helped break the tension or only added to it.

Jake offered me a sympathetic smile. "I don't know everything." After a brief hesitation, he added, "What do you want to know?"

I thought about it for a moment, wondering which, of all my questions, I wanted to ask Jake the most. "What were you like before the Ending? I mean, what did you like to do for fun and that sort of thing?"

He looked at me with an amused grin.

"I know it's probably not the question you were expecting, but I figured I'd start with the basics…"

Leaning down, Jake pulled a piece of wild grass from the field, and we continued walking. "For fun?" He shrugged. "I traveled a lot, took a lot of odd jobs, and got into a lot of trouble instead of going to college." Jake paused, and I could feel a sudden sadness filling him. "I came back when Gabe's sister passed away from leukemia and decided it was time to get my act together. I needed to be there for Becca."

"I'm sorry about your friend," I said. "At least you still have Becca and Gabe, I guess…" I'd seen enough of Gabe's memories to know that was sort of a sticky situation.

Jake nodded, and I could tell he *was* grateful. "I just wish I hadn't taken so long to do the right thing. I finally found a good, steady job as a mechanic, bought a house, and figured out how to stay out of trouble."

"Yeah? That's good." I had a hard time picturing Jake getting into trouble, but then, I had no idea what *I* even did before the Ending. "And how was it that you managed to stay out of trouble?"

"Reading…a lot."

"Oh…"

He gave me a thoughtful, sidelong glance. "'Oh?'" He smiled. "What were you expecting?"

"I'm not sure, I just didn't picture you as a reader, I guess."

He shrugged. "I couldn't picture you as a gallery assistant."

"A gallery assistant? I can't really picture it either." We ambled along, Tavis a dozen yards ahead of us, rolling the wheelbarrow into camp, and Cooper exploring the sparse woods nearby.

"I wish you could ask me a question, or rather, that I could answer one," I said quietly. "And I'm sorry you have to tell me all of this again."

"Actually, we've never really talked about this sort of stuff before."

"No? But I thought…"

Jake shrugged. "Pasts don't matter so much when your whole world is ripped away from you. We just weren't like that…we didn't dwell on the past."

It was hard to miss the longing in his voice. "Oh," I said.

"Sorry, that probably wasn't very helpful."

Since he was closer to me than usual, I had an easier time feeling his emotions. I knew he was sad and hopeful and confused, which I understood and tried not to hold against him. I felt the same way.

"Maybe one day you can tell me more about myself?" I joked, realizing how idiotic that sounded. Too bad it was true.

"Or, maybe…" He stopped walking, and I automatically stopped as well. "Maybe we can just start over."

I faced him and stared into his eyes, trying to see the truth, not just feel it. "Do you want to?" I was picking up mixed signals from him, and I wasn't really sure what my *own* opinion was.

His expression turned skeptical and he searched my eyes for answers I didn't even know the questions to. "Do *you* want to?"

I thought about the dreams I kept having and how unsettling they were—how exciting and frightening and…confusing. I nodded once, nervous about what starting over entailed. Then in a bout of self-consciousness, I looked down at my feet. I didn't want him to see the blush caused by the thought of doing all the things we'd done in my dreams.

"You don't seem sure," he said, narrowing his eyes when I glanced back up at him.

"No…I mean, I am." *I think.*

"Is it Tavis?" The question seemed to come out of nowhere. "You guys get along well. I'm not sure—"

I shook my head. "It's not him, not really." Jake eyed me as I continued, "We get along great, don't get me wrong. It's easy being around him. He's easy to talk to, and there's no history to navigate, there's no pressure…" Peering up at Jake, I tried to act more certain than I was, but failed miserably. "Who I used to be… she's just a lot to live up to," I admitted.

Jake's eyes lingered on mine before he scanned the small patch of field separating us from the others. "I don't want you to feel uncomfortable around me," he finally said.

I smiled up at him. "I know, and I don't, I just…" I had no idea what I was trying to say to him. "Things aren't complicated with him."

I couldn't help but feel the slight sting my words caused Jake, but I had to tell him the truth, if for no other reason than to remind us both that whatever had been between us before was gone now. It was going to be a lot of hard work to get back a semblance of what we once had—hard work I wasn't willing to turn my nose up at, but hard work I also wasn't sure either of us was ready for.

But it didn't mean we couldn't try.

8

DANI

MARCH 29, 1AE

Cahone, Colorado

It was late afternoon, and I was sitting beside our burgeoning campfire, staring into the flames and generally despising myself while I built the fire up for Sarah. I prodded the burning logs with a stick to rearrange them before adding a few more hunks of freshly gathered firewood.

I was becoming a horrible person, possibly the worst person I'd ever met. Okay, maybe not the *worst* person—I was no Mandy, no General Herodson, no Clara, no Dr. Wesley—but lately, I'd felt like I was on my way. I certainly wasn't a *good* person, not anymore. I was a horrible friend, a deceiving girlfriend, and a child-killer. But of my mounting flaws, it was all of the lying that had started to erode my soul.

I hadn't been lying because I enjoyed the taste of deceit on my tongue, or because I felt a thrill hurting others; I'd been lying to protect the people I loved…to protect myself. But the problem with telling so many lies was this: it's so easy for one little lie to spawn a dozen more, which in turn birth their own litters of little lies. And when the first lie, lie zero, is a whopper, the horde of untruths and not-saids grows much, *much* faster. My core lie was as big as they get.

I was lying to Jason about his mom, Dr. Wesley. After Camille's revelation, I'd made a promise to myself to never tell him that she was alive and relatively well—considering—and that she was living in the Colony, loving companion to the man who'd orchestrated the destruction of human civilization. I would never tell him that I knew why she left him, Zoe, and their dad over twenty years ago, that General Herodson had threatened to kill her children if she didn't give him everything he wanted, do every single thing he requested of her, and that she'd come to love her captor. I would never tell him that she was the person who created the virus that killed almost everyone, including their dad.

And I would never show him the letter she'd written, the one addressed to him and Zoe that supposedly explained everything; it was stuffed in the bottom of my left saddlebag in the manila envelope with the rest of the garbage she'd given to Zoe, directly beneath my emergency stash of tampons. Jason would never look there.

Maybe if that was the only lie—or *set* of lies—I was maintaining, I would've been able to deal with the guilt. But there were the other lies, ones that had nothing to do with Dr. Wesley. They, too, were lies of omission. I'd yet to tell Jason that I kissed two men while I was in the Colony, one to steal his gun and keys, and one—Gabe—simply because I wanted to. For some reason, "the General took control of my mind and made me do it," sounded like the lamest possible excuse, regardless of it being the absolute truth. There was definitely a reason I was avoiding Gabe. *Awkward…*

On the other side of the fire, Sarah was sitting at the folding table, staying warm while she chopped vegetables for the rabbit stew that was going to be tonight's fresh offering.

I poked the burning logs again, simply for the sake of stabbing something with the stick. Letting out a heavy breath, I looked around camp.

The tents were set up in a rough ring around the fire, the carts and wagon in a half-circle on one side, blocking some of the dusty wind, and the horses munching on whatever roughage they could find in the sparse fields of wild grasses on either side of the tiny creek we'd plopped down beside. Everyone was busy—down in the creek's ravine washing clothes or dishes, filtering safe drinking water, gathering firewood, or hunting and foraging to bulk up our fast-depleting food supply.

"I still can't get over the fact that we have a covered wagon—a legitimate covered wagon," Sarah said. "I feel like a pioneer woman every time I climb up onto the thing!" She shook her head, her curly brown ponytail bobbing.

Biggs strolled over to the campfire, carrying a fresh load of firewood. "Hey, babe!" He quickened his step as he neared, stopping by Sarah's prep table to drop a quick kiss on her cheek on his way to the dwindling pile of sticks and branches beside the fire. He offered me a nod as he set down his burden, then returned to Sarah. His hand darted out, and he snagged a carrot nugget the size of my thumb off of Sarah's chopping board.

"Hey! You thief!" Sarah laughed, making a shooing motion.

Chuckling while he crunched, Biggs moved around the table to stand behind her. He wrapped his arms around her, resting his chin on her shoulder and his palms on her belly. "How's the little guy today?"

"*She* is fine. Kicking a bit more, but Harper said that was normal…or as normal as we can say…" Doubt weaved through Sarah's words, despite what I figured was a valiant effort to remain positive.

Biggs kissed her neck, then started murmuring reassurances against her skin.

I felt like a voyeur, but I couldn't tear my eyes away from them, from such a genuine display of affection…of love. A yearning ache sprouted in my chest, sending out tendrils that spread envy and loneliness throughout my body. Before I'd been abducted by the Colony, Jason had shown just as much affection toward me as these parents-to-be, but after…with each passing day, I could feel him drift further away from me. Soon, I'd be just another member of the group to him. Just another survivor.

"Hey," someone whispered near my ear, and I started. I felt hands on my shoulders and looked back to find Ky studying me, his eyes pinched with concern and possibly a little bit of pain. "It's just me," he said as he crouched beside me, partially blocking my view of the oblivious, adorable couple. "Thought you heard me coming."

I met his eyes, then looked into the flames and shook my head. "Guess I zoned out."

There was a long stretch of silence between us. Eventually, Ky took a deep breath. "You feel like shit."

I snorted quietly and scrubbed my good hand over my face before meeting his eyes again. "Listen, Ky—I'm a mess…I know it, and I'm sorry, I really am, and I know it's not easy for you when I'm all crazy like this, and I really appreciate whatever insightful words you're planning on sharing," I said in a rush. "But this isn't one of those times when talking about my feelings is going to make all the bad ones disappear, so…"

He turned his face to the fire, staring into the flames like they might hold some hidden secret. "I like you, D. I like you a lot, you know that." He shot me a sideways glance, then returned to staring into the crackling flames. "But if you don't figure out a way to deal with whatever's eating at you, and I mean this in the least dicky way possible, I'm not going to be able to be around you *at all*."

I exhaled heavily. Honestly, I wasn't surprised.

"You're my friend, D, and in case you haven't noticed, those are"—he squinted—"a little hard to come by these days. I don't want to cut you out of my life…"

"I—I—" I shook my head. "I'm sorry, Ky." Laughing bitterly, I sent out a halfhearted wish for the universe to send someone like

Clara my way, someone who could erase certain unwanted memories and droplets of corrosive knowledge from my mind.

Ky flashed a weak version of his usual mischievous grin. "And now for those insightful words you mentioned…" Leaning forward, he rested his elbows on his knees and held his hands out to the flames. "Sometimes the people who seem the strongest, who seem the most in control of their shit…sometimes they *have* to be that way on the outside because what's inside them is so wild, so extreme, so far beyond too much, that if it was ever unleashed, they'd never be in control again."

I swallowed hard, cleared my throat, and poked the burning logs…again. "I'm assuming you're talking about Jason…"

Ky nodded.

"So what are you saying? That Jason's dealing with too much on the inside, and that's making him push everyone away?"

"He's not pushing *everyone* away."

"Oh," I said. "Right. Just me. Awesome…" A chilling thought gave rise to a wash of goose bumps. Did that mean that Jason knew about the lies? Had Zoe told him? Or had Mase or Camille let it slip?

Ky lifted one shoulder, offering me a small smile.

"How do you know any of this? Or…have you felt something from him?"

Ky laughed dryly. "Hell no. He keeps me cut off from feeling his shit permanently. And thank God, 'cause I have a feeling that whatever's going on inside him right now…well, let's just say I wouldn't enjoy having a front-row seat on *that* joyride. I've got enough to deal with from you, Zoe, and Jake…not to mention everyone else."

This time when he looked at me, his dark brown eyes were so focused and intense that I held my breath. "But I've been friends with Jason for over a decade, and I know him well enough to tell when he's working through something. And right now, he's working through something big, and I *know* it has to do with you, because you're the only woman—the only *person*—who's ever gotten so deep under his skin."

He clapped a hand on my knee. "So, since the only thing that *ever* seems to unplug your emotionally constipated relationship is to talk things out and then run off and do whatever it is you crazy kids do, I'd suggest you sit down for a chat as soon as possible. If not for my sake, at least fix this for Zoe, because she doesn't seem to be able to block *anything*, and you know the poor girl's got to be drowning under the weight of all these crazy emotions, hers included."

All I could do for five breaths, ten breaths, was stare at Ky. He was right. He was so very, *very* right. Saying nothing, I looked across the fire at the table where Sarah had been sitting, but both she and Biggs were gone.

Ky gave my knee a squeeze before standing. "Look…I saw him and Sanchez on the other side of the carts, inventorying ammo or some shit like that. You should take the evening off, talk to him, fix whatever's wrong, or *don't* fix it, I don't care…just do something, 'cause this headache is killing me."

Internally, I resisted, and that made me realize how big of a baby I was being. Ky was right; Jason and I needed to talk. And my resistance to do just that made me reevaluate some of my assumptions about what was happening to our relationship. Maybe Jason wasn't the only one pulling away, building walls; maybe I was doing it, too. Maybe it was the secrets…leeching the vitality out of our relationship. Maybe Jason could feel the strain just as much as I could. Maybe he thought my feelings had changed, just like I thought his had. So many maybes…

There was only one way to know for sure, only one way to fix things. I stood, patted Ky's arm, and said, "Thanks…really." Then I started across camp toward the carts.

Jason and Sanchez weren't inventorying ammo. They weren't doing *anything*, so far as I could tell. They were sitting on a fallen log, apparently deep in conversation. Sanchez had one of her legs pulled up and her chin popped on her knee, facing Jason, while he had his elbow planted on his thigh and was resting the side of his face in his hand.

I paused, between the front of the wagon and the back of one of the carts, suddenly not so sure of myself. Maybe all of my maybes had been worthless. Maybe we were already done, and he was moving on. Maybe I was the most pathetic woman in the world.

Sanchez noticed me first, then looked at Jason and nodded in my direction. When Jason straightened, when his eyes met mine, I had a total deer-in-the-headlights moment. My heart pounded, and blood whooshed in my ears with each beat. I couldn't blink.

"I should get back to…that thing," Sanchez said as she stood. She offered me a tight-lipped smile and strode off toward the creek.

Jason stared at me across the dozen or so yards separating us. For several seconds, that was all he did. Stare. Watch. Assess. Until, placing his hands on his knees, he stood.

I gulped. I hadn't been so ridiculously anxious—so uncomfortably aware of my own awkwardness—around him since I'd been in middle school. Taking a deep breath, I took a step toward him, then another. And another. I forced myself to keep my eyes on his face, to keep moving.

Jason studied me as I approached, his expression giving no indication of his thoughts or mood, and I couldn't help but wonder if Ky had been right. Was Jason so closed off, so controlled, because he felt too much and was, for whatever reason, afraid of the intensity of his own emotions?

I stopped a few feet in front of Jason. The skin around his eyes tightened the barest amount.

After a fortifying deep breath, I raised my hand, reaching out to brush my fingertips over the exposed skin of his forearm. I stopped short of touching him. *When was the last time we even touched?* I thought it might have been the previous afternoon, when my Ability flared back to life, and my eyebrows drew together. That we'd gone a whole day without physical contact seemed impossible.

But I was fairly certain it was true. We hadn't been intimate in weeks—not with my kidnapping, resulting in a broken arm and many bruises, and the still-healing gash crossing Jason's face from hairline to jaw—and though we'd been sleeping *near* each other in our tent, our sleeping bags remained separated. I'd been telling myself it was because he feared hurting me while we slept. Now I suspected *that* was only part of the reason for the physical restraint.

I searched the sapphire depths of his eyes. "Can we talk? Somewhere more private." Another deep breath. "I—there's some stuff you need to know."

The tightness around his eyes increased, but he nodded. He held out an arm, indicating that I should lead the way.

Taking a deep breath, I squeezed my good hand into a fist and turned to head toward the tiny creek. There was a sharp bend a short ways downstream, and the rocky walls of the shallow ravine and the scrubby pines lining it would provide us at least a semblance of privacy. I had no way to gauge how Jason would react to what I was about to tell him, but I wanted to give him the opportunity to process away from the others.

Silence was our only companion as we descended one of a myriad of paths leading down to the creek. The creek itself was only several feet wide and easy enough to cross. By the time we were hidden from our camp, from our companions, by the ravine wall, I was a ball of anxiety; my hand was shaking, my heart was beating a fast staccato rhythm against the inside of my rib cage, and I didn't feel like I could draw in enough breath.

I wiped my suddenly damp palm on my jeans and stopped in front of a knee-high rock. Turning to face Jason, I pointed to the rock. "Sit, please."

Jason did so silently, his eyes never leaving me. His gaze was a tangible thing, burning into my flesh, flaying me open, and laying out my fetid soul for the whole universe to witness…to judge.

I pulled my braid over my shoulder and wrapped my hand around its end, giving a gentle tug. *I can do this. I can* do *this. I* have *to do this!* My stomach twisted, knotted, lurched, and I started pacing. Back and forth. Back and forth.

"Dani." Just that single word, my name on Jason's lips, halted me mid-step.

I opened my mouth, swallowed, pressed my lips together. There was so much I hadn't told him about my time in the Colony, so much I hadn't told anyone, that it seemed an impossible task to pick a place to start. But I had to tell him something. I had to let him know that I wanted to fix *us*.

I met your mom, she's in the Colony, and she created the Virus.

Taking a deep breath, I tried again. "When I was at the Colony, you—do you remember telling me to do whatever it took to survive?" I stared at the rough rock wall behind Jason, just over his shoulder, too chickenshit to actually look at him.

"Yes." His voice was carefully controlled.

Another deep breath. "Because of the issues they've been having with pregnancies making it to full term, one of the regular commands the General gives newcomers is to actively attempt to procreate…" My voice sounded hollow, dead. "…with pretty much anyone."

Jason's jaw clenched, and it remained that way.

"The men are encouraged to approach any woman they desire, and the women are discouraged from denying them." A disgusted laugh caught in my throat. "God, he's such a chauvinistic bastard—he doesn't even give *that* choice to the women. It's just, 'If someone wants you to spread your legs, spread 'em.'"

"Dani…did someone—"

I shook my head once, sharply, and whatever Jason saw in my eyes silenced him. "The night I met Mase and Camille, I was searching the warehouses, doing my first round of scouting out their supplies. I—there was a soldier, a yellow-band, who I *may* have antagonized just a bit when I first arrived." My hand clutched the side of my jeans. "He propositioned me, I said no, and when he found me wandering around the warehouses that day, no longer mind-controlled—though he didn't know that—he decided to take advantage of those particular commands.

"He forced me into one of the warehouses and—" I looked down at my hand; my nails were digging into my thigh painfully. I embraced the sensation, drawing strength from it. "He was big and armed, and I wasn't." I raised my gaze to meet Jason's; his eyes were bottomless pools of midnight set in granite. "I stopped fighting him, and..." I cleared my throat. "I stopped fighting him...let him believe I wanted him...so I could steal his sidearm." A soft laugh. A one-shoulder shrug. *I was thinking about you the whole time,* I didn't say. "I managed to nab his key, too."

"What did you do to him?"

"Nothing." I refused to look away. As the words had come out, I'd started to realize that my actions weren't something to be ashamed of. I *had* been doing what I had to do to stay alive...to survive. "Mase did all the heavy lifting, really. He was going to kill the guy, but I asked him not to."

"Why?" So very, *very* cold.

"He was a yellow-band." I shook my head again. "You don't know what it's like, to have no control over your actions, but to believe everything you're doing is your own idea, that it's what you want, your choice. The guilt once you remember...he was only doing what the General commanded him to do."

"So you spared him."

I didn't have a response to that, so I simply stood there. I'd spared a man who'd had every intention of forcing me to have sex with him, but I hadn't hesitated to shoot—to kill—a little girl to protect Zoe. *She was a Crazy,* I told myself. *She was going to attack Zo...*

Seconds passed in handfuls until, finally, Jason said, "Tell me what it's like."

I blinked several times. "What *what's* like?"

"Having no control over your actions…being mind-controlled."

"I—it—" Mouth still open as though the words might form at any moment, I shook my head. "I don't know how to explain it. It doesn't seem bad until you're awake, *really* awake, and you realize what you've done. When I was under—" I pressed my lips together and squeezed my eyes shut. Panic was a living thing inside my chest, a trapped bird flitting around, making my heart skip beats and stealing the space my lungs so desperately needed.

I took several steps and knelt on the rock-strewn ground before Jason. Resting my chin on his knee, I met his eyes. His face softened minutely, and he brought his right hand to my head, smoothing back the flyaway curls that had escaped from my French braid and running the backs of his fingers over my unbruised jawline. His body, however, was humming with tension.

Turning my head, I rested my cheek on his knee. "The General made me forget everything that happened once I got sick," I said softly. "I thought I had amnesia, and since I was told I'd been found alone—other than the Crazies who'd supposedly been attacking me—I assumed that everyone I knew was dead. I didn't remember the journey from Seattle to Bodega Bay, or the one from there to Colorado, and I didn't remember us ever being…*us*."

The soft brush of Jason's knuckles against my skin stilled, but I couldn't bring myself to look up at him. I didn't think I would be able to continue if I saw his expression, and I *had* to keep going. Things wouldn't be right with us until I'd shed at least *some* of my secrets.

I took a deep breath. "Gabe"—Jason's tense body stiffened further—"was the only person I knew. He was the only familiar thing in a terrifying world, and I was so, *so* lonely."

"Did you—did he…"

I shut my eyes. "No. I—we kissed, that's all. He stopped things before it could go any further than that." Trembling, I pulled away so I could look up at Jason.

He was staring at the opposite side of the ravine, jaw clenched and nostrils flaring.

"Jason, I swear that whatever I felt for him when my mind was twisted to hell and back, it pales in comparison to what I feel for you. It means *nothing*."

"It means something to me," he said quietly. "Is there anything else?"

I met your mom, she's in the Colony, and she created the Virus.

"No," I whispered.

With a gentleness born of great strength and intensive training, Jason pushed me away from him and rose, not even looking down at me before walking away.

I wanted to call after him so badly, to stand and chase him down and beg him to stay and talk to me, to help me fix things between us. But I couldn't. I watched him go, grief silencing my voice, paralyzing my limbs. I watched him walk further downstream, my heart crushed in his fist, and I couldn't even fight for us, for what we could be.

This is what I deserve…to be alone. Jason, Zoe, Camille, even Gabe…I only hurt whoever gets close to me. I was wrong; my secrets aren't poison. I *am poison.*

But there was one thing I could do that wouldn't hurt anyone, one place I could go where I wouldn't feel the waves of desperation caused by having my heart torn out, and where neither Ky nor Zoe would have to feel the reverberations, either. There was only one way I could escape.

"Jack," I said in my dog's mind. He was on the other side of camp, frolicking over the barren land with Cooper. I crawled one-handed closer to the ravine wall and, leaning my back against the rocky surface, pulled my knees up to my chest. *"Please, Sweet Boy, let me in. Let me run with you."*

"Yes, Mother. Run. Chase. Hunt."

With a sigh, I slipped out of my shivering body.

I was Jack.

The moon was high and bright, and the night was filled with promise. My prey ran ahead, its heartbeat rapid. I could taste its terror on my tongue.

Abruptly, it changed direction, heading upward. It was climbing a tree. No!

I lunged at the tree's trunk, standing on my back legs and scratching at the rough bark with my front claws. I opened my mouth and barked, begging my prey to come back down and play some more.

"Dani!"

"What?" I blurted, sitting bolt upright and jostling my broken arm. "Ow!" I curled in on myself, clutching my sling with my good hand. My eyes were shut tightly as though that act alone could block the pain.

"Dani—Red…"

That voice. My eyes snapped open. "Jason?" *He came back?*

His hand was clasping my shoulder, and his face, which I could barely see in the darkness, was mere inches from mine. "You're shivering."

"I'm cold," I said, with an extra big shiver that made my teeth chatter. "What time is it?"

"Late…everyone's asleep back at camp." His hand moved up my neck, and the pad of his thumb brushed across my lips. "We missed dinner."

My pulse was suddenly racing, and I shivered for another reason entirely. It took me a moment to speak. When I did, it wasn't much. "We?"

"Yeah."

So he's been gone all this time? I took a shaky breath, a

byproduct of the nighttime chill and my anxiety. At first, I couldn't believe that nobody had come looking for us, but then I realized they probably thought we'd snuck off for some amorous alone time. Boy, were they wrong.

I cleared my throat. "Where'd you go after I, um—earlier?"

Ever so carefully, Jason nudged me forward, wedging himself between my back and the rock wall, and my God did he feel good—so warm and firm and *there.* He cocooned me with his body, his chest to my back and his legs propped up on either side of me. His left arm slid around my middle, just under my sling, and he raised his right arm, tracing a slow line along my collarbone, up my neck, and along my jawline with his fingertips.

"Walking," he said. "I just walked around. I couldn't be here."

"Why?" I whispered.

Jason held me, kindling a gentle, sizzling promise I hadn't felt in weeks. Warmth blossomed in my lower abdomen, his touch arousing my desire with embarrassing ease.

"Needed a breather." His fingers clasped my jaw tenderly, and he turned my head so the side of my face was pressed against the worn brown leather of his coat. He lowered his head and nuzzled my neck, and when he next spoke, his breath tickled skin made overly sensitive by weeks of neglect. "I need to know one thing. Why didn't you tell me earlier…and why now?"

"That's two things," I managed to say, though the words were breathy.

He chuckled, the sound fanning the flames of desire. He was doing a really good job of warming me up, inside and out. "Tell me," he said against my neck.

I sighed. "I was afraid."

"Of…?"

"You." I felt Jason tense, his lips stilling on my neck, and rushed to explain. "I mean, saying 'do whatever you need to do to survive' and actually being cool with me making out with some other guy so I could steal his gun are two entirely different things.

And then the thing with Gabe, I—it terrified me every time I thought about telling you."

"But you did tell me."

I laughed, a dry, bitter sound. "I had to. I—the secrets, the guilt—I couldn't be around you without thinking about the things I *wasn't* telling you." *Like about your mom.* I took a deep breath, still not sure I would ever tell him about her, because despite how understanding Jason was being about the other secrets I'd divulged, I wasn't worried the one about his mom would break us; I feared it would break *him*. "At first, I thought you were pulling away. I thought you'd changed your mind, that you didn't want to be *us*. But it wasn't you; it was me." I tried to sit up, intending to turn around so I could see his face, but his arms tensed, holding me in place.

I had no choice but to relax back against him. "I was distancing myself from you without realizing what I was doing, and once I *did* realize it, I knew I had to, you know, confess…because I missed you. I *miss* you."

Jason made a rough noise low in his throat. He raised his head, and the hand holding my jaw moved lower, his strong fingers dancing along the side of my neck. "Did either of them touch you here?"

"Yes," I whispered.

His lips replaced his fingers, a searing brand on that sensitive skin. His hand moved lower, dipping under the collar of my sweater. His fingertips traced the edge of my bra. "And here?"

"Just a"—my voice hitched as he pushed the thin fabric out of the way, his fingertips trailing a blaze of pleasure—"just a little…bit."

His lips, still on my neck, curved, and imagining his possessive smile was like lighter fluid on my burning desire. The arm he'd wrapped around my middle shifted lower, his hand slipping under the hem of my sweater. He ran charged fingertips up and down my side, from my hip up to my bra and back. "And here?"

"I—I don't—"

That hand, those fingertips, moved to my stomach, sliding ever so lightly over the skin of my lower abdomen, just above the waistband of my jeans, and I whimpered. Jason's responding chuckle was so knowing, so male, so heated. "Here?"

Breaths coming faster, I shook my head. My hand clutched his thigh in an effort to stave off my mounting, needy ache.

Jason popped the top button on my pants, then drew the zipper down more slowly than I would have thought possible. My hips lifted off the ground, seeking, wanting.

He tsked me. "Patience, Red."

With a low groan, I moved my hand higher up on his thigh. His arousal showed in the unmistakable hardness pressed against my lower back.

My hand was just below his pocket when he stopped unzipping. "No, Red."

The fingers on my breast pinched in a way that would have hurt had I not been so painfully aroused. The pleasure-pain earned another whimper from me.

"Just feel." He lowered the zipper the rest of the way with a quick jerk. "Close your eyes and just feel."

Thankfully, he stopped teasing. He thrust his hand into my pants, and I groaned, and again my hips lifted off the ground. I shifted my hand closer to his knee, my fingertips digging into his jeans. To say my body ached for him would be a gross understatement.

"Jason…please. I need…"

He laughed, low and rough, then shoved that final barrier out of the way. "Tell me if I'm hurting you," he said as he finally gave me what I craved. Remotely, I registered that he had to be talking about my arm, but at that moment, with his fingers doing such tantalizing things between my legs, I really didn't care. His fingers were *everywhere* in the most delicious ways. Mounting pleasure was my whole world.

I gasped as Jason's touch hurtled me off the top of a mountain of bliss, and I was free-falling into heaven, or maybe into hell.

I lay in his arms for minutes, breathing hard and basking in the afterglow. Craning my neck, I peered up at his shadowed face. "So you're not mad?"

"No, Red," Jason laughed. "All the proof I need that you're still mine is right here." His forearm flexed, and he did something with his fingers that sent echoes of pleasure through my body.

I moaned and arched against him, but in my chest, a very different ache blossomed. *I want more than this…more than lust,* I didn't say. *I want you to love me, because I love you,* I didn't say, despite feeling it in my every cell.

With a satisfied exhale, Jason withdrew his hands from my pants and shirt and quickly refastened my jeans. His powerful arms wrapped around my middle, and he rose, bringing me up with him.

Once I was on my feet, I turned and slipped my hand under the hem of his t-shirt, tracing the outline of his abs. I moved my hand lower, fully intending to return the pleasure he'd just lavished upon my body.

He caught my wrist in an iron grip before I reached the top button of his jeans. Shaking his head, he said, "Let's go to bed."

My eyebrows drew together. "But…don't you want"—I glanced lower on his body—"you know…?"

Leaning down so his lips brushed my ear, he laughed huskily. "More than anything. But we can't risk me nulling everyone; it's too dangerous. Ky's keeping watch, but without his Ability…" I felt him shake his head. "After what happened last time, I'm not willing to risk it for anything…not until I know we're safe."

I flushed. Last time we'd really been together, he'd lost control of his Ability—nulling the general area, as usual—and I'd been abducted. "Oh, right. If you're sure…"

He shifted, trailing his lips along my jawline until he pressed a gentle, almost chaste kiss against my lips. "I am. And trust me, Red—it'll be worth the wait."

I'm sure, I thought. *But I want more than that, too.*

Jason captured my hand and led me back to camp. We retreated into our tent, where Jack was already waiting for us, and settled into our sleeping bags—closer to each other now, but still far enough apart that Jason wouldn't accidentally hurt my arm while we slept. Jason was asleep within minutes, his breathing deep and even, and not long after, Jack snuggled close on my other side. He inhaled deeply, exhaled in a sigh, and was out.

I watched Jason, studied the way the moon shadows played over the sharp angles and planes of his face and softened the harshness of his scar, until sleep tugged my eyelids closed. But my mind refused to give in to the coaxing pull, despite my body being utterly exhausted and more relaxed than it had been in weeks. I lay there, willing myself to fall asleep.

After an hour or two of trying, I gave up. I opened my mind, seeking out a companion for the wee hours of the morning. Wings was napping in the pasture, and thousands of other creatures were slinking and scurrying through the field around camp, but none of them were the mind I sought.

Finally, I found Ray, perched on one of the top branches of a lodgepole pine a few miles away. The falcon fluffed her feathers in anticipation as I relaxed into her mind. She spread her wings and launched into the night before I was fully detached from my own body, and I felt myself exhale a sigh of relief.

Yes! This is what I need.

9

ZOE

MARCH 31, 1AE

Great Basin Desert, Utah

My heart raced, and my body trembled with a thrilling sort of panic; an aria of desire and excitement and fear sung through me, sensations so raw and real it was as if I was feeling them for the first time.

He braced me up against a wall, a woolen blanket the only thing sparing me from the hard surface of the rough, wooden slats. Momentarily, my eyes flitted open. I was in a barn washed in the pale dawn light seeping in between wood planks.

A low, possessive groan preceded his hot breath, burning against my neck. I shuddered as instinct took over, and my eyes closed again. He trailed urgent kisses along my jaw before finding my mouth, his lips both soft and bruising. His hot body against mine sent a curling ribbon of anticipation spiraling through me.

How could something so wild feel so right?

A throbbing need flooded my insides, filling even my deepest, most forgotten hollows. It was nearly too much to bear as his strong fingers knotted in my hair, his silken tongue burning against my skin, and I could feel his muscles flexing with every determined thrust of his body. His fingertips explored my curves, leaving fire trails in their wake and setting my body ablaze with an appetite for something I didn't understand but desperately wanted to fulfill.

A devastatingly greedy hunger rippled through me, and my immediate fears and uncertainties vanished as I let all my inhibitions go. Feeling so full and overwhelmed with lust, I gripped him closer and struggled to catch my breath...

He thrust, and I cried out.

Feeling awakened and near bursting with a coiling, aching fever I thought might bring me to my knees if I didn't give in, I shuddered against him, holding on for dear life as the world dissolved around me. And as though my body couldn't contain the roiling sensations a moment longer, my insides swelled with a pulsating intoxication that left me near tears.

I was falling...losing myself in a swirling blackness of passion.

"Jake..."

Starting awake, my insides still clenched in wanting and my heart nearly jumping out of my sweat-dampened chest, I looked around the tent's interior. I took a deep breath, steadying my nerves. I'd expected to see Becca still asleep beside me, but thankfully I was alone. *Did I [illegible]?*

Hearing hushed whispers outside by the campfire, and with only dim light filling the tent, I assumed it was still early morning. I sighed in relief. This dream, like the many I'd been having as of late, seemed so real that I felt like I was losing my mind—or, rather, like I might be finding it again. I ran my fingers through my hair and lay back down, heaving a sigh of relief that I was alone in the tent. I couldn't imagine what Becca might've overheard had she been asleep beside me. *Get a grip, Zoe.*

I unzipped my sleeping bag and let the cool air assault my exposed skin. Although my arms were covered by long sleeves, I'd been growing too warm most nights, and had decided shorts were a better option. As I sat there in the brisk spring chill, I realized the dreams were most likely the cause of my body's confusion. I shivered, welcoming the distraction, and I hoped it would help stir me awake and out of my apparent sex fog.

My dreams had become more frequent and so much more...*real*. As a result, it was increasingly difficult to be around Jake—to look at him and not see his hard, naked body and the hunger illuminating his copper eyes that I saw so frequently in my sleep. As long as we weren't too close or touching, I found it easy to be around him. But when I came close enough that I could feel his longing for the woman I'd once been, I was torn. I wasn't her, I likely never would be again, and I wasn't sure how he was going to deal with that when he finally accepted it.

Determined to get my day started, I dug through my duffel and pulled out a set of clean clothes. After unfurling my favorite black t-shirt, I shook the wrinkles out of it and pulled it over my head. Amused, I considered how foreign my clothes had felt to me a little over a week ago, and that at some point I'd deemed a knee-high pair of soft, pink socks, the black, well-worn t-shirt, and a pair of snug, faded blue jeans my favorite ensemble. Had that always been the case? Given the fact that I'd been a gallery assistant of sorts like Jake had said, I highly doubted it.

Standing as straight as was possible in the two-person tent that was Becca's and my current bedroom, I tugged my jeans up, pausing as my eyes lingered on the tattoo on my hip. I'd often wondered why, of all things, I'd decided to get a Celtic knot inked on my skin—the same Celtic knot I'd apparently painted on pretty much all of my worldly possessions. *What does it mean?* I'd seen its twin on the inside of Dani's left wrist when Harper had been examining her broken arm. I'd wanted to ask her about it on numerous occasions. I knew, deep down, that it was important to us, that it symbolized something that I would probably never fully comprehend, but I wanted to at least try.

Unzipping the side pocket of my bag, I pulled out my brush, running it through my hair before tossing it back down. Jake's voice rumbled in the still air outside my tent, and I froze, listening and waiting. I wasn't sure I had gathered my wits enough to see him just yet. Straining to listen, I heard his heavy, unhurried footsteps dawdle by what I assumed was the fire pit. He chuckled softly at something one of the other campers whispered, and I heard a folding chair creak beneath his powerful body. The image of his strong, possessive arms wrapped around me flashed in my mind, and I groaned.

Searching the side pocket of my bag for my toothbrush and a tube of toothpaste, another smoldering image of his fingers gripping my hair flashed in my mind. Despite my efforts to explore the comet trail of desire and curiosities left behind by my frequent dreamy sexcapades, it was proving difficult to find my backbone when it came to initiating anything between Jake and me. The pressure to be *her*, and the fear that I would grossly disappoint him, trumped all of my own intentions and desires.

Finally, I found my toothbrush and toothpaste and grabbed my bomber jacket before steadying myself to leave my safety zone. Unzipping the tent, I stepped out into the chilly morning and let the cool, high-desert air assault my hyperaware senses.

So as not to be rude, I glanced over at Jason and Jake, who were sipping their morning coffee by the fire. "Good morning."

Jake's back was to me, but Jason's wasn't. My brother looked exhausted, but who wouldn't be after having second watch—scouting the camp perimeter while the rest of us slept soundly in our tents. Jason nodded at me and Jake craned his neck as I passed by.

"Morning," they said in unison.

Under the heat of Jake's stare, I couldn't help but blush. *Can he tell I just woke up from a scandalous dream about him?* The way my face reddened and I fumbled around whenever he was nearby, I assumed it was nearly impossible for him not to notice how much his presence affected me.

I walked over to the water station Sarah and I had set up on the back of the temporarily nonoperational and very rickety covered wagon. Taking a couple days of respite while Jake and Jason worked on repairing it was a welcome break from long days of boring riding; it allowed everyone—horses and riders alike—time to rest and gave me the opportunity to appreciate the expansive high desert landscape that surrounded us.

I dipped a small, plastic cup into a galvanized tub of water, filling it as much as I could before heading over to the washing station a few yards away. I stopped at the folding table set up near a small cliff that overlooked a canyon, stuck my toothbrush inside the water cup to wet the bristles, and squeezed on a healthy dose of much-needed minty paste.

Appreciating the small luxuries, I brushed my teeth, grateful to carry out such a mundane task with such a spectacularly eerie view. With the sun illuminating the dense fog that settled between the towering sandstone mesas scattered below our camp, it was like the fog acted as a barrier between two worlds—two realities.

I felt like *I* was caught between two realities—the one I'd awoken in after the incident at the golf course, and the one I *should've* been in.

"Did you sleep well?"

I jumped mid-brush and pivoted around to find Jake wandering up behind me. His coffee mug was dwarfed in his large hand as he took a sip. His eyes met mine briefly before shifting to my mouth and back. Clearing his throat, he averted his gaze as he tried not to laugh. "You have some toothpaste…right here," he said and pointed to the corner of his mouth.

Mortified, I hurriedly wiped away the white, pasty foam with my sleeve.

"*Did* you sleep well?" He stepped past me, his gaze fixed on the canyon surrounding us.

When he looked back at me, expecting an answer, I nodded. With a final quick brush, I spit over the edge of the cliff. "You?"

Amused, Jake watched me as I swished around a final

mouthful of water. “Jason and I had second watch last night,” he said.

I spit again. “Oh, right. How was it?”

He shrugged and took a step toward me, a crooked smile parting his lips. “I found something I want to show you,” he said, bringing his hand up to my cheek. Unbidden, images from my dream flashed through my mind, and once again I felt a thrilling sense of panic. With the pad of his thumb, he wiped away what I assumed were the final remnants of my morning routine.

“Thanks,” I said, feeling self-conscious under the weight of his stare.

His smile broadened. “What are you doing today?”

I grabbed the jacket I’d hung over some sagebrush and shrugged it on before gathering my things. “Umm, after breakfast, I was going to practice some more with Sam and Tavis. I think I’m finally starting to get a teensy bit better with the whole archery thing.”

“Good,” he said.

“I’m free after that, unless you want to help me with my self defense again.” I gave him a playful flutter of my eyelashes. “Because last time worked out so well…”

Jake grinned and rubbed the side of his face like he could still feel where I’d smacked him. “Jason and I need to put the front wheel back on the wagon, but we can practice after.”

“Perfect,” I said, and we started walking back toward camp. “So you guys figured it out then? Whatever was wrong with the wheel, I mean.”

Jake stopped just outside camp, dumping the final remnants of coffee from his mug out on the dirt. “I think so. We tweaked a few things, so hopefully it’ll help.”

“Well, that’s good news,” I said, smiling at Sarah as she waddled past us. “I’m gonna help Sarah with breakfast. Come find me later?”

Jake studied me, his expression bordering on amused. “You got it," he said, and I felt a surge of hope as he walked back toward the fire pit.

Dropping my things off at my tent, I headed over to Sarah, who was bustling around by the food tubs as she gathered her morning ingredients. "What can I do?" I asked, ready to be put to work.

She glanced over at me. "Hey, Zoe." She flashed a bubbly smile, an expression I'd come to rely on each morning. "Can you wash and chop the potatoes for me? Pretty please, with extra chocolate syrup?"

A laugh burst from my mouth, and I felt the tension Jake had inspired in my body instantly ease. "Cheap shot, Sarah," I said, shaking my head with feigned regret. "I never should've told you about my chocolate addiction."

She batted her eyelashes at me for show and offered me another silly smile. "The potatoes…?"

"Of course I'll chop potatoes," I said, sidestepping around her to the oversized basket of what was left of the potatoes we'd brought with us from Colorado Trails. "I'm assuming we're gonna need all of them, right?"

"Yes, please."

I heaved the basket up, pausing to figure out the best place to clean them.

"Go ahead and just use the water in the tub, Zoe. It'll be easier that way. I'll ask Biggs to get us fresh water later, after we do the dishes."

"After *I* do the dishes. You don't need to be lugging around cast-iron skillets and bending over so much." I shook my head. "In case you forgot, you're pregnant," I added dryly.

"Am I? Geez, that would explain a lot."

I shrugged, "Just thought I'd remind you." I offered her a playful smile. Happy I didn't have to lug at least fifteen pounds of potatoes somewhere else to scrub and chop, I placed the basket on the ground beneath the ledge of the chuck wagon, where the water tub sat. Reaching for the large Ziplock bag of sponges, SOS pads, and miscellaneous brushes tucked inside one of the wagon's little cubbies, I picked through the contents before choosing a palm-size bristle brush and began scrubbing.

"So, what's on Sarah's Roadside Menu this morning?" I asked. "The boys came back empty-handed last night…that doesn't mean we're having, like, roadkill or something, does it?"

"I would've considered it if we'd seen any that was fresh, but nope, we're going with spam in our breakfast burritos this morning." Sarah sighed. "Honestly, Zoe, I'm beginning to run out of ideas. There are so many of us now, I think I've exhausted all of my sort-of-quick-but-good ideas, at least if I want to feed everyone before it's time to start preparing lunch."

"We're traveling, Sarah. No one expects a five-course meal. We're lucky we have you cooking for us at all, and besides, I've never heard anyone complain." I put a scrubbed potato on the cutting board Sarah had delivered to me before reaching for another potato.

"Thanks. I guess it's just that cooking is really the only thing I can contribute at this point. I just don't want to disappoint."

From my periphery, I watched her pour oil into three cast-iron skillets and carry them one by one to the campfire, placing them beside one another on the metal grate Biggs had set up for her.

As she waddled back, wiping her hands off on her apron, she glanced around. "Where's Becca this morning, anyway? Is she getting tired of me already?"

I laughed. "No, I don't think so. She's probably with Mase and Camille. She was gone this morning when I woke up, so don't take it personal."

"I'll try not to." She bustled around behind me for a while, leaving me to my thoughts as I scrubbed one potato after another.

"How are things going with Jake?" Sarah asked after a few minutes.

I felt my body tense. "They're good," I said as nonchalantly as possible.

Lazy footsteps, followed by a sigh and Sarah's shadow approaching, brought my scrubbing to a stop. I looked over to find her staring directly at me, head tilted to the side and hands on her hips. "Tell me," she demanded. "What's wrong?"

Giving in, I sighed. "Nothing's *wrong*."

"Something's…something. You're lost in thought, which is more of an old Zoe thing than a new Zoe thing."

My head snapped toward her. "Is it?" I couldn't help feeling a burst of hope.

With a curt nod, she crossed her arms, resting them on her belly. "Now spill." The curious gleam in her pale, brown eyes betrayed her hard-set features.

Rinsing off the newly scrubbed potato in my hand, I set it aside and turned to face her. "It's the dreams." I wiped my wet hands off on a towel haphazardly draped over the edge of the chuck boxes. "You know…about Jake?"

Sarah grinned. "I remember. Does that mean you finally did something about it?" Her eyebrows danced suggestively.

"No," I said, exasperated.

Sarah's excitement vanished, replaced with sympathy. "I'm just teasing you, Zoe."

"What's wrong with me, Sarah?" I leaned against the fold-out work table, rubbing my temples as if it might help the answer form.

She sighed heavily. "You haven't even talked to him about your dreams?"

"God no!" I blanched. "What the hell would I say?"

"Okay, well"—she threw her hands up—"this situation is clearly bothering you," she said flatly, shielding her eyes as she squinted into the sun burning through the morning fog. "If you won't *talk* to him about it, what *are* you going to do?"

I threw my own hands up, feeling foolish and naïve. "Haven't you ever been so scared that you'll fail at something, that you'll be rejected? I know it sounds silly, but—"

"It doesn't sound silly." Sarah stepped closer to the wagon, into the shade, and the tension around her eyes lessened.

"What if taking that next step makes me feel closer to him, but pushes *him* further away from me? I'm not the same, Sarah. The next step could easily ruin what we're slowly putting back together—"

"Or make it better." She watched me for a long moment, clearly considering my situation. "You know what I think?"

I stared at her blankly.

"I think you just need to take the chance—not with sex or kissing or anything you don't feel comfortable with, but you need to be more open with him. Let's be honest, it's Jake, which means he's not going to push things between you guys…he's waiting for *you*." Sarah placed both of her hands on my shoulders. "If you want things to change, you need to make the first move—and soon, by the sound of it, or these dreams are going to drive you crazy." Sarah gave my shoulders a squeeze. "You're torturing yourself, Zoe. I know it's scary, but you need to do *something*. You're letting your fear get in the way of your relationship with him."

I groaned, nerves making me feel nauseous. "I know." As much as I knew she was trying to help, it was easy for her to encourage me; she'd been with Biggs for months—they were having a baby together even. They'd come to know each other organically, whereas I woke up in a relationship I couldn't remember ever having been in.

"For what it's worth…I don't think you'll regret *trying* to be with Jake. I just hope you don't hurt him in the process. He's a good guy, Zoe." Sarah turned away, smiling to herself as she ambled to the food trunk.

Multiple images of her and Biggs flashed through my mind. Although I'd gotten a bit better at distracting myself so I wasn't solely focused on everyone's memories and emotions all the time, some were more difficult to ignore than others. And sometimes curiosity got the best of me, and I couldn't help but pay too much attention. *What's it like...really* being *with someone?*

Refocusing on Sarah, I realized that she was watching me intently and that I'd been thinking out loud...again. I cleared my throat, feeling like I'd been caught lurking in the dark corners of her mind. Because, in a way, I had.

"What's *what* like?" Her eyes narrowed and then widened. "Are you in my head, Zoe?"

Biting the inside of my cheek, my hands found their way to my temples again, and I attempted to rub the swirling questions I had away. "Yes...sorry."

She only tossed her head back and let out a boisterous laugh. "'What's it like?' It's *amazing*, Zoe."

I smiled timidly, relieved she wasn't offended by my prodding.

"Which is why I think you shouldn't run away from whatever you and Jake might still have just because you're feeling lost. I think you should try to figure things out. Biggs makes me feel beautiful and special, even when I'm as big as a whale. He makes me feel alive." She smiled, more for herself than for me. "I don't know how I would've gotten this far without him. Granted, I wouldn't be like I am now, near bursting and hormonal as all hell, without him..."

Sarah's thoughts drifted and she glanced over to the tents, where Biggs and Sanchez were standing with Jason. "Being with someone you love makes you feel important," she said wistfully. "It makes you feel like everything will be okay because you have someone to face your problems with. Jake used to be that for you, at least I think he was. But you won't know if he still is until you try."

In spite of my uncertainty, I longed to have with someone what Sarah had with Biggs. Jake was amazing, I knew it innately, even if I wasn't sure how or why I knew it. Determined to find out if he really was someone I could love, I decided that today *had* to be that day—the day we would take things a step further, regardless of how small and seemingly insignificant that step might be. I needed it. *We* needed it.

"You're getting faster," Jake said, helping me to my feet after our final round of blocking and kicking. I excelled at the blocking, although any sort of offensive strikes had proved to be more difficult.

"Yeah?" I said, genuinely curious. Cooper trotted over to us, and I rubbed his head while he paused from his exploring.

Jake nodded. "But speed was never a problem for you."

I frowned. "What was my problem?"

Jake only chuckled as he took in my expression. "Let's just say you weren't very strong."

"*Weren't*? You mean *not*…?"

"Weren't," he clarified and gestured to my exposed biceps. They were nothing to write home about. "You're stronger now. All you need is to remember—" He stopped himself. "You just need to learn how to use that strength again."

Again. The fact that he'd probably spent countless hours teaching me, doing the same training exercises we'd been doing together the past couple days, was aggravating.

Luckily, Chris and Harper strode by, deep in conversation, giving me something else to think about. *Them.* I smiled. They weren't overtly affectionate, but they spent a lot of their time together, and I'd seen Harper come out of Chris's tent on more than one occasion.

"We're heading up to the ledge after this," Jake told them. "We'll be back after sundown."

Chris nodded. "Have fun."

"See you in a couple hours," Harper said, and they both continued toward camp.

I glanced behind us toward the canyon below and then back to Jake. "Excuse me…the *ledge*? Are you going to throw me over?"

Jake took my hand in his, a gesture I hadn't quite expected, and we walked toward the mass of boulders at the southwest edge of camp. "Not exactly."

"Umm…"

Jake stopped. "Are you afraid of heights now?"

"Why? I wasn't before?" That was surprising.

Jake shook his head. "Not that I'm aware of."

"Oh."

Smiling, he squeezed my hand tighter in his. "It's not as bad as it sounds, I promise. Come on, Coop!"

I bit at the inside of my cheek. Jake wanted to do something special with me today, alone, and I wasn't about to complain. "Alright. But remember, Harper and Chris know I'm going to this *ledge* with you, so if anything happens to me…"

Jake laughed softly, and we fell into step beside one another.

After a few minutes of walking hand in hand, I lost sight of camp, but I didn't mind. We really were completely alone, and I felt strangely at ease about it. Something was different about us this time; whether it was the fact that I was adamant to step out of my comfort zone or the fact that this seemed the closest thing to a date I could ever remember having, I wasn't sure. But I was both comfortable and content.

"I found this place last night during my rounds," Jake said, leading me up onto a large, lichen-covered boulder. He stepped up and reached down to help pull me up, too. He was squinting even though his back was to the lowering sun. "I thought you might like it."

"I'm excited," I said truthfully. He guided me up onto another large rock, but this time my foot slipped, and I flailed forward.

Jake caught me, his hands gripping mine with a firm, reassuring hold.

"Are you alright?" His hands were rough and warm and strong around mine, one small detail to add to the list of things I'd been noticing about him the more time we spent together.

I let out a disgruntled grumble. "Yeah, thanks. I guess I'm not very good at this hiking stuff."

"You've never been very agile," Jake teased and helped me step onto the next rock. "It's just over here." He nodded toward the tallest boulder as his fingers tightened around mine, trying to keep me from toppling over.

As if they were carried on the gentle breeze, a stream of memories filled my mind, and I couldn't shut them out.

I saw myself on the ground, struggling beneath a very aggressive and determined soldier as he straddled me, grinning.

I was sobbing and screaming.

A little ways off, Cooper stood beside Jake at the edge of the woods; Jake's attention snapped between the soldier and me.

In a blink, I watched another, older military man fall to the ground, a bullet between his eyes, and Jake [illegible] against a tree, bleeding and in pain.

Jake had saved me. I could feel his disgust and astonishment acutely. There was something about physically touching each other that made our connection stronger.

Another memory flickered to life.

Jake was holding me against his chest. I was unconscious as we rushed toward a truck, Harper and Sanchez hobbling along nearby.

"How many Crazies was that?" Sanchez groaned, limping as she leaned against Harper. Blood covered the front of her shirt and

was all over Harper's hands and clothes, as well. "The bastards came out of nowhere..." She cringed. "Ah! Shit!"

"Stop talking and concentrate on getting back to the truck," Harper said.

Sanchez retorted with something sarcastic, but I was distracted by Jake's perpetual glances down at me, cradled in his arms as I was, and the way he absently stroked the side of my face, resting against his chest.

"Here," he said, stirring me from his memories. "Put your foot right here."

I smiled at how careful he was with me. I could imagine how being around him had made me feel. His hands tightened reassuringly around mine, and I had no doubt that he'd made me feel safe.

Without warning, another memory assaulted me.

I saw myself, crumpled on a cement floor in what appeared to be a cafeteria, my face blue and bile and sweat covering my body. But Jake didn't seem to mind any of that as he gathered me into his arms. I could feel his fear, anger, and self-loathing as he called for help and rushed me away to find Harper.

And then another…

I was lying on a hospital table, unconscious, with IVs in my arms and tubes up my nose and down my throat. Jake paced back and forth, desperately waiting.

"It was your blood," I whispered, resisting as he pulled on my hands, urging me forward.

Jake let up. "What?"

I shook my head, amazed every time I learned something new about him…about us. "Do you ever get tired of saving my life?"

Though the question was little more than a whisper, it was still a question I needed him to answer.

With the exception of Dani and how much we'd relied on each other growing up, I was suddenly certain that no one had ever done as much for me in my entire lifetime as Jake had done in the few months we'd known each other. "Do you?" I persisted.

He furrowed his brow.

"Even after Dr. Wesley found me, you tried the transfusion again—you tried to help me. It seems I'm always getting myself into trouble, and you're always having to get me out of it. Do you ever get tired of saving my life?" I repeated, barely noticing Cooper chasing a lizard in the crevasses in the rocks beneath our feet.

Jake stared at me a moment longer before looking away. "It's just the way it is." I could feel a hint of irritation coming from him.

"But it can't be easy for you…"

His eyes found mine again, an unsettling disquiet burning within them, scorching any remaining questions off my tongue. "No," he said carefully. "It's not. But I'm glad I can be there when you need me, regardless of how much it bothers you."

"It bothers me?" I asked, more than a little curious. It seemed unlikely that I would be annoyed at having my own knight in shining armor.

"I could be wrong, but I don't think you're used to relying on other people."

"It makes sense, I guess." I stepped up to stand on the rock beside him. "And what about you?" I asked more playfully. "Are you a habitual hero, or am I just one lucky girl?"

Jake's expression hardened, and he stared down at our joined hands. "I'm still getting used to having someone I"—he paused and let go of my hand—"someone I *want* to take care of."

I barely heard the words as the wind whooshed past my ears, but I *had* heard him, and my heart skittered in my chest. "I—" I cleared my throat. "I see."

We continued our climb to the ledge.

"Well, whatever's happened in our past," I ventured. "I hope I've told you that I appreciate all that you've done for me."

Finally, he smiled again, and my heart felt a little lighter. "I know you do," he said, pulling me toward him. "This has been a learning curve for both of us."

We stood there quietly for a long moment, staring at one another.

"I'd probably be dead right now if it weren't for you," I said. After all I'd seen, it was obvious.

Jake narrowed his eyes the barest amount, no doubt gauging what my reaction to his answer might be. "Probably," he said. "But then, I don't think you would've had so many close calls if it weren't for me, either." Jake peered out at the view and reached for my hand once more. "Stop distracting me, would you?" I was relieved by his lighthearted tone. "I promise, you're going to like this."

Stepping up onto a flat rock, I froze beside him, gripping his arm to steady myself, and gaped in awe. I didn't care how high up we were, the desert was the most picturesque, undisturbed landscape I'd ever seen. It stretched on as far as I could see, eroded sandstone towers standing vigil over the valley floor, casting protective shadows over every fissure etched in its basin. Fuchsia cactus flowers edged down the mountain we stood atop of, meeting a valley floor with bursts of yellow and purple wildflowers. The reddish hue of the late afternoon created an almost alien glow over the horizon, and I felt like I was on another planet. It was amazingly beautiful, and standing there, looking up at Jake, his eyes glowing golden brown, I never wanted to leave. This place was ours.

"It's so beautiful. Thank you for bringing me here." I took both of his hands in mine. The urge to kiss him, to create new memories between us, was almost too intense to resist. So I didn't.

Leaning forward, I appreciated the soft smile that pulled at his lips and lost myself in his asking eyes, and my excitement trumped my lingering uncertainties.

But with another surfacing memory, I hesitated.

We stood in an old house, blood covering me as I peered up at him with a pained expression on my face. Moving tentatively in to kiss me, Jake yearned for forgiveness and a sense of familiarity. His kiss was controlled, but desperate and full of more emotion than he knew what to do with. He needed me—her. *He wanted* her...*he loved* her.

My mind filled with emotional vomit I couldn't process, and I took a step back, unable to bring myself to follow through—to try to be *her.* Feeling something cool on my cheek, I blinked and wiped a lone tear away. I couldn't do this; I couldn't take the chance—not right now, not yet.

"What's wrong?" Jake asked, concern creasing his brow and an expression of longing on his face.

Reaching out to hold his hand was the most I could offer him. I flashed him a weak smile and turned toward the sunset. "The sun's setting," I said hoarsely. "Let's get comfortable."

APRIL 1 AE

10

DANI

APRIL 20, 1AE

Great Basin Desert, Nevada

For almost three weeks, we traveled across Utah and into Nevada in relative peace. We encountered no Crazies, no megalomaniacal dictators, no mind-controlling cult leaders. No human enemies crossed our path, which seemed almost miraculous. But in a wasteland as expansive as the Great Basin Desert, there was no need for *human* enemies. The desert itself was enemy enough.

The first horse fell before the sun even reached its zenith. It didn't matter that it was early spring and the days never reached blisteringly hot temperatures; what mattered was that we hadn't encountered freshwater in two days, and our reserve supply was dangerously low—too low for a caravan of over two dozen horses, nineteen people, a few goats, and two dogs. The last "town" we'd passed—it was really little more than a cluster of farms—we actually had to circumvent widely due to a large population of Crazies who, according to Zoe, were exceedingly bloodthirsty, and the last three bodies of water we'd come across were saltwater, not fresh. The Fates, it seemed, had turned against us.

I was riding beside Jason and his as-yet-unnamed horse at the front of our column when Sarah shrieked. Jason and I exchanged wide-eyed glances and quickly guided our horses back down the length of the caravan to find out the cause of Sarah's shriek. If she was going into labor…now…

Near the back, just ahead of the covered wagon, Houdini, an older palomino thoroughbred who'd been with us since leaving Bodega Bay months ago—who I'd befriended years ago, when I worked at the Bodega Bay Riders' Ranch—lay on the gravel shoulder. He was partially on his side, his legs slightly curled and his head resting limp on the ground, and some of the stuff sacks and a duffel bag that had been strapped to his pack saddle were strewn around him on the gravel. His sides heaved with each too-quick breath.

"Oh God, no!" I swung my leg over Wings's rump and jumped down, not caring that the sharp movement jarred my broken arm. I lunged toward Houdini, dropping to my knees by his head. "Dini…" My fingers brushed over his forehead, moving his blond bangs away from his eyes so he could see. Those brown eyes were wide and filled with terror.

I strengthened the telepathic link between us automatically, needing to comfort him, to ease his mounting panic. *"It's okay, Houdini…it's okay,"* I murmured in his mind. *"I'm here. You'll be fine. Just breathe, old friend. Just breathe, and you'll be okay. I'll take care of you."*

Lies. All lies. He wouldn't be okay. And the worst part was that he knew it.

I reached for the nearest buckle on his pack saddle, the one over his shoulder, but my fingers were trembling too badly to be effective. I balled my hand into a fist and glanced up at the humans standing in a loose circle around us. I didn't understand why they were just standing there.

"Help me!" I said, tugging ineffectively at the buckle once

more. "Get this damn thing off him." The words came out broken, an almost sob. "Please!"

Jason was suddenly there, and Zoe and Carlos and Mase. Everyone moved closer, wanting to help. But they couldn't help, not in any way that *really* mattered.

I scooted closer, lifting Houdini's heavy head up onto my knees awkwardly with only one arm, and huddled over him. I hugged his neck and whispered empty reassurances in his mind.

As his pain increased, so did his panic, and he started fading in and out of coherency.

"Red? Dani?" Jason touched my shoulder. "We did what we could with the saddle, but he's lying on part of it, so…"

It didn't matter anyway. I raised my head and met Jason's eyes. He knew. Or at least, he suspected.

"Dehydration?"

I nodded. I couldn't speak; anything I attempted to say would come out garbled and incomprehensible.

"What else can we do?"

I stroked my hand along the length of Houdini's neck and took several deep breaths. Clearing my throat, I said, "Give the horses the rest of the water."

Jason stared at me for a few seconds, blinking but not speaking. Finally, he shook his head. "We'll give each of them a drink, but we have to save some…"

I felt my expression harden, but I didn't argue.

Again, he stared and didn't respond for long seconds. "What do you want to do now?"

I swallowed. Talking about water was making my throat feel painfully parched. "Tell the others to keep moving until they can't see us anymore…and to take Wings and Nameless with them." I wiped my cheek on my shoulder. "And *nobody* gets back in the saddle. We're walking until we find freshwater."

Jason nodded before standing and striding toward our other companions, who were clustered behind the wagon. I couldn't spare much attention for them, not with Houdini growing more and more afraid with each passing minute. I did what I could for him, reminding him that I was still there, that I wouldn't leave him, that I loved him and would always be there with him. That I would never abandon him, not while he still breathed.

I was vaguely aware of someone, possibly multiple someones, gathering the items that had been on Houdini's pack saddle.

"Dani?" It was Zoe.

I continued to stare into Houdini's wild eye, continued to murmur nonsensical things, impossible things, aloud and in his mind.

Zoe touched my shoulder. "Do you want to give him some water, too?"

I sniffled and shook my head. There was no point, and we couldn't afford to waste it.

Crunching gravel, receding footsteps, and then Houdini and I were alone again.

I wasn't sure how long it took—maybe fifteen minutes, maybe more—but the caravan started to move west again, leaving Jason, Houdini, and me behind on the shoulder of the highway.

"Where's the best place to do it?" Jason asked softly as he knelt behind Houdini's head.

I touched my fingers to a spot on the palomino's forehead, then leaned over and pressed my lips against his bristly hair. "I love you, old friend," I whispered. Maintaining the telepathic connection, I continued to soothe Houdini, even as I stood and took several steps backward.

"You don't have to watch," Jason said.

"Yes, Jason, I do."

On his exhale, Jason nodded and pulled the pistol from his shoulder holster. His aim was true, and Houdini was gone almost as soon as the bullet entered his skull.

"Goodbye, old friend."

By the time we caught up to the caravan, the sun was directly overhead. Our companions were clustered on the side of the road, talking over one another. Jason and I didn't notice it at first. Maybe because we didn't want to, and maybe because it didn't seem possible after what we'd just been through. It wasn't until we were just several dozen yards away and I was in the process of checking in with the rest of the horses that I felt it: panic—pain—terror.

Two more horses were down.

It was one of the driving teams, which explained why the humans were clustered beside one of the carts. One of the cart horses had collapsed, and she'd dragged her companion down with her, fracturing the other mare's leg in the process. Carlos and Jake were working on freeing the healthier horse, not that it mattered, while the others were arguing about what to do next.

Jason's hold tightened on my hand.

"—that lake we passed a couple miles ago," Ben said.

"Yeah," Ky agreed. "Couldn't we, I don't know, boil it and capture the vapor or something. That would be freshwater..."

Grayson shook his head. "The amount of wood required to boil enough water...it's too inefficient. It won't produce enough drinkable water fast enough."

"So we go to this next town," Sanchez said, holding up a partially folded map and shaking it. "No matter what, we go here, clear out any Crazies—"

"But what if there are other people?" Sarah said.

Sanchez pressed her lips into a thin line and took a deep breath. "If there are other people, we'll make them see reason." She raised her eyebrows. "This is the only option. We didn't survive this long just to die of dehydration in the middle of a fucking desert."

Silences settled over the group.

Jason and I stopped on the periphery, earning hasty glances and tight smiles. They'd all heard the shot; they knew Houdini's fate and knew the cart horses—along with any other horse that collapsed—would suffer the same fate.

"I'm with Sanchez," Jason said. "I think heading for the nearest town and doing whatever it takes to get access to their water supply is our only move at this point." He looked at me, and when I nodded, he shifted his focus to Grayson. "Daniel?"

The eldest and undeniably wisest member of our group nodded as well, and one by one, so did the others.

By the time we reached the "town"—the label was even less applicable to this one than it had been to the last—we'd lost another horse and were down to only one cart and the wagon. As far as I could tell, it appeared to be a single farm, lonesome and dried up in the middle of the high desert. We stopped about a quarter of a mile away to assess any possible dangers before diving in.

"Do you sense anything?" Jason asked Zoe as she walked to the front of the caravan. When she shook her head, he shifted his focus to me. "And your scouts still aren't picking up on anything?"

I, too, shook my head and, staring up at the sky, watched the pale pinpoint that was Ray grow as she glided closer.

Jason exhaled heavily and nodded in slow motion. It was clear that he was reticent to believe we'd caught a break. Eager, but reticent.

I started salivating at the thought of gulping down water. How I still had enough moisture in my body to salivate was beyond me, but I couldn't wait to suck down as much water as my stomach could hold. I hadn't had to pee since just after waking, and even that had been a lackluster effort—not overly encouraging regarding my own state of dehydration. And the dark spots taunting me as they danced around the outer edges of my vision…I didn't think those were a great sign, either.

By the time we reached the farm, our pace slow to exert as little effort as possible, the spots were no longer only on the outer edge, but creeping across my vision like ashes floating in the drafts of heat over a campfire. We sought refuge in the largest, shadiest building—a slightly rundown barn. Most of us worked together to unburden the horses while Jason, Carlos, and Jake split off to work on gaining access to the remote farm's water supply. Carlos's Ability was more than strong enough to power a well pump, as he'd started doing pretty much everywhere we stopped that had a well so we could stock up. Unfortunately, the deeper we plunged into the Great Basin Desert, the fewer and farther between those places seemed to be.

While I moved from horse to horse in the barn alongside Zoe, I imagined the sensation of water filling my mouth, cool and refreshing…trickling down my throat…dripping down my chin…over my head…

"I hate to have to say this…" Jason's voice was low, even.

I looked up, focusing with some effort on the barn doorway. Jason, Carlos, and Jake stood, silhouetted in the opening by the late afternoon sun. I didn't need to be able to see any of their shadowed faces for dread to sprout and flourish inside me.

"…but the water's no good."

I noticed the others straighten, turn to face him, exchange a confused look with whoever was nearest to them.

"What do you mean?" Sanchez asked. She took several steps toward the trio, away from the wagon team she was helping Grayson unharness.

"There are bodies in the house." Jason paused. "And in the water tank."

Grayson joined Sanchez. "We can disconnect the pump, and—"

"Won't work," Jake said from beside Jason. "Someone disabled it. It's gonna take some time to fix, and there's no guarantee…"

Sanchez placed her hands on her hips. "What about those pickups over by the house? At least one of them's gotta be—"

Jake shook his head, his expression grim.

"Someone clearly wanted to cut off these people's access to water," Jason said. "There's no water here."

No water. It wasn't possible. I shook my head as my knees gave out, and I plopped on my butt on the dirt floor. This couldn't be happening. We couldn't die here…not after everything. But we would.

We're going to die here.

I rubbed my hand over my mouth.

We're going to die *here.*

I felt whiskers tickle the side of my neck, closely followed by the warmth of a velvety muzzle. *"No,"* Wings said in my mind. *"We will not die here. You will lead us to water. We trust you."*

Which made the whole situation so much worse, because I couldn't do a damn thing.

I blinked.

But I *could* do a damn thing. I could slip into Ray's mind…into the minds of any other creatures for miles around. I could hop from mind to mind until I found freshwater.

I leaned my cheek against the side of Wings's long face. *"I will try, Pretty Girl. I will try."*

I was Ray.

I flew away from the tainted two-legs den in circles. My quarry was not my usual prey, but it was no less important. My quarry was water. Without it, she-who-flies-with-me would cease to be. I had to find it. She-who-flies-with-me is part of me, now. She-who-flies-with-me cannot cease to be.

I suggested life-water, warm and thick and sustaining, but she-

who-flies-with-me claimed consuming such would make her ill... make her more likely to cease to be. That could not happen.

I flew until the sun neared the storm clouds on the horizon. I flew until my wings ached. I flew until I had to hunt, or I, too, would cease to be.

I came "awake" with a start. I'd been sleeping less and less as the days passed, spending more and more time flying with Ray, or running with Wings or Cooper or Jack. It was so easy now, so relaxing. Usually.

"Did you find anything?" Jason asked. My head was on his lap, as it had been when I'd first drifted away, and his fingers were stroking the wispy flyaways at my temples. He looked down at me, hope gleaming in his eyes.

I glanced at the doorway. It was still light out, but dimmer than before. I looked up at Jason. "What time is it?"

"A little after seven."

I stared into his sapphire eyes for a little bit longer, savoring the hope they still contained. Because as soon as I spoke, I knew it would disappear.

Taking a deep breath, I whispered, "Nothing close enough." I closed my eyes and felt a tear escape, sliding across my temple only to be stopped by his fingertip. "I'm sorry."

Jason leaned down and pressed his lips to my forehead. "Me too."

11

ZOE

APRIL 20, 1AE

Great Basin Desert, Nevada

I'd come to appreciate the cool evenings in the high desert, a welcome contrast to the warm and wearisome days. And after a day as long, hot, and emotionally trying as this one had been, tonight was no different. The sun was finally setting behind the mountains, offering the group and our animal friends a reprieve from the threatening sun. I felt a slight sense of rejuvenation as the sun's rays lessened, allowing people to scramble around in their desperation to find water without the added burden of heat.

Feeling useless and overwhelmed by everyone's mounting emotions, I couldn't stay in the barn stewing in everyone's fear and anxiety any longer. So, leaving Sarah, Ben, and Sam to continue making room for everyone to roll out their sleeping bags in the barn, I slipped away to clear my mind, to harness my own emotions and rid myself of everyone else's.

What are we going to do?

Stretching my legs, I walked to the pump house, stopping just outside the crumbling doorframe so as not to bother Jake as he,

Carlos, and Mase cranked and banged on the piping and machinery it housed.

"Carlos, there's a roll of duct tape in that bin over there." Jake pointed to a storage tub resting by my feet. I bent down and picked it up, handing it to Carlos. "And there should be a tube of silicone, too." On the outside, Jake was all calm confidence, but I could feel his wavering ease beneath the surface.

"To seal up the cracks?" Carlos asked as he took the bin from me.

Jake nodded and turned back to Mase. "On the count of three, I'll turn to the left, you twist to the right, but be careful. I couldn't find any piping to replace this one."

Mase nodded.

"One. Two. Three." Both men wrenched and strained, Jake more than Mase, until finally the piping twisted apart. I felt Jake's wave of relief as he examined the intact pipe. Then his relief fizzled. "Shit." He ran a hand over his head. "I hope to God we have enough silicone to fix this."

Unable to watch frustration harden Jake's face, I wandered over to the workbench on the side of the barn, where Sanchez, Grayson, Harper, and Biggs were standing. Inching my way into the circle, I stared down at the three maps they had unfurled and laid out, overlapping one another.

"If we go south," Sanchez said, "we'll find more shelter—caves and such—but there's absolutely no indication of there being any water."

"We know there are three bodies of water here," Harper said, pointing to an aerial map of the westernmost side of the desert.

"True," Grayson said. "But we don't know if they're saltwater or—"

"We can't steer clear of possible water because we're assuming they're salt ponds," Harper said. "It's a chance we might have to take…"

With thinning patience lacing each of their voices, I left the four of them to debate which route to take. There were no words of advice I could offer, and I decided hanging around would only worry me more and aggravate them further.

I passed Dani, who was lying quietly in Jason's arms inside one of the stables. I could feel her mind in both an awakened and hibernating state. Jason glanced up at me as he held her, amplifying her Ability as she no doubt soared or roamed or slithered around with her animal friends in search of water.

With heavy limbs, I schlepped to the edge of the farm, found a lone juniper, and nestled myself against it. Had our day not been filled with death and turmoil, I might've thought the storm clouds looming over the mountains miles and miles away might be our saving grace, but instead, I felt as if we were being taunted, teased. Even the sunset that stretched across the expanse that separated us from our salvation seemed to have a greater meaning. It was truly remarkable, a melody of reds and yellows and oranges so vibrant and alive I couldn't help but wonder if it was there as an accompaniment to our swan song.

"There you are," Tavis said as he strode up behind me. "I was wondering where you'd run off to."

I smiled, knowing it didn't reach my eyes, and scooted over so he could plop down beside me. "Where have you been?"

Tavis nodded back to where the herd stood languidly. "Helping Becca and Camille give the animals what little water we could."

"Water," I said quietly. "It's so close…" My eyes fixed on the dark clouds moving even further away from us as the breeze picked up.

"True. Wouldn't it be nice if the breeze was moving in the opposite direction…"

I nodded.

With a sigh, I gazed out at the most barren stretch of land we'd stumbled across yet. There was less scrub brush, fewer trees and cacti. Instead, jagged, crumbling rocks and cavernous mountains seemed to stretch out as far as I could see.

A deep humming and what sounded like yodeling startled me. I turned to Tavis. His eyes were closed, his legs crossed in front of him, and his palms were facing up.

"What are you doing?"

He opened one eye and looked at me. "It's a rain chant the Aborigines used back in the day when they thought the gods would hear their pleas."

"A rain chant?" I listened more closely. "What are you saying?"

"I'm calling to the rain, asking it to come and replenish our bodies, to provide the sustenance we need to thrive and continue on our journey."

I looked at him askance. "Really? It sounded more like gibberish to me."

Despite Tavis's efforts, he chuckled. "It was. I was just joking."

I hit his shoulder. "That's not funny."

"Ouch," he groaned and rubbed his arm, but he was grinning.

"Well, then stop joking around." I nearly started laughing as his smile grew. "This is serious stuff."

"Yeah? More serious than everyone dying of the flu? Of the world coming to an end? Of Crazies and Re-gens and—"

"I get it," I said. "But yeah. A little bit. This could be it for us."

Tavis shook his head. "We've all weathered worse. We'll figure something out."

Although I wasn't sure how Tavis could be so certain, so upbeat, he was. For a man who had absolutely no idea of his family's fate back home in Australia, he had an ever-optimistic air about him.

He climbed to his feet. "Come on, let's go see if we can help the others."

Standing, I dusted off my backside and straightened, affording one last glance behind me. It was probably my imagination, but I could've sworn the wind had shifted.

"Come on," Tavis called, and I followed after him.

A thundering rumble startled me from sleep. I sat up and peered around at the rest of the group as they too began to stir in their sleeping bags.

"What was that, Babe," Sarah said groggily.

Another, not-so-far-off rumble shook the ground beneath me.

Nobody said anything for a heartbeat…a breath.

"Is that thunder?" Dani said, scrambling as best she could with one hand to get out of her sleeping bag.

"Easy, Red," Jason said as he climbed out after her.

I sat still in my sleeping bag, listening, too scared to hope amid everyone else's mounting excitement that our prayers had been answered.

Sam ran by me, Cooper running after him toward the sliding barn door. With a grunt, Sam helped Jason and Jake push the door open.

Becca and I simply looked at one another. After another rumbling peal of thunder, a cacophony exploded in the room as everyone chattered and clambered to their feet, me included.

We crowded in the doorway, one by one, and stared into the early morning, waiting with bated breath.

"There's no rain," Becca said, and she stepped outside, staring up at the inky sky. Jason and Dani followed, then Tavis and Sam, Sarah and Biggs. Soon everyone was outside but Jake and me; he sidled up beside me, his arms crossed over his chest.

"Come on," I breathed. "Maybe you need to do another rain chant, Tavis," I called half-jokingly, but remembering the way the wind had shifted hours before, I couldn't help but wonder if his ancestors had really been listening.

Tavis only shrugged. "Rain," he jestingly commanded the clouds overhead.

There was another deep rolling of thunder and the whistle of the breeze zipping past my ears, but there was still no rain.

Plip. Plip-plip.

I heard the hollow sound of raindrops on the roof, and those standing out beneath the clouds held out their hands.

"Oh my God!" Dani cried. "Jason, it's raining!"

Everyone stood there in silence—in disbelief—as they stared up at the sky.

After a flash of lightning, everyone seemed to stir from their stunned trances. Jason wrapped his arms around Dani, lifting her feet off the ground and laughing as he twirled her around. As the rain poured more steadily, Dani howled with laughter.

Hooting and laughing resounded, and I could see the outlines of my friends in the predawn light, streaming raindrops glittering all around them. Jack and Cooper frolicked in the quickly forming mud puddles, barking and yipping.

Jake stared down at me. "What are you waiting for?"

"Oh, I'm fine, I'd rather watch—" Before I could finish, Jake crouched down and heaved me over his shoulder, eliciting squeals of laughter and shouts of profanity I hadn't meant to let escape my lips as he stepped out into the rain.

"Such language," he admonished, and I only laughed. Despite my reservations, the rain felt good, rejuvenating. As was usual when touching Jake, I saw a collage of memories, most notably one of him tossing me over his shoulder down by a lake and carrying me into a large, plantation-style home while I squealed and wiggled in his arms.

"I think I'm going to be sick, Jake."

"You always say that," he said, and as he loosened his hold on me, I pushed against his shoulder and slid down his chest. The fabric of our shirts bunched between us, but I was too excited and relieved to care. Jake grinned down at me and tucked a strand of stringy, wet hair behind my ear.

I saw the memory of us in a creek, of me in his arms, skin against skin, and I took a step away from him. “One of these times I’m actually going to throw up on you,” I joked. Then I caught a glimpse of Tavis and Sam on the outskirts of our early morning celebration, staring up at the clouds. Tavis was dumbfounded, and I couldn’t help but laugh.

“I’ll be right back,” I told Jake, placing my hand on his arm as I stepped past him and weaved my way through my jubilant friends. “Tavis,” I called to him.

He turned to me and shrugged.

I widened my smile. “You did this,” I said loudly over the rain and pointed skyward.

He shook his head. “I made up that rain chant, it wasn’t real.” I could hear the confusion in his voice and felt it muddling his mind. “It wasn’t real,” he repeated. “It’s just coincidence…”

I knew Tavis didn’t fully believe that. “You sure about that?”

He sighed and shrugged.

“You did a rain chant?” Sam seemed confused.

“Not really, no.” Tavis held out his hand, pouring rainwater collecting in his palm.

“I felt the wind shift, Tavis. I saw the water move when you walked by it back at the retention pond…I *know* you did this.”

I could see Sam’s head whipping back and forth between us. “Try to make it stop,” he said. “Then we’ll know.”

Tavis’s eyes remained locked on mine.

“Let’s wait a little while,” I said. “Just in case you can’t make it start back up again…”

And that’s exactly what we did. After our water jugs were filled, the troughs overflowing, and we’d played in enough water to satiate our fear of dehydration, Tavis made the rain stop, leaving everyone in complete, awed silence.

“She was right!” Sam said. “You’re not a Crazy after all.”

I laughed at Sam's quick tongue, and before I knew what was happening, Tavis was hauling me up into his arms for a giant bear hug, so relieved he'd been able to help save us all.

"I'm not sure I would've put two and two together," he said, a renewed lightness to his voice I appreciated.

I laughed. "That's what friends are for."

12

DANI

APRIL 27, 1AE

Great Basin Desert, Nevada

I sneezed, then blew into a red and white paisley hankie, expelling mostly rust-colored dust, and grimaced. "Dusty brains." And my brain already felt dusty enough without all of the added, well, *dust*. Slipping into animal minds at night wasn't quite as rejuvenating as sleeping, but sleeping wasn't nearly as comforting, and I craved the deepened telepathic connection I shared with whichever animal I was merged with even more after losing some of the horses.

"What was that?" Jake asked, glancing my way. He was on "Dani duty"—akin to guarding me while most of my attention was funneled into splitting my own consciousness among my avian scouts—and had been riding nearby on Highway 50 all morning. The task was usually Jason's, but he'd been convening en route with Sanchez, Chris, Grayson, and Harper all morning and had asked Jake to take his place before we'd packed up camp.

We were still moving through the Great Basin Desert, the endless expanse of parched earth and sagebrush stretching out on either side of us, but we'd managed not to repeat our near-catastrophe via dehydration of a week earlier.

Jake guided his horse, a robust sorrel gelding whose reddish-brown coat looked overly vibrant in the sun-bleached high desert, closer to Wings's side.

"What? Dusty brains?" I laughed as I stowed the hankie in my jacket pocket. "It was just something Grams—my grandma—used to say to me whenever I sneezed." Adopting her age-roughened tone and Irish accent, I said, "Bless you, child, you and your dusty brains..." With a quick look around, I added, "Though it seems particularly appropriate here."

Jake's lips twitched, and a faint smile cracked the usually austere set of his face. "Dusty brains...I knew someone who used to say that." Jake stared ahead at some point beyond where Ky and Ben were riding, his eyes distant as he spoke. "But that was a long time ago."

I watched him, watched the way nostalgia altered his features, softening them. "Another life," I said softly.

Jake's eyes met mine, his gaze intense in a way that made me self-conscious. "It seems like it sometimes, doesn't it?"

Feeling my cheeks warm, I shifted my attention to the road ahead. The highway was empty of all but a few vehicles—some abandoned, some *not*—making the passage of the cart, wagon, and herd fairly easy.

"Your grandma," Jake said, his voice tentative. "She's the one who raised you?"

Surprised by the personal question—I didn't know much about Jake, but a prier he was not—I looked at him, head tilted to the side and eyes wide. "She is...Grams." I forced myself to smile, automatically raising my right hand to touch my fingertips to Grams's Claddagh medallion through my shirt.

Seconds passed with nothing but the sounds of horse hooves on pavement and cart and wagon wheels rolling along behind us.

Surprising me again, Jake said, "Zoe used to talk about her. Said she was like a mother to her."

Running my fingers through the streak of white hair at the base of Wings's mane, I nodded, recalling the countless days Zoe had passed at my house under Grams's attentive, motherly watch. During middle school, when the tension at home between her dad and Jason had escalated to an unbearable level, Zoe had spent more nights at Grams's house with me than at her own.

Lifting my right hand, I brushed my fingertips over the part of my cast that covered the tattoo on the inside of my left wrist; it was the Celtic knot that symbolized the unbreakable bond between sisters. Zoe had the same tattoo on her hip, though she neither knew what it meant nor remembered the day we'd suffered through their creation together.

Staring ahead at nothing, I cleared my throat. "I miss her."

"She raised you," Jake said evenly, and I had the impression that it was his way of saying that he understood…that he could relate. Of course, he didn't know I hadn't meant Grams; I'd meant Zoe.

I blinked a little too rapidly. "Yeah, uh…my mom died when I was born, and I guess my dad didn't want to stick around"—he hadn't even written his name on my birth certificate, and he'd been gone by the time Grams arrived—"so Grams moved to the States to raise me." I laughed softly, a ward against the decades-old sense of rejection. "I used to daydream about what my life would've been like if she'd taken me back to Ireland and raised me there."

"You were lucky."

Brow furrowed, I sent Jake a sideways glance.

He smiled, just a little, and shook his head. "Not about your mom and dad; you were lucky to have your grandma."

My eyebrows lowered, and I frowned, sensing that I'd just stumbled upon a kindred spirit in the least likely of places. "What about you?" I asked, not really expecting much of a response. Jake wasn't known for his verbose insights into his past…or for being verbose *at all*.

Grip tightening on his reins, Jake stared ahead. "My dad left when I was six, but not before he nearly beat my mom to the point of miscarrying."

I glanced over my shoulder, seeking out Becca. I found her on the cart, sharing the bench seat with Camille. "Becca?"

In my peripheral vision, I saw Jake nod.

I returned to facing forward. "Did he ever come back?"

Jake looked at me askance. "Nah." He shot a quick glance behind us at Becca. "He didn't want us in the first place, and he sure as hell wasn't going to come back to take care of us once she was gone."

I didn't think he meant that his mom had left him and his sister, too. "How'd she die?"

"Overdose," he said, the single word a blade. After a quiet, tense moment, he added. "Becca found her."

"Jesus…how old was she?"

"Four."

I brought my hand up to my mouth, covering my horrified expression.

"Sometimes I wonder if it wouldn't be for the best if she never remembers her life before," he said quietly.

"That's not your decision." My voice was sharper than I'd intended, making the words sound like a reprimand. When Jake turned widened eyes on me, I rushed to say, "Sorry—didn't mean to snap at you."

He said nothing, just stared at me, his expression wary. There was something wild about him, like a mustang who'd been broken but still remembered the days when he could run free through endless rolling hills and prairies. Cracking his shell was going to be a challenge. I smiled on the inside; I'd always liked challenges.

Finally, after neither of us spoke for some time, Jake broke the silence. “What if Zoe doesn’t want to remember?” There was a challenge in his eyes.

I stared at him, refusing to look away. “*If* we find a way to fix—I mean, to return her memories, it’s her choice,” I lied.

Jake raised his eyebrows the barest amount.

Snapping my mouth shut, I sighed. “Yeah, okay, you’re right. There’s no way in hell I’d let her choose *not* to remember. One way or another, I’m getting my Zo back.” I gave him a sidelong glance. “How’d you know?”

Again, he chuckled. I never would’ve pegged him as a chuckler, but if the shoe fit… “You’re the only person who loves her as much as I do.”

For a long time, I simply watched him, assessing. I hadn’t known things were quite so serious between them before the Clara-induced mind-wipe.

His horse, a few steps ahead of Wings, veered a little bit closer to us. Wings swung her head to the right, extending her neck.

“Don’t,” I warned before she could nip at his shoulder.

With a snort, she shook her head. *“Spoilsport”* was the general gist of her response.

I caught Jake splitting his attention between me and my horse, a quizzical expression on his face. “Wings considers herself my second-in-command of the herd, and she gets a kick out of keeping her”—I raised my right hand and made air quotes—“‘charges’ in line.”

Jake looked like he was trying not to laugh. “So she was trying to show Brutus who’s boss?”

I nodded. “Pretty much, yep.” Squinting, I looked over the sorrel from nose to flank. Only a tiny white star on his forehead and white socks on his hind legs broke the unrelenting red-brown of his coat. “So…Brutus, huh? Are you, um, expecting him to stab you in the back?”

Jake smiled and shook his head. Rubbing the back of his neck, he said, “Don’t laugh.” He was quiet for a moment, and I was about to badger him for more of an explanation when he said, "Our neighbor, Joe, he took us in for a bit after our mom..." Jake raised one shoulder in a halfhearted shrug. "I used to watch college football with him. Ohio State was his favorite team, which didn't ever make sense to me because he was from Indiana...but the mascot's name was Brutus." He met my eyes briefly, a self-deprecating half-smile on his face. "It was the first thing that came to mind."

"It's sweet," I reassured him. "What was he, anyway—Brutus the mascot?"

"A Buckeye—it's a nut."

I snorted. "You are such a geek," I said without thinking. Worrying I'd gone too far, I peeked over at Jake. He was smiling.

Carlos pulled his hands away from *almost* touching Mase's head and shook them out. It always amused me when he did that, because every time his fingers touched, they emitted a faint crackling sound, and when he did it in the dark, little blue sparks accompanied the crackle. I smiled.

Mase stood from his perch atop a knee-high rock and stretched his thickly corded arms over his head. It was late in the evening, and Mase, Camille, and I were sitting by the stream near our camp —a freshwater supply like that wasn't one we could pass up —"washing dishes." Which was code for helping Carlos hone his electrotherapy skills in semiprivacy. He was still reticent, bashful even, to show this new facet of his Ability to the others, but I didn't think we could make much more progress without a certain member of our group's help.

Camille took Mase's place and closed her eyes, a small smile curving her lips. Both she and Mase seemed to *enjoy* the sensations caused by Carlos's version of electrotherapy, which was utter lunacy to me. Not that I said so out loud. Often, anyway.

Mase moved several yards upstream to crouch beside me and grab a plate from the stack of dirty dishes I'd been working through for the past fifteen minutes. "He's getting really strong," Mase said quietly, his eyes flicking toward Camille and Carlos. "And his control—" He shook his head. "The way he can focus it so precisely…contain it…"

I met Mase's murky gaze. "You think he's ready?"

Mase nodded. "I know he is, but I think the only way for *him* to know that, too, is to bring Gabe in on what we're doing."

Narrowing my eyes, I nodded slowly. "You can be incredibly insightful sometimes, you know that?"

With a shrug, Mase once again glanced at Carlos and Camille. "He has more in common with her than I do…now." His voice was that of someone letting go.

I touched Mase's thick forearm. "They may be around the same age and be able to relate to each other's troubling pasts, but she loves *you*, Mase."

Mase was quiet for a moment. When his eyes met mine, they were glassy. "She's different now."

I shook my head and laughed softly. "But she *still* loves you."

"How do you know?"

I rolled my eyes and bumped his arm with my shoulder. "Because I see the way she looks at you, doofus."

He frowned, apparently not buying *my* skills of observation and insight.

Sighing, I said, "Fine, don't believe me. But you should talk to her about this. If you don't, you'll never know…"

Mase opened his mouth, but he was interrupted by Ray, who'd been circling overhead as my lookout. "Kak-kak-kak." She swooped just over our heads. "Kak-kak-kak."

I watched her land on a rock directly across the creek from us, ruffling and settling her black- and gray-speckled white feathers effortlessly. "Someone's coming." I translated *stalk-of-wheat two-legs* and, laughing, said, "It's Gabe."

"I need a few…more seconds," Carlos said between clenched teeth. His hands were covering around Camille's head like a flesh and bone skullcap.

I pivoted on the dusty rocks so I was facing Jack. My dog's ears perked up, but he remained on his belly. *"Please go after Gabe and distract him."*

Jack sprang to his feet and trotted away.

Mase watched the German shepherd go. "I can't imagine being able to communicate with other creatures like that."

A smile spread across my face, and I shook my head. "I can't imagine facing the prospect of going through life *without* being able to talk to them—or fly or run with them—but it's more than that. It's like I'm a *part* of them."

It was Mase's turn to shake his head. "Like I said—I can't imagine."

"Okay, I'm done," Carlos said, straightening and, once again, shaking out his hands and making that faint crackling sound.

Camille stood and stretched much more languorously than Mase had done before picking her way across the uneven rocks toward us.

"Thank you, Sweet Boy. Now, please bring Gabe to me," I told Jack.

The crunch of rocks and dirt under boots alerted us to Gabe's approach. Jack slinked ahead of him, loping the last few yards to reach us first. With a sigh, the German shepherd lay back down, rolling on his side in universal dog-speak for "rub my belly."

"Good job, Sweet Boy," I told him, scratching a spot that prompted him to kick out his leg in pleasure. I patted the side of his tummy before standing to greet Gabe. "Hey…do you have a minute?" I asked him, fiddling with my fingers. I still felt awkward every time I spoke to him, courtesy of all that had happened between us at the Colony.

Gabe leaned his shoulder against a scraggly tree, eyeing Carlos, Mase, and Camille with curiosity and a hint of caution. His pale blue eyes flicked to me, and he nodded.

I smiled shakily. "Right, so…" I glanced at Carlos, then back at Gabe. "I—*we* wanted to talk to you about Carlos's Ability. It seems to be, um, *evolving* a bit, and—"

"Evolving how?" Gabe asked.

"Well…" Carlos picked up a twig and rolled it around between his fingers. "At first I could just turn stuff on and off, like radios and lights and stuff." He paused, staring at the twig with intense focus. "But now…" There was a crackling sound, closely followed by sparks and threads dancing around the twig like blue lightning. Smoke drifted up from the twig, carrying the scent of burning wood, and Carlos dropped it on the dirt. "Now I can do *that*, too."

Slowly, Gabe stepped closer to Carlos. He sank to a crouch a few feet from the teenager and reached for the twig. The second his fingertips made contact, he sucked in a sharp breath and pulled back. "Impressive…but why are you showing *me*?"

"Because he can do the same thing to a person, at the same intensity or much lower," Mase said.

I crossed my arms over my chest and raised my eyebrows. "Remind you of anything?"

Standing, Gabe looked from Mase to Carlos to me, his eyes lighting up with interest. "It most certainly does." He stepped closer to Carlos and held out his hand, palm up. "Show me."

Carlos glanced at me. When I nodded, he extended his hand, holding it about an inch above Gabe's. "Don't move," he told the older man. "And *don't* touch me." When Gabe's head tilted to the side, Carlos said, "The twig."

"Ah…so direct contact is more intense while you're using your Ability?"

"And for a little while afterward," I added.

Carlos pressed his lips into a thin line, and a few seconds later, Gabe's breath hitched.

I watched, seeing no visible sign of Carlos's Ability, but I could almost feel the hum of electricity flowing over Gabe's skin.

"Don't extend it any further up my arm," Gabe said, his voice slightly hoarse. "I don't want to risk you actually knocking my Ability out for who knows how long."

Carlos shrugged and stepped backward, shaking out his hand for the third time that evening.

Gabe did the same and met my eyes, excitement shining in his. "What a pleasant surprise."

Giving Gabe a tight smile, I nodded. "He thought of it and figured it might help give us an advantage down the road, especially if we come across any other people like Herodson. He's been practicing pretty much every day with Camille and Mase." I tapped my index finger against my lips. "The only problem is that he's a *little* bit deadly if he accidently touches anyone at the wrong time."

"We'd have to figure out a way around that…otherwise it'd be too dangerous to be practical." Gabe's gaze grew distant. "But I do think it could be useful, and for more than just your standard Ability-increasing electrotherapy."

I frowned. "Like what—use Carlos as a weapon?"

"Not exactly what I was thinking, but it's a definite possibility." Gabe paused, taking a ponderous deep breath. "Electrotherapy is similar to part of the process that creates Re-gens." He glanced at Camille and Mase. "We know that you two experienced an excessive amount of self-administered electrotherapy, and that by doing so, you regained some access to the memory centers in your brains, diminishing the retrograde amnesia we'd previously believed was an unavoidable side effect to the Re-gen creation process."

I glanced at Carlos. "So…what? You think this could help Mase and Becca remember more of their lives *before*?"

Gabe grinned, his eyes gleaming with such fierce intelligence that he was almost frightening. "That, and it might help us with Camille's little speaking problem…as well as a few other things."

He looked at Carlos. "Let's take a walk, shall we? I have a few questions…"

That night, I lay beside Jason in the tent we'd been sharing for months and stared up at the green nylon roof, unable to think of anything but my desperate need to slip into another creature's mind. I focused on the ever-present connection that stretched between myself and Ray, who was soaring through the night sky a mile or two to the west. With a sigh, I slipped into her mind.

I was Ray.

It was moon-time, and I was soaring among the stars. The cool night wind sliced between my feathers, reminding me how good it felt to be alive, to fly. I beat my wings once, twice, three times, climbing higher. And then I dove, ecstatic as she-who-flies-with-me made happy sounds.

CRACK.

Pain in my right wing. Too much pain. A flash of white.

The ground was growing too close. I beat my wings, needing to slow my descent, but my right wing refused to move. I tried again. Again. Again. Again.

Too late. As the ground rushed toward me, I pushed she-who-flies-with-me away.

I slammed back into my body with a scream.

Scrambling out of my sleeping bag, I only remotely felt Jason's arms wrap around me, one around my middle and one around my shoulders. I fought against him, needing to escape, to get outside, to get to Ray.

"Red! Dani! You have to calm down!" Jason said, his voice harsh and demanding.

Like his words had flipped a switch inside me, I went limp, sagging back against him. "Ray…they shot Ray," I sobbed. "Ray…"

"What—*who* shot Ray?" When I didn't respond, only sobbed harder, Jason shook me. "Dani! *Who* shot her? Are we in danger?"

I took gasping breaths, trying to quiet the convulsive sobs wracking my body. "I—I don't know. I don't know…Ray…"

"Yeah?" Jason said, raising his voice. "No, we're okay. Get everyone up and gathered—no fire. Something's happened." He relaxed the arm he'd wrapped around my shoulders and gently stroked my sweat-dampened hair, brushing back pieces that were stuck to my face. "What happened?" he asked, his voice dropping to barely a whisper.

"Ray…we were flying, and there was…" I swallowed several times. "A crack. And pain." I squeezed my eyes shut at the remembered agony. "Her wing…someone shot her wing, and we were falling, and then I was back here…"

Pressing his cheek against the top of my head, Jason exhaled heavily. "Why weren't you sleeping?"

"Why wasn't I—" I wriggled out of his hold and turned on my knees to face him. "It doesn't *matter*!" I said, shaking my head vehemently. "She's out there. I can still feel her. She's hurt badly, but she's still alive. We have to go find her. We have to *help* her!"

Jason didn't say anything for a long moment. He blinked. Watched me. Blinked. Stared. Measured. Blinked. "Alright. The others are gathering. Let's go talk to them."

I was yanking down the tent door's zipper before he finished speaking. Barefoot and dressed in sweatpants and a way-too-big t-shirt I'd borrowed from Jason, I jogged to the center of camp where everyone was gathering, half-awake, half-dressed, and half-armed.

"Ray's been shot!" I said as I reached them. "We have to go find her!"

"Shot?" Sanchez looked at me so intently that I felt certain we would be able to get to Ray in time. Sanchez was a woman who could get things done. "How far away?"

I pointed to the west and a little south. "A couple miles that way."

Sanchez looked past me, and I could hear Jason's footsteps as he jogged up behind me. "We've got potential hostiles to the southwest—armed," she said to Jason. She glanced at the eastern horizon; it was just starting to lighten. "It'll be another two hours at least until full light. We can either sit tight until we know more or move out now."

My heart sank like lead in water. "We have to go after Ray," I repeated.

"Wait, which one is Ray?" Sarah asked.

"She's the white falcon," Zoe said as she skirted around the group to reach me. She slipped an arm around my shoulders and squeezed gently. "How badly was she hurt, Dani?"

"I don't know." I focused on my mental connection with the falcon, opening myself up to more input. I shook my head as I listened to Ray's terrified babbling. "She's in a lot of pain. Her wing's useless…she can't fly, and her body hurts. She wants me to stay with her. She's scared."

I looked around at my companions, my friends, seeing pity on their faces, but not a single ounce of determination. *Nobody* intended to help Ray. I shoved away from Zoe with my good arm, a wild sort of energy pulsating through me. "We *can't* just leave her out there."

"Red…"

"It's a bird," Sanchez said. "I'm sorry, Dani, but we're not risking our lives to rescue a damn bird."

I rounded on her. "A damn bird?" I shouted. "A *damn bird*?" My chest heaved with each breath, indignation a living thing inside me. "That *damn bird* has done everything I've ever asked her to do for us. She left her territory…scouted for us day and night… warned us of other people…helped us find safe places and food… almost killed herself looking for water…" My fingers curved into claws; I wished they really *were* claws. "That *damn bird* is part of the reason we're all still alive!"

Sanchez raised her hands defensively.

"Dani, calm down," Jason said, stepping between Sanchez and me, blocking my view of the other woman. He placed his hands on my shoulders and repeated my name, drawing my eyes up to his face. "Let's think about this. Maybe there's another way. Could you use some of the other animals? Are there any you can send to retrieve her?"

"I—I—" I shook my head, searching his eyes. "Maybe, okay…maybe."

I was in the process of scanning the area around where Ray had fallen when the falcon's fear and panic quadrupled. Slipping into her mind, I immediately understood why.

I was Ray.

A two-legs stared down at me, his face inches from mine. I couldn't move, and I didn't know what to do. I didn't want to be alone, and I wasn't, now that she-who-flies-with-me had returned. She was with me. I wasn't alone. At least I wasn't alone.

The two-legs showed me his teeth, then opened his mouth and made two-legs sounds. "I see you, she-drifter."

He reached for me, and I tried to get away from him, but my body wasn't working right.

"Hush now. Sleep."

His hand stroked the feathers on my neck as his other hand covered my head. There was darkness. I felt—

"*No!*" I screamed, falling to my knees. "No…"

13

ZOE

APRIL 27, 1AE

Great Basin Desert, Nevada

"*No!*" Dani screamed, falling to her knees. "No…"

My eyes flooded with tears as I tried to swallow the anguish pouring out of her, one tormenting wave after another. It was almost more than I could bear. Attempting to comfort Dani, to help her quell the emotions burning a hole inside her, I knelt down and wrapped my arms around her shoulders.

"I'm so sorry, Dani." She was completely despondent, but she let me hold her this time, and I rocked her in my arms as she sobbed. "Shhh…" I murmured. I couldn't help the tears escaping down my cheeks as her grief consumed me. "Shhh…" I knew better than to tell her it would be okay—she was inconsolable, and even I would be forever changed by what she felt.

As I rocked her, I brushed stray curls out of her tear-dampened face every so often, trying to keep my own wild emotions in check. The rest of the group whispered around us. Some people left to give us our privacy, while others, like Jason, stood nearby, unwilling to leave Dani in such a distraught state, but also determined to give us space. His eyes were filled with untamed emotions, but his face remained blank.

Only hazily could I feel the sharp concern and unease breaking through the forbidding walls he'd so meticulously constructed around himself. Dani, it seemed, was the one person who could breach them.

I closed my eyes and held her tighter against me. "Shhh…" I whispered, and when my eyes opened, they briefly met Sam's. He still lingered in the fading shadows of dawn, awestruck by the scene that had unfolded. He appeared more frightened than I'd ever seen him before. Quietly, Tavis nudged Sam's shoulder, and with a nod toward their tent, the two of them retreated.

Though her body continued to tremble in my arms, Dani's sobs eventually lessened. Leaning away, I glanced down at her red, swollen face. She didn't seem to notice the distance I put between us any more than she registered the chilled air sending goose bumps over her bare arms; she simply stared past Jason with dull, glazed-over eyes.

She was numb. It was as if the life inside her had been emptied, like the way my life before had been stolen from me, leaving behind an unfillable void. There was nothing I could say to take away her pain. There was nothing I could do but hold her, reminding her that she wasn't alone.

Rubbing my hands over Dani's exposed skin to help keep her warm, I glanced at Chris and found her watching us intently. I nodded at her, silently requesting her help.

Quickly she approached us, clearly eager to do whatever she could. "I'll get something to keep her warm."

"Dani," I said, but she didn't seem to hear me. Her thoughts were far away. I could see vivid images of her flying through the star-filled sky with Ray—the wind against her feathered face, the air crisp and smelling of damp earth. Together, Dani and the falcon felt free…wild…alive.

"I'm so tired. Stay with me?" Cam, Dani's late boyfriend, rasped and pulled the blankets tighter over himself. They were lying in bed, sick and exhausted.

In a blink, the scene shifted, and Dani was sitting on top of him, hitting his torso with her hands and pleading with him to stay alive, to come back to her.

And then, the little girl appeared, her eyes crazed and a snarl on her face before her body crumpled into a heap on the ground, fresh blood soaking through the front of her nightgown.

"It's not your fault," I whispered to her, my eyes flicking to Jason of their own accord. "None of it is." I wondered if my brother—the love of Dani's life—had any idea how deep her scars ran, or if he knew the weight of regret she carried.

Chris came up behind us and handed me a sweatshirt, socks, and a pair of shoes for Dani. "We need to get on the road soon," she said quietly. Her words served as both a warning and an explanation for what she was about to do.

Gradually, Dani seemed to thaw, blinking and peering around at the commotion in our camp instead of out into nothingness. Her emotions went from nearly uncontainable to a steady stream of muted turmoil, and I knew we had Chris to thank for that.

While everyone bustled around camp, packing and readying the horses, I helped Dani change into her warmer clothes. After pulling her hair back into an unruly ponytail, I squeezed her shoulder. "I'll be right back. I need to get dressed."

Dani's only response was a slight dip of her head, and with a final squeeze, I left her with Chris.

"Is she alright?" Becca asked as I unzipped our tent and stepped inside.

I shrugged and hurriedly dressed, tearing through my duffel in search of a pair of jeans and a clean, long-sleeved shirt. "She'll be okay eventually, but right now, I just don't want her to be alone."

Becca offered me a sympathetic smile. "I'll pack your stuff for you and ask Mase to help me load it. You should return to Dani."

Beyond grateful, I closed my eyes and took a deep breath. "Thanks, Becca. That would be awesome." I searched through my bag, vaguely aware of the fact that I was making a bigger mess for Becca to clean up, but desperate to find a hair tie.

"Here," she said, handing me the one from around her wrist.

"Thanks," I said and gathered my hair away from my face.

I unzipped the tent and stepped back outside. I found Dani and Jason having a stilted conversation by their tent, and I had to force myself to stop a few yards behind them so not to intrude.

"—should ride in the cart with Zoe," Jason said.

I watched as Dani's dulled, green eyes widened infinitesimally. "No," she said quietly. "I'm fine."

"Please, Dani," he breathed. His back was to me, but I could hear the plea in his voice.

"No, Jason," she said simply and ducked into their tent.

Rubbing the back of his neck, Jason turned around, glanced at me warily, then headed over to the horses, where Ben, Grayson, and Carlos were readying them.

I wasn't comfortable with Dani riding Wings either, but I knew better than to argue with her about it. There had been a controlled sort of desperation in her even tone that I could feel bubbling beneath the surface. She wasn't going to budge, regardless of anything anyone said.

I stepped inside her tent and helped her pack. We were mostly silent, saying no more to one another than was needed, but I hoped my presence offered her some sort of comfort all the same. As we finished folding, stuffing, and zipping, Chris came back to help Dani load her and Jason's things into the covered wagon.

"Thank you, Zo," Dani said, barely meeting my eyes.

I gave her a quick hug, and her self-loathing and despair felt more acute with the physical contact. I struggled to keep the emotion out of my voice. "Let me know if you need anything," I said quietly.

Dani nodded and stared blankly ahead as Chris led her toward the wagon.

Unable to hold it in any longer, I strode away from the group and toward the stream to cry in privacy. I couldn't help the emotions blaring in my mind, making me feel raw and unsettled.

The tears came willingly, the remnants of Dani's emotional maelstrom nearly choking me as I sobbed and gasped for air. Her emotions were too much, and too many. Bracing myself against a tree beside the creek, I tried to steady myself, worried my legs might give out if I didn't. How could she do it? Was this what life was like for everyone, a convoluted mess of unwanted memories and sorrow and pain that clung to them, following them around for the rest of their lives? How could Dani—how could *anyone*—hold it all in, live with so much wretchedness every day?

"Zoe?" I faintly registered Tavis's voice amid my violent sobs. I didn't bother trying to hide my distress. I knew it was pointless.

"Zoe, what's wrong?" His bucket thudded to the ground, water sloshing over the rim, and he wrapped his arms around me.

"I can't feel like this anymore," I gasped, not knowing what else to say.

Mumbling reassurances, Tavis held me tightly against him. I lay my head on his shoulder, his arms a protective shelter around me, and I focused on the methodical drum of his heartbeat and the soothing motion of his hand rubbing circles on my back. It felt good to be in strong arms, to be held.

"I can't do this anymore," I bawled. "I…"

"Shhh…" Tavis whispered. "It's okay…you'll be okay."

The crunch of debris underfoot alerted me to the approach of someone behind me, but I didn't bother trying to collect myself. I didn't care who saw me a blubbering mess.

"Tav?" Sam called out, and his footsteps ceased shortly after. "Zoe?"

"Is she alright?" Jake asked. Hearing the soft rumble of his voice, I slowly peeled my eyes open. I wished it were him holding me, but I didn't move; my cowardice wouldn't allow it.

"Do you want me to get Dani?" Sam asked, and I nearly cried harder at his thoughtfulness.

"No, thank you, Sam. I'll be fine," I managed. "I just need a minute."

"I don't mean to rush you," Jake said. "But they're waiting." A moment later, I heard two sets of retreating footsteps.

Pulling away from Tavis, I wiped away the hair and tears that clung to my face. "I'm okay."

"Are you sure?" Tavis asked. Until now, I'd been so lost in my emotional downpour that I hadn't picked up on Tavis's concern… and his *other* burgeoning feelings.

"Yeah, I'm fine," I said, sobering and stepping further away from him. I didn't want him to get the wrong impression. "Thank you, Tavis." Using my sleeve, I wiped the moisture from my cheeks again before taking a few much-needed deep breaths. "We should go," I said and abruptly started back toward camp.

As I tried to rally my morale, I scanned the caravan for Jake, but I didn't see him. When I spotted Sam, who I was scheduled to drive the cart with today, sitting on horseback, I grew confused. The expression on my face must have indicated as much because Sam shrugged before shifting his attention to what I assumed was Tavis finally walking up behind me.

"I guess I'm driving alone today," I said with more animation than I felt before climbing up into the cart. As I took a few more steadying breaths and tried to ignore the curious, watchful faces around me, I stared out at our now-abandoned camp. It amazed me that only an hour ago, the space had been our temporary home—the area cluttered with a rainbow of tents, people buzzing around and chatting comfortably. A nomadic lifestyle was all I'd ever known, making it feel normal to me, but everyone else seemed to have acclimated to it just as well as I had.

The cart creaked and shook as someone climbed up onto the bench seat beside me. "Hey," Gabe said.

He'd been keeping his distance from me, like most people had been, so I was surprised to see him sitting only a few inches away. But my surprise was quickly overshadowed by the barrage of memories that flooded my mind. I saw Jake and Becca in some of them, and my interest piqued.

"Ah…I know that look," he said, a line appearing between his eyebrows. "There are some matters I'd like to discuss with you, and I'd appreciate it if I could do so without you rifling through my memories." He gave me a pointed look. "They're private."

My eyes widened. "It's not intentional," I said a little defensively. Although I understood why everyone felt uncomfortable around me, that didn't make it less frustrating. "But, of course, I'll try."

Gabe dipped his head in gratitude. "That's all I ask…and that if you *accidentally* see something, you'll keep it to yourself." His eyes bored into me, a silent demand.

I gave him a quick nod to reassure him and lifted the reins, commanding the cart horses, Clyde and [illegible], into motion. With a jerk, the cart creaked and began to roll forward. "I guess that makes us riding buddies for the day," I said, thinking it was going to be an interesting ride.

"Indeed." He was quiet for a moment. "There have been some new developments"—he shot me a sideways glance—"that could prove very relevant to your current situation."

Intrigued, I looked away from the stretch of highway in front of our caravan and up at his knowing blue eyes. "Developments?"

He nodded. "Of course, the last thing I want is to get your hopes up only to fail miserably, but…" He drew the word out, increasing my curiosity. "We don't really have a choice. You're an integral part of the hypothesis I'll be testing…and more or less the reason I'll *be* testing it." He leaned in a little closer and whispered, "So let's hope I don't fail."

I couldn't help but smile as I resituated myself on the padded bench so my knees were angled toward him, anxiously awaiting his explanation. "Fail…just what every test subject wants to hear." The cart creaked and swayed beneath us. "So, are you going to tell me what it is we're testing, or am I just supposed to comply and hope for the best?"

"Oh, right—I may have found a way for you to regain access to your memory."

My heart skipped several beats, and I opened my mouth to unleash a barrage of questions.

Gabe held up a hand, cutting me off before I could ask any of them. "But we won't know anything until we get a chance to try a few things out. It's far from a sure thing."

It's far from a sure thing. I understood that, but I couldn't help the hope his words summoned. At first, we'd all *hoped* that my memory would eventually come back, but after weeks of waiting, I'd begun to assume that who I was now was who I would *always* be. Suddenly, the day—my future—seemed a little bit brighter.

"How…what do we need to do?"

"I won't bore you with all the neurology babble," he said with a kind smile. "Basically, we're going to immerse your mind in an electric field and slowly increase the intensity while Chris keeps an eye on how the, uh, treatment is stimulating the memory centers in your brain."

"An electric field? Is it going to hurt?" I wasn't sure I cared so much, as long as I could be me again. Once more, hope swelled inside me. *Everything would be so much easier…*

Gabe's smile returned, but this time, it had a distinctly apologetic edge. "At the lowest intensity it'll feel odd—sort of tingly and fuzzy—but as we increase the intensity, it could become quite painful."

Given that there was no electricity to make such a process

possible, I knew it was ridiculous, but I couldn't help the image my mind conjured—me, hooked up to a horrifying contraption with electrodes stuck all over my body. I cringed. "And *how* exactly are you going to create this electric field?"

"You're aware that Carlos has some control over electricity?" When I nodded, Gabe continued. "He's recently developed the ability to create and manipulate an electric charge with enough precision that he can actually surround anything—a stick, a house, a person, *your brain*—with an electric field." The side of his mouth tensed. "We just have to work on his control a bit, make sure he doesn't accidentally fry any of us…"

I took a steadying breath. "I see." I sat there a moment, wading through the dozens of questions I wanted answers to. "I know you're smart and this sort of thing is your specialty, but I have to ask—what makes you think it will even work?"

Gabe glanced over his shoulder, and I followed his line of sight to Camille, who was riding in the wagon with Sarah. "There's a marked correlation between Camille regaining memories of her former life and her extensive exposure to electric fields, so it's not too great of a leap to hypothesize that the same result would occur in a non-Re-gen mind. I've spoken to Wes—"

"Wait, you talked to Dr. Wesley—my mom?" It took me a moment to remember that Gabe could visit people in their dreams.

Gabe shut his mouth and stared at me for a few seconds. "I forget sometimes…that you're her daughter." He raised one shoulder. "How it's possible for me to forget is beyond me, considering the resemblance, but…somehow I do."

"So, *she* thinks it will work, too?"

"She agrees that if Chris monitors the neurological response and guides Carlos to direct the point charge…" He shook his head. "The point is—Wes agrees that with Chris and Carlos working together, we *might* have a shot." He shrugged. "And we'll at least be able to tell fairly quickly whether or not this 'treatment' will even work on you. *And*, even if it doesn't restore your memories, at least it should increase your Ability enough that you'll have better control over it."

It was clear Gabe's "might" served as another warning that failure could be a likely outcome, but I was stuck on the fact that it also *might* work. Optimism and elation trumped my apprehension that Gabe's theory wouldn't work.

"Have you already talked to Chris and Carlos? Are they willing to try?"

"Yep," he said.

My mind reeled with gratitude, hope, and fear. I glanced at Gabe, who was leaning forward with his elbows on his knees as he stared out ahead.

"Thank you," I said. "When the transfusion didn't work, I sorta lost hope…" I cleared my throat, trying to rid my voice of unwanted emotion. "You have no idea what this means to me. I—I know it may not work, but the fact that you're going to try, that you care even a little, means a lot to me."

Gabe nodded.

"And…" I was torn to say the next words. "I don't think we should tell anyone, not until we know if it's really even possible."

Gabe glanced at me again, eyebrows raised.

"I wouldn't want anyone to get their hopes up and then have it not work…" I pictured the look of disappointment on Dani's and Jason's faces, then on Jake's. *I* would be disappointed enough; I didn't want to have to feel their disappointment as well.

With a curt nod, Gabe turned his attention back to the road.

For a few minutes we sat there, the sound of distant chatter, clomping horse hooves against the asphalt, and the creaking wagon and cart filling our silence. We were both lost in thought, which was a bad thing; with his mind wandering while he was sitting so close to me, it was difficult to prevent myself from seeing too much. It was going to be a long ride, and if I was going to honor his request to stay out of his head, I needed to keep myself busy.

I cleared my throat. "Can I ask you something?"

"Hmmm…?"

"What's she like?"

"Who?" Gabe asked absently.

I swallowed, uncertain he would want to talk about her. "My…my mom."

Gabe looked at me, his eyebrows raised. His mouth curved in a thoughtful frown, and he straightened, extending his arms over his head and arching his back in a stretch. After a deep breath, he settled back in the bench seat. "Wes is…" He scanned the way ahead. "To say she's complicated would be an understatement. I worked fairly closely with her for a few years, but sometimes I still think I barely know her." He shook his head. "I've never met somebody with as many secrets as her. How she manages to juggle them all without falling flat on her face is beyond me."

"I'm assuming Jason and I were one of her secrets…"

"Ah…no. At least, not one of the secrets she kept from me." He laughed wryly. "When I first figured out the Virus's origins—*her*, essentially—I was *not* happy." With a meaningful look, he said, "We had words. But, when I found out the reason she'd done it, the reason she'd worked so diligently to help Herodson with his 'Great Transformation'…" For a long moment, he simply stared out at the road in front of us and shook his head. "I couldn't really blame her. I can't say I'd have done the same thing in her place, but I also can't say I wouldn't have."

I wondered what my reaction to the truth about her and the Virus would've been a month ago. "It's difficult to wrap my mind around it," I thought aloud. "She did all of this…for us." *And Jason still doesn't know.*

Gabe nodded. "Which tells you quite a bit about her right there. She's protective of those she loves, and arguably loyal to a fault." He smiled, the corners of his eyes crinkling the barest amount. "She's the most intelligent person I've ever met, and more than a little uptight—the woman can't take a joke to save her life." He rolled his eyes. "But considering everything Herodson's put her through, it's impressive that she can even manage a smile now and again."

I remembered her kindness the night she found me with Clara, and it upset me to think what the General might've done to her, especially as I recalled how he'd tortured Becca, Mase, Camille, Dani… "Is he unkind to her?" I asked tentatively.

Gabe eyed me, his expression guarded. "If you consider forcing her to play house for two decades, forcing her to pretend to love him, unkind, then yeah"—he laughed bitterly—"he's unkind to her." Gabe's coiling hatred settled in the pit of my stomach, and after a moment, he added, "Maybe it wouldn't seem so bad if his mind control actually worked on her and she was blissfully unaware…" He sighed. "But she's not."

I still had questions, tons of them, but I wasn't sure I was ready for the answers, so I kept them to myself. We rode in affable silence for a while, my thoughts lingering on the possibility that soon I might have all my memories back.

14

JAKE

APRIL 28, 1AE

Humboldt-Toiyabe National Forest, Nevada

Unwilling to mill around by the campfire, watching Tavis and Zoe act like lifelong friends or more, Jake decided to walk the perimeter of their camp in the hopes of clearing his head. With Cooper tagging along, Jake made his way down to a small, stagnant pond in a gulch that dipped below their camp. The further away he drew from the sound of everyone meandering around camp with routine and purpose, the clearer the truth became. Jake knew he'd been grasping at straws, trying to hold onto something —to *someone*—that hadn't been his for weeks.

The headway he'd been making with Zoe simply wasn't enough. She'd needed a shoulder to cry on after Dani's breakdown, and she'd gone to Tavis. But if he was being honest with himself, things with Zoe had been strained since the moment they'd found her in her altered state. It seemed like every time they were alone together, she would pull away from him, just like she'd done on the ledge overlooking the canyon…just like she'd done the night of the rainstorm.

Whether she pulled away from Jake because she was scared,

torn between him and Tavis, or simply not interested, Jake had no idea. Regardless, it was time for him to stop living in his dream world of what-ifs and maybes.

He crouched by the pond's edge and stared out at its glassy surface. Zoe had woken up in a world she didn't understand. There was uneasiness in her eyes when she was around Dani, her supposed best friend, and hesitation when she was around Jake. Everything about her was different.

Grabbing a few rocks from the edge of the pond, Jake rose and chucked one off into the water as far as he could. Zoe had admitted herself that being around Tavis was easier. It was a difficult truth to swallow, but Jake knew, deep down, that whatever had been between him and Zoe before, Tavis and Zoe were more compatible now.

Jake heaved another rock. His stomach churned with an aching longing as he realized that she was no longer his and accepted that she might never be again.

How exactly he'd fallen so absolutely in love with his Zoe, he didn't know. From the first moment he'd seen her, something had stirred inside him—a purpose…a curiosity…a desire. And as he'd come to know her better, her stubbornness had challenged him and her determination had inspired him. But she was different now.

With the burning sting of acceptance, Jake knew he had to let her go. He tossed the last rock further than the rest, and anger hardened inside him. Turning on his heel, he headed back toward camp.

His jaw ached and his teeth clenched as he considered how often he would have to watch her with Tavis. His heart tightened at the mere thought of her never sleeping in his arms again. It would be easier to leave, to run away like the coward he'd been so many times in his life. But he couldn't do that, he couldn't very well leave, not with his sister carving out a place for herself in the group.

Running his hands over his head, Jake let out a despondent groan.

After too many resentful thoughts, he reached camp. As he approached the campfire, Cooper left Jake's side and pranced over to the Re-gens, who were sitting in a tight circle around Ben. He was gesturing wildly, no doubt dramatizing some story about him and Ky in their youth.

With a few hours to kill before his watch started, Jake left Cooper to be fussed over by Camille and Becca and headed past the group toward his tent. The little voice inside his head wondered where Zoe was, causing his hands to clench into fists. He needed to stop seeking her out.

Rubbing the tension from the back of his neck, he glanced up and froze.

Zoe was pacing back and forth in front of his tent. Her hair was braided, trailing down her back, the ends just brushing the waist of her jeans. One arm was wrapped around her middle, the other raised so that her hand clasped the back of her neck.

She continued to pace, giving him no indication that she'd even realized he'd approached. She looked just like she always had, statuesque and thoughtful with each long stride, but inside she was fractured—pieces of her old self clinging to the new, unwilling to let go. He saw glimpses of her old self every now and again, and that made it all the more difficult to accept that everything had changed, that he'd lost her.

When she finally looked up to see him standing there, she stopped mid-step. "Something's changed, hasn't it?" she asked.

Jake remained silent, her urgency catching him off guard and the tremble in her voice thawing his anger and frustration.

She took a step toward him, her eyes searching his. "You've been keeping your distance, and I can't tell why."

What could he tell her? Their long, heavy silence only echoed the distance that had been growing between them.

Jake took a deep breath. "I have to let you go" was all he could say, but the words tasted ashen on his tongue. He hated how confused he felt around her. "This isn't right. You're different now—"

"Yes," she said and took another step forward. Finally her brilliant teal eyes met his, and she stared back at him with an injured gaze. "I'm fully aware that I'm different."

"You can't be something you're not." He hoped speaking the words would make it easier to accept the truth, but when her eyes gleamed and her features hardened, he felt deplorable for saying them at all. "We're not the same as we were before. I have to accept that—"

"Do you still care about me?" she blurted. "The way I am now…do you still want to be with me, at all?"

Jake's heart began to race, and he was about to open his mouth when she continued.

"Because after what happened with Dani…" She shook her head. "I've felt more pain and regret and loneliness today than I *ever* want to feel again." Tucking a loose hair behind her ear, she took another, more fortifying step toward him. "I've lost more in the last few weeks than I may ever be able to fully comprehend, but I don't want to have any regrets in this new life." She said each word pointedly, that strong will and resolve he admired so much flaring to life. "You don't get to make choices for me," she said.

Questions thrashed around in Jake's mind.

In his long, pregnant silence, she added more tentatively, "But, if it's too difficult for you to be with me, if it's not what *you* want, then that's your choice…and I understand."

"No you don't," he muttered, shaking his head.

Her eyes narrowed. "Excuse me?"

"You don't understand." His tone was harsher than he'd meant, but he needed to speak the truth. "You have no idea how difficult this is."

She straightened, her head shaking and her glare boring into him. "Difficult…for *you*? Every time I think we're taking a step closer together you think of *her*. I'm not her, I'm—"

"I think about *you*."

"No, it's different." Zoe's hands fisted at her side and she took two more obstinate steps closer. "You know it is. I can't *be* her, Jake. I can't live up to that. I can't be someone I'm not."

"Which is why I should let you go," he said. The words hung, suspended in the quiet that followed. After a few steadying breaths, he continued, "This is torture, Zoe. I love you so much, and it's killing me that I can't have you." He slumped his shoulders and cursed. "I can't do this anymore."

"Does what I want matter at all?"

Jake let out a bitter laugh. "I know what you want."

"Obviously not."

He was growing impatient. "Tell me then, what is it that you want, exactly, because I'm confused. Tavis is always around—"

"So you're 'letting me go' because of Tavis?" She looked shell-shocked. "It's not what you think," she said, pointing vehemently toward the campfire. "It's easier to be with him, but—"

"Exactly." Jake's voice was a low growl, and he was on the verge of walking away so he didn't say something else, something he would regret. "That's why this isn't going to work."

Zoe recoiled.

Jake's heart was pounding violently, and his hands began to shake. He didn't want this, he didn't want her to hate him, but it was too much to keep locked inside anymore.

"Despite what you may think," she started, "I didn't go to him this morning—it just happened that way." Her voice cracked. "I wanted him to be you." She closed the distance between them, her eyes shimmering and her heaving chest mirroring his. "If you don't want to be with me, I understand," she said. "But I don't want to waste any more time sidestepping everything because I'm scared that I won't live up to her memory. I don't want to feel the kind of regret that's simmering inside you…that's consuming Dani. I don't want to be the reason I'm not happy."

Jake was awed by this tenacious, uninhibited side of Zoe. She was stunning.

Swallowing, she said, "Do you still love me, even though I'm different?" Her eyes searched his, and she bit the inside of her cheek.

Jake's hand reached out and cupped the side of her face. Yes, she was different, but she was still Zoe. "Of course I do," he whispered, emotion making it difficult to speak.

She covered his hand with hers, the electricity of her touch rippling through him. "Good, because no matter what you may think, right now, being with you is the only thing I want." She closed her eyes.

As Jake digested her words, his chest tightened almost unbearably with immense joy. Standing so close together, with only inches separating them, he felt more intimacy with her than he could ever remember feeling before.

It's still Zoe, he told himself, knowing he might never get the *old* her back; they were still connected in some intrinsic way. He could feel the heat radiating from their bodies and gravity pulling them together, making it impossible to let her go. He moved closer to her until their chests were touching.

When she opened her eyes, a tear escaped from between her lashes.

"What is it?" Jake asked, and he wiped the rogue tear from her cheek with the pad of his thumb.

Blinking, Zoe closed her eyes again, another teardrop sliding down her face. "I know this sounds so stupid," she said and let out a small, self-deprecating laugh as Jake brushed away the second tear. "But I've never felt something like this before." When she gazed back up at him through her dark, fanning lashes, her radiant eyes seared into his soul.

Zoe placed her open palm on his chest, staring at it intently. Her fingers tensed against his thermal shirt, then relaxed again. "It feels right." Slowly, she leaned toward him, her eyes searching his before her lids flitted shut, and she pressed her lips to his.

Automatically, Jake's arms wrapped around her waist, and he stifled a groan. The tension in his neck and shoulders dissolved, and his wild, corrosive thoughts tamed. She was his, and like always, they would figure everything out.

Zoe brushed a featherlight kiss against his lower lip and then the corner of his mouth, like she was exploring him. He reveled in the moment, letting her tender touch force back every derisive thought and assumption he'd allowed himself to harbor. He'd missed feeling the soft pressure of her lips. He'd missed the close proximity of her body. He'd missed *her*.

Returning her kiss, Jake gently pressed his lips to hers. He took his time reacquainting himself with the way they felt, with the way her fingertips swirled small circles on the back of his neck, and with the way she slowly rose onto her tiptoes, bringing her up even with his height so she could kiss him deeper and hold him tighter.

Jake's arms tightened around her as his heartbeat droned steadily. He couldn't think. He didn't *want* to think; he just wanted to feel her, to be in the moment and never second-guess their relationship ever again.

But all too soon, she pulled away.

Opening his eyes, Jake saw a spark of hope enliven hers again, replacing the hurt reflected in them only moments ago.

"So," she said huskily, eliciting a strumming desire through his body. "We try then?"

With more relief than Jake knew how to handle, he lowered his forehead to hers, tightened his hold around her, and closed his eyes as he whispered, "We try."

15

DANI

APRIL 28, 1AE

Humboldt-Toiyabe National Forest, Nevada

I ran a curry brush along the curve of Wings's back, over and over again. The rest of the horses were already rubbed down and turned out in the field of wild grasses that spanned the acres between the highway and the sprawling forestland to the south. It was the first time we'd been somewhere so green in weeks, let alone near a creek that held enough water to actually clean ourselves. I didn't know where the others were, but I assumed the creek had captured their attention.

Not that I really cared, other than being glad they weren't nearby. It was a relief to finally be alone with Wings and Jack. I planned to stay with them until the sky darkened and I was too tired to keep my eyes open, and then I would slip into their minds and spend the long hours of the night with them as well. I basked in the comfort only they could provide, because only *they* understood what I was going through. The others—my *human* companions—they tried to comfort me, but all of their pitying eyes and concerned expressions only made me feel worse.

And then there was Chris. She'd volunteered for "Dani duty"

this morning so she could ride in the front of our caravan and meddle with my brain chemistry. Usually, I appreciated the brand of soothing that was unique to her, but this time I didn't. I'd let her take the pain away after Cam died, mostly because for days, weeks even, neither of us realized what she was doing. I hadn't been able to mourn Cam, not fully and not while the feelings were still raw, and I was determined *not* to let the same thing happen with Ray. I didn't think I would be able to continue on with another burden of half-closure looming overhead like a thundercloud, always on the verge of bursting and showering me in misery.

"I'll talk to her tomorrow," I told Wings and Jack, knowing they would understand my meaning. I'd looped them in on my inner monologue, not wanting to keep any unnecessary barriers between us. Because one day, I would lose them, too.

I stayed with them while the sun slipped behind the tree-lined hills, while the sky turned orange, then red, and then darkened, and while the stars winked into existence overhead. I stayed with them until Jason showed up and pulled me toward our tent, where he tucked me in before heading back out for first watch. But even then, while I lay alone in the tent, I stayed with them.

My eyelids snapped open as a strange blip appeared on my telepathic radar.

"What the hell?" I murmured, closing my eyes to make focusing easier. I was used to random animal minds flitting here and there, coming closer and moving away on the ground, *under*ground, and in the air, but I could always recognize what sort of creature I was sensing. But this mind…it was completely unrecognizable.

It wasn't overly close, maybe a mile to the south, but it was heading in our direction.

I opened my eyes again, sat up, and crawled out of my sleeping bag. Jason wasn't tucked in his sleeping bag beside mine, which meant it was still first watch, still before two in the morning. I slipped my feet into my boots and unzipped the tent door. As I exited, I telepathically called Jack to me.

He trotted through the darkness, Cooper right beside him.

"Quiet, boys," I told them both as they drew closer. *"We don't want to wake everyone."*

The German shepherd and husky sniffed my legs and wagged their tails while I took a moment to scratch each behind an ear.

"Where's Jason?" I asked them.

Jack grunted and yawned, his version of a whisper, before turning and trotting toward the wagon and cart, which were parked just outside our circle of tents.

I rarely had watch, considering I was *on watch* via the animal minds pretty much all day and, to some degree, all night anyway; that alone nearly exhausted me, so I'd never had the chance to sit with Jason in the wee hours of the morning, guarding our slumbering companions. I didn't know his patterns, his favorite lookout spots, his strategies for staying awake.

Splitting my consciousness between my own mind and Jack's, I could make out a person's silhouette on the wagon's bench seat a short ways ahead. I allowed my consciousness to become whole again as I neared the wagon, and the shadow that was Jason became visible to my own, less sensitive eyes.

"Jason," I whispered. "It's me. Don't shoot me."

"I saw you get out of the tent," he said, his voice low, dry. "*And* heard you stomp over here. I know it's you."

"I didn't stomp."

Jake, who I hadn't noticed sitting beside Jason, leaned forward. They looked like two heads coming out of the same body. "You didn't tiptoe, either."

I glared at them both, not that they could tell.

Chuckling, Jason hopped down from the wagon. "What's up?"

"I felt something…" I focused on the strange mind again. It was closer, maybe a half-mile away now, and still headed toward us. "But it doesn't feel like any animal mind I've ever sensed…and it's coming our way."

My eyes had adjusted to the darkness enough that I could just make out Jason's frown. "Any guesses?"

I answered with my own frown and a shake of my head.

And then I felt another of them—no, two more. They, too, were heading toward us, a short way behind the first one but closing in quickly.

"There's more." I squinted, concentrating. "Two of *something* chasing another of their own kind." Again, the corners of my mouth turned down, and I shook my head. "I don't know what they are. They feel sort of familiar, like—"

A horse screamed, and I instinctively slipped part of myself into Wings's mind. She was standing in the grassy field with a handful of horses from our herd, all sniffing the air and tossing their heads.

"What is it?" I asked her.

"Danger," she said. *"Two-legs. They hunt other two-legs."* She focused her eyes on a shadowy shape rushing across the field, then on the cluster of similar shapes several dozen yards behind it. "*They hurt herd-mate."* She lowered her head and sniffed the writhing body of one of the pack horses, who appeared unable to stand.

Eyes wide, I reached for Jason, my fingers digging into his forearm. "It's people." I didn't waste time wondering *how* I was able to sense some of them. All that mattered was relaying the message. "They're coming here…chasing another person, and there's more of them than I can sense—maybe six? Or seven? They hurt one of the horses."

Jason's eyes searched mine. "Where?"

I pointed to the portion of the field Wings had shown me.

Jake jumped down from the wagon and whistled three times, paused, then repeated the sound. It was our holy-shit-we're-under-attack signal. We'd sounded it before, but it had always been a false alarm. *This* wasn't.

"Get under the wagon," Jason ordered, pushing me in that direction. I could hear the others moving around in their tents and the sound of zippers in the suddenly restless night.

"I'm not hiding!"

Jason dragged me toward the chuck wagon despite my protests. "You can do more from under there than you can do out here, so get under the fucking wagon." It took me an especially dull moment to understand what he meant—the animals. He meant I could call in outside help, raise an army of teeth, claws, and talons.

Staring into his eyes, I nodded and whispered, "Don't hurt the one in the lead. It's their prey."

"I'll do what I can." Jason kissed me, hard, then more or less shoved me under the wagon.

I didn't resist. I was already searching the forest to the south and the desert to the north. If this had happened during daytime, my resources would have been limited, but not at night. Night was when the most dangerous creatures came out to play. Of course, it didn't matter how dangerous they were if they weren't close enough…

A female mountain lion was hunting in the desert, about a half mile north of our camp, and a pack of coyotes were hunting a few miles to the east. The coyotes were too far away to bank on, but the mountain lion's location was a lucky break. And just beyond Wings's field, several bobcats were watching the pack of not-quite-humans stalk after their prey. A human who, like the other two I could sense, could communicate with the bobcats. Like me.

A second was all I could spare to be utterly dumbfounded, to wonder if that was why I could sense these three humans' minds—because they could mind-meld with animals like I could. I was getting the impression that my Ability was the only similarity I shared with this roving pack of wild humans.

The mountain lion hissed when I told her what—or rather *who*—was attacking my camp. She was already sprinting toward me, her leaping strides consuming the distance with astonishing speed. I just hoped she made it in time.

Flat on my stomach under the wagon, I took a deep breath. Reinforcements were on the way. I rolled onto my side and reached for my gun. Which wasn't there. I no longer had to wear the sling for my broken forearm, but the cast made it almost impossible to don my shoulder holster by myself. My only weapon was the combat knife in my boot sheath, which I never went without—*not ever.*

I reached down to my calf and drew the half-foot blade just as I felt the first like-me mind—the prey—reach the outer circle of our tents. I squeezed my eyes shut and hoped that Jason had found a way to alert the others that *that one* wasn't the enemy.

Footsteps, short and quick, rushed toward my hiding spot. My eyes snapped open and my muscles tensed, ready to strike. Except I couldn't sense the mind of whoever was approaching, which meant it was more likely a friend than a foe.

"Dani," Zoe whispered. "I've got Sarah. Can you help me get her under there before—"

There was a gunshot, closely followed by a screech from Sarah.

Another gunshot.

I could feel the prey in the center of our circle of tents, stationary but unharmed, as far as I could tell.

Sarah wiggled under the wagon so quickly that I didn't have time to even think about trying to help her; all I had time to do was move out of the way. Zoe followed, and within seconds, the three of us lay side by side, Sarah on her back, cozy to the point of being claustrophobic.

"What's going on?" Sarah asked, her voice thready and too

high. "Jason sent us here…" Though I couldn't actually see much of her face, shielded as it was from the dim moonlight by the wagon overhead, her terror was palpable.

"He said we're under attack," Zoe added.

"Shhh!" I hissed. Because at that very moment, the other two human minds I *could* sense neared the edge of our camp.

There were a handful of them; I'd gleaned as much from the horses as the strange humans had passed through their pasture. And tapping into Jack's and Cooper's keen senses, I could tell that these intruders were hanging back several dozen yards, staying low and hiding in the tall grasses and behind stray boulders and trees around the outskirts of camp. If they continued to move like that, slow and incredibly quiet—like wolves—they'd be almost impossible to find in the moonless night.

Another pair of footsteps crunched closer, coming from the circle of tents. More of our people, I assumed, but I still gripped my combat knife tightly, preparing to strike.

I watched the darkness as they neared. Knees landed on the ground by the front left wheel just before Ky's face, a mask of silvery light and shadows, appeared less than a foot from mine. "D—you under there?"

"Shhh…," I repeated. "They're really close."

"We can't get a lock on 'em," he said, lowering his voice to the barest whisper. "Ben's on the other side of the wagon. We'll keep you safe." Ky paused. "Any chance of some wolves or something…?"

"No, but a mountain lion's on her way."

A low-chorused growl started from right beside Ky. Jack and Cooper had arrived, and feeling their mind signatures so close was immensely comforting. Abruptly, the dogs' growls intensified, and both moved around the back end of the wagon.

"Shit!" Ben shouted just as one of the strange minds rushed straight toward us.

There was a loud thud, and the wagon creaked and groaned overhead. I heard a wet, tearing sound, and then a thump.

Ben was lying on the ground on Zoe's side of the wagon, his limbs floundering and his neck glistening in the faint moonlight. Blood as black as tar gushed out of a gaping hole in his neck.

Sarah sucked in a breath, likely for a scream, but I slapped my hand over her mouth before she could actually propel the shrill sound into the night and alert any of the other attackers as to our location. I should have been paying closer attention to my own reaction.

A low rumble started in my chest. A growl. *I* was growling, and it felt like the most natural thing in the world. It merged with the vicious snarls coming from Jack and Cooper as they circled Ben's attacker, pushing him away from the wagon.

"Ben..." Ky's voice was low and pained. I could just make out his boots as he took slow steps along the length of his brother's body.

Ben was no longer floundering; he wasn't moving at all anymore. I refused to think about what that meant.

"You killed my brother." Ky's voice was rough, harsh. "You fucking piece of—"

There was a gunshot, closely followed by another loud thud, another moment of groaning wood over the three of us, then vicious grunts and snarls. It sounded like Ky was grappling with a bear, though I knew, based on what I could sense telepathically, that it was one of the like-me two-legs. And I couldn't do a damn thing from under the wagon. But I had other resources.

I handed my knife to Zoe and closed my eyes, focusing on Jack. I slipped into his mind completely, becoming a single, unified entity with him in seconds.

I was Jack.

My hackles were raised, my lips retracted. I licked my teeth, eager to feel them sink into flesh, eager to protect my pack.

"Help me, dog," *the enemy two-legs ordered silently as he wrestled with one of my two-legs pack-mates.* "Fight with *me*, dog."

I snarled and snapped my teeth at him. The desire to bite—tear—rend—was so deep. It was a need. To protect. I had to protect my pack.

Beneath my paws, I felt the ground shudder. One of my larger pack-mates. I raised my nose high and inhaled deeply. Wings. She was coming. Good.

Thud-a-thump.

Thud-a-thump. Closer.

Thud-a-thump. Almost here…

I lunged for the grappling two-legs. I sank my teeth into my enemy's arm.

Thud-a-thump. So close…

My enemy swung his other arm, hitting the side of my head.

Darkness.

"Jack! No!" Without thinking, I crawled out from under the wagon and lunged for my dog. My lips retracted, and an inhuman snarl crawled up my throat as I wrapped my good arm around his limp body.

Our attacker paused, halfway to his feet, and cocked his head to the side. *"She-drifter…"* He watched me, but not for long.

The sound of hooves pounding on earth drew his attention, and he snapped his head to the side. My mind was linked with his, and I could hear him ordering the horse to stop.

Wings trampled him without hesitation. He fell, bones crunching under her hooves, and she turned, rearing up and stomping on him a few more times for good measure. She snorted and tossed her head, then met my eyes. *"Protect herd."*

I nodded. *"Protect herd."*

I loved my herd—my pack—humans, horses, dogs, goats, birds, and even the wild animals I spent time with only fleetingly.

But I'd never loved them as much as I did when I saw them spread out in the dark field behind Wings.

There were still several enemy two-legs, skulking in the cloak of darkness...laying wait. I could sense them through the animals and could still feel the mind of one just beyond the opposite side of camp. I'd heard a bevy of gunshots and shouting while I'd been in Jack's mind, but only a few had actually hit home. Our attackers' tactics were too wild, too unpredictable, and it seemed it was far too dark for my people to be very effective with their guns.

As the mountain lion neared, I warned her to leave the horses alone while I let them know the predator was a part of our herd, at least for a short time.

More gunfire. Another shout. An inhuman, human snarl.

I dragged a limp Jack closer to the wagon, where Ky was kneeling next to his brother's body. I swallowed roughly, forcing back a wail. Ben...was gone. But I had to focus. Mourning could come later; we didn't have time for that now.

"Zo!" I whisper-shouted. "Keep Jack safe."

She tried to hand me my knife, but I pushed her hand, knife and all, back under the wagon.

"Protect them," I told Cooper before I stood and faced Wings.

She was prancing nervously, eyeing the graceful, deadly creature slinking closer.

"Thank you for coming to our aid," I said to the mountain lion.

She was huge, far larger than either Cooper or Jack. She sat on her haunches and opened her mouth, emitting a soft, almost purr-like growl. *"Your enemy is my enemy."*

I nodded. *"Come,"* I said, both to her and to Wings. I turned and led them around the back end of the wagon, toward the heart of our camp, picking my way across the uneven ground carefully. "Don't fire," I called ahead as I touched the single enemy mind I could sense. *"Which one of you is pack leader?"*

"I am, she-drifter." He was on the opposite side of the ring of tents.

"Stop attacking."

"Your pack-mates killed three of mine. Only one thing could make us stop."

I assumed he meant killing us all. *"And what's that?"*

"A female, she-drifter. You."

Surprised, I blinked. And then I smiled. If he wanted me, then he could have me. *"Fine. Deal. Gather your pack. I will come to you now."* Of course, I never said I would come alone. "Jason?"

"Yeah?" he said from almost dead center inside our camp.

I continued forward, shifting trajectory slightly and aiming for where I'd heard his voice. "They've agreed to a ceasefire." As I entered the circle of tents, Wings remained outside, but the mountain lion trailed after me. I could sense my other human pack-mates' eyes on me, on *her*. Soon I was standing in front of Jason, my hand resting on his forearm and my eyes scanning his moon-shadowed face.

But he wasn't looking at me; he was staring at the mountain lion flanking me.

"Ben…he's dead," I said softly. Pain and sorrow were overshadowed by the absolute need to protect the rest of my herd—my pack. This had to end.

Jason's eyes shifted to me, grazing over my face before traveling lower, scanning the rest of my body. "Zoe and Sarah?" His voice was barely a whisper.

"They're fine. Everyone else?" I glanced around at the shadowed forms of our other companions, barely visible as they crouched within the circle of tents.

"Jake's wounded." Jason nodded toward the ground, toward a smoking body.

I focused on the man's charred face, and for a moment, I feared that it was Jake's.

"That one took a chunk out of his arm when he dragged him in here, before Carlos got his hands on him," Jason said, and I exhaled in relief. "What's going on?"

"I can speak to their leader—telepathically," I said as quietly as possible. I hesitated. "They're like me," I told him, holding my head high and keeping my gaze steady. "So is he." My eyes flicked to our attackers' prey, huddled in by the flameless fire pit in the center of camp. "They agreed to stand down if I went with them."

"No."

"Jason…this has to end. Ben's already dead. He's *dead*."

"There's no fucking way you're—"

I dug my fingernails into his arm, wishing they were claws. "I agreed to go with them, but I didn't say how long I would *stay* with them."

Jason shook his head. "I'm not letting you—"

Irritation flared, and beside me the mountain lion stood, lashed her tail, and roared. I offered him a small, sad smile. "You can't stop me."

Starlight glinted in his eyes.

"I have a plan, Jason. Trust me. Please."

He didn't respond, so I released his arm and pushed past him, but he grabbed my wrist before I'd taken two steps. "Don't fucking die."

I grinned. "I wouldn't think of it."

Nobody else tried to stop me while I moved through camp. I could hear Jason speaking to the others behind me, too far away and his words too hushed for me to make out what he was saying.

"Be ready," I told Wings.

"Protect herd," she said. *"Protect you. Destroy enemy."*

When I reached the leader of the enemy pack, he and his remaining companions stood, one by one. There were four of them in total, and they were all male and of various ages, as far as I could tell, and the leader appeared to be the youngest, a tall, sturdy man in his prime.

I stopped a few yards away from the leader, my feline guard still at my side me. "Here I am."

"She-drifter," the leader said as he stepped forward. He moved closer, until he was standing less than a foot away from me, and my blood turned into liquid nitrogen, then lit on fire. His face, though shadowed, was one I would never forget. It was the last thing Ray had seen before he'd snapped her neck.

Shock. Recognition. Rage. "You." A sound started, a low rumble that was nowhere near human. The growl was coming from me, from somewhere deep inside my chest, born of a sudden, desperate hunger for vengeance. "You killed her."

The man's eyes shone with awareness of what he'd done. "Had to get your attention. You belong with us. With *me*."

My growl ceased, and a grin spread across my face. Anticipation melded with my hunger for vengeance. With my lust for blood. "Do I? Then take me away from here."

The pack leader returned my grin and held his arm out for me to walk beside him…away from my old pack. "We will worship you." He touched his hand to my lower back, and I fought the urge to twist around and tear his arm out of its socket. It didn't matter that I was far from strong enough to accomplish such a feat, the desire still swelled.

I walked with these strangers, this small pack of apparently wild men, for minutes. When we were halfway to the tree line, when I was certain that we were far enough away from camp that all of my people would be safe, I spoke to Wings. *"Now."*

Thunder filled the air.

The earth quaked under the beating of dozens of sets of hooves.

And as I slipped out of my body, the mountain lion pounced on the pack leader.

I was Wings.

I led the herd, racing through the night toward our enemy. Close.

So close.

There.

I skidded to a halt while the rest of the herd stampeded onward.

I guarded her body from the horses trampling the rest of our enemies, guarded my predator-ally while it tore into the enemy leader.

Rearing up onto my hind legs, I screamed in triumph. The battle was done, and the enemy was no more, nothing but lifeless flesh, bone, and blood under our hooves. We won.

I made it back to camp less than ten minutes after I'd left, feeling numb, both mentally and emotionally. My feline companion had already gone her own way, returning to her regular routine of nocturnal hunting.

The horses, however, moved as a mass behind Wings and me, clingy in their post-fight euphoria. They remained just beyond the ring of tents as I, alone, entered camp.

I felt exhausted, wrung dry of energy and emotion. "It's done," I said hollowly. "They're dead."

Jason strode toward me, closing the distance between us in three steps. His arms wrapped around me so tightly I could barely breathe, but at the moment, I didn't really care. I wanted him to hold me like that, suffocate me with the strength of his relief, for all eternity. Possibly longer.

Seconds later, he set me back on me feet. His mouth covered mine, his lips gentle, but demanding.

"Why couldn't you fucking warn us?" Ky shouted, and the kiss ended abruptly. Jason and I turned our heads in time to see Ky stalking toward Becca. "My brother is *dead.* You see the fucking future. What the fuck is wrong with you? You should have warned us! You should have fucking warned us!"

Jason and I exchanged a wary look.

"Back off, Ky," Harper said, stepping in front of Becca and

blocking her from Ky before the irate man could reach her and do something *really* stupid. "It doesn't work like that."

Jake joined Harper in shielding his sister.

"I didn't know," Becca said, a tremor in her voice. "I swear it…I do." I'd never heard the chronically composed Re-gen sound so distraught. "I'm so sorry about your brother, I—"

Ky threw his hands up in the air. "You know what? Fuck you." He pointed around Harper at Becca, then aimed his finger first at Harper, then at Jake. "Fuck you and you." He swept his arm around in a broad, sweeping gesture. "Fuck you all, very much."

Jason took a step toward him. "Ky—"

But Ky flung his hand up, turned, and stalked out into the night. "I'm taking Ben. I'm done with all this bullshit."

Again, Jason and I exchanged a look, bafflement this time. "He'll be back," I said, my chest clenching.

"Yeah," Jason agreed.

But neither of our voices contained any amount of certainty.

A dog barked, a second joined it, and I felt Jack's mind as he and Cooper trotted into the ring of tents. My eyes closed, and I exhaled in relief. At least Jack was okay.

16

ZOE

APRIL 28, 1AE

Humboldt-Toiyabe National Forest, Nevada

It was the dead of night. Ben was dead, Ky was gone, Becca had practically been assaulted *by* Ky, and a piece of Jake's arm had been torn off; sleep was the last thing on any of our minds. Well, except for Dani. She was exhausted after melding with the minds of the animal battalion that had come to our aid.

Sitting by the fire, I tried to collect myself. My mind had already felt a little fried after sneaking in a quick, headache-inducing electrotherapy session with Gabe and Carlos early today. And after I'd seen Jake's arm—a bloody mess that needed tending—followed by the mental replay of the wild man who'd literally torn a piece out of him with his teeth, it was all I could do not to burst into hysterics.

Other than questioning the guy who'd been fleeing from the pack of wild men, a middle-aged man named Ralph, Jason hadn't said much; his concern for Dani had become all-consuming. *My* concern for her was heightened as well, but for another reason. *What's to stop Dani from becoming like them?* I knew she'd been drifting more and more, and now that I'd seen some of Ralph's memories, I knew Dani wasn't safe…from herself. Even as she lay inside her tent, trying to sleep, I could feel her mind drifting.

Hearing Jake's rumbling voice behind me as he thanked Carlos for frying the man who'd gnawed on his arm, I glanced over my shoulder at him. I could see that Jake's sleeve was dark with blood, and I knew someone needed to look at the wound. Harper had taken a walk with Becca, trying to reassure her that there was nothing she could've done for Ky or Ben, leaving me a sorry stand-in.

Whether it was overexertion or his body actively regenerating itself, I could feel Jake's exhaustion, prompting me to head over to the chuck wagon. I dug around inside one of the cubbies for the medical kit I thought had been crammed in there somewhere. I was considering where else it might be hiding when I finally found it behind a stack of paper plates and napkins.

Ready to put on my nurse cap and attempt to look like I knew what I was doing, I turned back toward the fire, my gaze automatically gravitating to Jake, who was still standing with Carlos by his tent.

I made my way over to them, then stopped a few yards away and waited for their discussion to end. When Carlos noticed me, he nodded in my direction, and Jake turned around. I held the medical kit up and gestured toward the fire that was ever present in the center of our camp. It wasn't usually blazing in the middle of the night, but tonight was obviously an exception.

After Jake dipped his chin in acknowledgement, I headed over to the campfire to find a place for us to sit. I knew he was different than the rest of us, that he could heal faster than everyone else, but that didn't mean he wasn't in pain or that he didn't need to take care of himself.

Plopping down into an empty folding chair, I anxiously waited for him to join me. Mase had built the fire to roaring, and its flames would provide ample light to tend Jake's wound. Losing myself to the sound of crackling fire and the undulating flames, I thought about how many other times he'd been injured, about the memories I'd seen of his burned body…

"This seat for me?"

My gaze slipped away from the mesmerizing pull of the fire and met Jake's. He offered me a lopsided smile, but it wasn't reassuring. I could feel his exhaustion even more acutely with him standing beside me and could see it plainly enough on his face. He needed rest.

"Of course," I said, leaning forward in my seat. "Now, how are we going to do this?" I asked, holding up the kit again as he sat down.

Using his good arm to tug the long-sleeved shirt over his head, Jake grimaced as he gingerly pulled the blood-dried fabric off his arm. "You playing nurse again?"

Suddenly, I realized Jake had removed his shirt. I cleared my throat and busied myself as I opened the medical box. "Nurse? No, I have no idea what I'm doing."

"That's comforting."

I glanced over at him with a smirk, in time to see Jake's smile…and exposed chest. It was the first time I'd ever seen Jake without a shirt on, the first time I learned of the light brown hair dusting his chest and leading down his lower abdomen.

But as much as I wanted to study his body, I zeroed in on the chunk missing from the inside of his forearm—a fleshy, gaping hole layered with folds of blood-crusted, unevenly torn muscle and tissue, some of it more pink than red, a sign of his quick healing. Even the traumatized skin surrounding the wound was colored with faint green and yellow bruises, as if they were already days old.

While *I* felt my heart seize at the sight of the bite wound, Jake seemed unfazed. "You sure you want to do this?" he asked. "I can have one of the others—"

"No," I said quickly. "I don't mind, really." I squeezed his hand before turning my attention back to the medical kit in my lap. "I want to make sure someone tends to it before it heals wrong or gets infected or something."

"It won't heal wrong," he said, "and it won't get infected." I saw an image of him lying in the snow, a bullet in one hand and his other palm against his chest.

I glanced up at his torso, seeing no scar from a bullet wound. "Maybe not, but it still hurts, doesn't it?"

"Like hell."

"Well then, let's do what we can to help your body instead of making it do *all* the work."

I evaluated the contents of the kit, trying to decide where to start. "I suppose cleaning it is the first order of business," I thought aloud. I curled my lip as I examined the flesh once more. "I take it you've not done that yet…"

Jake tried not to smile. "No, I haven't had the chance."

I cleared my throat and swallowed. "Clearly." Removing an alcohol pad from its wrapper, I cleaned the skin around the wound, which was half the size of my palm.

Jake chuckled softly.

"Am I entertaining you?"

"Your determination is very…you."

My eyes met his for a brief a moment. "Thank you, I think." We were quiet for a few breaths, the fire and the chatting around us only white noise. I held up a small bottle of rubbing alcohol. "What do you think?"

Jake frowned. "I don't think you need to go that far."

I smiled, happy to be the one amused this time. I gave an innocent shrug. "I'm just trying to help."

"Helping or hurting?" he asked glumly.

Shaking my head, I relented. "You're no fun." I exchanged the bottle of alcohol for one of saline solution and squirted around in the wound, repeating the action a few more times until I felt it was sufficiently clean. I reached for the alcohol pad to wipe the excess saline solution dripping from his arm. "I'll wrap this up for you and then you can go rest."

Jake shook his head. "I can't. Ralph has some information he wanted to—"

I glared at him. "Can't you let Jason talk to him? Or at least wait until the sun comes up, when you have some of your strength back? No offense, but you look like you're about to fall over. You think you can keep going at this rate with your body trying to heal itself?" As I wrapped the clean gauze around his forearm, both his amusement and exhaustion flowed into me. "Can we at least go lie down for a little bit?"

I struggled with the small role of adhesive tape but finally managed to tear a piece off. When I looked back up at Jake, his expression seemed part perplexed and part entertained.

"What?" I asked, giving him a sidelong glance.

He raised his eyebrows. "We?"

"We what?" Then it hit me. Realizing what I'd said, I busied myself by taping down the bandage and putting the supplies back into the medical kit. "Well, *you* at least. I'm not trying to be obnoxious, but I really don't feel like you're taking this whole regenerating thing seriously. You're not superhuman, you know."

Jake turned his shirt right side out.

"In all seriousness," I added in his silence, "have you considered at all how much your Ability has changed you?"

"What do you mean?" Exhaustion and pain getting the better of him, Jake struggled to lift his wounded arm.

"Here," I said, gently peeling the half-donned shirt back off of him. "We'll get you a zip-up sweatshirt, that'll be easier." Jake sat there patiently while I manhandled him. "If your body regenerates itself, will you stop aging?"

He chuckled weakly.

I smacked his good arm. "I'm serious. You can't die—"

"I'm sure that's not true," he said. "Just like your Ability has limitations, mine has to as well. I'm just not sure what they are, and I don't really want to test any theories." He obviously didn't want to talk about it, and I had to admit that it was too deep of a conversation for us to be having when he could barely keep his eyes open as it was. "Come on," he said. He stood and, taking the kit out of my hand, set it on his chair and intertwined his fingers with mine.

Without a word, I followed him to his tent. I'd never been in it before, and the thought of being in his private space *with him* was thrilling.

He unzipped the door and stepped inside, guiding me in gently behind him. His tent was larger than the one I shared with Becca; ours was snug, barely fitting the two of us and our things. I was fine with it, though; it was what I was used to, and it made me feel safe. Jake's tent, on the other hand, was big enough for four people, which I thought was sort of strange. It was only him, a single, open duffel bag, which his clothes were perfectly rolled and stacked inside, and his sleeping bag. Granted, it was actually two sleeping bags conjoined, but still. It seemed a big tent for one man.

"Shoes off," he said, standing slightly slouched by the entrance, which apparently served as his designated "shoe" area. "That's my *one* rule," he said. "And don't try to get out of it. I'll hold you to it this time."

I was confused. "Wait, what?" As far as I knew, we'd never once talked about a "no shoes in the tent" rule. But then I realized…he was talking about *before*. Surrendering, I toed off my tennis shoes and moved to the side, nearly able to stand up straight at the tent's peak.

Jake zipped the door shut and, favoring his right arm, lay down on the sleeping bags with a groan. I hadn't realized there were two pillows until he wadded one of them up beneath his head.

"One of the pillows is mine," I thought aloud. I felt stupid for not making the connection earlier. The joined sleeping bags, the bigger tent—this wasn't just *his*, it was *ours*.

"Yep," he said, his eyes meeting mine. The campfire outside, only a few yards away, brightened the inside of Jake's tent enough for me to see how intently he was watching me.

"And, let me guess, I don't like the 'no shoes' rule."

A weak smile pulled at his lips. The firelight cast shadows against the tent's blue nylon walls. The flickering light and dark made the brown stubble on Jake's jaw glow then turn sable before it began glowing again.

"No," he finally said. "You don't like my 'no shoes' rule."

I smiled. "I don't think it's so bad now."

He made a derisive noise and patted the area beside him. "You're making me anxious standing over me like that."

"I need to get you a sweatshirt," I said a little warily. I stepped over to his bag and stared at the items rolled and folded inside. "Since this is organized immaculately, I have a feeling you know exactly where your sweatshirts are."

"There should be one tucked in the right corner."

Just as he'd said, I felt the cool zipper against my fingertips and carefully pulled out a black, zip-up, hooded sweatshirt so not to mess up the rest of his clothes.

"Here you go," I said, lowering myself down to him. "You need to sit up, just for a minute. I'll make it fast, I promise."

With a grunt, Jake sat up and held his injured arm out first. After I pulled the sweatshirt on as gently as possible, I helped him with the other sleeve, and then he lay back down. Lifting his good arm, Jake welcomed me to lie against him, and I automatically accepted his offer.

My head fit perfectly in the crux of his arm, and I leaned into him, draping my arm over his middle. My entire body eased, the tension fleeing my muscles as I was consumed by Jake's warmth. He smelled smoky, like campfire, and the faint sound of his heart was steady and reassuring.

"What *do* I like?" I asked.

A small smile pulled at Jake's lips. "Well, you like sleeping with two pillows. At least you say that, but you only ever really use one. So I gave one of yours to Camille and Mase." His voice was velvety.

"Sneaky." I smiled. "What else?"

Jake's hand drew languid circles in the middle of my lower back, and I felt my mind start to drift. "You like to leave your clothes all over the tent, and you never fold anything…not really, anyway. You claim it's pointless."

I thought of the disarray my side of Becca's tent was currently in. "What else?" I whispered.

Jake was quiet a moment, and for a second I thought he might have fallen asleep, but then he spoke. "You hog the bed, and…"

I peered up at him, the intensity of his gaze making my stomach flutter. Admiration and affection stirred within him, lulling as it passed over me like a warm blanket of promise and hope and safety.

He was hesitant, scared even, to love me the way he once did, but for some reason, it didn't upset me. Maybe I finally understood, or maybe it just didn't matter anymore. Either way, he was trying. I could feel his vulnerability: longing—desire—uncertainty—wonder. It was the most amazing thing I'd ever felt, and I had to resist the urge to tell him that Gabe and I were working on a plan for me to get my memory back. I couldn't bear to think about his disappointment if it didn't work.

"You also do this all the time," he said, rubbing his sock-covered feet against mine. "Every single night, you rub your feet against the bottom of the sleeping bag until they finally find mine…and then you fall asleep."

I glanced down at my feet, which were tangled with his, and realized how deeply I could fall in love with Jake. It wasn't his emotions or guilt making me feel obligated this time, and it wasn't a looming pressure to be someone I no longer was. It was a simmering love I'd felt since the first moment I saw him, the sad man standing in the doorway of the abandoned house.

Propping myself up on my elbow, I leaned in without hesitation and kissed him, more fervently than the last time. I wanted Jake to know how I felt, wished I could share with him the feelings he, unbeknownst to him, had shared with me.

"I love you," I whispered against his mouth, not wanting to let another moment pass without him knowing how I felt.

Afraid to open my eyes, to see his reaction illuminated on his face, I kept them closed and pressed my lips to his once more. "I love you," I repeated.

Ignoring his pain, Jake pulled me closer with his injured arm, his kiss tender and his body exuding waves of unmistakable relief.

17

DANI

APRIL 29, 1AE

Humboldt-Toiyabe National Forest, Nevada

I "woke" with a groan. I hadn't been sleeping; I'd been stalking squirrels with some bobcats. And I'd *meant* to be sleeping.

I'd essentially passed out in the wee hours of the morning, intent on remaining asleep and resting my mind and *not* drifting into any animal minds. But I *had* drifted, and because my subconscious had been in charge when I left my body, I'd drifted from creature to creature like a sleepwalker, unwilling, or possibly unable, to return to my body by choice.

Jason trailed his fingertips over the sensitive skin on the side of my neck, giving rise to goose bumps. I could feel the heat of him close against my side despite the two insulated layers of sleeping bags separating our bodies.

"Good dream?" he asked.

Opening my eyes, I stared up at the green nylon canopy of our tent and frowned. "I…I can't remember," I lied, glancing at him. He was lying on his side, his head resting on his curled-up arm. "Why do you ask?"

Jason's piercing blue eyes held a hint of the sparkle that usually accompanied a smile. "You were hard to wake." He rolled onto his back.

I forced a smile and shrugged. I hadn't been having a good dream—or *any* dream—because I hadn't even been asleep. But I didn't want to worry Jason or anyone else with such a minor problem compared to what had just happened the night before. Ben was dead, Ky was who knows where, and one of the mares had a bad gash on her rear that Harper feared would become infected. And I'd led the horses in what could easily be called a slaughter-by-stampede. Suddenly, *child-murderer* and *liar* didn't seem to be the worst things I could be called.

I sighed and rubbed my hands over my face, wiping away the crusty sleep in the corners of my eyes. "I need some fresh air." I crawled out of my sleeping bag and toward the tent door.

"Wait," Jason said when I had the top part of the flap unzipped.

I glanced back at him.

"Aren't you forgetting something?"

"What?"

His eyes trailed down the length of my body, zeroing in on my butt. The attention to my nether parts made me notice the draftiness around my lower half. I'd fallen asleep in only one of Jason's t-shirts and my underwear, and that was still all I had on.

The blush started on my chest and burned its way up my neck. I cleared my throat and shot a cursory glance around the tent before I remembered that we'd had to burn the sweatpants I'd been wearing the previous night because they'd been soaked through with blood…and *bits*. Which sucked so much more because they were my last pair.

"Here," Jason said, reaching for something on his side of the tent. He handed me a pair of black leggings. "Camille gave these to me after you conked out…thought you might need 'em."

"Oh…" I took the soft, stretchy pants. "Thanks."

He lifted one shoulder. "Thank Camille."

"I will." I pulled the leggings on quickly, then fished a pair of clean socks out of my duffel bag and wiggled my feet into my boots, which were much cleaner than they'd been when I'd removed them earlier that morning. "Did you clean these?" I asked, noting that the combat knife had been replaced in the boot sheath.

Jason nodded.

I offered him a grateful smile. "Thank you."

He held my gaze, not returning my smile. "You scared the shit out of me last night."

I licked my lips. "I know." I'd scared the shit out of *myself*, too.

"Your eyes…" He shook his head. "They were different. *You* were different."

I looked down at my hand, watching my fingers toy with the leather at the top of my boot. When I spoke, my voice was quiet. "I know."

And I did know; I'd been less like me, and more like *them*.

"Excuse me, um, Dani?" Ralph, a.k.a. *prey*, said from behind me.

I was perched on a rock at the edge of the creek near camp. The afternoon sun shone high overhead, but its rays couldn't warm the part of me deep inside, chilled with fear over what I was becoming. I glanced over my shoulder as I heard Ralph's footsteps draw nearer.

"Do you mind if I join you? I thought we might have a little chat sometime before you and your people continue on your way."

Widening my eyes, I brushed my palm against my borrowed leggings and bit my lip. I wanted to talk to him and had been planning to hunt him down later. "Now's as good a time as any."

Ralph smiled, bowed his head, and crossed the creek. He sat on a rock a little larger than mine and scratched his graying beard.

I picked up a small handful of pebbles and started tossing them into the water one by one. "So…what'd you do to get on their bad side?"

"Scott and his *pack*?"

I met Ralph's eyes for the briefest moment. "Yeah." I hadn't known the leader's name, Ray's killer's name—hadn't wanted to—and now I felt like even more of a murderer. So much for vengeance being sweet…

"Existed," Ralph said bitterly. "Me and my son, Bobby—he was a drifter, too—we came out here after we realized how much we'd changed. I've had a cabin in the area for years, and living in a place secluded from people but teeming with animal life…" He shrugged. "It just felt right."

I nodded, finding that I could relate a little too well to what he was saying.

"Scott caught wind of us a few weeks back and wanted us to join his 'pack,' but Bobby and me didn't like the way their minds felt, especially not Scott and the other drifter in the pack." He squinted up at the sun. "Like they weren't quite human anymore. We thanked him and passed on his offer and returned to our new, secluded way of life." He lowered his gaze, his warm, brown eyes meeting mine. "We'd already noticed the changes in ourselves when we drifted too much, and we decided it was time to use some restraint before we ended up turning into wild men like Scott and his pack."

I swallowed roughly. This was exactly the kind of thing that I wanted to talk about…that I was terrified to talk about.

Ralph sighed and shook his head. "But it was too late for Bobby. He couldn't stop. Every time he went to sleep, he ended up drifting, and every day, instinct ruled him just a little bit more… until about a week ago."

"What happened?"

"He disappeared, and I found him two days later…at the base of a cliff."

"Was he, um…"

Ralph raised his eyebrows. "Dead?" He nodded slowly.

"Scott?"

He continued to nod. "He didn't mind us so much when we hadn't 'fully embraced the gift,' as Scott liked to say, but once Bobby *had*, Scott claimed that he couldn't allow a competitor in his territory." Ralph sighed. "And then he decided his pack needed some entertainment, so they started hunting me." He flashed me a weak smile. "When I felt your mind, I knew you'd be my only chance…that Scott wouldn't be able to resist the pull of a female drifter."

I scowled, and when I spoke, my voice was flat. "So I was meant to be a diversion."

"I hate to admit it, but yeah." He frowned. "But here you were with an army of humans *and* animals…couldn't have guessed that." His head tilted to the side. "Your connection with the creatures is different—deeper—and they trust you more, seem to genuinely care about your well-being, even accept you as one of their own, where they just tolerate the rest of us drifters playing at being a part of their kingdom. But then, it's not like I've met many of us, and you're the first female drifter I've met, so…" Again, he shrugged. "Makes sense that that sort of thing would matter to the animals."

A harsh laugh escaped from my throat. "Great…so when I turn wild, I can frolic around with all my animal friends and be their lady Mowgli. Awesome."

Ralph studied me for a long, uncomfortable moment. "So it's started for you, too, then, has it?"

I nodded. "Last night—or this morning, I mean—was the first time." Another humorless laugh and shake of my head. "Went to sleep and woke up drifting." I stared across the creek at him, pleading with my eyes. "Do you know how to stop it from happening?"

Frowning, Ralph shook his head. "Once that starts happening, it seems to be inevitable that you'll, well, you know…change."

I blinked, and a few tears escaped over the brim of my eyelids. "I don't want to change; I want to stay *me*." I hugged my middle and squeezed my eyes shut

"I wish I could tell you how to manage it, but it seems that's something each of us has to figure out on our own. The best two pieces of advice I can give you are these: you've got to want to stop drifting with every fiber of your being, or else that part of you that takes over when you sleep is going to keep pushing you out into the critters—and you have to stop, *now*. If that means you try not to sleep for days, then you try not to sleep for days. Maybe the compulsion to drift will lessen the longer you go without doing it. Maybe…"

I took several deep breaths, trying to collect what little remained of my tattered composure. My voice shook when I spoke next. "I see." I was terrified, because I knew that a part of me never wanted to stop drifting, and I had no idea how to convince that tiny, stubborn part of me to give it up.

Sometimes, I really hated myself.

Standing beside Wings, I took a tiny bottle of caffeine pills out of my saddlebag, opened it, and shook a pill out to pop into my mouth. For the fifth time today. I hadn't even tried to sleep the previous night, and even with the aid of the caffeine pills I'd lifted from Harper's medical supplies while everyone was fussing over a returned and repentant Ky, I'd almost succumbed to the pull of sleep three times during the day's ride; the resulting imminent fall could have been devastating.

I dry-swallowed the caffeine pill, then tucked the bottle back into the saddlebag, glancing around to make sure nobody was watching me. At least we were done traveling for the day, so I wouldn't have to risk sliding out of the saddle for another twelve hours. Of course, that also meant I had to get through my second consecutive night of resisting sleep.

Tomorrow night, I told myself. *I'll try to sleep tomorrow night.*

"Red…"

Startled, I jumped and spun around, only to find Jason standing a few feet away, watching me. His eyes were tight with concern.

"Yeah?" I said, skirting eye contact. I wasn't sure if he'd seen me gulp down the pill.

"Take a walk with me?" he said, holding out his hand.

I looked over my shoulder at Wings. "But I have to—"

"Carlos'll take care of her."

"Yeah," Carlos said, walking up and coaxing Wings's attention away from me with the promise of an apple. "She's an easy one."

"But…" I trailed off as I realized that only a few horses remained in the area near the paddock we were using to store the tack for the night while the rest roamed around, unburdened as they grazed. A glance off to my left told me the tents were already up in the corner of a tiny farm's parched hay field, and the fire was well on its way to roaring. "How…?"

"You must've zoned out," Jason said, reaching for my good hand and linking our fingers when I showed no sign of intending to meet him halfway. "You were just standing there, staring at your saddlebag."

I closed my eyes in a prolonged blink, letting Jason lead me away from Wings and Carlos and our camp. He headed for the solitary, one-story farmhouse located on the other side of the almost nonexistent creek. A single row of tall, skinny trees covered in scraggly new growth lined the property as a windbreak. Jason led me around the house on a lawn that was so brown and patchy it blended in almost seamlessly with the barren desert floor surrounding it, only stopping once we reached the opposite side. He stared down at me, looming unintentionally.

Sighing, I rubbed my eyes; they felt grainy from lack of sleep. "What are we doing out here? I still have to check in with all of the horses and set up scouts for—"

"You're off scouting duty," he said quietly, calmly. "We can do it the old-fashioned way for a few days." And still, he stared down at me. I felt like a preserved specimen in a jar.

"What?" I blurted, first widening, then narrowing my eyes. "Why?"

Jason stepped closer, his usually stony face finally showing some emotion. And his emotional displays were a lot like the desert climate we'd grown used to over nearly a month of travel: when it rained—especially when Tavis made it happen—it poured. "You're exhausted." Jason raised a hand and placed the crook of his index finger under my chin, angling my face upward. "Have you slept at all since Ben…since Ray—"

I pulled my hand from his, taking several steps backward, and crossed my arms over my chest. It was a gesture of protection more than a gesture of defiance. I looked away—at the farmhouse behind him, at the dirt and dead grass beneath our boots, at the trees surrounding the yard—anywhere but at him. I couldn't let him see the tears stinging my tired eyes. "Not really," I said softly. *Not at all.*

"You're not eating, not sleeping…you've got to take better care of yourself."

I shrugged, trying to appear nonchalant, but inside I was screaming, *I'm trying! I don't want to lose my humanity! I'm trying to fix me!* I both wanted and refused to tell him about my current predicament…about my apparent addiction to drifting. Having his support would mean everything, but he had enough on his plate without having to deal with my problems, especially when they were problems I practically dove into headfirst.

"You don't understand," I said.

Jason sighed. "But I *do* understand. Losing first the horses, then Ray, and now Ben…it's hard. And then with those drifters, and what you did…you're dealing with a lot."

"A lot?" I scoffed, a harsh, ugly sound. "Jesus, Jason…" I shook my head. "You couldn't *possibly* understand."

"Then why don't you explain it to me," he said, his tone level.

If he thought me sharing my feelings would help me move on, then fine—we could talk about Ray, and drifting, and…*not* about my soul-sucking addiction to it.

I started pacing, the caffeine pill making me jittery. "When I drift, it's like…like…" I threw my arms up in the air. Explaining the connection I shared with the animals—the connection I'd shared with Ray, that I'd *been* sharing with her at her moment of death—seemed impossible.

"When I merge with them," I said, "it's like I'm a *part* of them and they're a part of me…like the essence of who we are—our souls, or whatever—join together, and when I'm just me again, a piece of my soul is still with them, and a piece of theirs is with me."

I paused and looked down at the ground. "Ray was more than a pet, more than a friend…she was part of me, and when she died, I lost that part of me completely. It's just…gone. And killing Scott didn't bring her back…didn't make the hurt go away. So now I have to deal with crushing guilt, too." I raised my eyes to meet Jason's. "So tell me again about how you *get it*, about how you *understand*."

Jason's jaw clenched, and his Adam's apple bobbed as he swallowed. "I care about you more than I've ever cared about *anyone*," he said, his voice low and cold despite the heartfelt words. "And when you were gone, you took a piece of me—*my* soul—with you." He moved closer, his strides consuming the distance separating us. "So yeah, Red, I get it."

I stared at him, slack-jawed and slack-brained. "What?"

"I didn't mean to fall in love with you," he said, as though that explained anything.

"Fall in love…with me?"

He let out a harsh laugh and ran his fingers through his short, dark curls. "It was never something I wanted—with *anyone*." He looked at me, his eyes aflame with too many intense emotions: accusation—desire—anger—fear—love…

He loves me?

"I thought if I just got a taste of you, had my fill…" He shook his head, staring down at me with eyes of luminous blue fire. "I never wanted to fall in love, because I've seen what it does to a person when it's taken away." His eyes widened, like he'd just realized that I was both the monster in the dark and the hero who could chase it away. "And now I've felt it." He squeezed his hand into a fist, then stretched out his fingers. His hand was shaking. "So don't tell me I don't get it." His gaze hardened. "*I* get it."

Turning, he started to walk back toward camp.

My arms slipped lower until they hung at my sides. "Jason…wait."

He stopped, his back to me and his body flush with the corner of the house. He turned his head, showing me his profile…his perfect, strong profile.

"I'm sorry," I whispered.

Everything about him relaxed noticeably.

I took a step toward him. Another. And another. "I'm sorry I'm such a mess, and I'm sorry that you have to deal with it, but I'm not sorry that you fell in love with me. I will *never* be sorry about that." I stopped a foot or two behind him, making no move to touch him. "Please turn around."

He did so, slowly. When he finally faced me, he gazed down at me with familiar, guarded eyes. Somehow, the red in his scar only intensified the blue in his eyes.

I couldn't help but smile. I felt drunk and giddy and muddle-brained, and I couldn't believe any of this was really happening, that he'd really just told me he loved me. It was the best possible thing at the worst possible time.

"I thought I was in love with you when I was younger," I said. I felt my smile grow, and I glanced away, embarrassed. I had to force myself to meet his eyes again. "And then when I got older, when I was with Cam, I convinced myself that I'd only fallen in love with the *idea* of you…that it had only been a crush, and that I'd barely known you, and that my feelings only *seemed* so strong because I was a teenager and *everything* is so extreme then." I laughed softly and shook my head. "I convinced myself that I barely knew the real you."

Jason clenched and unclenched his jaw repeatedly.

"But I was lying to myself. I think I was the only one besides Zo and your dad who you let catch even a glimpse of the real you." I took a shaky breath. "I love you, Jason…*so much*. I've loved you for a *very* long time."

I watched as his guarded mask cracked, fragmented, and fell away, baring the full force of his emotions to me. His eyes were so full of hope and wonder and desperation, his lips of promise, and his entire face was softened by what could only be called adoration…and love. He searched my eyes, back and forth. Back and forth. Back and forth. The intensity of him stole my breath.

Wait…wait…wait…there's something else…something I have to tell him…

Before I knew what was happening, Jason's hands were cradling the back of my skull, his fingers unintentionally tugging pieces of my hair from my braid, and his lips were on mine. His kiss was not patient, not kind. It envied and boasted and was proud…so damn proud. His kiss sought to dishonor me, and I sought *for* it to dishonor me and would have been angered beyond reason had it stopped. A cessation of the kiss would have been unforgivable. This, these lips on mine, this tongue dancing with mine…this was the first real, honest kiss Jason and I had shared.

Except that it's not *an honest kiss,* the very tiny coherent voice in the back of my mind said. *You're still lying to him, about yourself* and *about his past...his mom.*

Jason pressed me back against the house's weathered siding, and I placed my palms on his chest. With a groan, I pushed, but instead of breaking the contact between our lips, Jason kissed me harder, deeper, more urgently. And damn it all to hell if I didn't want him to stop. His hands were *everywhere*, and he felt so good, so strong and real and all mine…

Again, I pushed against his chest. He froze, pulling back just enough for me to gasp, "Wait…stop…just wait."

Tension was a living thing vibrating along every tendon, through every muscle in his body. "Red…" Pain—desire unfulfilled—made the word a desperate groan.

I squeezed my eyes shut, loathing myself for what I was about to do. "Before this goes any further, I have to tell you something." I didn't know why—maybe it was the lack of sleep, or maybe it was a desperate need to save face—but suddenly my knowledge of his mom didn't seem like the biggest secret standing between us.

Jason lowered his head and grazed his lips over the side of my neck. "Later…"

"No, Jason, *now*. It has to be now." Because I wouldn't forgive myself if I started this new phase of our relationship with *that* lie hanging over us, and I doubted that he would forgive me either. As it was, I didn't know if he would feel the same about me after I told him—but I wouldn't trade the chance to have a lifetime of love for a few moments of bliss. I wouldn't.

With a rough, knowing noise, Jason wedged his leg between my knees and slid his hands down to my hips. He moved against me, taunting me. Damn him for knowing exactly how to please my greedy body.

My head fell back against the side of the house, and I moaned.

"What were you saying?" Jason whispered against my neck.

I swallowed, cleared my throat, whimpered. "Your mom… she's alive."

He stilled instantly, a new kind of tension humming through him.

"I met her," I said, breathing hard. "In the Colony."

Ever so slowly, Jason raised his head and met my eyes. "What?" His voice was cold…so very cold.

"It's not what you think," I rushed to say before he could draw false conclusions…or *any* conclusions. Pretty much any conclusion would be a bad one. "She really didn't want you to know about her, and I thought about telling you…so many times—"

"Then why didn't you?" That tone…that tone could freeze the sun.

"Because I didn't want to hurt you."

"And how, exactly, would telling me that *my mom* was alive and *within reach* have hurt me?" His eyes narrowed, spearing me with accusation. "Or was it just that you'd have to admit to lying all this time?"

"What? No!" I pushed against his chest again, and this time he lifted off me enough that I could duck under his arm and slip out from between him and the side of the house. "Do you really think that little of me?"

With a roar, Jason punched his palm against the wood siding. "Then tell me, because right now I don't know what to think. What possible reason could you have for *not* telling me?"

"She created the Virus," I said, my voice barely audible.

Jason turned his head, looking at me with eyes filled with utter revulsion. "Why would you say that?"

My arms itched to wrap around my middle, but I held them rigid at my sides, my hands in shaking fists. "Because it's true."

Jason's eyes slid off me. "You're wrong. It wasn't her. You don't know what the fuck you're talking about."

Indignant, I straightened my back and held my head high. "I'm going to ignore the fact that you're being a huge asshole, because I know this is a shock." I inhaled harshly. "Your mom *was* at the Colony, and she *did* create the Virus."

Jason was shaking his head. "Then she didn't know. It was an accident."

"No, Jason, it wasn't."

"So what are you saying?" He pushed away from the side of the house and started stalking toward me. "What the fuck are you saying—that my mom's evil? That she's some sort of evil genius working with that—that fucking General…to *what*? To take over the world?" He stopped less than a foot from me, all hard muscle and menace and anger towering over me.

I refused to look away, refused to back up. "No," I said, expending every ounce of control I had to keep my voice even. "I'm *saying* that it wasn't an accident, and that she knew exactly what she was doing." I took a deep breath, and before Jason could launch into another tirade, said, "She did it to protect you, because if she hadn't helped Herodson create the Virus, he would have killed you and Zo."

Jason staggered back as though I'd punched him. In seconds, his expression transformed from irate man to lost little boy. "What?"

My chin quivered, and I blinked rapidly, refusing to cry. "After your mom left you guys, General Herodson stationed watchers around you and Zo. You were collateral in case his mind control failed on her, except—" I wanted to look away so badly, to not bear witness to Jason having one of the pillars of his childhood ripped out from beneath him. But I couldn't leave him to face this alone, not when I was the one who'd landed the first blow. "He didn't know—still doesn't—about the other half of her Ability."

"I don't…" Jason shook his head. "I don't understand."

"Your mom's just like you, able to increase, decrease, or block other people's Abilities, but Herodson only knows about the boosting part. She was never under his mind control. The only control he ever had over her was you…you and Zo and your Dad. And then she fell in love with him." I blinked, and a tear snuck out from between my lashes. I swiped it away before it could start its journey down my cheek and took another deep breath. "There's something you should see," I said, walking past him. When I didn't hear footsteps behind me, I paused and looked back at Jason.

He was standing exactly where he'd been for the last few minutes, exactly *as* he'd been.

"It's from your mom—a letter."

His head snapped around, his eyes seeking mine, eagerness and terror making them too bright, too wide.

"Come on," I said, continuing back toward camp. It wasn't immediate, but I finally heard Jason's footsteps behind me and exhaled in relief. If he was following me, it meant he believed me. It meant there was hope that he could accept this…and possibly *not* hate me for all eternity.

We walked in silence, Jason always a few steps behind me. When we reached our tent, I quickly dug through my saddlebags until I found the manila envelope containing the letters and documents from Dr. Wesley. I fished out the smaller envelope with "Jason and Zoe" written on its face in Dr. Wesley's elegant but barely legible handwriting. Inside, it contained a letter from a mother to her children…and the confession of a mass murderer.

"Here," I said, handing the sealed envelope to Jason. "I haven't read it, so I don't know how much she explains."

Jason sat carefully on his sleeping bag. His face was washed out, and his hands were shaking as he flipped the envelope over to look at the unbroken seal. He peered up at me, his eyes unfocused. "Zoe?"

"She hasn't seen it. She doesn't actually know about the letter—not that it would do her much good as she is right now." I shrugged uncomfortably. "But, um, she *does* know about your mom."

"What?" His gaze sharpened. "How?"

"Dr. Wesley—your mom—she's the one who saved Zo from Clara and left her at the house for us to find, as per Becca's instructions." I waved my hand weakly. "It's all very confusing…*everything* with Becca is confusing…"

Staring down at the envelope, Jason said, "All her life, Zoe's been searching for clues about our mom, and now she knows…and she doesn't even care." He chuckled hollowly. "It's all such a fucking mess."

Hysteria bubbled up from my chest in the form of a laugh that turned into a desolate sob. I dropped to my knees before Jason, taking one of his hands in both of mine. "I'm so, *so* sorry, Jason. If I could spare you this…" I shook my head. "You're pissed. You *should* be pissed. I screwed up. I should have told you sooner… when I first found out…I should have—but I didn't want to tell you. I *never* wanted you to know, because some things really are worse than death. I thought…I don't know. I guess I thought I could protect you from that." I laughed bitterly. "I can't do much, but I thought I could do that…"

"I'm not pissed—not at you." Jason chuckled again, the sound devoid of all emotion. "Most of my life, I was miserable because I thought she was dead. Then I found out about the accident—that it was all crap—and I hated her for leaving us…for leaving *me*. And now *this*?" He blinked slowly. "Now I wish she really had died in that car accident." For seconds, he said nothing, simply stared at the envelope. "I can't be mad at you, not when I know I'd have done the same thing if our roles were reversed."

I stared at him, wide-eyed. "You don't hate me?"

He shook his head the barest amount.

My eyebrows rose. "Do you—do you still love me?" My voice increased in pitch as I asked the question.

Jason glanced up at the roof of our tent. "If love were something that could be turned on and off whenever we wanted…" He laughed softly, a sound absolutely devoid of humor. "But it can't."

He lowered his eyes, a spark of something flashing in their desperate, blue depths. "I think my dad was proof of that." Surprising me, hope washed over his face. "Do you think my dad…that he might still be—"

"He's gone, Jason. Grams found him, remember?" I gave his hand a supportive squeeze as I watched the hope fade away. It was such a fickle, fleeting thing, hope.

"Right." He shook his head, dispelling any lingering hope. "No, I know that. I know."

"Well, um…" Clearing my throat, I glanced down at the envelope in his hand. "Are you going to open it?"

With trembling hands, Jason unsealed the envelope and pulled out the tri-folded letter. He unfolded it, and I watched his eyes as he read, skimming quickly from side to side, devouring his mom's words. The letter was three pages long, and it only took him a few minutes to read through it.

"Holy shit," he murmured when he reached the bottom of the third page. "Holy fucking shit."

I tightened my hold on his thigh. "I know…it's a crazy story," I said, shaking my head.

"No." Jason pointed to the second to last paragraph, and I started reading.

<u>This is very important</u> —These Monitors may still be with you. They would have had the gene therapy and already been familiar with their Abilities by the time they were implanted into your lives. They would still have fallen ill when infected by the Virus, but it would have been nothing more than a bad case of the flu to them, as their genetic code would have already been altered. It is possible that they don't even know what they are. Herodson has people like your father who can alter perception as well as memories; they are, after all, the heart of the T-R program. Your Monitors could be sleeper agents, programmed to carry out their mission and eliminate you only when they've

been triggered. If this is the case, those triggers <u>*will*</u> *include any sign that I've been in contact with you.* <u>*Be very careful about who you share this letter with.*</u> *Better yet, share it with no one. Burn it.*

"Holy shit...*eliminate* you," I said, echoing Dr. Wesley's words. If she was right, if her information was trustworthy, then one or more of our companions could really be agents of the General. Only Chris and Ky had been with Jason from the beginning, and only Sarah had been with Zoe. *None of them can be*...that. *And why the hell didn't Dr. Wesley tell* me *about this?*

I met Jason's eyes, the horror I felt mirrored in his. Chris and Ky were his two closest friends. The idea that one of them could be working for the General, planted near Jason for the sole purpose of executing him should the need arise, was obviously killing him.

"We have to talk to Zo and Gabe," I said. "Right now."

Zoe and Gabe were sitting on one side of the rectangular Formica kitchen table inside the farmhouse Jason and I had visited earlier. Someone had died in the bedroom, but the five months that had passed had shifted the odor from putrid to merely pungent, and closing the door made it tolerable. Jason was standing at the end of the table, arms crossed over his broad chest and the letter from Dr. Wesley clutched in fingers, and I was pacing back and forth along the side opposite Zoe and Gabe. The manila envelope with the packet of documents and papers the doctor had left with Zoe, along with her letter to me, was on the table in front of Gabe.

"Why didn't you mention Wes's little care package earlier?" Gabe asked, tapping the manila envelope. "There might be something in here that can help with..." His eyes flicked to and away from Zoe so quickly that I wasn't positive I hadn't imagined it. "Things."

"I know…I should've shown all that stuff to you. But when Camille told me about how Dr. Wesley was *actually* in love with Herodson—"

Gabe's eyebrows shot upward. "What? Wes despises him, I assure you."

I shook my head. "But she doesn't, not really. Before Camille was turned into a Re-gen, she overheard Dr. Wesley telling someone that she couldn't leave the Colony because she wouldn't abandon him…because she *loved* him."

Gabe took a deep, even breath. "And did Camille happen to mention whether Wes stated Gregory Herodson, specifically, as the recipient of her love?"

I blinked several times, searching my memory. "Um…no. She just said 'him.'"

Gabe's answering smile wasn't overly kind. "And you just leapt to the conclusion that she was talking about Herodson." He shook his head. "You must truly despise her."

"Of course I do," I snapped. "She killed *everyone*. God, it's like you're suffering from Stockholm syndrome or something." I pointed to Jason, and then to Zoe. "Even *if* she created the Virus just to save them"—I glanced at my boyfriend and amnesiac best friend—"no offense, she still did it. She still killed billions of people." I skewered Gabe with a raging glare. "That's not something you do that deserves forgiveness or pity. There's no repentance for that."

Gabe blinked slowly. "She's not the enemy, Dani."

"Yes. She is."

"She was talking about her son."

"What?" Jason, Zoe, and I said in unison. Both Zoe and I glanced at Jason, who frowned and shook his head.

"Peter," Gabe said. "His name is Peter, and Herodson is his father."

Crickets filled the room. Or rather, the absence of crickets. I was pretty sure we were all holding our breath.

My cheeks flamed and shame filled me. I'd assumed wrong and put us all in danger, and now I felt like the biggest moron in the world.

Jason cleared his throat. "As disturbing as that is, it's not the most important thing at the moment. Can we get on with this?"

Right...the letter. "Yeah, of course."

Uncrossing his arms, Jason raised the letter and started to read.

Dear Jason and Zoe,

I wish I didn't have to write these words to you. I wish things were different. Some of the things I've done...I wish I hadn't, but I didn't have a choice. Now we all must live with the fallout.

If you're reading this, it means Dani decided you should know the truth. I can't say I agree with her decision, but I also can't say that I haven't yearned for this day since I left both of you and your father. Whatever else you glean from this letter, know this: I love you. I always have, and I always will.

Over two decades ago, Gregory Herodson, who you know as General Herodson through Dani and Gabriel, threatened both of your lives. If I hadn't left you to join him, hadn't created a virus that would spread the gene therapy like wildfire, and hadn't helped Gregory begin his "Great Transformation," then you would have been killed. Please don't fool yourselves; I knew exactly what would happen once the Virus was unleashed on the general population. I knew that those infected would either die or go through a genetic mutation that would leave them forever altered, for better, or—in the case of most people—for worse. I knew all of this, and I created it anyway.

I'm not asking for your forgiveness or even for your understanding. I'm fully aware that I deserve neither. It is reward enough to know that both of you are still alive. Nothing is more important than family. Please don't blame yourselves. This was my decision, and the blame must fall on my shoulders. I accept it, even welcome it.

Now, I have consulted with RV-01, and she has advised me in what I must tell you if you're both to continue to survive. According to her, whether or not you read this letter is essentially a fork in the road—the future will be drastically different if you don't read it than if you do. I just wish she'd told me which is the better path to take. But she didn't. What she did tell me is this—it's imperative that I explain the effects the gene therapy has on our ability to procreate. I don't know why this knowledge is so important, but according to her, it's a matter of life or death.

One of the side effects of the gene therapy is that the gametes (eggs and sperm) of the survivors will be unstable after the initial mutation. The time it takes for them to stabilize is different for everyone—some never stabilize, and some stabilize in around three years, at which point the survivor can reproduce. When genetic stability has been reached and procreation is once again possible, gestation will occur at an accelerated rate. Gregory has had me experimenting with treatments to speed up the stabilization process, though I've yet to be successful. You will find a summary of the data I've collected so far enclosed with this letter—these documents have "Project Eden" on the header. Please give them to Gabriel, as he will understand them best.

Children of two mutated parents are mutated as well, gaining some combination of their parents' Abilities. I inserted a genetic block into you both when you were young to prevent your Abilities from manifesting. They remained latent until activated by a trigger

I built into the Virus. As you are second generation, your Abilities should, in time, prove to be some combination of mine (being able to affect the potency and effectiveness of another's Ability) and your father's (being able to alter another's perception as well as view, and even change their memories and sense their emotions).

From what Dani told me, Zoe, you take after your father, which will be difficult for you. Tom learned—over a very long time, I might add—that the key to controlling his Ability was to not fight it, to not even think about it, but to let it become an extension of his senses, as integral and second nature as his senses of hearing, sight, smell, touch, and taste.

And you, Jason, apparently take after me. We're valuable, which means we must always be cautious. People who desire power will seek out those like us, because no matter how much power they have, they will never be satisfied. They'll always want more, and we can give them that. Case in point: Gregory Herodson.

You must be asking yourselves why I've stayed with Gregory for so long. I let him use me as an instrument of [illegible] way to increase his power for several reasons, but chief among them was to protect you. Gregory placed a Monitor close to each of you, intended to carry out your execution should I step out of line. At the first sign that I wasn't absolutely under his control, he would have sent word, and you would have died. If I'd attempted to contact you or your father, and the Monitors found out, you would have died. I couldn't allow that.

<u>This is very important</u> —These Monitors may still be with you. They would have had the gene therapy and already been familiar with their Abilities by the time they were implanted into your lives. They would still have fallen ill when infected by the Virus, but it

would have been nothing more than a bad case of the flu to them, as their genetic code would have already been altered. It is possible that they don't even know what they are. Herodson has people like your father who can alter perception as well as memories; they are, after all, the heart of the T-R program. Your Monitors could be sleeper agents, programmed to carry out their mission and eliminate you only when they've been triggered. If this is the case, those triggers will include any sign that I've been in contact with you. Be very careful about who you share this letter with. Better yet, share it with no one. Burn it.

I'm so sorry that you have to deal with the fallout from my decisions, but I'm not sorry that you're still alive. The hope that we will meet again one day is one of the few things keeping me going. I love you both, so very much.

Love,
Mom

There was a long moment of silence after Jason finished reading. It was Gabe who finally broke it. "Well, at least we know who one of these 'Monitors' is."

Jason, Zoe, and I all exchanged narrow-eyed glances with one another, not quite sure where Gabe was going with his proclamation.

And then I understood. It was the very reason Becca had advised Dr. Wesley to include the information about procreation. "Oh crap."

"Sarah," Jason said softly, setting the letter on the table. He looked at Zoe "Yours has got to be Sarah."

"But…she's my friend," Zoe said. "She wouldn't hurt me, I know it." Her hands clung to the edge of the table in a white-knuckled grip. "I mean, I *know* it."

I sighed and, shaking my head, pulled out a chair and sat heavily. "But if *Sarah* doesn't even know it..."

"So she's a sleeper agent," Gabe said. "It's the only explanation." He looked at Jason. "What do we do?"

Jason placed his palms on the table. "We get Sarah alone and interrogate her."

"But she's pregnant," I said. "Whatever she's done—or might do—it's not the baby's fault. We can't *hurt* her." I looked to Zoe, hoping for her support.

She was biting the inside of her cheek, her gaze distant with thought. "I can get inside Sarah's head, rummage around to find out the truth and, I don't know"—she shrugged—"try to get rid of it or something?"

"Deprogram her," Jason said with a nod. "Good plan."

"And how precisely will we mentally interrogate and deprogram her without setting her off?" Gabe's voice was calm, composed; it was his problem-solving-research-genius voice, which was awesome. Because we really needed a problem-solving research genius on our side at the moment.

"Sedative?" I suggested. "One that won't hurt the baby?"

"I think Harper's got some in his med kit," Jason said. "But I don't know how safe they'll be."

"There's another option," Gabe said, and all eyes focused on him. "My Ability seems to be expanding, and I might be able to force her into an unconscious state."

Jason straightened. "Define 'might be able to.'"

"Fine." Gabe took a deep breath. "It'll take a lot out of me, but I can *definitely* do it."

"Works for me." Jason looked at me, and I nodded, as did Zoe when he shifted his questioning gaze to her. "Let's do it."

"No matter how you look at it, that leaves Chris and Ky," I said, glancing from Jason to Gabe and back. We were sitting in the living room of the farmhouse, staying out of Zoe's way while she sifted through Sarah's mind in one of the bedrooms. "Either of them could be your Monitor—"

"—or it could've been Dalton," Jason said. Dalton had died back in Bodega Bay, before we ever left for Colorado. He'd been with Jason from the beginning, making him the only other feasible candidate. We'd already eliminated Holly, Hunter, Cece, and all of the others who'd left the base with Jason as candidates to be Monitors because they'd chosen to go their own way, away from Jason. We agreed that a Monitor, sleeper or not, wouldn't just give up on a mission like that. We were certain. Fairly certain.

"So…do we do this all again?" Gabe nodded toward the kitchen.

"It's going to be a lot harder to pull something like this on one of them," Jason said.

I rubbed my eyes, then took a deep breath. "This might be crazy, but what if we don't do anything? If they're set to activate *only* if we mention your mom contacting you guys, then maybe we can just keep going as we are…"

Jason leaned forward, his elbows on his knees, and rubbed the back of his neck. "It'll be like playing hot potato with a live grenade."

"At least it would still have a pin in it," I mumbled.

All three of us looked up as Zoe appeared in the mouth of the hallway. She shook her head before dragging her feet across the carpet and plopping down on the floor beside me. She rested her head on my shoulder and yawned.

"Anything?" Gabe asked.

"Nope." She yawned again. "Nothing but Sarah."

Gabe frowned. "Which means either she's a blip and her DNA

miraculously stabilized quickly enough for her to carry a child to term, or you can't sense the sleeper part of her."

"I think we have to assume the latter," Jason said. "We'd be fucking idiots not to."

Groaning, I rubbed my eyes. "So if we go with that—Zo can't uncover the truth—then we can't rely on her to weed out and unmask any *other* sleeper agents, either."

Gabe leaned back in his recliner, popping up the footrest. "We could trigger them on purpose, flush 'em out…"

Jason shook his head in sync with me. "Too dangerous," he said. "We can't assume they'd immediately go berserk and rush us or anything like that. We have to remember that Chris and Ky are trained fighters with years of experience in combat tactics and strategies. Even if they were triggered, they'd wait…they'd have a plan, and we can't bank on Zoe picking up on it. Especially with Sarah, because we don't even know what her Ability is."

I leaned my cheek against the top of Zoe's head. "So we wait. We keep going as we are, keep our mouths shut, and pretend everything's normal."

Gabe and Zoe nodded.

Jason met my eyes, everything about him weary, and nodded as well. "We wait.

MAY 1 AE

18

ZOE

MAY 1, 1AE

Fallon, Nevada

The sun was just setting, filling the sky with the most vivid, ethereal waves of purple and orange I'd ever seen—an unexpected welcome to the mountain-rimmed patches of forest we would be trekking through for the next week or so. The awe-inspiring sunset was a tranquil ending to a tedious day of cart-driving and thinking, thinking and cart-driving, along Highway 50 through the high desert. We were a little less than a week outside of Tahoe, finally.

Sitting beside the campfire, I watched Jason intently. I watched everyone more intently. For someone who always seemed to arrive to a party early—to know my companions' secrets before everyone else—this time, I felt like I was the late arrival. *Why couldn't I sense the Monitors, sleeper agents or not? Why can't I now?* I could sense everything else, including Jason's dejection as he sat on the other side of the fire, quietly lost and drowning in his own misery. *I* should have been miserable. But I wasn't.

I wondered if I should be grateful for not being able to

remember my past, for not being in the same wretched state as Jason. But I wasn't grateful; rather, the reminder that I was so far detached from what used to be my reality was disconcerting. Instead, all I could feel was gratitude for my mom's timely intervention, that she'd stopped Clara before she could finish whatever else she'd been attempting to do to me. Without her interference, I most definitely wouldn't be sitting around the fire with a beer in my hand, relaxing with my friends. Well, relaxing might not have been the right word, but I was alive and mostly intact, which was more than I could say for Clara.

I took a swig of my beer.

"That bad?" Sarah asked, plopping down into the camp chair beside mine. I tried not to let any hint of last night's clandestine exploration of her brain show on my face. I hated that I'd been digging around her mind, and even more, I hated that, after finding nothing, I still couldn't trust her.

Sarah pointed to the bottle in my hand. "You keep making a"—she twisted her features into a grimace—"face."

I couldn't help but laugh. "Oh, come on. I'm not that bad."

She started shaking her head before I could defend myself. "Zoe, trust me. That's *exactly* what you looked like."

I held the bottle of beer out and studied it. She was right, I didn't enjoy the taste, and I didn't understand why everyone else did. "Even if it was cold, I don't think I'd like it. I'm not sure how the guys drink this."

"It's because we're men," Harper said, sauntering over. He had a cowboy hat on and a piece of straw between his lips, an ensemble he'd readily adopted during our travels through Utah and Nevada. He stopped beside me, waggled his eyebrows, and smiled. "'Evenin', ladies." He dipped his hat, and once again, I started laughing. This time, Sarah joined me.

"Nice hat," Sarah said with a snort. "Where'd you find that old thing?"

"*Old thing?*" Harper's hands thudded against his chest and he displayed mock offense. "This is vintage, ladies. *Vintage.* Do you know what that means?"

"Yes," Sarah said, snorting again before tossing her head back for a belly laugh. "It means it's old, ugly, and was purposely left wherever you found it. Trust me, you should toss that thing into the fire." She rested the paper plate holding her fourth helping of cornbread on the mound of her stomach.

I studied Harper's hat while he poked and prodded at the fire with a thick stick, still mulling the piece of straw between his lips as he listened to Sarah's playful teasing. The hat was tan felt, with a wide rim and a tattered, navy blue band. I kind of liked it. Although I'd probably never *wear* it—it was a little hideous—I was perfectly content with him doing so.

"Where did you get that thing, anyway?" I asked.

"I scavenged it. My grandmother used to tell me I would've been a good cowboy. It must've been my chivalry and good looks." As usual, his eyebrows danced. "Anyway, it was time for a changeup."

"I don't see it…" I said, eyeing his dark, olive-colored skin and sable features. He seemed more islander, more exotic.

Harper shrugged, but he was right, it *was* time for a bit of a changeup. Like everyone else, the long days of riding, of meeting other survivors every now and again, and of having to deal with unexpected injuries, were wearing on him.

"What's on your mind, Zoe?" Sarah asked. When I glanced at her, her eyebrows rose suggestively at me. "Jake again?"

I smiled. "No, not this time."

"How are things going between the two of you? Are they getting any better?" She grunted as she leaned forward and tossed her paper plate into the fire.

I nodded. "Yes, actually."

"Then what is it?" she asked, the playful lilt in her voice replaced with concern.

Sarah's eyes were imploring when I looked at her, and unwillingly, I wondered why she was so curious. Digging around inside her mind for a brief moment, I found no malicious intent, nothing that would indicate her as a Zoe-assassin, so I tried to forget about the pact I'd made with Dani, Jason, and Gabe the night before, about the letter from my mom.

Leaning back in my chair, I opened myself up to my friend. "It's more difficult than I thought."

Sarah's brow furrowed. "Am I supposed to read minds as well as be pregnant with twins? Or are you going to help me out?"

I straightened. "What? Twins? But—when...?"

Sarah smiled. "Harper heard two heartbeats during my morning checkup."

I searched Sarah's face for any indication of how she felt about the news…the *huge* news.

"Don't look at me like that, Zoe," she said and shook her head. "I'm fine with it."

"Are you sure?"

She heaved a sigh before leaning her head back. "I think I sort of expected it. I mean, there's a *lot* of movement in here." She pointed to her belly. "Plus, Harper's been extremely attentive lately. I think he already suspected but wanted to be sure before he broke the news to me."

I saw a memory of her bursting into tears, completely despondent when she'd first received the news that she was pregnant.

"Well, I'm happy for you. At least now they'll have each other…being the first post-apocalyptic baby would be a lot of pressure." I smiled, offering her what little jest I could in hopes it might make her smile in return.

"Thanks, Zoe." She nudged me with her elbow. "So tell me, what's eating at you?"

Mind still reeling from baby news, I shook my astonishment away and leaned back in my chair again. "Not that it's nearly as exciting as having twins, but"—I stared out at the group of friends that surrounded me—"I'm starting to loath my Ability, I guess… trying to fit in, to be accepted. It's all more difficult than I thought it would be."

"Really?" She let out a slow, even breath.

Again, I nodded. My Ability was proving to be my biggest enemy, making it difficult to get closer to people because they still tended to avoid me, and it forced me to know things I didn't want to know and to keep secrets I didn't want to have to keep. It was ruining everything.

"I'm just tired of being in people's minds, that's all. I wish I could control my feelers a bit better." I watched her, waiting for a reaction. "I wish I didn't have to carry so many secrets."

But Sarah sat there, oblivious, picking at the food crusted on the hem of her shirt. "Look at me," she groaned. "I'm such a pregnant mess!" Her voice was nearly a hiss, and again, I fought the urge to laugh at her expense. "I'm sorry things are so hard, Zoe. I know there's probably nothing I can do, but if there is, you'll let me know, won't you?"

Offering her a quick nod and a grateful half-smile, I watched as she struggled to her feet.

"I better go change, I'm exhausted." She gathered my hair up off of my neck, then gave it a gentle, playful tug. "Nighty-night, Zoe. See you in the morning."

"'Night," I said, and I watched her waddle away. Sarah was so uncomplicated, or at least she seemed that way. She spent most of her time thinking about Biggs and babies and sleep and food.

Jason, on the other hand, wasn't. His mind was toxic most of the time, a reservoir of overflowing, dangerous emotions that would eventually suffocate him. Among his outrage and disbelief at what our mom had done was his constant concern for Dani. Over the past month, I'd learned a lot of things about my brother—he kept his emotions hidden, had a foul mouth, and was beyond stubborn most of the time—but stupidity wasn't one of those things. He knew something wasn't right with Dani, and although his guarded expression gave nothing away, I could feel his disquiet regarding her, as messy and convoluted as his emotions were.

Dani was *trying* to get better, I knew that much. What she'd seen the night we were all attacked by wild drifters and her conversation with Ralph had spurred her toward trying to take better care of herself, trying to overcome her drifting problem…*trying*. But she was failing, and that was why I needed to tell Jason. He needed to know what the hell was going on with her, and she needed him if she was going to get any better.

Setting aside my nearly full beer, I walked around the fire toward Jason, Sanchez, and Biggs, hoping Dani wouldn't decide to return from her walk with Mase, Camille, and Carlos until after our conversation ended. I wanted to avoid getting caught in the act of tattling, because no matter how necessary I tried to tell myself it was to get Jason involved, I still felt like I was betraying her.

Jason's body tensed as I approached, his gaze questioning.

"Hey," I said and cleared my throat, readying myself to say what I knew I should but feared Dani might hate me for forever. "Can I talk to you for a minute?"

Jason frowned minutely. "Is this about…?" He gave me a meaningful look. "Did you discover something?"

Glancing from Sanchez to Biggs and back to Jason, I shook my head. "It's sort of personal…" I hoped that would squelch any formulating questions from our audience.

Taking a deep breath, he searched my face. Whatever he found must have convinced him that what I wanted to talk about was important, because he nodded once, slowly, and stood. "Alright. Where to?"

Without another word, I walked away from the fire, away from prying ears and distracting chatter, toward a shack that temporarily housed our things. Jason's footsteps were heavy and methodical behind me, but stopped as I slowed in front of the shack and turned to face him.

"It's about Dani," I said. "I didn't want the others to know… she's going to be upset that I've told you as it is."

Jason's jaw clenched, and I could feel the concern rolling off him in waves.

Biting the inside of my cheek, I considered my words carefully. "I know things have been beyond crazy lately, but I also know you've been worried about her—"

"You saw how she reacted the night of the drifters—of course I've been worried."

With a curt nod, I said, "Right, but it's more than that, Jason."

"She's having a hard time dealing with all the loss…" He shrugged one shoulder, clearly trying to seem less concerned than he was. "I think she's just been through a lot and needs some time to work through it." I felt a spike of defensiveness come from him.

I shook my head slightly and tried not to sound too sympathetic as I explained, knowing he wouldn't appreciate it. "She can't stop drifting. It's become an addiction for her, something her body seems to want, even if she doesn't. But once she saw what happened to Scott and the other drifter in that band of wild men…let's just say it doesn't matter how badly she wants to stop, she's not in control of it when she's sleeping. She can't fight it on her own." I paused, allowing myself to breathe and letting Jason absorb the truth.

"Why—" He shook his head, both understanding and denial battling within him. "Why didn't she tell me?" His composure cracked, making his voice hoarse.

I felt like I should comfort him, but I didn't dare. "She's embarrassed, Jason. She hasn't told *anyone*. I'm the only one who knows anything about it at all—and not because she's confided in me." I peered into his troubled blue eyes. They were almost glowing in the moonlight. "I know Dani needs you."

Jason took a long, deep breath and then another. "Yeah, okay. Just tell me what to do." From the desperate plea in his eyes, I could tell that he would do *anything* to help Dani.

"You can null her, like you did with me. You can make it so she can't use her Ability at all, right?"

Jason began pacing, running a hand through his hair. "Yeah, I can null her."

"Okay, so I'll go find her, then? Bring her back here so we can talk to her together?"

He shook his head. "No," he said. "I'll go." He started striding back toward the carts.

"I think she's by—" I started to say.

"I know where she is," he said over his shoulder. "Meet me in the shack."

Ten minutes later, I was leaning against a stack of Rubbermaid tubs of food and cooking utensils when Jason and Dani entered through the open doorway. Dani seemed more than a little surprised to find me waiting inside.

Pausing in the doorway, she looked at me, her eyebrows drawn together. "Did you figure out who the Monit—"

"No, Dani," I said. "This isn't about that."

After a brief moment, shock and betrayal played on Dani's exhausted features, and my guilt thickened. I felt like I was a horrible friend. *She* needs *our help,* I reminded myself.

Jason tried to pull her further inside, but she dug in her heels, glaring at him and me in turn, suspicion emanating from her. "What is this?"

"We came up with a plan…a plan to help you stop drifting," I said.

Her eyes flicked up to mine, little more than narrow slits of emerald, and she pulled her hand free from Jason's grasp.

I cleared my throat, trying to ignore the hurt and anger and shame radiating off of her. "I couldn't *not* tell him, Dani. I'm sorry."

"So this is—what?" Again, she took the time to glare at each of us. "An intervention?" She laughed, harshly at first, though it quickly became high-pitched and despondent. "It won't help. Nothing will."

Jason reclaimed her hand. "Red…"

"No!" Dani shook her head rapidly and shoved him, or *tried* to shove him. "You don't get it. I'm *trying*. I can't make it stop!"

"We know, Dani," I rasped, stunned by the feral sound that had emanated from her. Her desperation and fear brought tears to my eyes. "Jason…" I looked to him, unable to speak.

He stepped forward and took hold of her upper arms. "I'll null you for a while, help keep your mind with you instead of drifting."

She stared at him, her eyes wide. "You—you're sure you should do that? What about everyone else? What if they can't use their Abilities—"

"We'll make it work, Red. I'm stronger now, I can control it more. I'll make it work…"

Without warning, she flung herself at Jason, clinging to him as her body shook. She was crying, but all I could feel coming from her was a sense of overwhelming relief.

Lying in my sleeping bag that night, warm and cozy beside Jake, I stared up at the stars through the netted top of our tent, succumbing to every thought that filtered into my head. My mind failed to do what my body so desperately wanted—to rest.

If I wasn't thinking about my secret electrotherapy sessions with Gabe and Carlos and the dwindling hope that my memory would return, I was thinking about what had happened with Dani a couple hours earlier. Or I was thinking about my mom and the danger we were all in, or about Jason's anguish and Sanchez's and Carlos's and Camille's traumatizing pasts. I didn't want to be the one who knew so many disturbing secrets, but I had to keep quiet because they weren't my secrets to tell, they weren't my problems to fix. At the moment, I just wanted my Ability to go away.

With an audible exhale, Jake rolled over to face me.

I looked at him, finding his shadowed eyes in the inky darkness.

"What's wrong?" he asked quietly, his hand clasping both of mine, which were folded on my chest. "Are you worried about Dani?"

I turned onto my side to face him completely. I could've lied, I could've told him that I just couldn't sleep. After all, he would never know what I was really thinking. But I didn't want to pretend nothing was bothering me anymore. "I'm thinking about secrets, actually, and how much I hate them."

"Secrets?" He said it with a hint of intrigue.

"Not the good kind," I clarified.

Jake was quiet for a moment. Over the last few nights, we'd been slowly slipping into a routine that was familiar to him, but was strange to me, and, at times, awkward for both of us. Although he was happy enough being with me, I knew it wasn't the same for him. Still, he tried, and he did love the new me in his own way, which was as much as I could've hoped for.

"I know things about people, too many things," I whispered, not wanting to think about *me* a moment longer. I wanted to get the corrosive thoughts out of my head…I needed to get them out in the open.

Jake was quiet.

"Dani's losing herself to drifting. Jason's going to try to help her overcome it, but…" I listened to Jake's deep, even breaths before I continued, hoping that airing out the haunting thoughts in my mind would make me feel better, lighter. "Dani's contact at the Colony, the woman who saved me back at Colorado Springs, is my mom. She created the Virus, and that night you found me in the house, she'd left me with a letter for Jason and me." I balled my pillow up underneath my head, wanting to be at eye level with Jake. "She has another family now…she says we're in danger, that some of the people we trust might try to hurt us…"

I knew I shouldn't be telling him any of it—these were dangerous secrets, private, powerful secrets, and the more people who knew them, the more danger Jason and I were in—but simply voicing them made it easier to breathe, like my lungs could finally expand fully and the tension in my mind could ease.

"Please don't tell anyone."

Jake squeezed my hands and wrapped his arm around my back, pulling me closer to him. "I won't," he promised. I entwined my legs with his, feeling more solace lying in his arms than I'd ever felt before. "But if you're in danger—"

"There's nothing you can do. There's nothing any of us can do. We just have to pretend we don't know."

"But, Zoe…"

"I've got my feelers out, and Jason and Dani and Gabe are on the lookout, too. I'll be fine."

Although I could sense Jake's extreme dissatisfaction, could feel the tension it caused in his body, he left the topic alone, his touch soothing me despite his internal struggle.

"I'm sorry," I whispered. "I shouldn't have told you. There's nothing you can do about it, and it's not your burden to bear."

"Shhh," he murmured. "I'm glad you told me. I just wish I could do something to help…"

After an hour of us lying there silently, Jake comforting me, my mind finally relented, and I drifted to sleep. My dreams were a patchwork of nonsensical images—images of Becca surrounded by an army of Re-gens mixed with images of Dani and Jason, and of Jake and me, the *other* me…

In a barn filled with morning sunlight streaming in through cobwebbed and broken windows, Jake and I lay on a bed of sleeping bags, laughing uncontrollably. I wriggled in his arms, trying to get away from his relentless tickling. His baritone laugh and my squealing were an ear-piercing chorus, but I savored the sound nonetheless. Our combined laughter resonated painfully deep.

"Seriously, Jake, stop! I'm going to pee my pants!" I pulled at his arms, trying to pry them from my body, but he tightened his hold and buried his face into the crook of my neck.

"You're mine today…all day," he said, his voice held a hint of promise, and my insides warmed. I ceased my wiggling and looked over my shoulder at him. Jake's amber eyes were gleaming. Keeping his eyes on mine, he smiled and placed a kiss on my shoulder. His hold on me loosened, and I rolled over to face him.

He grinned wolfishly, melting my heart.

"You're a bad influence," I said as casually as possible. "Who will do my chores if I stay in here with you?"

Jake shrugged. "You can say I held you hostage."

"Oh, I kinda like that idea," I said and sat up. Slowly, I pulled off my t-shirt to expose my bare chest and flung my shirt into the corner of the barn. "But what if we change it up a bit?" I pushed him onto his back and crawled up on top of him.

"Yeah?" he asked. "How so?" His eyes danced with a combination of desire and amusement.

"What if it's me who won't let you leave? I'd be the captor, you the victim."

Jake chuckled. "I don't think that's very realistic…sorry."

I tilted my head, ignoring his taunt. "Are you sure I'm so innocent? Black widows—"

"I never said you were innocent," Jake clarified, sitting up and rolling me over onto my back. "You definitely aren't innocent." He pulled me beneath him, his strong legs entangling with mine, holding me in place while his gaze trailed from my mouth to my chest and over my exposed breasts. A salacious grin spread over his lips. "But I'm definitely the captor."

I laughed eagerly this time, impatient to feel his lips on mine, to feel his body pressed against me.

Equally impatient, he lowered his mouth to mine, one hand knotting in my hair while the other slid down the length of my body to squeeze my thigh.

He groaned in wanting.

My eyes fluttered open. The tent was still encased in darkness. That hadn't been *my* dream; it had belonged to Jake. He'd been dreaming of *her*.

He groaned beside my ear, and my blood heated to near boiling. I'd never been so aroused. Dreaming about him on my own was one thing, but sharing a dream was another matter entirely. I wanted to feel adored and loved and coveted like *that* Zoe. I wanted to feel his hands on my body and his lips devouring me.

Hearing him groan again was too much. Feeling what he was feeling as he dreamed about me was too much. I couldn't ignore it, not this time. I wanted to reclaim *something* of my old self.

Rolling over to face him, I tried to gather the courage to wake him up, to do something—anything—that would satisfy the emergent, burning need inside me. I trusted Jake more than I trusted anyone, so why hadn't I given him this? Why hadn't I given it to myself?

"Jake," I said quietly, not wanting to frighten him awake. I perched on my elbow, watching him closely. "Jake."

He didn't stir.

I tried again, this time leaning closer. "Jake, wake up."

When he still didn't, I swallowed my apprehension and did what I thought *she* would've done. I leaned down and brushed a kiss across his lips, hoping that would wake him. It was both petrifying and enlivening. While part of me feared he would reject my advances, another part of me felt a thrill of excitement that he wouldn't. The possibility of acceptance outweighed my hesitation, and I kissed him again, this time letting my tongue sample the curve of his soft lips. It was a kiss that felt different than others we'd shared; it was sneaky and felt dangerous, but I liked it.

Finally, Jake stirred. His lingering desire quickly gave way to confusion and then to a hazy curiosity.

His curiosity was reassurance enough for me. I leaned in further and kissed him again, more fervently, and this time, he kissed me back. His lips were soft and warm, and the whiskers around them tickled my mouth as I leaned deeper into him, as I kissed him harder…more desperately.

In the darkness, with my eyes flitting open and my heartbeat pounding in my ears, I felt one of Jake's hands cup the side of my face. He exuded the barest amount of pressure as he gently pulled away. The soft pad of his thumb rubbed my cheek, a tender, asking gesture, before he leaned in and rested his forehead against mine, letting out a steadying breath.

Not wanting to give him enough time to push me away, I pressed my mouth to his again, seeking out his tongue with my own. He needed to know that this was what I wanted—that *he* was what I wanted.

Placing my hand against his chest, I let his growing lust fuel my own. The desire to feel his hard, naked chest beneath my fingertips flooded my thoughts, and I reached for the hem of his t-shirt.

Understanding what I wanted, Jake sat up, pulling his shirt off over his head and tossing it out of the way. His sudden haste was intimidating, and I hedged as he leaned into me. Despite the fantasy I wanted to play out for him, the dream that was still so vivid in both of our minds, I couldn't bring myself to do it. I felt inadequate, and as much as I yearned to feel him inside me, I was petrified.

Slowly, Jake reached forward, tucking my hair behind one ear. His tenderness was an unspoken promise that he understood my fears, that he would be gentle. With another world-altering kiss that left me feeling lightheaded, I nearly melted into an aroused, malleable heap in his arms.

Guiding me down onto my back, Jake lowered himself onto his elbow and leaned over me, covering part of my fully clothed body with his. His fingers trailed around the outline of my face, his lips brushing against mine before he kissed the tip of my nose and the sensitive skin beneath my ear, each offering putting my nerves at ease and sending my heart soaring.

I tilted my head, giving him access to more skin, while my hands explored the planes of his chest—the soft skin and corded muscle—soliciting a delicious, aching feeling I never wanted to forget…that I never wanted to go away.

I let everything Jake was feeling drive my instincts. When his breathing quickened, so did mine, and my heart pounded so loudly I was certain he could hear it. When he pressed his hips against me, I pulled him closer. When he groaned, I tightened my grip on him. When he removed my clothes, running his rough hands over my stomach and breasts, immortalizing my body, I did the same with him.

I memorized the feel of the muscles spanning over his shoulders and back. Every single touch was euphoric, every hot puff of breath against my skin devastating. And every quiver of his body sent ripples of exhilaration through mine.

I inhaled the alluring smell of him. I tasted him. I finally, truly *felt* him.

Just as he'd silently promised, Jake made love to me like it was our first time—like I was the virginal novice I felt like. His touch was tender, but skilled and greedy, his movements slow, but impassioned.

And when we were through, when I could no longer think and our bodies trembled with fatigue and satisfaction and we lay in each other's arms, I tried to ignore his emotions. I wanted to bask in my own euphoria, get lost in my own thoughts, and replay every moment of what we'd just done, but that was impossible. Jake's emotions were amplified and raw.

Although he wrapped his arms around me, nuzzling the inside of my neck, I couldn't help the burn I felt as, inside him, his contentment warred against an insatiable longing for someone else, for someone I could never be.

19

DANI

MAY 1, 1AE

Fallon, Nevada

"You're mad at me," I said as I pulled off my jeans, exchanging them for black leggings.

Jason was kneeling in the corner of the tent, his back to me as he rummaged through his pack. He didn't say anything, didn't confirm or deny my statement, but his shoulders stiffened, and his back straightened.

"Because I hid my—my *problem* from you?" I unclasped my bra and slipped it off without removing my t-shirt.

Jason exhaled heavily. "You should have told me." He'd said those exact words to me once before, when we'd finally reunited in Bodega Bay after I received Cece's death threat and fled with Jack and Wings.

He faced me, the emotionless statue I'd come to know so well. "You should have told me about the note when you first read it. We could have figured it out together."

"I know." The realization may have come slowly, but I knew that whatever happened, whatever threat loomed ahead, Jason and

I would face it together. He needed to know that I believed in him... depended on him...trusted him. "I'm so sorry, Jason. I won't leave you again."

Though barely four months had passed, it felt like that conversation—that first kiss—happened four *lifetimes* ago.

"You should have told me."

Once again, I'd let him down...I'd failed to confide in him.

I could think of hundreds of responses: *You're right, I know. I should have told you. I'm so sorry. I don't know why I didn't tell you.* But they all felt hollow. Jason deserved better, so I said nothing. I simply stared at his back, at the way the fabric of his t-shirt strained against his broad shoulders with each inhale.

He exhaled loudly. "Why do you hide things like that? What are you so afraid of?" After a moment, he turned on his knees and sat back on his heels. Staring at me, he shook his head. "If you don't trust me, maybe we shouldn't be—"

Eyes wide with horror at what he was suggesting, I lunged toward him, dropping to my knees in front of him. "Shut up!" I covered his mouth with my hand. "Just shut up."

He tensed, but he didn't pull away.

It took me a few heartbeats to collect my thoughts. "I love you, Jason, and I trust you, more than anyone else. It's just—" I pressed my lips together and shook my head. "This drifting thing...it's embarrassing. It's always embarrassing, these stupid predicaments I get myself into, and, I don't know, I thought if you found out I was a drifting junkie, you'd finally realize that I'm more trouble than I'm worth...that being with me's just not worth all the effort it takes to actually *be* with me." Ashamed, I looked away.

Reaching up, Jason gently curled his fingers around my wrist and pulled my hand away from his mouth. "Red—" He placed his hands on either side of my face and turned my head, forcing me to look at him. "Dani, I love you. Whatever problems you're having, you can tell me, and it won't change *that*."

I bit my lip.

He blinked, dropped his hands, and pulled back. "You don't believe me."

"What?" I asked, my eyes widening. He was right, sort of; part of me didn't *want* to believe that he loved me, because I knew how he felt about love, especially after having a front-row view of the tragedy that was his family. To Jason, love was a weapon; it was the single most powerful way to destroy a person—or worse, to control them.

Jason frowned. "You're afraid…?"

"How could you possibly know that?" I whispered.

He opened his mouth, then closed it again and shook his head. "I don't know; I just *do*. Are you afraid of me?"

"No," I said. "I'm afraid *for* you. I'm afraid that loving me will kill you."

"That's ironic." He smiled wryly, coaxing a timid smile from my own lips. "I've never felt more alive."

I slapped his chest, laughing softly. "I'm serious, Jason." My eyebrows drew together. "Promise me—promise that if something happens to me, if nulling me while I sleep doesn't work and I become as bad as Scott, or if something else happens to me, you won't end up like your dad. You'll keep on living…*really* living."

Jason's teasing expression sobered, and his eyes pulled me in like cerulean quicksand. "Only if you promise me the same in return."

I bit my lip again and nodded.

"Deal," Jason said as he leaned in. He claimed my lips in the gentlest, most tender kiss. It was sweet and delicate, and I wanted so much more…until he pulled away and said, "Are you ready?"

I sighed, my shoulders drooping. "What if it doesn't work and you have to null me while I sleep…forever?"

He smiled, and his eyes consumed me. "I don't think I'd mind that."

I couldn't help but return his smile. He'd just said he was

willing to remain by my side, being my tether to humanity, for the rest of his life. I sighed as I reached for my sleeping bag. I unrolled it, and Jason did the same with his, arranging it right beside mine. And for the first time in over a month, he zipped our sleeping bags together.

I slipped into my side of the joined sleeping bags and sighed in pleasure. By the time my head touched my camp pillow, my eyes were already closing.

Still kneeling, Jason moved onto his sleeping bag, taking up a position with his knees flush against my hips. "I miss those sounds." He brushed a stray curl away from my face, and I opened my eyes just enough to catch a glimpse of his gentle smile. "Do you have any idea how badly I want to be with you…to feel you?" He groaned, a rough noise deep in his chest. "But I can't give in, not until we're somewhere safe for good."

Oh, right…because if he unintentionally nulled everyone, we'd all be in danger for who knew how long. I blinked up at him groggily. "Until we're safe," I mumbled.

"Yeah, until we're safe. Sleep well, Red." I felt Jason's lips brush against my forehead, felt his fingertips trail down my cheek, and then sleep claimed me.

I blinked awake to the first rays of morning sunshine glowing through the green nylon of my tent, feeling both sleepy and rested. Groaning, I stretched in my sleeping bag, then turned onto my side. Jason was, of course, already awake. After all, the sun had already started to rise.

He smiled lazily. "'Morning." Raising a hand to my face, he brushed the backs of his fingers down my cheek and along the line of my jaw. "You look better. How do you feel?"

I frowned, taking quick assessment of myself, starting at my toes and working my way up. "Better. Not awesome, but better," I said through another yawn.

Jason laughed. "I *think* you just said 'better.'"

I smiled sheepishly, but it contained genuine happiness… because it had worked. Jason had nulled me all night, and I'd slept and dreamed and remained in my own body the entire time.

Five mornings later, I woke to the feeling of Jason's body pressed against the back of mine, to the tickle of his fingertips drawing lazy designs around my belly button. Giggling, I squirmed into him, and heard his answering chuckle.

His hand started moving lower, and I tensed, grabbing his wrist and moving his hand back up a few inches. "Jason…"

"Red…" The desire contained within that single syllable, the sheer force of need, almost made me release his hand.

"No, Jason." I moved his hand higher, snuggling it against my chest. "No. It's too dangerous. You said so yourself…over and over and over…"

Jason groaned and held me more tightly against him. "Right now, I really don't give a fuck."

My heart skipped a beat or three. "Yes you do." I held my breath for a few seconds, then said, "Maybe I should start sharing a tent with Zo…at least until this is no longer such a, um, *painful* issue…"

"If you tried that, I'd throw you over my shoulder and bring you right back here," he whispered near my ear.

Craning my neck, I stared into those intense eyes, as clear and blue and luminous as any tropical sea, blinked several times, then burst into laughter. "You are such a caveman sometimes, you know that?"

He watched me, amusement making his eyes dance and his lips curve upward. "You make me crazy."

I grinned like the cat who caught the canary, leaned in for a quick kiss, then sat up and stretched my arms over my head. "Good," I said with a nod. "My life's work is complete." With one final stretch, I pushed my sleeping bag down and out of the way and crawled to my folded pile of semi-fresh clothes. I exchanged my leggings and t-shirt for a sports bra, black tank top, long-sleeved shirt, and somewhat faded jeans, then headed for the tent door to slip on my boots before heading out.

"You're in a hurry," Jason said as he finally emerged from our sleeping bags.

I paused with my fingers pinching the zipper and shrugged. "I'm excited to get moving." It was a big day, a milestone day, and we couldn't afford to waste time.

Today, if everything worked out, we would reach Lake Tahoe. *If* everything worked out, we would meet up with Holly and Hunter, our two companions who'd remained behind with the liberated cult followers the last time we'd passed through, enjoy several days of rest and recuperation, then continue on our way.

The coast, Bodega Bay—my hometown—was mere weeks away, and it felt so close that I could almost reach out and touch it. Tahoe was one step closer to home, and I wanted to be there, *now*.

I stared at the white letters carved into a rustic sign on the left side of the highway as Wings and the other lead horses clopped past it: *TAHOE WOLF AND WOLFDOG RESCUE*. A long cinder-block building, a small barn, and several sheds stood on the land beyond it, with various fenced-in areas and cages arrayed around, between, and behind them. It looked like a miniature ranch, set in the most beautiful, wooded setting, and that wasn't even accounting for the view.

We were traveling south on Highway 50, along the east shore of Lake Tahoe, and a faint breeze was making the lake's surface glitter like an enormous cache of sapphires, diamonds, and blue topaz. The rescue, located on the opposite side of the highway, had one hell of a view. I laughed softly, my lips curving into a closed-mouth smile. *Lucky dogs…*

"Find some new friends?" Carlos asked, and when I glanced his way, I found his eyes studying the small cluster of buildings.

I shook my head. "They're gone."

"Dead?"

"Dunno." I looked away from the rescue center, focusing on the road ahead and my sense of the animal minds around me. I had dozens of open telepathic connections, and keeping myself from drifting to each and every one of those creatures' minds took more effort and concentration than it used to take. "I hope not." I shrugged. "They're intelligent enough that they could've found a way out…I think."

"Hmmm…" Carlos steered Arrow further away from Wings, scanning the alpine forest on either side of the road.

"Careful, now," I said to Wings. *"I'm going to be a little distracted for a minute or two."*

"Take good care of you," she said, her mental voice smooth and reassuring.

I ran my hand down the side of her neck, feeling the gentle flexing of her immensely powerful muscles with each step. *"Thank you, Pretty Girl."*

She whinnied and raised her head, purposefully becoming more attentive to our surroundings.

Closing my eyes, I extended the radius of my Ability beyond the mile or so I'd been maintaining. Thousands upon thousands of minds flooded my awareness, and I noticed a less dense spot a little over a mile south of us. I assumed that was Zephyr Cove, where, as Gabe had discovered one night while scouting the dreaming minds, Holly, Hunter, and the formerly mind-controlled cultists had relocated.

I narrowed my focus, searching only for the minds with the distinctive canine feel that belonged to the Canidae family of animals. Dogs, formerly domestic creatures forced to fend for themselves once their owners passed away, were the vast majority of what I sensed, but there were also a fair number of coyotes and foxes. I didn't actually notice the wolves at first because their minds were clustered with those of some of the dogs, forming an unusual pack, both in terms of its mixed-species makeup and its large size. There had to be at least a dozen wolves and even more dogs.

And there was something else…another mind that felt at the same time hauntingly familiar and utterly unique. *Like Ralph,* I thought. *And Scott and the other drifters.*

It's another one of us. The realization sent a thrill of fear-laced excitement racing through me. I wasn't sure why, but I'd felt a kinship to Ralph that I hadn't noticed until I was away from him. I'd chalked it up to him being able to understand me unlike any of my survivor companions, even Jason, but now I was starting to wonder if it was something more.

Was it possible that the gene therapy changed our DNA more than Dr. Wesley had intended? Had she unknowingly given rise to dozens of new subspecies? Instead of all of us making up one Homo sapiens sapiens group, had we been broken into Homo sapiens telepathicus, Homo sapiens regenerativus, and Homo sapiens psycho-mind-control-megalomaniacus?

Whatever the cause, I felt drawn to this new mind.

Opening my eyes, I looked around. Carlos appeared to be the only person who'd noticed my momentary lapse of attention. He watched me, curiosity and something else shining in his eyes.

When he noticed me looking at him, he smiled uncomfortably, then returned his attention to the pines surrounding us.

At first, I thought his behavior was odd, but then I remembered that while I was excited by the prospect of seeing people I'd once called companions, if not friends, Carlos would be reuniting with people who'd been around him during the worst month of his life.

Fifteen, maybe twenty minutes later, we were guiding the horses off the highway and into the parking lot of an old lake lodge. The long, three-story building had been painted a dark brownish red with forest-green trim, and an enormous stone chimney ran up along the exterior of the north side. And standing in an uneven column on the porch spanning the entire front of the lodge were more people than I'd seen in one place since leaving the Colony. Holly and Hunter stood foremost, waving and grinning like little kids.

Any eagerness I'd been feeling had faded, or possibly had just been overshadowed by my desire to search for the drifter whose mind I'd sensed among the dogs and wolves. As Jason and the others dismounted and crawled down from their perches on the wagon and cart benches, I remained in my saddle. My attention kept returning to the expanse of pines stretching out on the east side of the highway. Somewhere in there…whoever I was sensing was somewhere in there.

"Jason," I called.

Halfway to the lodge, he stopped and glanced at me over his shoulder.

"I'm going to get the horses situated in that stable up the road," I said, nodding back the way we'd come. "I'll meet back up with the rest of you in a bit."

Jason frowned, glancing at the cart and wagon. "What about the teams?"

"We'll get them unhooked and bring them up," Zoe said, looking first at Sam, who was standing next to her, then at Carlos, who was holding his horse's reins just a yard or two away from Wings and me. "Right, guys?"

When both Carlos and Sam nodded, I smiled at Jason. "See. All taken care of." I asked Wings to turn and head back up the road, then looped in the rest of the horses and requested that they follow us. I looked back at Jason. "I'll have the whole herd around me. That's about as safe as it gets, and I'll come back in a bit… after all the hubbub has died down." I made a shooing motion and laughed softly. "Go—talk to Holly and Hunter, see what their plans are. I'll be fine."

"Okay…"

With one last reassuring smile, I faced forward, and Wings started clip-clopping back up the highway. We reached the stable without trouble, the herd fanning out behind us.

Thanks to Harper having removed my cast and given my no-longer-broken arm the okay a few days ago, I was finally able to really use both of my hands again. I unsaddled first Wings, then Jason's unnamed horse. It was when I was sliding Arrow's saddle off his back that I felt it; the mind was drawing nearer. Whoever it was had sensed me.

Smiling at the fact that now I wouldn't have to go hunt the person down, I sent out a tentative greeting.

"Friend?" The mental voice that responded was tiny and high-pitched and very clearly belonged to a child.

A kid? It's a kid? If the mind really belonged to a child, and the little kid was out here all alone with only the animals to help it survive…

"Yes, of course I'm a friend!" I started walking toward the woods beside the stable, where I could feel the young drifter's mind. *"I'm Dani. What's your name?"*

"Annie." A distinctly childlike giggle came from further in the trees, and I was extremely grateful that the ground had little cover, because I hardly paid any attention to where I was placing my feet

as I picked up my pace. *"Dani and Annie."* I heard the giggle again, closer this time.

"I'm here," I called out. Going by her mind's signature, the little girl—Annie—was just up ahead, and some of the canines who'd been around her when I'd first sensed her were scattered throughout the woods around us both.

Most greeted me warmly in my mind, but it was the pack's alpha female who showed herself first, slinking between the trees as she approached. She had a snowy white coat, and blue eyes that were so pale they almost appeared silver. Those eyes never left mine.

"I'm honored to meet you," I told her, making a point *not* to lower my eyes. She was testing me, and I wasn't about to fail. Among her kind, this wolf held as much power as was possible.

She stopped a few yards in front of me and, after several more seconds of intense staring, sat. *"You take young two-legs?"*

"I—I don't know."

She half-stood, then settled back down. *"You must take young two-legs. Be mother to young two-legs. Cannot survive here. Cold too dangerous in time of longer night. Nearly lost young two-legs."*

Did that mean that the kid had been out here, alone for all intents and purposes, for most of the winter? Had she been out here since the beginning?

"Yes," I told the wolf without thinking. *"Of course, yes."* Remotely, I wondered what the hell I'd just agreed to.

"I am pleased," the wolf said, then stood, turned, and trotted back through the trees.

As she left, a tiny girl wearing the dirtiest clothing I'd ever seen on a child ran past her, directly toward me. She was laughing as she ran…until an even dirtier person lurched through the woods behind her. It was a woman—a *young* woman, I thought…maybe—and her adult legs carried her toward me faster than Annie's could.

I was so stunned that I didn't register her as a threat until it was too late for me to draw a weapon.

She lunged at me, her dark hair a tangled halo, her face covered in a layer of dirt so thick it almost qualified as a mud mask, and her tattered jeans and sweatshirt barely recognizable for what they were. And she *reeked*, almost as badly as some of the dead bodies I'd come across, which was really saying something.

"You can't have her," she shrieked mid-leap.

She hit me hard, taking us both down to the ground, and proved to be surprisingly strong for a woman who appeared to have spent the past few months living in the woods like an animal. I was just lucky that she was about my size. Had she been any bigger, I'd have been at a severe disadvantage.

"You can't take her away from me! You can't have her!" There was no doubt in my mind that she was a Crazy.

Annie was wailing like a banshee, but at least the sound told me she'd halted far enough away that neither of us would accidently kick her while we grappled on the ground.

"Would it hurt you…to brush…your teeth?" I grunted as I wrestled with the Crazy. Her breath was *horrendous*.

Rolling us both, I managed to get the insane woman beneath me and yank my knife from my boot sheath before she could overpower me. I held the knife to her throat and—

"Dani! No!" Carlos shouted from behind me.

The crazed woman and I both froze, the edge of my knife's blade just beginning to slice into the Crazy's flesh. My chest heaved as I sucked in air. "What?"

"Don't hurt her," Carlos said. He skidded to his knees beside us, pushing my knife hand away from the woman's neck.

I stared at him, dumbfounded. "Why the hell not?"

He glanced down at the filthy woman, seeming to be at a loss for words.

She stared up at him, and recognition shone in her unstable gaze. She started cackling maniacally. "Mom! Jesse! Did you see?"

She tilted her head back, looking at empty space. "Carlos came back!" She giggled, the sound soon turning into a full-blown laugh, and she flashed the grimiest teeth I'd ever seen.

I had to turn my head away to keep from gagging from the stench of her breath. "Carlos…?"

The young woman's laugh cut off abruptly. "You can't have him! He's *my* brother! Mine!"

20

ZOE

MAY 7, 1AE

Lake Tahoe, Nevada

When Gabe left me a note to meet him down by the lake at lunchtime, I knew he had either great news or terrible news. Since he'd asked me to meet him in private, I assumed it had something to do with my electrotherapy sessions. Like maybe he wanted to take a break for a while.

Maybe he wants to focus on fixing Vanessa? Helping Carlos's long-lost sister, who they'd found the previous afternoon—and who was also a definite Crazy—seemed more important than administering more failed attempts to recharge my memories.

As I wandered down the cement path to the lakeshore, I hoped that if Gabe *was* planning to take a break from our sessions, he wasn't going to pull the plug completely. They weren't going well, not in the least. There had been absolutely no advancement on my end, and we'd been trying for almost two weeks. In fact, Carlos's Ability was improving quickly, growing stronger and more focused, but I was left with nothing more than a headache now and again and a temporarily out-of-service Ability. Regardless, we couldn't stop now. A break I could handle, but I wanted us to keep trying…I *needed* us to keep trying.

I spotted Chris a few yards away, sitting on a large rock on the beach, Gabe pacing back and forth in front of her. I quickened my steps, trying not to let their bland expressions worry me.

"What's wrong? Is everything alright? Is it Carlos?" He was the only one missing from our undercover electrotherapy group. Forcing myself to look away from Gabe's pinched expression as he continued to pace, I focused on Chris.

She offered me a reassuring smile. "Carlos is fine, Zoe, don't worry. He's out with Dani and his sister."

Gabe looked up at me like he finally realized I'd arrived. To my surprise, his keen eyes widened, and he smiled—not just a polite hi-how-are-ya smile, but an *aha!*-by-Jove-I-think-I've-got-it smile. "Ah, great. You're here."

I let out the breath I'd been holding onto like it would've made any impending bad news less knifelike. "Wait, what happened? Why are you so…" I tried to pinpoint his emotions. "Excited?" I wasn't sure that was even the right word.

Gabe lifted his shoulder. "I had an idea…something different. Have a seat, and I'll explain." He gestured toward a smaller rock beside Chris's.

I looked at Chris, and when our gazes met, she shrugged and shook her head. "You know as much as I do."

With a sigh, I sat on the rock.

"So," Gabe started. He was pacing again, back and forth in the sand, creating a trail of obscure, overlapping footprints in front of us. "I've been an idiot." He ran his fingers through his long blond hair.

"What?" Chris and I asked in unison.

Gabe let out a soft chuckle. "It's so obvious, I can't believe I didn't think of it sooner." He was quiet for a minute, deep in thought.

When he looked up at me, prudent and appraising, I could only stare back at him in wonder. I tried to control the increasing hope that he might've found a way to help me get my memory back, but it was difficult while he was keeping me in such suspense.

Chris glanced at me in my periphery, and I could feel her hope perking up alongside mine.

"Please tell us, Gabe." I dropped my head into my hands. "I'm dying here…"

"Sorry. I'm just trying to wrap my mind around all the possibilities." He exhaled heavily. "We've been treating your memory loss like amnesia. Essentially, Carlos has been going in and trying to jumpstart the memory centers of your brain, trying to spark them back to life, right?" A small grin tugged at the corner of Gabe's mouth. "But what if there's nothing wrong with your memory centers? What if it wasn't actually Clara who did this to you…at least, not completely?"

Bewildered, I frowned.

"Hear me out," he said and crouched between Chris and me. "What if you did this to yourself?" When Chris and I remained quiet, Gabe continued, "Dani's Ability is mental, like yours and like mine. She can communicate with animal minds. Your Ability is similar. You can't communicate with other minds, but you can feel them, you can *see* inside them."

As much as I appreciated his attempt to help me understand, I was still confused.

"Are you going to spit it out, Gabe, or—" Chris said.

"I'm getting to it." He flashed us a cocky smile. "When Dani was in the Colony, she was in extreme danger. To save herself, she drifted into Ray, remember?"

I nodded. I'd seen what Dani had been subjected to while she was in the Colony, what Clara and the General had done to her toward the end. Her memories were vivid and frequent, in spite of her attempt to forget her time there.

"What if your mind did something similar? What if you shut parts of your mind down to protect yourself from Clara?" Gabe's gaze was intense and filled with a spark I hadn't seen in it for a while.

"Are you thinking that if Zoe did this to herself, she's the only one who can reverse it?" Chris asked, rising to her feet. She glanced furtively from Gabe to me.

"Maybe. I have an idea of what *we* can do to help her reverse it, but, yes, a lot of it might be up to Zoe. If we stop thinking of your condition in terms of amnesia and instead think of it more like repressed memories, it makes sense." He looked at me intently. "Don't you think?"

I nodded. "I think so…"

"Your body's natural instinct is to protect itself. In fact, people's minds do it all the time, blocking traumatic memories and such. And I have no doubt it was traumatizing to have Clara prodding around in your mind, threatening to destroy the very essence of who you are." Gabe paused, considering something before he continued. "Depending on what she was trying to do to you, it might simply have been too much, and your mind locked your memories away as a defense mechanism."

A chill raked over my body as I thought about her meddling with my mind. I never really thought about that night, but suddenly I could feel the cool, night air and Clara's looming presence like I was there again.

"So…how does she *un*-repress her memories, then?" Chris asked.

"We need to figure out what triggered the reaction in the first place…what caused the repression."

Brow furrowed, I glanced first at Chris, then at Gabe. "Clara, maybe?" Although I obviously couldn't remember her from my past, I'd seen her in other people's memories and knew she was pure poison, and I could only imagine how terrified I must have been while she was cerebrally raping me. But I couldn't actually remember.

Gabe nodded. "Exactly. How much have you thought about that night?"

I pulled my knees up against my chest and shrugged. "Not much. I try not to, actually."

"Well, it's time to try," Gabe said.

Studying him and Chris for a moment, I wondered how I was supposed to suddenly remember such specific details if I really had repressed all of my memories from that moment backward. "Every single day, I try to remember even a smidgen of my past...what makes you think it's magically going to work this time?"

"Because I'm going to help you," Gabe said, offering me his hand. I stared at it, wondering if this was the final moment of being *this* me, or if it was another step closer to defeat and desperation. Accepting his hand, I stood.

"Are you thinking about conducting some sort of hypnosis?" Chris asked, an intrigued gleam in her clear blue eyes.

Gabe nodded. "It's our best bet." He looked back to me. "If I can put you into a dreamlike state, we can try to work backward to help you unlock everything you've repressed. We can free your mind." He was nodding and smiling enthusiastically, trying to increase my comfort level. "I think this could work, Zoe."

The general atmosphere around me shifted. Not only had Chris suddenly grown more hopeful, but Gabe seemed completely rejuvenated as well.

"Are we trying it now?" I asked.

Gabe turned to Chris. "Do you mind sticking around? If this works the way I hope it does, Zoe's going to be quasi-awake, but totally focused on what I'm asking her to do. I'm not sure what latent memories or emotions will surface; you might need to soothe her."

"Of course," Chris said with a curt nod. "I'll do whatever you need me to do."

My eyes shifted back and forth between them. "Thanks, you guys," I breathed, wiping my clammy palms off on my jeans. "I really appreciate all your help with this. Whether it works or not, it wouldn't even be an option without you."

Chris smiled. "I like projects." Her eyebrows danced. "Especially ones that have to do with brains."

Gabe made a noncommittal noise and stared at me, deep in thought. As we stood face to face, I realized how important this moment was…or *might* be. His pale blue eyes were fierce, holding a glint of both apprehension and resolve. I could feel his certainty that if this didn't work, I would never get my memories back. This was his final hope.

With a heavy exhale, he raised his eyebrows and smiled. "Shall we?"

Offering him my own weak smile in return, I gave him a quick nod. "Ready as I'll ever be." Goose bumps were already inundating my body at the thought of what he might uncover inside my mind, should his theory prove correct.

"Alright." Gabe pointed to the shady base of an evergreen at the edge of the shoreline. "Have a seat over there. I want you as close to the ground as possible in case you collapse."

I let out a nervous laugh, and on shaky legs, I walked over to the shady patch beneath the tree.

"Chris," I heard Gabe say from behind me. "I'd like you to be next to her to hold her up in case she loses consciousness completely."

"You worried she'll pass out?"

"That, or I'll push too much and put her to sleep. I need her to be partially coherent for it to work. But, again, I've never done a procedure quite like this before."

"That makes three of us," I muttered and sat down, propping myself up against the base of the pine tree that would serve as my psychiatrist's chair while my mind was invaded one last time.

Gabe crouched down in front of me, and Chris sat to my right. Her mere presence was reassuring.

"No matter what you hear, Zoe, no matter what you see, I need you to listen to my voice and do what I say, okay?" Gabe said.

After taking a deep breath and nodding, I settled into a comfortable sitting position, my legs folded in front of me and my eyes closed. To rid my mind of anticipation and doubt, of fear and excitement, I focused on the gentle breeze tickling the back of my neck and the grating call of the jaybirds off in the distance. I could almost smell the crisp freshness of the melting snow from the mountains surrounding us as I let the warmth of the sun lull my senses.

My mind was suddenly lighter, almost like it was floating away, and remotely, I wondered if it was Gabe sending me into a half sleep.

"Alright, Zoe," Gabe said softly. "Think back to your very first memory."

Letting out a deep breath, I felt my body wilt as I unwound my limited memories like a spool of thread, the days and weeks unraveling into frayed images and incohesive thoughts.

One of my earliest, blurred memories was from that first night, when I'd been found in the abandoned house.

I felt fear and uncertainty...I saw Dani's wide, green eyes and Jake's horror as I stepped out from the closet. I felt what I now understood was Chris's soft, cerebral touch lessening the edge of uncertainty filling me. I saw Jason's hardened features, which made me question Dr. Wesley's decision to leave me with them—complete strangers, or so it seemed to me.

"Who do you see?" Gabe's voice was a velvety cord of trust and reassurance, binding me between this time and a not-too-distant past.

"Ja—" I cleared my throat. "I see Jake and Chris, and Dani and Cooper...we're in the house in Colorado Springs." I was vaguely aware that I was sitting on the hard ground, surrounded by towering evergreens, and that Gabe and Chris were sitting with me, but my mind was drifting somewhere far away…

"What happened before that?" Gabe asked quietly.

Holding onto the tether that was Gabe's voice, I tried to reach further back, to delve deeper into the past. A slight pain blossomed in my temples, making me hesitate. "It's not working…"

The more I tried to focus, the sharper the pain became, making me wince. *I've felt this before…*

"Who brought you to the house?" Gabe asked. His voice was a bit more distant now, but just as persistent. I strained to hear it over the images fading in and out of my mind.

Although I knew it was my mom who'd taken me to the abandoned house, my mind had been hazy that night, and only bits and pieces lingered in my memory. "It was Dr. Wesley—my mom—but I…" There were only splotches of memories, nothing connected or coherent.

Details. I needed to remember details.

I latched on to what I *did* remember: the feeling of the cool, night air against my skin when I first awoke and the sound of my mom's footsteps behind me as we walked—no, ran—into Colorado Springs. *What did she say to me in the forgotten moments?* I feared it was something important, but I couldn't remember. All I could think about was the fact that the woman who'd saved my life, a stranger, was also my mom. For the first time since I'd learned of it, I felt sad.

I was back at the golf course, kneeling on wet grass. Someone stood beside me, their warm body shielding me from the nighttime chill. The person was humming. She *was humming. I felt cool fingertips against my skin, followed by an excruciating pain that lanced through my head, making me gasp for breath. But I couldn't gasp for breath. I couldn't move.*

Unable to open my eyes, I began to panic.

It wasn't the first time I'd panicked. I wracked my brain, trying to remember why such an acute, helpless feeling felt so familiar. I had been afraid before, but not for me… "Dani," I breathed.

"Is Dani still there with you, Zoe?" Gabe asked. Although his voice was faint, it was warm and soothing in the swallowing darkness of my mind.

I felt something wet on my cheek, but still felt paralyzed, unable to move. A set of triumphant blue eyes flashed in my mind's eye, along with blonde hair and pale skin…

There was sickening sweet laughter and an eerily calm voice whispering nonsensical things in my ear, and a deep, innate sense of terror consumed me. When I realized I still couldn't move, I tried to scream, but nothing came out, and I felt hot tears burning down my cheeks.

"Zoe," Gabe said quietly. "Where are you? What do you see?" I could barely make out Chris and Gabe whispering as my mind tumbled with confusion and fear.

"I can't see anything," I croaked. "I can't move…"

I heard Dani's voice echoing around me, and my heart raced. I needed to help her. She was afraid, she was alone, and she needed me.

Emotion bubbled up in my throat. "I'm on the golf course…Dani…"

"Dani wasn't with you, Zoe." Concern deepened Gabe's voice.

I shook my head the barest amount. I was confused. "But I can hear her. I can hear her voice, it's all around me…she's hiding."

"It's only a memory, Zoe. Don't let it scare you. It's not real. Dani is fine."

Part of me knew it was a memory, a distant part of me that was overshadowed by a fear I didn't understand but was impossible to ignore. "I was trying to find her."

Another sharp pain shot through my head, and this time, my body tensed. I felt gentle fingers against my wrist, alleviating some of the panic and emptiness that swelled inside me. I could still hear Dani's voice, crying out to me, but I couldn't move, I couldn't do anything. I was frozen.

I felt the pressure of Chris's hand squeezing mine, and it helped to keep me grounded. "Zoe, are you okay?" she asked, and with those four words, my trembling ceased.

"Zoe, are you okay?"

I opened my eyes to see a woman—a doctor—crouched down beside me. She reached out for me tentatively, her eyes filled with sadness and longing and unshed tears. Seeing her tears made my heart ache.

"She's mine!" the blonde woman shrieked beside me.

The doctor took a few forceful steps forward. "I'm warning you, Clara," she said.

Clara. I knew she was familiar.

"Get your fucking hands off my daughter or I'll—"

My insides knotted. I'm the doctor's daughter...

I gasped and doubled over as a clawing pain seized my heart.

"Shhh...they'll find you. You'll be safe." My mom reached out and cupped the side of my face with trembling hands. Tears spilled from her eyes and ran down her cheeks. "I'm sorry I couldn't get here fast enough...I'm so sorry, Zoe."

A barrage of images and emotions assailed me, and I tried to stifle a violent sob. I fought for breath as they overtook my senses, unable to stop them.

I saw evil.

Clara.

She laughed and simpered and schemed…and she poisoned me.

I saw the fire…she killed Stacey and Dave and Tanya, and nearly killed Jake.

Now she was gone…I hit her over the head with a branch. Once. Twice. She didn't get back up.

I killed her. I *killed Clara…*

"…can you hear me?" *Is that Gabe?* I couldn't tell anymore.

Jake was holding me, an embrace so protective and warm I thought I'd never feel so loved again.

He saved my life—the men in the woods—the poison.

But then he was leaving—he was going to break my heart and leave me empty and alone.

"Jake…" I rasped. Arms were around my shoulders, someone holding me against them.

"Zoe, can you hear me?" Gabe asked, his voice earnest.

"You need to answer him, Zoe." It was Chris holding me, I vaguely realized. Her voice was like a warm blanket I wanted to wrap around myself.

I tried to nod, to reassure them, but I couldn't.

I could hear Chris whispering and feel her voice reverberating in her chest. The deafening pain and emotional onslaught was muted by her touch, but not gone. It thrummed through me, impossible to avoid.

More memories suffused my mind, and I lost myself within them.

I saw my friends.

Sarah flashed in my mind. She was laughing and grinning from ear to ear.

She was my only constant in the ravaged, lonely world we lived in. She trained beside me, faster and stronger…and pregnant. She was my friend now, the days when she'd been a thorn in my side long gone.

…she brought me comfort in Dani's absence.

Dani was in my arms, her wild hair clinging to my tear-dampened face. Her wide, shrewd green eyes luminous with fierce love.

I'd thought I had lost her. I thought I would never see her again. But there she was, standing in front of me.

…she was upset.

"I know about the box, Zoe."

Familiar whispers danced around my ears, talking about getting help and finding someone, but I couldn't pay attention…all I could see was the box.

Dad's box…Mom's letter to Dad.

Jason and I opened it. We learned the truth.

She'd left us. She'd abandoned us and Dad had lied. We'd been cheated out of the truth for so long…we'd been cheated out of a real family.

There was so much pain, so much misery and loneliness. I cried out as I remembered the desperation I'd felt to learn the truth of what happened to her, to have closure. I cried out at the realization of what our lives had become—nothing but a patched-up quilt with tattered emotions and relationships hanging on by mere threads. There was so much strain, so much distance…

I was lying in bed, a little girl, scared after a bad dream—the bad dream about the faceless woman I wanted to know so badly.

I saw my disheveled dad trying to explain to me why I couldn't see pictures of my mom…that she was gone.

Now he *was gone. I would never see my dad again.*

My mom's face appeared in my mind again. Her eyes boring into mine, the emotion now so clear, so haunting.

She was real.

She was the creator of the Virus.

She was the mother I never had and the mom I'd always wanted.

She was alive.

She had another *family.*

I had met her, but...

I'd never felt so near to bursting. The heartache and anger and despair were alive and gnawing inside me, overwhelming me until I felt hollow and raw. My throat burned with each violent sob. My chest ached from lack of air.

Chris's arms were around me, holding onto me as if I was about to crumble away.

I saw her boys, and I saw me in her arms.

I felt her fear melding with mine, her regret tasting sour in my mouth, and her concern, that which a mother might have for her daughter, made it impossible to breathe. I wanted my mom. I was angry and *afraid* of my mom.

I grasped onto Chris desperately, tearing my eyes open, needing to see light in the darkness. Blurred trees and brightness filled my vision.

"Take a deep breath," she whispered, and shakily, I did. The softness of her voice soothed me as my mind began to settle, each memory falling back into place as if it had all simply been a bad dream. But it was real, all of it. It was my life.

I had Dani and Jake and Jason. But my mom was out there, a stranger who'd abandoned me in order to save me—more than once. I'd met her. *I wasn't even* me... A new sense of desperation and regret sprouted inside me, but I buried it away.

"Where's Gabe?" I asked hoarsely, trying to control each breath.

"He went to find Dani," Chris whispered.

I let out a choked, happy sob at the thought of having *my* Dani with me. With a steadying breath, I righted myself, trying to harness the emotions overcrowding me. *I just need to let them settle again...*

21

JAKE

MAY 7, 1AE

Lake Tahoe, Nevada

Jake stood at the supply cart in the Zephyr Cove campground parking lot, across the highway from the lodge, ready to take inventory of the weapons in the duffel bag he and Jason had filled during their morning scavenging trip to Emerald Bay with Hunter and Holly. The sun was warm on his back, and although the snow was still melting off the mountains surrounding the lake, making the air crisp in the shade, the sun was shining intensely enough to stave off the chill.

Unzipping the duffel, Jake rifled around inside for loose ammo. Against his better judgment, he'd been thinking a lot more than was productive. Ever since Zoe told him about her mom, Dr. Wesley, thinking about the doctor brought his anger to near boiling, and the unfathomable truth about what she'd done turned his anger to rage. Of course Zoe's mother would end up being alive and the destroyer of all that Jake held dear in his life. And Zoe didn't need to feel that living, churning hatred every time she was around him. He didn't blame *her*, not in the slightest, but he couldn't change what he felt about her mother, either.

So Jake clung to the few happy memories he had left of the past, memories of Joe's farm, of rebuilding tractor engines, working on cars, and patching fences around the property. But then Jake wondered if Joe was even still alive, and his thoughts went full circle, back to Zoe and Becca…back to the doctor.

For months Jake had blamed himself for bringing Clara along with him when he first left Colorado Springs—he still did—but he wasn't the only one to blame. It was Dr. Wesley's fault that Clara had been able to manipulate people the way she could in the first place, and essentially it was the doctor's fault that Zoe was only half the person she'd once been, and that his sister was a Re-gen. Jake paused from unloading the bag, forcing himself to loosen his grip on the hunting knife he held in his hand.

Hearing hurried footsteps on the asphalt in front of him, Jake ignored their approach and set the hunting knife and then a bundle of arrows and a new crossbow he'd collected for Zoe on the cart bed.

"Jake," Gabe called, breathless as he jogged nearer.

Jake looked up, and upon seeing Gabe's eyes opened wide and filled with what looked like a frenzy of concern and excitement, he straightened. "What is it?"

Gabe rubbed the back of his neck and let out a calming breath. "Ah, I think Zoe's memory is back. She's—"

"What?" Jake frowned. That didn't seem likely, and he was scared to hope. "How?" With the back of his hand, he wiped away the sweat beading on his brow.

"I've been working with her on this for a while, and—" Gabe stopped himself and sighed. "It doesn't matter right now. I'll fill you in later." He pointed across the highway, toward the beach.

When Jake saw two figures coming up through the interspersed evergreens blocking most of the lake view, his heartbeat quickened. Zoe and Chris were walking closely, slowly, with one of Chris's arms around Zoe's shoulders. Zoe's ponytail was disheveled, and there was something about the way she walked, like the weight of a wretched lifetime took the bounce out of her step.

Jake's mouth went dry. Swallowing, he glanced back to Gabe, incredulous.

His friend watched the women approach, hands in his pockets.

Jake's attention shifted back to Zoe. The soles of her tennis shoes—not her boots—softly padding against the pavement, and the black t-shirt she'd been wearing most frequently—not her favorite purple one—were just a few of the many reminders that she was different from the woman he'd first fallen in love with. Or was she?

After a few seconds of silence, Gabe met Jake's gaze again and shrugged. "It just sort of happened," he said, and even though Gabe smiled, it wasn't cocky and confident like it usually was.

Jake felt uneasy. If Gabe wasn't sure exactly what had happened, maybe it wasn't entirely a good thing.

"Just go," Gabe said, pointing toward her.

Wiping his shaking hands off on his pants, Jake took long, slow strides in Zoe's direction. Her eyes were locked on the ground, and he could faintly hear the sound of her voice as she chatted with Chris.

He couldn't tear his eyes away from Zoe, hope and guilt mixing into a poisonous concoction inside him. If Gabe was wrong, Jake wasn't sure he'd be able to forgive himself for hoping she'd returned to the person she used to be, for letting this Zoe feel his disappointment.

Fisting his hands at his sides, Jake stopped in the middle of the highway. He needed more time to process what might be happening. But the moment Zoe's gaze met his, her steps faltered until, like him, she was still. He searched her face for recognition, for some indication of what was going on in her head, for proof that she'd returned.

His brow knitted together as he watched her bright eyes widen, her dark eyebrows raise, and her mouth open slightly as if she were about to say something. Three agonizingly long heartbeats passed before she moved.

At first, she seemed to hesitate, like she was trying to compose herself, but she quickly gave up and ran to him. A choked sob escaped from her throat as she jumped into his arms, wrapped her legs around his hips, and encircled her arms around his neck, gripping him so tight, so unrestrained, and with so much emotion he thought he *must* be dreaming.

Stunned into disbelief by the woman trembling against him, Jake wrapped one arm around her back, pulling her away from him slightly with the other. He needed to *see* her to understand.

Searching her eyes, Jake found the old spark he'd missed, the determination and tenacity he'd seen only on rare occasion over the past weeks, but most importantly he found recognition of the two of them and everything they'd been through.

Her teal eyes, red-rimmed and swollen, were no longer cast in uncertainty and frustration; instead they were cisterns of unbridled torment and longing, filling with so much emotion he couldn't deny the truth: she was back.

In his silence, her eyes frantically searched his.

"How…" Jake couldn't tear his gaze from hers, didn't *want* to. "I didn't even know…"

Pushing against his hold, she wrapped her arms around his neck again, leaving not a hairsbreadth between them. "I didn't want you to know," she sobbed. "In case it didn't work."

For the first time in weeks, he could feel her, *his* Zoe. She was more real to him now, shaking in his arms, than she'd seemed in weeks.

Though he tried not to, Jake's mind sifted through their more recent time together, some of the memories knotting up and burning deep in his gut. Suddenly, everything that had happened between them while her memory had been gone felt…*wrong*.

"Don't," Zoe said softly, her lips brushing against his neck. "Don't think about it, not right now."

Squeezing her tighter, Jake breathed her in, the scent of her hair, the feel of her body against his…*this* felt right, and he let himself revel in the moment.

"I don't understand how that's possible," Sarah shrieked. "How'd she get her memory back? And if she did, the last thing she's gonna want is all of you fussing all over her." Her voice echoed among the trees lining the road as she drew closer, the mumbling of the others drowned out by her scolding.

Hesitantly, Jake opened his eyes, reluctant to let Zoe go.

She leaned back, a fierce glint in her eyes as she looked at him. He never wanted to look away, never wanted to leave the sanctuary he found in her familiar gaze.

"You didn't give up on me," she said, offering him a brief smile before she pressed a hungry kiss to his mouth. "I'm so sorry I ran off. I didn't mean to. Clara tricked me. I heard Dani's voice, and—"

"Shhh…" Holding her against him with one arm, he wiped the drying tears from her cheeks with his free hand. "It doesn't matter anymore." Cupping the back of her head, Jake brought her mouth to his once more, his kiss slow and deep and reassuring, showing her all that he couldn't say. But then he stopped and frowned at her. "But please, don't do it again."

She smiled and made a disparaging noise at first, but then she frowned. "My mom—Dr. Wesley came to save me…but I killed Clara…"

Jake brushed a loose strand of hair from her face. "I know. Now she can't hurt you anymore," he said, trying to offer her a beacon of light in the darkness shadowing her eyes.

Hearing the others approaching, Jake released her, allowing her to ease her feet down to the pavement, and was relieved when he felt her fingers lace through his.

He gave her hand a gentle squeeze. "Will you be alright?"

Zoe nodded, eyes lazily blinking closed as she let out a deep breath. "I'll be fine. It's just a lot to take in."

"Zoe!" Sarah squealed, stopping short behind Jake, with Harper, Biggs, and some of the others in tow. The click of Cooper's nails on the asphalt preceded him as he loped toward them.

Zoe rubbed the top of his head. "Hey, Coop."

Gabe called the husky back, giving Jake and Zoe their last few moments together before the swarm.

Cooper obeyed, and Zoe straightened, quickly wiping any remaining wetness from her face and taking another deep breath.

Jake offered her a sympathetic smile and nodded behind him toward the bickering voices. "I'm not sure I'm ready to lose you to the mob yet." He wished he could hold her a little longer…forever.

Stepping into him, Zoe rose to her tiptoes and pressed another long, promising kiss to his mouth. "I'm not going anywhere," she whispered. "After all," she added, "we have to make up for lost time and all that…" Her eyes drifted to his mouth as she pulled her bottom lip between her teeth.

Jake groaned and squeezed her hand tighter. "Jesus, Zoe."

When she stepped away, she smiled impishly, making his heart squeeze with extreme happiness. But despite her playfulness, Jake could still see the tumultuous emotions roiling behind her stormy eyes.

"Zoe?" Sarah called again.

As the seconds passed, and Zoe didn't move past him to greet their friends, Jake leaned down, his lips brushing against her ear as he asked, "What are you doing? They're waiting for you…"

She let out a nervous laugh. "I don't want to start bawling again."

"Zoe! Are you ignoring us?" Sarah huffed. "You better not be. I'm not as nice as I used to be. I might just freak out or something."

Jake smiled and moved out of Zoe's line of sight so she could see her friends. "She was just collecting herself," he explained as he turned around to face them as well.

"What's the point?" Sarah asked, throwing her arms around

Zoe. "We're just going to make you cry again, anyway."

Jake smiled as he watched the two women hug, but their interaction was different than he'd expected. It was no surprise to him that Sarah was sobbing within seconds, but even though Zoe was trying to comfort her, she seemed a little hesitant.

"It's not that I didn't like the other you," Sarah blathered. "But it wasn't the same, and then I thought about the babies, and I know Harper needs you, and I need you. I'm…" She let out a despondent wail and sobbed harder.

"It's alright, Sarah." Zoe gave her another squeeze before pulling away.

Biggs smiled at Zoe, offered her a nod, and wrapped Sarah in his arms to soothe her.

Jake watched Zoe slowly grow more and more comfortable around everyone as they bantered back and forth, doing their best to make her feel at home and welcome once again.

What must it have been like for her over the past month and a half? He could only imagine how much more difficult it had been for her than for the rest of them…so much so that she'd been trying to get her memory back in secret.

Ky wandered up and said hello and teased her, but only until Harper came pushing through the crowd and swooped her up into his arms. "It's about time, Baby Girl. I was beginning to worry I'd never have you back again. I need another pair of hands." Harper smiled at Jake as he spun Zoe around.

Cooper barked and scampered around excitedly as they twirled, and Jake laughed at the sight of them, feeling like everything might actually be falling back into place.

With a final squeeze, Harper set Zoe back on her feet, then smiled and kissed her forehead. "Hurry up and say your hellos, I have work for you to do."

"Gee, thanks." Zoe returned his smile, but faltered when she noticed Sam and Tavis standing on the outskirts of the group.

Jake's heart skittered a bit. He was surprised when Zoe simply nodded to Tavis, then shifted her attention to Sam as a broad grin filled her face.

Excitement enlivened Sam's eyes, though he offered her a casual smile.

"Drawing tonight?" Zoe asked him, and Sam gave her a quick nod before they were swallowed up in the excitement of the group. Sanchez offered Zoe a tight-lipped hello, allowing a slight smile to curve her lips, and Sarah rejoined them after she'd had a moment to compose herself.

After a few minutes passed, Chris came to stand beside Jake. The two of them watched the crowd of their friends with their happy faces and listened to their incessant chatter as they asked Zoe questions about what had happened to her, what it had been like, and what Gabe had done to help her.

"Any idea where Jason and Dani are?" Jake asked Chris, knowing they were the two people Zoe needed to see the most.

Chris placed her hands on her hips. "Sanchez contacted everyone; they should be here soon."

"Thank you for helping her," Jake said quietly. When Chris looked at him, he gave her a grateful nod.

Resting her hand on Jake's arm, Chris said, "I'm just glad I could be there. I—"

When she paused, Jake followed her gaze. Jason was wading through the group, his face uncharacteristically expressive as he drew closer to Zoe. Just as she noticed him and turned around, Jason wrapped his arms around her, and everyone grew silent, watching. Even Jake found it difficult to look away.

Jason's eyes were closed as he held onto his sister. "Don't ever do that to me again," he said so quietly that Jake could barely hear him.

Zoe wound her arms around her brother's back. When Jake noticed her body quaking in Jason's arms, Jake, Chris, and everyone else turned to leave the siblings in a silent reunion that was long overdue.

22

DANI

MAY 7, 1AE

Lake Tahoe, Nevada

"*But I don't* want *to!*" Annie whined in my head. "*It's* cold*!*"

I knelt in front of her on the sandy beach and reached for her little hands. We were both wearing swimsuits; mine was a purple-and-white-striped bikini and Annie's a one-piece covered in inch-wide neon polka dots. I'd "scavenged" them from the tourist shop in the lodge, thinking that "going swimming"—ahem, washing the months of filth off Annie—would be the perfect way to stay out of Jason's hair while he, Grayson, and Sanchez spent the morning meeting with Holly, Hunter, and a few others from the Tahoe clan. They were discussing the possibility of setting up some sort of self-reliant, self-sustaining community together on the coastal farmlands.

As I stared out at the lake, I was just grateful that it was a moderately balmy day. Not that the high-sixties air temperature did anything for the *extremely* cold water, but the sunshine was a nice perk. I'd stuck my toes into the lake, and I had to agree with the little girl; it was *freezing*.

"Annie, sweetie, remember to use your words," I told her.

She'd only spoken out loud a few times since I'd practically adopted her the previous afternoon, and even when she had, she'd only used one or two words at a time. I feared that the months she'd gone without actually speaking had hindered her ability to use human language…but not as much as I feared that she'd lost her humanity completely.

It was clear that she'd embraced being a drifter wholeheartedly, but she didn't feel quite so far gone as Scott had, like she'd somehow managed to find a happy medium between embracing the ability to drift into other creatures' minds and rejecting drifting altogether—something Ralph had believed impossible.

"Cold!" Annie said, crossing her arms and stomping her foot. Zoe—*old* Zoe—would have backed her up, possibly arguing that dirty and stinky was better than clean if frigid water *had* to be involved in the bathing process.

I sighed. "Believe me, Annie, I know. But I promise, I'll be right beside you."

Annie stuck her lower lip out in a pout. When I didn't react, didn't relent, she sucked it in between her teeth. *"Snowflake"*—I assumed she was referring to the female wolf I'd met in the woods who'd been more or less taking care of Annie—*"says I have to do what you say."*

At least I've got the wolf's support… "Great! Awesome! Okay, let's get cleaned up, hmmm?"

I released one of Annie's hands and stood, walking with her to the water's edge, where I'd set my handy bottle of all-in-one shampoo, conditioner, and body wash. It smelled like tropical fruit, which was a whole lot better than Annie's current eau-de-wolf-musk scent.

I glanced over my shoulder, giving Carlos a quick thumbs-up; he was sitting on the beach about a dozen yards back, his partially restrained and still-filthy sister, Vanessa, sitting beside him chattering nonstop to her imaginary friends, which seemed to include her mom, her other brother, Jesse, and someone named "Rosie"—

all of whom Carlos assured me were deceased. Which wasn't creepy or anything…

Looking down at the little girl holding my hand, I raised my eyebrows and grinned as widely as I could to show her how excited I was. "Alright, we're going to run in, dunk our heads, then run back out as quickly as we can, okay?"

Smiling wide enough that her chubby cheeks appeared even fuller, Annie nodded.

"Okay! Ready…" I crouched down like I was getting ready to run a race. "Get set…" I met her eyes, grinning with genuine anticipation. I was actually starting to have a little fun. "Go!"

Giggling and squealing and gasping, we lunged into Lake Tahoe side by side, ducked our heads under the water to wet our hair, then scrambled back out of the lake.

"Oh my God…oh my God…oh my God," I said, shivering and rubbing my arms.

Annie was doing the same, all the while looking up at me and giggling.

I bent over to retrieve the bottle of suds and flipped the top open, squirting a hearty dollop onto my palm. "Let me get your hair soaped up first, okay? Then I'll let you do the rest while I wash myself." I didn't really think I needed to explain the whole bathing process to her—Annie was a little wild and young, but she wasn't an imbecile—but I wanted to speak to her as much as possible, to help her remember what it was like to interact with people who weren't Vanessa. Everyone was wary around my brand-new, unrequested wild child, and I desperately wanted her to fit in, to be accepted, and to *not* be alone for the rest of her life.

Annie nodded, accepting my washing routine without argument.

It seemed to take ages to wash her hair. I lathered the liquid soap up until it formed a grimy, fruity helmet around her head, then dropped my hands to my sides and sighed. "I hate to say it, kiddo, but we might have to have a round two."

Annie didn't seem upset by the idea; she simply stared up at me and blinked her big blue eyes every few seconds. I thanked my lucky stars that she wasn't a complainer. The whole insta-kid situation would have been a lot worse if she had been.

About ten minutes later, we were in the middle of our final, icy rinse, when Sanchez's voice reverberated in my mind. *"Come to the highway…we're between the lodge parking lot and the campground parking lot. Zoe's back."*

Head barely above water, I froze. *Zoe's back…from where?*

A heartbeat later, I thought, *maybe*, that I understood. *Does she mean that Zo—*my *Zo—is back?* Heart racing, I spun around to look at Carlos. "Did you hear—"

"Sanchez? Yeah." He stood, brushing off the back of his jeans before reaching down to grab his sister's wrist bindings and pulling her up to her feet as well.

"Do you think—does she mean…?"

Carlos shrugged. "Only one way to find out."

"Come on, Annie. Time to go." I captured her hand and pulled her back to the beach, ignoring my shivers as we raced across the sand toward Carlos and Vanessa.

"Can you take her?" I asked, holding Annie's hand out to Carlos. I glanced at his sister, who was quiet for once as she stared down at the freshly clean little girl I'd uncovered under all of the dirt, then back at him. "Dry her off and—and—" I shook my head, incapable of thinking clearly. I was just too damn excited. *Zoe's back….*Zo *is back!*

"Yeah, it's fine. Go," Carlos said. He pulled Annie's hand out of mine and gave my shoulder a little shove, pushing me in the direction of the lodge's parking lot. "I got this."

"Thanks!" I called over my shoulder as I started to run. I didn't think my legs had ever moved so quickly, especially not on bare feet.

Every other member of our group was clustered in the middle of the highway, looking like they were starting to disperse. Jake and Chris were walking away, toward the campground, Gabe close behind them, and Harper, Sarah, and most of the others were headed to the lodge. And between them, in the middle of the highway, Jason was embracing Zoe in a fierce hug.

The pavement was rough under my feet, and every few steps a tiny rock would jab into my skin, but I hardly noticed. "Zo!" I called. "*Zoeeeeeee!*"

I reached Zoe just as Jason released her. I threw myself at her, locking my arms around her neck and doing my own unique combination of laughing and crying.

Her arms wrapped around me, and she hugged me so hard that she lifted me off my feet. She was laughing, I thought, until I heard the distinct, rare sound of Zoe giving in to tears.

"Hey, D." Her voice was a rough whisper. After another tight squeeze, she set me down and pulled away. Wiping the tears from her cheeks, she appraised my appearance and smiled. "Did I interrupt something?"

"Huh?"

"You're all wet…" She glanced down. "And wearing a bikini."

I waved one hand dismissively. "I was getting Annie cleaned up—she's a little girl I found yesterday when—"

"I know, D," Zoe said with a small chuckle. "I remember."

I frowned, and then my eyes widened. For some reason that didn't make any sense to the logical part of my brain, I'd assumed she didn't remember any of the things "new Zoe" had experienced. In my mind, they were two different people.

"Everything?" I felt a surge of shame.

She nodded once before offering me a slight smile. "We can talk about it later."

Looking down at my feet, nearly rubbing a hole in the asphalt with my big toe. "Okay…"

"Hey," Zoe said, poking my shoulder, and I raised my eyes to hers. "Want some company down at the lake? I could use a little rejuvenation."

"Really?" I smiled wanly. "Yeah, okay. That'd be great." I didn't actually need to get back in the water, but I *did* need some alone time with my best friend. Perking up at the thought, I linked my arm with hers and tugged her in the direction of the lodge.

"Um, D, the water's that way." Zoe pointed to the lakeshore beyond the parking lot on our right.

"I know, but you need a swimsuit."

"But I already *have* a swimsuit…"

"I know," I repeated. "But camp is *so* far away—"

"It's just across the street…"

"—and besides, you could use a new one. You've had that old green bikini *forever*." I dragged her up the stairs to the lodge's front porch. "And I know just where you can get one at a freemium price."

Zoe laughed as I pulled open the glass double doors. "You're such a dork…I missed you."

I forced a smile and met Zoe's eyes briefly. "Me too, Zo. Me too."

Zoe and I managed to splash around in the water for all of *maybe* a minute before running back onto the beach, screaming like little girls. Zoe stole my bottle of shampoo–conditioner–body wash and took an impressively quick "bath" using as little lake water as possible. When she finished, she took lurching steps up the beach and huddled in an oversized towel—also liberated from one of the shops in the lodge—beside me on the bright yellow hull of an overturned kayak. I was already snuggled cozily in my own towel.

"So…still hate cold water?" I asked.

Zoe shrugged. "Yes and no," she said, wrapping her towel

more tightly around herself. "But mostly yes."

"Zo, I—" I hesitated, closed my mouth, then took a deep breath and opened it again. "I know I probably could have been a better friend to her—you—" I shook my head and frowned. "To the other you…the not *you* you." I stared out at the lake's shimmering surface, squinting slightly from a thousand shards of reflected sunlight.

"D…"

"It was just…she wasn't *you. You* weren't you." Again, I shook my head, irritated at myself for fumbling so much with my words. "But I should have treated you like I normally would have, and I didn't, and I feel like such a jerkface." I sighed. "I don't think that made any sense."

Zoe laughed halfheartedly, ending in a sigh of her own. "It's okay, D." She stared down at her toes sticking out from beneath her towel. "It's not like I knew any different anyway," she said. "And it's not like anyone else treated me like, well, *me*."

Except for Jake, I thought, recalling the handful of mornings I'd seen Zoe emerging from his tent recently. *He* seemed to have figured out a way to see her as the Zoe he'd fallen in love with. So why hadn't I been able to do the same?

Zoe closed her eyes and tilted her face up to the sun, basking in its warm rays. "Looks can be deceiving," she said, her voice so quiet that I barely heard her. "Jake tried, but I knew the whole time that it wasn't the same for him…as much as he wanted it to be." She snorted and let her head fall back. "At least I know he prefers *this* me."

"Did you guys…you know…?" I asked, wiggling my eyebrows suggestively.

Her head shot up, and she looked over at me, biting the inside of her cheek like she always did when she was anxious.

"Oh my God, you *did*." I giggled and blushed and really tried to stop, but I just couldn't. "Wow, that's just…wow. Talk about an awkward first time…"

Zoe shook her head. "It wasn't our first time, but it *was* a little awkward, at least for him." She rested her cheek on her knees. "I think I sort of blindsided him…I'm not sure he would've done it otherwise. I felt sorta bad."

"Wait, what? *When?*" I waved my hand. "Don't feel bad," I said with a laugh. "I'm sure he didn't mind." I took a breath before babbling on. "But I was only gone for like a week…when the heck did you guys have time for hanky-panky—I mean, *before*?"

"It *was* a pretty crazy week." Zoe shrugged. "It's not like it was planned, but it happened the morning we left for the golf course. In fact, Jason had just come out to tell me—"

"Hold on," I said, raising a hand. "Your brother found you when you were *having sex* with Jake…?"

She barked a laugh. "God no! But I guess it was a little bit of a close call."

I snorted, then doubled over in laughter. "Oh my God," I gasped. "Could you imagine…"

"Ah, no, thank you." She shook her head and groaned. "God, that was such a horrible week. Jason was a mess, Jake and I were barely speaking after Becca showed up…we'd finally gotten our shit together, and then I had to run into Clara…"

"And your mom," I said softly, sneaking a glance at Zoe.

"Yeah, and there's that. I'm not sure I'm ready to talk about that yet…I don't know what to think."

I leaned in, nudging her shoulder with my own. "No prob, Zo. But you know I'll be here whenever you're ready." I wrapped my arm around her waist and rested my head on her shoulder. A few wet strands of her dark hair stuck to my face, and I blew them away. "Your hair is crazy long."

I could feel the muscles and bones in her shoulder shift as she strained to look down at me. "You want to cut it off for me?"

Raising my head slowly, I pulled away from her, staring at her with eyes widened by shock. Zoe'd had long hair the entire time I'd known her. "Shut the front door! What did you just say to me?"

She smiled, clearly amused. “I could use a change,” she said. “And it’s something I’ve been thinking about for a while.” She shrugged a single shoulder. “But if you don’t want to…”

“Oh my God, shut up. I’m totally doing it. I’m going to *cut off your hair*!” I squealed, clapping my hands together like a wind-up monkey. Almost as long as I’d known Zoe, I’d been bugging her to give shorter hair a chance, knowing she would look *amazing*. Now she would look amazing *and* it would be so much more practical. “This is going to be so much fun! Eeek…I’ve got so many ideas. We could do a bob, like this long”—I held my hand up to my chin—“or maybe—”

“Not a bob,” she said adamantly. “Not like *hers*.”

I pressed my lips together and studied her face. “Okay, got it. Not like your mom’s.” I raised my eyebrows. “Oooh…what if we did, like, an A-line cut, just touching your shoulders and a little longer in the front? It’d be short enough to not get in the way so much, but still versatile and—”

“Alright, D,” she said with a rueful smile. “I trust your judgment.” She unfurled her body and rose to her feet. “I saw a pair of scissors in the swim shop. I’ll go grab ’em.”

“Okay.” I narrowed my eyes. “But you better not back out…”

“I won’t,” she said, shaking her head. “*I* asked you, remember?” And with a smile, Zoe jogged toward the trees separating the beach from the parking lot behind the lodge. I stared after her until I could no longer see her.

Exhaling heavily, I slid down the side of the kayak and settled on the sand, pulling my knees up against my chest and rewrapping the towel around myself so all but my head and toes were covered.

Zo’s really back. Joy swelled in my chest until I thought I might burst, spilling down my cheeks in the form of happy tears.

She’s really back…my Zo. Smiling and crying silently, I stared out at the lake and simply felt happy.

Zoe returned a few minutes later, placing a pair of scissors and a brush on top of my upraised knees before sitting on the sand in front of me, her back to me. "Have at it, D. And for God's sake stop crying." But she said it with a smile evident in her voice.

I freed my arms from my terrycloth straightjacket and wiped away the wetness coating my cheeks. "I know, I know…I'm *such* a crybaby."

"It's alright, D. That's why I love ya."

I cleared my throat and moved the scissors and brush to the sand beside me before shifting my legs so I was sitting cross-legged. I straightened my back and started brushing the tangles out of Zoe's ridiculously long hair.

"Ow," she said when I tugged on a particularly stubborn snarl.

Breathing out forcefully, I said in a sing-song voice, "Which is precisely why we're cutting it…"

We fell into companionable silence while I continued to brush. Minutes passed with only the sound of dogs barking in the distance and seagulls cawing overhead.

"So," Zoe said, drawing out the word. "How have you been sleeping?"

I paused mid-stroke. "Why are you asking me when you already know?" I said softly.

"Because I'd like you to tell me." She paused. "I don't want to snoop…unless I have to."

I finished the stroke, then started to part her hair down the middle. "I thought you couldn't help it…"

Zoe started drawing shapes in the sand to the right of her. "I guess it's different now. I can shut it off a lot easier, *thank God.*"

I sighed in agreement. "Seriously." I quickly added, "No offense."

"You should've told someone about drifting, Dani." Zoe's voice was harsher than I'd expected, but not harsher than I deserved. "If I hadn't known…"

Setting the brush down on my knee, I smoothed Zoe's hair down her back and picked up the scissors. "I know." I closed my eyes and shook my head, wishing I could make the weeks of drifting disappear so I no longer had to remember how *good* it felt. "Believe me, I know. I'm just lucky that you were still looking out for me, even if you weren't really *you* while you were doing it."

I put the scissors down on my other knee and wrapped my arms around Zoe's shoulders, pressing my cheek against her wet hair. "Thank you for saving me."

Zoe cleared her throat. "Please just promise me you'll tell me if you need me…if you can't do it on your own, or if Jason nulling you doesn't help…" She swallowed loudly. "I can't lose you, D."

I nodded, messing up the smooth, damp curtain of hair I'd so carefully arranged down her back. "I promise," I told her before pulling away and picking up the brush again to straighten out her hair.

Minutes later, I'd snipped off over a foot of hair and was setting in to evening out what would eventually be a decently fashionable, yet practical, shoulder-length haircut. I paused and peeked over her shoulder so I could see the side of her face. "Do you want to see how much I cut off?"

"I don't know, do I?" she asked rhetorically.

I picked up a chunk and tossed it over her shoulder so it landed on the sand in front of her.

"Holy. Crap. That's like a foot and a half…"

I laughed. "I know, right?" Under my breath, I grumbled, "Now, if I could only get Vanessa to let me chop off that rat's nest she calls hair…"

Zoe snorted and started to turn her head to look over her shoulder at me.

"Hold still, Zo…unless you want a funky asymmetrical hairstyle."

"Oh, sorry." She faced forward again. After a long pause, she asked, "So, has Carlos told you anything about them?"

I frowned. "Such as…?"

"I was just curious if he shared his story with you, is all…what happened to his sister and Annie…and his brother."

My frown deepened, verging on scowl territory. "Jesse? No, not really. Before yesterday, I knew he had a sister…but that's about all I knew about his family." I shook my head slowly.

"Maybe you should ask him about it. I'm sure he could use someone to talk to."

"*You* won't tell me?"

Zoe shook her head, and I had to retrieve the brush to straighten her hair out…again.

"Please, Zo…pretty please," I said, my voice purposely whiny.

"If you really want me to, I will, but I think you should talk to him about it first. It's not really my place, ya know?"

I nodded and, realizing she couldn't see me, said, "Yeah, okay."

As I finished Zoe's haircut, my mind whirled with possible scenarios for how Vanessa and Annie had ended up living with a pack of wolves and wild dogs in the mountainous woods to the east of Lake Tahoe. Whatever the actual story ended up being, I was certain it wouldn't be good.

"Hey," I said as I approached Carlos. He, Vanessa, and Annie were sitting at a picnic table just outside the stable, snacking on beef jerky and packaged cheese and crackers. The trio had been easy enough to find, what with Annie's mind being one of the few human minds I could actually sense.

"Thanks for taking care of everything," I told him.

Looking up, Carlos nodded. He finished chewing before asking, "How's Zoe? Is she really back to normal?"

I laughed softly and swung my leg over one side of the picnic table to straddle the same bench Annie was sitting on. "She's good. Really good."

Carlos was sitting directly across from me, keeping a close eye on his sister, whose hands were still bound, but not so restrictively that she couldn't feed herself. His features were drawn, making him look older and wearier than I'd ever seen him. He'd been keeping his distance since we first arrived in Tahoe; I'd assumed it was because of the unexpected appearance of his sister, but now I suspected it was more than that. Though we were a few miles from the place that had hosted what was undeniably the most traumatic month of his life, we were pretty damn close. It would've been stupid to think his proximity to *that place* wouldn't dredge up painful memories…wouldn't haunt him.

"So, how are *you* doing?" I asked tentatively. "Being back here and all…?"

Carlos lowered his eyes, looking at the ground beside the table. "I don't want to talk about it."

The wind shifted, and I caught a whiff of the delightful odor that was so distinctly Vanessa's. I wrinkled my nose.

"You don't have to stay with us," Carlos said, meeting my eyes then glancing at his sister. "I know it's not the, uh, nicest place to be right now…and you should be with Zoe."

I raised one shoulder and half smiled. "It's cool. I got her all to myself for the first few hours. It's time to share." I shifted my attention to Annie, who had processed cheese product smeared all over the lower half of her right cheek.

She grinned at me, still gnawing on a piece of dried and salted meat.

Pressing my lips together in a disapproving line, I said, "You're a mess, you know that?"

Annie nodded enthusiastically.

I snorted and rolled my eyes. "What am I going to do with you?"

Setting the remainder of her half-eaten jerky on the table, Annie declared, "Full!" She squirmed off the bench and ran toward the three canines—two wolves and one dog—who were lounging in the woods nearby. They were precisely the reason I'd left Jack back at the lodge with Jason, who was, once again, meeting with Holly and Hunter.

"Don't go far," I told Annie, then repeated the same command to the canines, adding a request that they keep her safe and bring her back before dark. All the members of Snowflake's pack were protective enough of Annie—*young two-legs*, as they called her—that I knew she would be safe with them, and more comfortable than if I forced her to be around the other *human* members of my group.

When I turned back to Carlos, I found him watching me. "You're not gonna go after her?"

I shook my head, frowning the tiniest bit. "They'll keep her safe, and she'll come back…even if she doesn't want to."

"Listen, Dani…" Carlos hesitated briefly. He stared down at the uneven wooden surface of the table. "Annie's not your responsibility. You don't have to take her in and, you know, be her mom or whatever…not if you don't want to."

"I don't mind," I said, pretty sure I meant it. "It's not like there's anyone else really cut out to take care of a kid like her. Except for Ralph, I suppose…" I shrugged.

Carlos's brow furrowed. "Well, you don't *have* to, so if you change your mind, I'll—" He took a deep breath, then sat up straighter as if the breath had given him strength, helped him decide. "I'll take care of her."

Now, why the hell would he say that? I studied the handsome young man with world-weary features sitting across from me, feeling nothing but compassion and sympathy and the kind of love I felt for Zoe…and one hell of a dose of curiosity. "Who *is* she, Carlos?" She had to be *someone* to him, based on what Zoe had implied.

He laughed dryly and shook his head, staring off into the woods near where Annie had disappeared. "Just some kid we found…at the beginning." He glanced at his sister, his lips curving into a smile filled with regret. “Nessa and me, all we had was each other at first. Then we found Annie, and then my brother showed up…and then we made the mistake of coming down here.” He looked at me.

I tilted my head to the side and searched his guarded eyes. “So, why *did* you guys come all the way down here?”

Carlos inhaled and opened his mouth.

“To be safe!” Vanessa exclaimed, cutting him off before he could say anything. “Huh, Jesse?” She was staring at a space beyond the end of the picnic table as though somebody were standing there. She cackled for a moment, which seemed to be her go-to response to pretty much anything, then grew serious and started nodding. “It *was* mean of that guy to shoot you.” Her eyes shifted, and she glared at Carlos. “It’s not nice to shoot people.”

“Uh…” I frowned. “What’s she talking about?”

Carlos heaved a huge sigh. “Jesse, our brother, kept talking about this place in Tahoe where there were a bunch of survivors and shit. So, when we realized there was nothing left for us up in Yakima, we decided to come down here.” He shrugged. “Turned out this guy—Cole—had *made* Jesse bring us down here…like with mind control.” Carlos cleared his throat, his eyes becoming glassy, his gaze distant. “He shot Jesse when we got here—killed him—and then made me shoot at Nessa, but the bullet barely touched her arm. At least she was able to get away with Annie before I could really hurt her.”

I stared at him and his sister, at a loss for words.

“I know she’s a Crazy,” he said, turning his face to watch Vanessa continue her conversation with a hallucination of their dead brother. “But I *have* to take care of her.” He returned his gaze to me, his expression sorrowful but determined. “If that means I have to leave the rest of you…”

I reached across the table and took hold of his hand, strip of beef jerky and all. “Don’t be an idiot. You’re family.”

23

ZOE

MAY 22, 1AE

Petaluma, California

With my eyes closed and my fingers playing with the onyx fringe of Shadow's mane, I turned my face to the sun and basked in its warm rays. I groaned in springtime-euphoria. I'd been impatiently waiting for spring for months, and now, like everything else that seemed to have popped up over the past month, it was finally here.

Amid my impromptu sunbathing, I could hear little blackbirds chirping. I knew from the couple of hours Shadow and I had been standing like sentinels outside the feed store that the blackbirds were hopping around the parking lot, looking for dropped seeds in and around the discarded food bins and perched on the forgotten forklifts behind the store.

Opening my eyes, I watched them, careless and oblivious to all that had happened in the world. One blackbird in particular had decided we weren't nearly as threatening as the rest of his friends thought, and he was venturing closer and closer…only to fly away when Shadow flicked his tail. *Maybe next time I should bring my sketchbook.* While what I was doing was important—keeping my feelers open for any approaching danger—it was a good time to sketch, to document and write down what we were finding, what we'd seen, and what we'd learned about surviving.

Typically, being on intruder watch meant I needed to be on high alert, but now I was so in tune with my Ability—a result of all the electrotherapy sessions—that it was easy to multitask, at least so far. It had been over two weeks since we'd left Lake Tahoe, two weeks since I'd told Dani that my Ability felt different, and only now did I know to what extent. Now, as we neared the coast, it seemed that using my Ability had become effortless.

I could cast my feelers out for any unsettling minds that wandered too close. I didn't need my eyes to know when danger was near because I could sense people—their emotions, their memories…the essence of who they were. I could reach further distances, a solid mile at least, and I didn't have to worry about learning things others wanted to keep private unless I was purposefully looking. I could separate memories from emotions like they were oil and water. I could turn my Ability on and off at will

Along with my memory returning, I was able to get back into a routine that felt more…me. I still helped Dani manage the horses each day and helped Ky scout for danger up ahead when we needed to find a place to rest each night, but I'd also earned myself a spot on a scavenging team whenever an extra scout was needed. I'd resumed self-defense and archery training just as intensely as I'd been doing before losing my memory and helping Harper gather and organize medical supplies when the opportunity presented itself. I had a purpose again, but even though I felt useful, something still felt off…

Leaning against Shadow, feeling his coarse mane between my fingers as I idly combed through it, I gazed out at the lowering sun. I'd seen many stunning sunsets over the past few months—traveling through Colorado, Utah, Nevada, and now through Northern California—but this sunset felt different, like it meant something. I figured it was just my antsiness that made it feel different, because tomorrow, I would go home.

Home. It was a place I both longed and loathed to visit. Returning there was one of the most petrifying things I could think of doing, more disturbing than seeing a wall of corpses and more unsettling than having a gun pointed at my face.

And my dreams had returned, haunting me like they used to. Sometimes my mom had a face, but it was distorted and permanently etched in a sneer, her voice cold and flat and menacing. Other times, she resembled herself—Dr. Wesley—but the malevolent gleam in her eyes continued to disturb me, even when I was awake. But none of those dreams were as horrible as the truth. *My mom is alive. She created the Virus. She lives with the General. She has a family with him...*

I let out a frustrated sigh. I *needed* to go home. It was all I had left of my dad, and I needed to say goodbye, and somehow I needed to leave all the disquieting memories of my past behind when I closed the front door for the final time.

No matter how honorable my mom's intentions had been twenty-five years ago, she still killed billions of innocent people to save Jason, Dad, and me. She took Becca from Jake, Grams from Dani, and Dad from me...and I hated her for that. Part of me wondered how I could hate her when she was my mom, but the rest of me wondered how I could possibly forgive her. Was I even supposed to try? The questions looped through my mind, making it impossible to think of much else. Every time I thought I'd come to terms with my feelings toward her, thought I'd settled in to despising her, forgiveness and longing threatened to wash away all my anger and fear.

Shadow turned to me, nudging my belt buckle with his nose. He let out a chuff of air, and his impatience made me smile.

"Uh-oh, was I neglecting you?" His eyes blinked sleepily as I began stroking his sleek, muscled neck. "So sorry. What was I thinking?"

...about Mom and why I can't forgive her. I had to continuously remind myself that she was a horrible person. I couldn't just forgive her for what she'd done...what she was still doing. But it was never as simple as black and white, because I couldn't truly hate her, either. She was also the person who saved me, who helped save Dani...she was my mom.

Diverting my thoughts to something less unsettling, I stretched my feelers a bit and focused on the mood inside the feed store, where Jake, Chris, and Ky were gathering the last of the horse tack, grain, and assorted pet food we needed for the dogs and goats. Inside, the team's mood seemed pleasant enough, so I let them be, happy to be out in the sunshine on my own.

It was nice to get away from camp every once in a while—mostly because I felt like an ass around Tavis, no matter how nice he was about my momentary fickleness and mixed messages. Nothing had happened between us, not really. But I was kicking myself for putting everyone in an awkward position. And being around Sarah was hard, too. She'd been such a loyal, kind friend, and I'd gone snooping around in her mind, finding nothing to make me feel uneasy, and yet I still did. She wasn't stupid; she knew I was acting differently around her, and I hated that I couldn't tell her why.

Wiping the moisture from my brow, I glanced down at Shadow. "Is it just me or is it getting too hot in the sun?" He simply stared ahead, his head hanging languorously as his eyelids grew heavier. "Come on," I said. "Let's park it in the shade."

Welcoming any form of movement, Shadow perked right up as we headed to the shade of a few eucalyptus trees lining the side of the lot. I loosened Shadow's reins so he could graze on a small patch of weeds growing beneath the trees.

At the sound of a dull thump behind me, I glanced over my shoulder to find Jake loading two large bags of dog food into the cart.

"Is that the last of it?" I asked. It was his ninth trip to the cart, and I wasn't sure how much more we could really carry.

Jake grunted. "Close, I hope. They're picking out a pair of chaps to take back to Harper."

I pouted my bottom lip. "And they didn't invite me?"

Wiping his hands off on his jeans, Jake walked toward me, a heart-stopping smile curving his lips. I liked the appraising way he studied me now—my old boots donned, my tank top and jeans, my new haircut. He acted like he was still trying to get used to me being back to *me*, even though it had been a couple weeks.

"It's going to be a beautiful sunset tonight," I said, trying to stay in the moment.

"Yeah?" Jake came around behind me and wrapped his arms around my waist.

"You smell like a barn," I said, wiping away the loose alfalfa flakes and grain dust from his arms.

He squeezed me more tightly. "Is that good or bad?" It was so wonderful to feel him again…not the Jake who'd accepted the other me and loved me the best he could, but *my* Jake.

"Oh, it's good," I said, a devious lilt to my voice. I craned my neck so I could see him.

"You're so weird."

I shrugged. "I can't help it. It's true. It's nostalgic, I think…it reminds me of when we were back at the ghost town." I eyed him, waiting for the memory of the morning we first made love to click into place in his mind.

Shaking his head, he let out a soft chuckle.

"Wanna sit down and watch the sun sink behind the hills with me?" I asked.

His amber eyes met mine again. They looked molten in the dying sunlight. He grinned wryly. "Aren't you supposed to be working?"

"Ha. Ha. You're so funny. I can do two things at once, you know. Watching a sunset isn't overly exerting."

"Only two things, huh?" His smile broadened. "Can you do *more* than two things at once?" he asked, his voice holding a seductive edge that made it impossible not to smile back. He kissed the side of my neck.

"I'm determined to," I said, closing my eyes and wishing we could be alone for a few hours. "Ky will feel anything I miss…" I lost my train of thought as Jake brushed my hair away from the back of my neck, trailing his lips up and down my skin, bringing chills to its surface. I felt him smile against my neck, and I shivered.

"I wouldn't want to risk your spot on the scavenging team," he said with feigned seriousness. "You're in a probation period right now, and you're already failing miserably."

I barked a laugh. "Entrapment, huh?" Prying his hands from around me, I stepped away and turned to face him completely. Jake's response was a mere wink, and I shook my head. "You're a horrible tease," I said and dropped his hands.

Entwining my fingers with Jake's, I plopped down against one of the tree trunks, tugging him down with me. Only, he resisted.

I looked up at him. "You joining me?" I asked, tucking my hair behind my ear.

He raised an eyebrow and gave me a sidelong glance. "You're gonna get me fired from the scavenging team. I'm supposed to be working."

I rolled my eyes. "Doing what? Shopping for chaps to wear with Harper?" I let out a tiny laugh at the thought. "We can enjoy a sunset while they're doing that. Besides…" I patted the space next to me. "We can consider this research."

"Research?" he asked, lowering himself down beside me. The scent of him filled my senses again, leather and hay and something minty.

"We can experiment," I said, letting my voice drop to a seductive purr.

Jake positioned himself behind me, leaning back against the tree trunk and urging me to rest against him.

With one of his arms across my middle and the other draped casually over his bent knee, I twisted around to see the face that made my insides burn with welcomed desire. "We can test the multitasking facet of my Ability…see how much I can exert myself while staying focused and alert."

He chuckled, a low, easy sound that made it impossible not to swoon. It was so good to hear him laugh.

"You don't think so?" I let out a soft chuckle of my own and leaned back against him again.

"I think it's a great idea…when we don't have an audience."

"If you say so," I said, only partially dejected. "Maybe next time." There was something thrilling about flirting with Jake. He was so strong and serious most of the time that goading him was like tempting a lion; beneath his rugged beauty was a physical prowess and hunger that made him dangerously alluring.

Refocusing on the lowering sun, I marveled at the bright orange already streaking across the sky, at the clouds cast in a rosy hue. "Look at that," I said, gazing up at the frosted sky that looked good enough to eat. "I couldn't sketch something so beautiful if I tried."

I rested my head back against his shoulder, losing myself in the sound of his deep, even breathing and the strong, thrumming bass of his heartbeat. I sighed in contentment and closed my eyes.

Jake lowered his lips to my ear. "What are you thinking about?" he whispered. Before I could answer, his mouth gently brushed the side of my neck again, sending another wave of shivers rushing over my skin.

"Is that so," he said, his voice light with amusement.

I could never get tired of this… Opening my eyes briefly, I saw the sky was glowing poppy red, and I closed them again.

"You're tired." Tenderly, Jake brushed a stray wisp of hair from my face.

I yawned in answer, and snuggled up closer to him.

Abruptly, his body tensed against me, and I opened my eyes to peer up at him.

"Is it the dreams?" he asked.

Righting myself, I let out a dallying breath and glanced around at the parking lot—the blackbirds had gone for the night, and Chris and Ky were still inside, Chris's laughter carrying on the light breeze. "I'm fine. It's just taking some time to acclimate, I think."

Jake remained quiet, thoughtful, which meant he didn't buy it. He knew about my dreams about my mom; he'd been the one to comfort me almost every night since my memory returned, despite his own feelings about her.

The longer Jake was quiet, leaving me with only the slightly increased thumping of his heart against my palm flattened on his chest, the more desperate and terrified I was to know what he was thinking. But I didn't pry…I didn't peek. I already knew how he felt, and as much as I could understand his resentment toward my mom, I couldn't bear feeling it.

Finally, he broke the silence. "We haven't talked about anything since your memory's come back." His fingers brushed the exposed skin on my arm.

Lifting my palm from his chest, I studied the dirt on both of my hands, uncertain what to say. Every topic would lead back to my mom, back to more reasons for him to hate her.

"We need to," he said, a hint of frustration in his voice. "Something's upsetting you…is it *her*?"

Sitting up, I turned to face him. "The shit I'm going through now is nothing you can help me with. I'm sorry, Jake, but it's…it's complicated."

"Your mom…" He frowned. "I know—"

"I can't hate her Jake, she's my mom. I've barely even talked to her…"

Jake's eyebrows drew together, and he leaned forward, his muscles straining as he pivoted me completely around to face him.

"You'd be surprised how easy it is." For a brief moment I saw the images of his own mother, a woman with a classic beauty that was washed out by years of drug use.

Jake's features relaxed, and his eyes turned pleading. "But I don't expect you to, Zoe. I know what it means to you to have her back."

Of its own accord, my mind opened itself to his, searching for the truth in his words.

"But *you* hate her," I said hollowly.

Jake didn't have to say anything, I already knew it was true.

"What happens if I can't hate her for what she did?" I asked, bitterness riddling my voice…bitterness at my mom for putting me in this fucking situation, and bitterness with myself for seeking what, deep down, I knew I would never have: a real mom. "What if I never can?" I'd finally asked him the single most important question I'd been obsessing over for the past week, but I didn't avert my gaze, and I didn't close myself off from him. I needed to feel the truth, to know if things were going to change between us because of her.

Our faces only inches apart, Jake asked me very softly, "What are you afraid of?"

A dark, loitering doubt harbored in my heart refused to go away.

"That I'll leave? That I'll resent *you*? Why can't you trust me—us?" His voice was gentler than I'd expected.

"Is it so hard to believe that I would worry about you resenting me because of who I am? What happens if I forgive her? What happens if I want her to be in my life?"

Jake shook his head. "That won't happen."

"And how do you know?"

"You could never truly forgive her, not after what she's done to you, to your family," he said. "I know you're scared, this is all new and confusing for you…I get that. But you won't forgive her. You won't *choose* her."

"You don't know that."

Jake leaned back against the tree, his body rigid and a scowl on his face. "I know you. You won't risk everyone you love, everyone who's been there for you, for her." He paused. "You won't risk Dani." Slowly, his arms wrapped around me, and he pulled me into him. "I'm in this with you. We'll figure it out as we go."

His tone was so adamant, his gaze so determined, that I could only trust him, trust my heart, despite the difficulties I knew lay in store for me…for us. Allowing my hope to bloom into a small smile, I shrugged. "You're probably right, but I won't know for sure until after tonight."

In the shadows of the dusk light, I watched Jake's eyebrows draw together. "What's tonight?"

I hesitated. "Gabe's taking me to talk to her."

"So," Gabe said, standing in front of me on the same stretch of beach he'd constructed the last time he'd entered my dreams, before Dani, Jason, and the others had joined us outside Cañon City. "Is it all you expected and more?" He glanced around at the dream world surrounding us.

I smiled nervously, my emotions a dangerous mixture that had me second-guessing my decision to do this. "At least there's no unnerving replica of Dani sitting beside me this time."

Gabe laughed. "I forgot about that. You didn't like my Dani avatar?"

I shook my head.

Gabe waited for a moment, no doubt giving me time to change my mind and go back to dreams that didn't include meeting my mom for the first time while I was actually me.

Finally, he said, "Are you ready?"

Taking a deep breath, I shrugged. I'd come too far to change my mind when I was so close. "Ready as I'll ever be."

He smirked. "I've heard you say that before," he muttered. "Let's go find her."

Reaching out, I touched Gabe's arm. "Hey, Gabe?"

He stilled mid-step, glanced down at where my hand rested on his arm, then at me.

"Thank you for doing this."

Gabe smiled. "Say my name when you're ready, and we'll try to visit some of the members of the Bodega Bay Town Council before we call it a night."

I nodded, and the next thing I knew, it was late afternoon, and I was standing in my backyard at my childhood home in Bodega Bay. A young Jason swung in the tire swing hanging from the cypress tree next to the deck. The sight made my chest tighten. There were so many memories in that house, so much loneliness.

I watched as Jason swung lazily back and forth, oblivious to me standing there. He was a pretty cute kid for being such a butthead, and part of me thought I could see a little bit of my dad in him at that age, something I'd never really picked up on before.

But as strange as it was to be home and to be watching my brother as a small child, it wasn't true to life, making it more disturbing than nostalgic. The difference was that my dad was standing behind Jason, playing the role of the attentive father spending time with his son in the yard after a day spent in his woodshop. His work clothes looked true to life, and the tousled, light brown hair he'd always run his fingers through was appropriate. But Dad standing with Jason while he played in the yard was unlikely. If anything, Jason often went to the tire swing to get away *from Dad—at least he had in his later years.*

Scanning the rest of the yard, I froze.

I'd tried to prepare myself to see her, but my heart still thudded in my chest when I saw my mom sitting on the edge of the deck. She wore dark slacks and a white button-down shirt as if she had just come home from work herself. She was watching my dad and Jason so intently, with such longing, I felt it bleeding my soul.

Unlike the single photograph I had of her, she appeared tired, her eyes devoid of the peaceful glow that I knew once filled them.

Like she could suddenly feel my greedy stare devouring the sight of her, she scanned the breadth of the yard until she found me.

Remembering the emotional woman who'd saved me in the golf course, I'd expected her expression to give something away, to show some sign of the emotions that had filled her eyes but that I hadn't been able to understand at the time. But now, her expression was surprisingly blank.

Slowly, she rose to her feet and took a half a dozen steps toward me, her eyes holding mine the entire time. She stopped a few feet away.

I tried to think about what I wanted to say to her. I had a hundred questions, each of which I was scared to learn the answers to: Does some small part of her love the General at all? Did she ever try to come back to us? Does she regret everything she's done? Will Jason and I ever be safe? Does she love Peter more than us?

"Zoe," she said quietly in greeting. "You seem...better."

I nodded absently but wondered exactly what that meant. Better? Than when—the last time she saw me?

"Are you alright?"

I looked up at her, and the weight of my trepidation, curiosity, longing, and confusion surged to life, nearly overwhelming me to the point of speechlessness. Just looking at her made me want to cry. I swallowed thickly. "I can't believe I'm standing next to you... after all this time..."

Her face softened, and she offered me a weak smile.

I stared into her piercing blue-green eyes and wanted so badly to know what she was thinking, to know what she was feeling, to know that my presence affected her more than the guarded expression on her face allowed her to show, but my Ability didn't work inside the dream world.

After studying me in return, she made a sweeping gesture toward the back deck. "Do you want to sit down?"

With only a couple feet that felt like a mile between us, we started toward the steps of the deck.

"I like the new haircut," she said, her voice lighter than I'd expected.

"Thanks." It was an automatic response. "I needed a change."

"I can imagine."

I knew I'd caught her off guard by showing up in her dream, but I'd expected our first real conversation would include more than idle chatter about my hair. Maybe some tears or an embrace, but she was composed and hesitant.

Slowly, she climbed to the top step and sat down. She clasped her hands together and rested them on her knee like we were two strangers having an uncomfortable conversation. We were *two strangers, but she was also my mom, and I was her daughter.*

I sat on the second-to-last step and leaned against the railing. "I didn't know it could feel worse," I thought aloud.

She straightened as if she were bracing herself for a verbal lashing. "That what could feel worse?" she asked tentatively.

"The loneliness."

Her brow tensed. "I don't pretend to know what you've gone through," she said a bit tenderly. "But I'm glad you came."

I felt a rekindle of hope. "You are?"

She nodded. "I assumed that once your memory returned and you truly understood everything I've done, well, I suppose I assumed you would never want to see me again. So you can imagine my surprise."

"But you're my mom," I said a little breathily. "I've wanted to know you my entire life." As I sat there with sweating palms and a racing heart, she appeared mostly unaffected, and I realized she

was right—she had no idea what I'd gone through without her, how I felt now sitting only feet from her.

Needing to look away, to grasp onto my thoughts and feelings before I lost myself to them completely, I stared down at the vibrant redwood slats beneath me. Her version of the yard, her version of my family, was so much different than I remembered it. "The back-yard doesn't really look like this anymore," I said.

"No?"

I shook my head, picking diligently at a blemish in the wood grain. "The deck's sun-bleached now and rotting in some spots. When Jason left for the Army, Dad sort of stopped taking care of the place."

Remembering one particular night of clandestine adventures with Dani, I leaned back and over the length of the step above me, searching the railing for a part of my past.

"What are you doing?" she asked, sounding genuinely curious.

When I didn't see anything but smooth wood, I sighed, unsure why I'd expected one of my memories to be reflected in her dream. "Dani and I carved our initials in this support post one day." I laughed softly, bitterly. "Dad pretended to be upset, but I knew he didn't really care. He didn't care much about anything..."

"I didn't realize he would take my leaving the way he did," she said. "If I would have known—"

"You wouldn't have left?"

She looked down to her hands, avoiding my gaze.

"Would you still have left us if you knew Dad was going to be such a wreck?"

Straightening minimally, she gave me a brief nod. "I didn't have a choice, Zoe." Her voice was low, but pleading.

"What about now? We know about you—what you've done—and we're willing to take the risk. You don't have to stay with him, you don't have to be a part of it anymore...we can try to salvage our family," I said, my vision beginning to blur.

"I'm sorry, Zoe, but I can't leave. Peter needs me and I—"

"You would stay with them, the General and his son, and forget about us?"

She seemed to deflate. "I could never forget about you and your brother," she said. Her voice was thin and her eyes gleamed.

"Then come back..." I hated the desperation in my voice, but I couldn't help it.

She reached out for me, her warm hand gently clasping my shoulder. "It's not so easy, Zoe, you have to understand."

"Then tell me. Why? Why can't you leave Peter? Leave the General? Why didn't you come with me when you saved me from Clara? Do you love your new life, your new family, so much? Do you—"

"He's sick, Zoe."

My mouth was open, but there were no words.

"Peter needs to stay at the Colony, and I won't leave him. Please, don't ask me to abandon another one of my children, to leave him in Gregory's hands." She shook her head, a tear escaping down her cheek, and she swiftly brushed it away. "I won't lose another child because of my past decisions." She hesitated. "I'm sorry." This time her tone was a bit colder.

I nodded. Not in understanding, but because I guess I never really thought she'd come back to us. Otherwise she would've already found a way.

"Bring him with you," I blurted. "We'll figure things out... you're all we have left. I don't—"

"He has to stay in the Colony, Zoe. There are things he needs, things I couldn't give him if we were anywhere else."

I struggled to swallow the lump thickening in my throat. I tried to feel sympathy for Peter, the half-brother I'd never met, but he was nothing to me. The knowledge that my mom was sitting in front of me and refusing to rejoin what remained of our family was too painful to ignore. "Now that you have Peter"—I wrung my hands in my lap—"do you still regret leaving us?" Despite the drumming of my heart and the sound of my own voice echoing in my ears, all I could focus on was her answer.

Her brow furrowed. "Of course I do. I wish things had been different—that I could've watched you and Jason grow up, that I could've been a part of your lives. But I don't regret leaving to save you. How could I?"

Trying to ignore the burning ache in my chest, I latched onto my resentment. "Why did you even have kids?" I bit out. "How could you when you knew you'd never be safe? Now, everyone's dead or crazy, and we're worried about Monitors and the General finding us." My voice ricocheted in the stillness of her dream.

Jason and Dad were suddenly gone, and it was just my mom and me sitting together in a setting she seemed so out of place in, my future juxtaposed with my past.

"I understand that you're angry," she said softly. "I don't blame you."

Shaking my head, a whimsical thought left my lips. "None of this would've happened if you'd just stayed."

"You all would be dead if I had stayed. I had to go." I could hear her frustration, but I ignored it.

I reminded her of her own words. "You told Dani that Horodson would've found someone else to create the Virus even if you hadn't." I stood, unable to sit so close to her any longer.

"There are always what-ifs and maybes. I can't go back and change my decisions. Knowing you're alive means more—"

"Alive? Barely," I spat. "Everything changed the day you left, can't you see that?" Resentment made it difficult to speak. "Dad, Jason, me...we weren't a family, not really. Dad was never around, and Jason and I never had a real relationship. All I had was Dani. While you..." I could barely say the words. "You started a new family...with him.*"*

"Please understand that I'm sorry, God am I sorry, for all the pain I've caused you and your brother..."

"But?"

"But this is my life now, and I have to do what I can to make things right."

"Just not right with us," I whispered.

Her eyes shimmered, and her lips tensed as she swallowed. After a brief moment, she descended the steps and stopped in front of me. Hesitantly, she reached for my face. Her eyebrows lifted the barest amount as she wiped a tear from my cheek.

I closed my eyes at the feeling of her touch; it was warm and comforting despite my mounting anger, and knowing it was the last time I'd ever see her, I burned the sensation into my memory.

"Zoe, I'm so…" Her voice broke. "I'm so sorry I—"

"Please don't," I said and slowly turned away from her before I completely lost control of myself.

She made no move to stop me, and after I whispered Gabe's name, my mom and the disturbing replica of my home disappeared.

24

DANI

MAY 23, 1AE

Bodega Bay, California

It was the morning of the final day of our journey—*finally*—and I was holding open the stuff sack for our tent, waiting for Jason to shove the rolled-up mass of dark green nylon into it. Every morning, it seemed to be a personal goal of his to roll up the tent even tighter, to make it fill an even smaller space. I smiled.

"Watch this," Jason said with a smirk. He slipped the rolled-up tent into the stuff sack like the interior was lined with butter.

I stifled my grin while I pulled the sack's drawstring to close it tightly. "Wow…that's a real talent you've got there." I tossed the tent on the ground with our packs, saddlebags, and the other stuff sacks containing our sleeping gear. "You should start a tent-rolling league."

Jason crossed his arms and watched me as I pulled my hair free of its hair tie and bent over to smooth the wild curls back into a more secure ponytail.

I straightened and stared back at him. "What? I'm absolutely, completely serious," I said, batting my eyelashes. "You should totally do that." My eyes widened, like I'd had a lightbulb moment. "It could be a game in the Post-Apocalyptic Olympics!"

Jason's eyes narrowed, the corner of his mouth curving up just enough to reveal the hint of a dimple. "You're hilarious," he said dryly and started toward me. He stopped with the toes of his boots almost touching mine, and simply stared down at me. "So damn funny…" His gaze flicked down to my lips, then returned to my eyes.

I licked my lips, feeling the charge of desire building between us, electric and pulsing.

Annie giggled and ran between us, causing Jason to take a step backward. He broke eye contact with me, looking around camp before bending over to pick up our camping gear. Briefly, his eyes met mine, still burning with unfulfilled desire and so much damn promise, before he started toward the barn where we'd stored the wagon, cart, and tack for the night.

"We're sure Bodega Bay's clear?" he asked over his shoulder. "Absolutely sure?"

Taking a deep, calming breath, I told my libido to shut the hell up and grabbed both sets of saddlebags, tossing one over my shoulder. I had to jog to catch up with Jason.

"Yeah…or as sure as we can be." Last night, Gabe and Zoe had met with some of the members of the Town Council, Bodega Bay's ruling body, alerting them of our imminent arrival plans and double-checking how safe the area had been over the last few weeks. Around our breakfast campfire, they'd relayed what the members of the Town Council told them: they'd been doing daily sweeps of the area in and around the town, and they hadn't seen any "Lost Ones"—the local survivors' term for what we called "Crazies"—for over a month.

Jason shot me a sideways glance. "And there's still no contradictory reports from any of your scouts?"

I shook my head. I'd confirmed the information Zoe and Gabe had passed on with the animals in the area. My furred and feathered informants hadn't caught a whiff of any off-smelling two-legs for weeks. Beyond that, Ky and Zoe would be doing their usual mental sweep of the area once we were close enough, and that would hopefully provide double confirmation. Besides, if we couldn't trust the survivors of our own hometown, who *could* we trust?

We reached the barn, and Jason propped the heavy wooden door open, letting me enter before he did. He placed the stuff sacks in their usual place in the chuck wagon, his expression thoughtful.

I watched him for a moment before setting our saddlebags on top of our respective saddles. When I turned to face him again, hands resting on my hips, I found him staring deeper into the barn, his eyebrows drawn together. Worry was written on his face, plain as day; he never allowed himself to be so expressive when the others were around.

"What is it?"

He looked at me and blinked, his usual guarded mask sliding back in place. "What if we lead him there?"

I tilted my head to the side. "Herodson?" I frowned. "I don't think we will, or at least, I don't think he'll follow us."

"You can't know for sure."

Shaking my head, I exhaled heavily and moved to stand in front of Jason. I reached for his hands and wove our fingers together. "No. I can't know for sure." *And if Becca can, she's not saying anything about it.* I peered up at him. "I can't know *anything* for sure, except that I love you, and I want to find a place where we can settle down and be together"—I laughed softly —"with our crazy new family of superhuman freaks and just *live.*" I sighed. "I'm tired, Jason. We can't run forever, and we can't pretend that everyone else's safety is our responsibility, because it's not. The only people we're responsible for are ourselves."

Jason's gaze softened. "And Annie…"

I smiled. "And Annie."

"Have you seen Jason?" I asked first Mase and Camille, who were moseying around the Bodega Bay Riders' Ranch collecting firewood; then Carlos, who was setting up a stall in the stable to be a comfortable living-space-slash-prison-cell for his sister while Vanessa remained locked in the neighboring stall, chatting nonstop with nobody; then Chris and Harper, who were inside the ranch house, cleaning up the gory remnants of the attack that had spurred our early departure months ago so it was at least partially habitable for the few days we would be camping there; then Gabe and Sanchez, who were unloading gear from the cart and wagon.

But nobody had seen Jason for nearly a half hour, not since we'd arrived at the ranch.

I found Zoe just outside the stable's pasture door, rubbing down the last of the horses with Sam. Her hair was up in a short ponytail, and she was wearing her usual dark, fitted tank top, jeans, and combat boots combo, making her appear both harder and more laid-back than she'd been the last few years.

The weeks since leaving Tahoe had really been the only time we'd had together since the outbreak, and I was enjoying finding out all kinds of new things about my best friend. She was stronger, both physically and emotionally—instead of emerging shattered from a situation that would have broken most people, she'd come out more decisive, willful, and sure of herself—and she was more capable and confident than the Zoe I remembered, which made me smile. Art gallery and bartender Zoe seemed like a washed-out reflection of the vibrant, vivacious woman standing in front of me.

I leaned one shoulder against the metal door frame. "Have you seen your brother?"

Zoe's face scrunched up, making her look constipated, before she turned away from me to continue brushing Shadow. I knew that face; it meant she was hiding something from me.

"Zo…" Squinting, I visually scanned the part of the pasture that I could see while I telepathically scanned the rest of the pastureland around the ranch for Jason's chestnut gelding. When I didn't feel the unnamed horse's mind anywhere, I expanded my search. Only then did I find him—in town, heading straight for our home street. "He's going home? Why?" *And why isn't Zo going with him?*

"I don't know?" Without looking at me, Zoe gestured inside the stable, indicating the stall immediately to the left of the doorway; it was the same stall that Wings had favored during our several-week stay on the ranch during the winter. "Just go after him already." Zoe glanced at me over her shoulder, smirking. "You know that's what you're going to do anyway, and I'm not crazy enough to try to stop you, so…"

Nodding, I strode to the stall doorway, where Wings stood with her head stuffed in a bucket that I could only assume contained oats or some other tasty snack. She lifted her head just enough to look me in the eye, murmured *"Yum"* in my mind, and returned to eagerly stuffing her face.

I couldn't bring myself to disturb her well-deserved rest by re-saddling her and asking her to carry me the mile or so between the ranch and Jason's house. If I asked her, she would do it, but that didn't make it right.

"Enjoy, Pretty Girl," I told her before leaving her to munch on her oats in peace.

When I turned back to Zoe, I found her cinching Shadow's saddle around his onyx belly.

"Take him," she said. "It was a short day, anyway, and he still seems a little antsy."

I frowned, feeling bad about delaying Shadow's relaxation time, but after receiving *his* reassurance as well as Zoe's that he would be okay with another short trip, I nodded. "Thanks, Zo."

She flashed me a grin that looked just a tiny bit forced. "Any time."

Several minutes later, I was riding Shadow down the gravel driveway at a walk. I left the stable through the door leading to the pasture. *"Jack,"* I said to my German shepherd. *"I need you."*

"With Pup," he said, showing me an image of Annie, flanked by two dogs—Jack and Cooper—while she carried on an intense telepathic conversation with a mama loon, who was floating in the pond behind the ranch house.

I briefly looped myself into their conversation, hearing the bird express her concerns about how much lower her pond was this spring than it had been the previous year.

"I'm going to be gone for an hour or two," I told Annie, interrupting her interspecies conversation. *"Stay with Cooper…and don't go any further from the house."*

Annie responded with the telepathic equivalent of a pout.

"I mean it," I said, a warning in my mental voice.

"Okay," she agreed without any more fuss. I wasn't sure if she was so easy to manage because her mind was more attuned to a pack structure like the mind of a wolf because of how fully she'd embraced drifting, because she'd lived among dogs and wolves for months, or because she was simply an easygoing kid, but I wasn't about to complain.

I let her know that I was pleased, then put our connection on the back burner, so I could speak only to Jack. *"Leave Annie with Cooper and come find me."*

"Yes, Mother."

About ten minutes later, I was swaying atop Shadow as he lazily clip-clopped down my street, the usual coastal fog hindering my view of the bay on the left, of the road up ahead, of the houses on the right…of pretty much everything.

I'd been paying attention to the location of Jason's horse while I rode. He'd been stopped several hundred yards up ahead, presumably at Jason's house, but suddenly started moving further away.

"That's odd," I mumbled. *Is Jason going to* my *house?*

The only other logical explanation I could come up with was

that he was heading out to the new town center, the marina near the end of the peninsula beyond our houses, to let the Town Council know we'd arrived. I shook my head. The Council already knew we were arriving today, and had given us permission to stay at the ranch until we met with them the following day.

Which brought me back to the deduction that he was going to my house and gave rise to a hoard of questions, the first among them being—*Why?*

Shadow, Jack, and I continued on through the fog, following Jason's horse. When I sensed him stop moving again, I was certain about Jason's destination.

The shape of Jason's horse formed in the fog as we approached my house. He was standing sentry in the front yard, his reins looped around the deck's bannister. I dismounted a few yards away and spent several seconds attempting to puzzle out what Jason was doing *at my house*. And still, I came up with nothing…zip…nada.

I glanced down at Jack, who was sitting patiently beside me. *"I'm going in. Can you stay out here and keep an eye on things with Shadow and Nameless?"* The poor horse's moniker, or lack thereof, had become well known among the other animals, amusing them to no end.

Jack barked as he stood and started wagging his tail.

"Let me know if you sense danger."

He barked his affirmative.

I made my way to the deck stairs, pausing to pick a sprig of lavender from one of the bushes bordering the railing before making my way up the wooden steps. I tried the doorknob but found it locked and quickly hurried back down the stairs and around to the back of the house, where Grams kept the spare key hidden in a flowerpot on the back deck.

When the sole of my boot touched the first stair, the back door creaked open, and I stared up at it. The doorway was empty.

"Jason?" I ascended the stairs and crossed the deck to the open door, the wooden boards groaning as I took each step. I paused in the doorway, peering around the bright, cheery—and *empty*—kitchen and adjoining dining room. There was no sign of Jason, other than the door being opened…*which had to be him, right?*

I stepped over the threshold, feeling a little creeped out. The quietness was eerie, as was Jason's apparent absence, and not even the comforting combination of cinnamon, chamomile, wax, and pine scents could ease my burst of anxiety.

"Jason?" I repeated, a little louder. "Where are—"

"Upstairs, Red," he called, his voice seeming to float down the stairs and echo in the hallway leading to the back of the house.

I jumped. Pressing my hand to my chest in a vain effort to still my now-racing heart, I hurried through the kitchen and down the hall, my footsteps sounding too loud on the linoleum and hardwood. I made my way up the carpeted stairway, taking the first few steps two at a time but slowing as I neared the top.

"Jason, wha—" I stopped in the hallway just outside my bedroom, my mouth falling open as I stared at Jason through the open doorway. The little sprig of lavender slipped out of my fingers.

There, in the center of the room, surrounded by my antique furniture and delicate ivory and lavender decor and wearing a pair of dark jeans and a white button-down shirt that looked far too pristine to be a part of his post-apocalyptic wardrobe, knelt Jason…on one knee…smiling a small, tight-lipped smile that altered the curve of his scar. It was a secret smile he only ever showed to me and, even then, only on rare occasions.

My breath was nonexistent.

Jason's eyes seemed deeper, bluer, more intense than usual as he stared back at me. "The world's gone to shit, and the only time I feel anything anymore is when I'm with you." He chuckled, letting his dimple show. "The messed up part is, I feel better, *happier*, around you than I ever did back when the world was whole. I never thought I was capable of this—this…" He shook his head. "Of caring about someone so much that I would do *anything* for them, *be* anything for them…*give up* anything for them. But that's how I feel every time I look at you."

Those sapphire eyes blazed into me. "As far as I'm concerned," he said, "there's you and me…and then there's everyone else. You're the only one I refuse to live without."

I swallowed, opening my mouth and shutting it again without saying a word.

"Which is why I want to give you this," he said, extending his fist. He turned his hand over and uncurled his fingers, revealing a tiny wooden circle resting on the center of his palm.

A ring. Does that mean—

"I can't stand the idea of another day, another *minute* going by without you knowing—I mean really, truly knowing, deep in your bones—that I love you." He fell silent, seeming to wait for me to do something, to say something.

When I did neither, simply stood in the doorway, utterly dumbfounded, he rose and slowly made his way toward me. He stopped in front of me and gazed down at me, his eyes filled with so much warmth and hope and love and passion too much.

Tears welled in my eyes from the intensity of the emotions shining in those *blue* blue depths. "I—I…" I couldn't find the right words, probably because I couldn't wrap my mind around *anything* he'd just confessed.

He reached his hand up to stroke the backs of his fingers down the side of my face. "Happy tears, I hope…"

I nodded dumbly. They were the happiest tears that ever existed. They were the kind of tears that would run circles around smiles and giggles and laughter.

Jason smiled, just a bit, and lowered his hand. "I've never been religious, and I know it's not your thing either, but I also know how much you value your grandma's culture"—he touched the Claddagh medallion lying snug and warm against my chest, then lowered his hand to brush his fingertips over the black Celtic knot tattooed on my wrist—"so I thought this would mean more to you than any ceremony or vows." He raised his hand and once again opened it, giving me a better view of the ring.

Made from a pale golden wood that was almost the color of honey and striated with slivers of brown, the ring had been carved by a deft hand into a more intricate and delicate piece of jewelry than I would have thought possible. Just like the silver medallion I wore around my neck at all times—a gift from my grandpa to Grams on their wedding night—the wooden ring had been carved into the shape of two hands holding a crowned heart. A Claddagh ring.

I stared at it, wide-eyed and even more astonished than I'd been when I'd first caught sight of Jason down on one knee. "Jason, I—did you…did you *make* that?"

"I did." His voice was a quiet, low rumble, barely more than a whisper. "And this one." Again, he raised his left hand, but this time he stopped short of touching my face. Another ring, twin to the one sitting on his palm in every way other than its larger size, had been fitted around his ring finger. The heart pointed inward, signifying that he was taken, that his heart belonged to someone. To *me*.

Slowly shaking my head, I raised my eyes to meet his. "But when did you…?"

"I had to do something during all those nights I was on watch." He shrugged, dismissing what was easily the kindest, most generous and thoughtful gift anyone had ever given me as unimportant. "Might as well have been making something to show you that when I say I love you, I mean it…that when I tell you I want to be with you forever, not just right now, I mean it."

I wet my lips with my tongue, swallowing roughly before speaking. "God, I love you…and I want to be with you forever, too." I raised my right hand, reaching for the little wooden ring with shaking fingers. I was breathing harder than usual, my heart beating faster than was necessary, as I slipped it onto my left ring finger, the heart pointing inward. It fit perfectly.

The happiest tears on earth spilled over the brims of my eyelids, streaking down my cheeks as I smiled at Jason. I reached up, placing my hands on either side of his face, drinking in the wondrous sight of him, reddish scar and all. "*And* I want to be with you *right now*," I whispered, standing on tiptoes as I pulled his head down.

Our lips touched without any hesitancy, igniting a kiss that was filled with so much love and passion and wanting, that was so sustaining, so fulfilling, that I didn't think either of us even needed air. Jason's hands were on my cheeks and jaw, behind my neck, on my shoulders, snaking around my waist, moving wherever he needed them to be to pull me closer to him.

We moved a few steps in some direction and suddenly a wall was against my back, and I was being sandwiched between it and the hard heat that was Jason's body. His kiss was relentless, demanding more from me. Always more. His hands traveled down the sides of my body, blazing hot trails of desire that pooled low in my abdomen, smoldering, aching, needing. Those hands ended up on my backside, and with a solid grip, Jason lifted me, guiding my legs around his hips.

We'd been here before, like this before, but we'd been interrupted by approaching Crazies. There were no more Crazies in the town, and I would be damned if I was about to let anything else get in the way of us consummating the epic exchange we'd just shared.

"If you…stop," I told him between gasping breaths and hungry kisses, "I will…kill you…so many…many…times."

Jason pulled me away from the wall and spun me around, carrying me further into the bedroom. I already had his shirt almost all the way unbuttoned by the time he lowered me onto the bed, only missing the bottom two buttons, which had been wedged between us. I quickly undid the final two, and he shrugged the shirt off, tugging his undershirt over his head in one smooth motion.

That simple unveiling sparked a flurry of disrobing, our hands fighting to unbutton, to unzip, to pull off…until finally, there was no more clothing between us.

As Jason lay atop me, nothing separated us anymore—not fabric, not secrets, not unexpressed emotions.

"God, I love you so fucking much, Red," Jason said, his voice hoarse. "So fucking much." With a grunt, he shifted his hips, and there was no more speaking, no more thought. There was only the two of us and the feeling of our bodies being joined together. Nothing else—*nobody* else—mattered. Just him and me. Together.

"So…what do I call you now?" I asked, snuggling closer against Jason's side as he wrapped the pale, vine-embroidered comforter and ivory sheets more tightly around us both. I felt like every bone and muscle in my body had been replaced with jelly—happy, tingly, satisfied jelly.

"Hmmm…" Laughing softly, he pressed his lips to the top of my head. "I know it's crazy, but…how about 'Jason'?"

I turned my face up to his, pretending to glare. "You know what I mean." Lowering my head, I rested my cheek on the firm muscle below his collarbone. "Are you still just my boyfriend, or are you my uber-boyfriend? My perma-boyfriend? My *partner*?" I wrinkled my nose, not liking the sound of the last.

"Husband?" Jason said, his voice so quiet that the single word was barely audible.

I gulped, and my heart rate quadrupled. "Husband," I repeated just as quietly. "Which would make me—"

"My wife," Jason said, louder and sounding more sure of himself.

I glanced up at him, and when I saw the sheer contentment softening his features, my heart soared. I couldn't stop smiling. I grinned so wide and for so long that my facial muscles ached and my lips trembled.

Minutes passed with nothing but the muffled sounds of our hearts beating and our slowing breaths, until finally, Jason sighed. "We've been gone for hours, and it'll be getting dark soon. We should get back."

I looked up at his face, resting my chin on his shoulder. "Can't we stay here for the night? I mean, isn't this technically our wedding night?" I giggled. "Shouldn't we stay here and do wedding night things?"

Closing his eyes and tensing his features into a pained expression, Jason groaned. "If only we could. But what if something happened to the others while we were—"

"No, no…you're right. Of course you're right." I frowned, disappointed that our moment of alone time would be so short-lived…memorable, but short-lived. I kissed his shoulder, then his neck and his jawline, and finally his lips. "Come on," I said, sitting up and tugging the blankets off of Jason in the process. "Let's go."

Ten minutes later, we were walking out the front door. Jason paused just outside the door, pulling a key out of the front pocket of his jeans and using it to lock the deadbolt.

I raised my eyebrows in a silent question.

"Your grandma kept a spare key in a flowerpot," he said. "Sort of an obvious hiding place."

I raised one shoulder, dropping it quickly. "Seemed like a good idea at the time…not that it matters anymore." Wrapping my arms around my middle, I turned to stare out at the fog blocking the view of the harbor.

Jason stepped up behind me, covering my arms with his as he hugged me from behind.

"I miss her so much," I said, my voice tight with sorrow, and I knew Jason would understand that I was talking about Grams.

"I know."

We stood like that for minutes, remembering those we'd lost, until finally, Jason released me and stepped to the side. He took hold of my hand and raised it slightly, looking down at my ring finger. "Do you like it?" There was hesitancy in his voice, hesitancy and a hint of worry.

I looked at him, widening my eyes in surprise. "Jason…I *love* it. More than I can ever express. I don't think I could ever come up with a gift that'll mean so much to you."

Jason gave my hand a squeeze. "You already have, Red."

I offered him a small, bashful smile and felt my cheeks heat.

Hand in hand, we descended the steps leading down to the front yard, and I was happier than I'd ever thought was possible. We led the horses back toward the ranch, Jack loping ahead, frolicking around bushes and between houses and cars that had been parked so long that most probably wouldn't start even if they had enough fuel.

The sun was just beginning to slip behind the rolling hills to the east when we started up the gravel driveway to the ranch. As we passed the rustic, old barn that stood slightly to the west of the stable, I caught movement out of the corner of my eye. I thought I spotted Annie, strands of blonde hair flailing behind her as she ran around the corner of the barn.

Annie giggled, and the bubbly sound was immediately followed by a loud "Shhh!"

I raised my eyes to meet Jason's. His face was absolutely blank…*too* blank. He'd planned the events that had unfolded at my house, leading to our spontaneous and unofficial-but-no-less-permanent-in-our-hearts marriage, and I was starting to wonder if that wasn't *all* he'd planned.

I craned my neck to see around the corner of the barn. "What's—"

But I didn't have a chance to get any more of the question out.

"CONGRATULATIONS!" shouted pretty much every living person I knew, which amounted to a small crowd of a little over a dozen people. Behind them on the faded red wall of the barn, the same sentiment was painted in enormous white letters, applied with enough embellishments—swirls, dots, and offshooting vines—to tell me that Zoe had at least had a hand in applying the finishing touches.

Again, I glanced up at Jason, then searched the small crowd for my best friend. I found Zoe standing between Jake and Sam, grinning like she was just a little too pleased with herself; I was almost positive I'd never seen her look so happy.

"Zo! You knew!" I said as we approached, pretending to be irritated though I knew she could feel every single wave of elation that poured out of me. I placed my free hand on my hip. "You knew, and you didn't tell me!"

Zoe's only response to my mock tantrum was to roll her eyes. She raised her arms, holding a bunch of flowers out in front of her. As we drew closer, I realized they weren't just a *bunch* of flowers, but a *crown* of flowers—bright orange California poppies and white and fuchsia ice plant flowers, looking like little sunbursts with a halo of long, slender petals. Beside Zoe, Sam held up his own handful of flowers, which turned out to be an even bigger, if less colorful, botanical crown.

I couldn't hold back the ginormous grin that spread across my face, but I also couldn't seem to find my tongue.

Zoe stepped forward, lifting her delicate burden so she could settle the crown on my head. She spent a few moments rearranging the curls that had escaped from my braid just so before leaning in and wrapping her arms around me in a strong, heartfelt hug. Zoe'd always been a good hugger.

Placing her hands on my shoulders, she pulled back and met my gaze, her blue-green eyes shimmering. "I'm so incredibly happy for you." Her gaze shifted to her brother, then returned to me. "For both of you."

"Really?" I said, the single word asking the thousands of questions I'd held in over the weeks since we'd left Tahoe, all variations of the same: *Are you okay with me being with your brother?*

"Really." She pulled me in for another hug. When she released me and stepped back, she was grinning from ear to ear. "Now show me the damn ring." Her eyes flicked to her brother. "Mr. Grumpy Pants refused to let me see it before you did…even if he *did* use *my* pinkie to gauge the size…"

I held out my left hand, showing her the immaculately carved oak Claddagh ring, and gave Jason's hand a squeeze with my right.

As Zoe lifted my hand higher to get a better look at the ring, her lips parted and her eyes widened. After several long seconds, she turned her gaze to Jason, finally focusing on him for more than a brief moment. "Jason, that's…wow. It's stunning." She smiled faintly and shook her head. "Even Dad would've been impressed."

I looked up at Jason, too, expecting to see the gleam of emotion —sadness and regret—that usually shone in his eyes whenever his dad was mentioned, but I found only pride.

"Zoe?" Sam said, stepping up beside her. "Do you want this one now?" He held out the larger, paler crown of flowers, clearly hoping she would relieve him of his duty as floral-crown-bearer.

"Oh, right." Zoe took the circlet of flowers from him and turned an obstinate glare on her brother. "Don't you dare argue about wearing this. You put me in charge of organizing this shindig with barely a day's notice, and—"

"It's fine, Zoe," Jason said. "I'll wear the damn thing." But despite his words, he didn't actually sound annoyed.

Zoe took much less time placing Jason's wedding crown on his head. When she finished, she reclaimed my left hand and pulled me toward the barn door, and I, in turn, pulled Jason. The door was shut, which made sense considering that the bottom half of the "U" and part of the "L" from "CONGRATULATIONS" were painted on its surface.

Zoe led Jason and me down a path formed of two curving lines of rocks only to stop and face us when she reached the door. "Close your eyes…both of you," she said looking from me to Jason and back. I did so immediately, grinning like a goofball, but based on her irritated "Jason…" her brother hadn't been quite so compliant. "Thank you," she whispered right before I heard the barn door creak open, and she tugged me forward.

After a few steps, she stopped again. I could smell candle smoke and flowers and food—possibly baked beans or something with barbecue sauce as well as something fishy, but good-fishy, not stinky-fishy. Since I'd grown closer and closer to the animals, I'd lost my taste for meat, but I still loved seafood. My mouth watered at the thought of what kind of fish awaited me.

Zoe arranged Jason and me carefully, making sure we were standing side by side and facing the same direction. "Alright, guys…open 'em."

Opening my eyes, I stared around the barn's interior, absolutely awestruck. Bursts of white hung from the crossbeams, and it took me a moment to recognize them as windsocks and spinners of every conceivable shape and size, their only common trait their color. A long table had been set up in the center of the cavernous space and draped with several overlapping ecru tablecloths. Bouquets of colorful spring wildflowers like those in our crowns filled mason jars spaced in a line down the center of the table. Mini-bouquets and individual blooms were arranged around and between the makeshift vases, splashing color along the table in an artful, elegant pattern.

Another long table had been set up against the right-hand wall, and several sizes of colored glass cups and wine glasses had been laid out on one half, while an impressive assortment of liquor, wine, and beer was displayed on the other. There were large crystal bowls scattered here and there on the table, and it took me a moment to realize that they weren't filled with colored pebbles, but with hundreds and hundreds of pieces of saltwater taffy.

My mouth started watering; saltwater taffy was a treat I adored, and one I hadn't had since *before*… "Where'd you get all of this, Zo?" I turned to her, eyes wide with wonder.

She snickered. "Let's just say that I had to get creative with my shopping…and that antique stores aren't people's first—or second or third—stop when it comes to scavenging." She gestured behind us, and both Jason and I turned to see that another long table had been set up beside the barn door, this one holding up a couple bowls and a platter of food. "We've got some more stuff coming, but this should get the party started." She leaned in closer to me, feigning a whisper. "And yes, D, that's trout, breaded and fried and too damn spicy, just the way you like it."

"Where—who—"

Zoe smiled. "Jake and Carlos took Annie to the trout farm while you were gone." She shrugged. "They said there were so many fish they could practically scoop 'em out with their bare hands." She waved her hands dismissively. "Enough of this, though. It's time to pop open the Champagne." She started toward the booze table, calling over her shoulder, "Come on in, guys!"

I looked back at the doorway to watch my friends pour into the barn, feeling happier and luckier and more alive than I'd ever felt before. Grinning, I shot Jason a sideways glance, earning another of his secret smiles, and before our friends could swarm around us, I mouthed, "I love you."

Jason lowered his head and pressed his lips to mine, and the barn erupted in hoots and cheers, making it sound like there were three times as many people as there actually were. When he broke the kiss, he rested his forehead against mine, and whispered, "I love you, too."

25

ZOE

MAY 24, 1AE

Bodega Bay, California

"Come, Zoe." The faceless woman was pulling me, her long fingers wrapped tightly around my wrist.

"No!" I shouted at her, trying to tug my arm away. My heart was beating so wildly I struggled to breathe. "Let go, please!" My little-girl legs were too weak against the strong hold she had on me, and they skittered on the ground as she dragged me along.

I held my breath and, with all the willpower I had in me, tugged my arm free.

The woman froze, turned, and stared down at me, her featureless face somehow menacing. "I said come, now!" She was furious, and I knew, deep in my soul, that she was going to kill me.

"What are you going to do to me?"

She only laughed, an icy, detached sound that sent a wave of dread over me, making my blood turn cold. "I need you..."

I whimpered. "For what?"

"You ask too many questions," she growled. "Shut up!"

Choking sobs burst from my chest, my throat. "Please don't hurt me," I begged. "I'll be good. I promise. I won't ask any more questions."

"It's too late for that." With a final tug, the faceless woman flung me into a dark room and slammed the door. The air seemed to thicken, and I grabbed at my throat, gasping. The inky darkness swallowed me. As I flailed, I watched my outline come in and out of view, like I was only partially in existence.

As the dream changed, my little sundress began to glow. My hands tingled, and I held them up in front of my face. They grew before my eyes, my palms getting bigger, my fingers longer.

Suddenly, light was shining all around me, and I was in a white, empty room. I stared down at my adult body, my little sundress exchanged for cargo pants and combat boots. I sighed with relief.

Hearing the clearing of a throat, I glanced up. I was standing in a room with my mom. A decrepit boy stood beside her, a hungry, maniacal gleam in his black eyes. He smiled, his teeth yellowed like his skin.

"Peter," my mom said. "This is your sister, Zoe. Her blood is going to save you."

His smile broadened.

"Be a darling and tie her up..."

I felt the color drain from my face. "My blood?"

My mom waved my question away as she glanced down at the clipboard in her hands. "You're my greatest experiment," she said, her casualness unnerving. "Peter, please..." my mom gestured to me, and the boy strode toward me.

I tried to step back, but my feet were glued to the ground. My heartbeat quickened. When I looked up, Peter was only inches from me, so I raised my hand to stop him. "Get away from me!"

But he kept coming, emitting a sinister laugh.

"Peter, don't do this," I pleaded, but there was nothing I could do, nowhere I could go. Before I knew what was happening, his

fingers skewered my chest, and the burning sensation of five sharp blades cutting into my flesh and bone made me scream out in pain.

In the late, foggy morning, with my hair up in a ponytail and the crisp sea breeze nipping at the back of my neck, Jason, Dani, Jake, and I sat atop our horses as they clomped lazily down the highway toward my childhood home. My stomach was in knots; the longing and familiarity I often felt when thinking of home tangled with the increasing ache of grief the closer we drew to my street. Haunting dreams and restless nights hadn't helped my nerves at all, either.

But I was being good; I clung to what I missed about being home. I focused on the calming, muffled sound of the waves crashing against the cove beyond the cypresses lining the highway and the occasional call of the seabirds perched on the rocky cliffs.

"Are you okay, Zo?" Dani asked as Wings fell into step beside Shadow. The two horses craned their necks slightly to meet the other's stare, and I wondered what silent conversation transpired between them.

"Yeah, just mixed feelings, you know?"

Dani gave me a quick nod and reached out to squeeze my arm. Her fingernails were just a little bit dirty, and her hands were coarse against my skin, two things the old Dani *never* would've let happen. I couldn't help but smile.

"What's so funny?" she asked, her hand dropping back to her leg.

Shaking my head, I smiled. "I'm glad you're here with me, D." We'd been through so much over the past few months, and we were *finally* together. I couldn't help but think about how lucky I'd been. I'd crossed thousands of miles to be with her and Jason, and now here we were, starting a new chapter in our lives together.

I turned in my saddle and looked back at Jake. He and Jason were strategizing about something; I could tell by the way Jake was nodding and offering a word here and there, while Jason drew shapes in the air. *I wouldn't have made it without Jake.*

Facing front again, I couldn't help the cheeky grin that engulfed my face as I spotted an old pump house through the fog, peeking out from a bramble of overgrown bushes and scraggly trees.

"What?" Dani asked, unable to resist smiling even though she was clueless as to why.

A parade of childhood memories danced through my head. "Remember that place?" I asked, nodding behind her. We'd decorated it as our summertime hangout after fifth grade, our no-bullies, no-boys-allowed fort.

Dani turned in her saddle. After an amused sigh, she said, "Yep. No boys allowed."

I grinned in a nostalgic haze. "It's so overgrown now, I can barely even see where it was…oh, what about the hideout we made under Mr. Boogieman's deck?"

Dani burst into laughter. Our horses spooked at the sound, but only momentarily before they continued around the bend in the road toward my house. "That was short-lived…and not the *smartest* place to hang out," she said.

"Yeah, poor Mr. Bergman. I feel sort of bad now. But he was *so* creepy…" I turned to my brother. "Jason, do you remember Mr. Bergman?"

He scoffed. "That old guy you stalked one summer?"

"Um, he was the *boogieman*," Dani said, trying to sound affronted.

"Weren't you guys like eleven? Who believes in the boogieman when they're eleven years old?"

"Uh, he was *definitely* the boogieman, Jason," I said, mimicking my eleven-year-old self. I remembered that summer so clearly, I nearly laughed again. "Remember the nights he would walk around town all creepy and in the shadows…in a *trench coat*?" I leaned forward and patted Shadow's shoulder.

"He was on the town watch," Jason said from behind me. "You guys knew that, right?"

"Wait…what?" Dani said. "We had a town watch?" We both turned around to see Jason.

He shrugged and averted his eyes. "Yeah, it was pretty much just Bergman."

"Oh, well…it's Bodega Bay. We had to do *something* to keep ourselves busy," I said, smiling as a wave of memories, of other Zoc-Dani adventures, bloomed to life.

We'd just gotten off at the bus stop and were walking home one afternoon when Kenny Monroe, the boy I had the biggest *crush on, ran up and stopped in front of us.*

Dani and I turned to one another and exchanged confused expressions for a moment, and when I turned back to Kenny, he kissed my cheek before running ahead, disappearing around a bend in the road. I barely had time to even comprehend what had happened.

Then there was the time in eighth grade, when Grams had to drive all the way to Tomales to pick us up after school. I'd gotten into another *fight, and Dani and I had missed the bus home. Grams had been angry, but once she learned that I'd only been protecting Dani from the Nasty Neilson triplets, the gleam in Grams's eyes contradicted her chiding words, and she offered me a silent nod in gratitude.*

"Good ol' Mr. Bergman." Dani sighed and shook her head.

"Yeah, he was a trooper," I said. "I'm sure he knew we were following him around, but he didn't say anything."

"Grams put a stop to that adventure real quick," Dani said, an unmistakable longing in her voice. Out of nowhere, she laughed. "Do you remember how pissed she was? I guess it wasn't very nice to tell everyone he was an evil monster who ate little kids."

Laughing, I said, "No, no I guess it wasn't. Especially because I think Judy and her little sister actually believed it."

"So," Jake said, startling me. I hadn't realized he'd ridden up beside me. "You've always been this much trouble?" he said ruefully, his eyebrow arched.

Between Jason's smirk and Dani's dying laughter, I couldn't suppress my own amused chuckle. "Yeah, I guess I have been. That was a fun summer," I said, trying to catch my breath. My stomach muscles hurt from laughing so much, but my heart felt lighter. It was a great feeling.

Aside from the difficult times I'd had growing up, there were a lot of good times, too. But time was a funny thing; it went by so fast that things changed in the blink of an eye. It seemed I'd already lived three lifetimes—my childhood, my time in Massachusetts, and now.

Dani must've lost herself in thought, too, because she and I both grew quiet as we watched the memories from our past disappear in the fog behind us. Jake and Jason's low chuckles and conversation were all that filled our silence.

My heartbeat quickened as my house came into view through the mist, and even the talk among the men quieted. The house—faded blue and weather-worn—was exactly how I remembered it, if a little more lonely and bleak.

With Dani and me in the lead, we clomped up the driveway, bringing Wings and Shadow to a stop outside the backyard fence. "Well," I breathed. "Shall we?"

Dismounting, I wiped my clammy palms on my jeans and walked toward the gate, slowly opening it and paying little attention to the others as I walked through. I led Shadow into the yard, and wrapped his reins around his saddle horn so he was free to roam among what little amount of grass and weeds were growing, before looking up at the house.

The others came into the backyard after me, but I was too busy losing myself in a rush of memories. I could almost picture Jason mowing the side lawn, cursing the tire swing for being in his way. I easily imagined Dani and me lying out on the deck, sunbathing in the only corner that wasn't completely covered in tree shadows, begging the sun god for just a few more minutes, and us eating our lunches at the outside table, music blasting from my stereo.

Stepping up onto the first stair of the deck, I thought of my dream two nights ago, the night I met my mom. The memory stung, but it also reminded me of something. I bent forward, searching beneath the railing for the carving Dani and I had etched into the wood over a decade ago. In a brief moment of panic, I'd worried it wouldn't be there. "It's still here," I said.

When I straightened, a smile pulling at my lips, I found Dani standing beside me, her smile equally as big. "You expected someone to search the entire deck, underside and all, for things to deface?" She scoffed, but merriment brightened her green eyes.

I'd told Dani about my dream meeting with my mom, but I hadn't thought about the carving until now. "No," I said a little self-consciously. "I guess not."

Glancing behind me, I noticed that Jake and Jason were a ways back, giving us our space.

"We'll be in the shop," Jason said, leading Jake toward the large shed our dad had built beside the house.

"So…" Dani eyed the sliding glass door. "You ready for this?"

"Yep," I said on an exhale. Taking Dani's hand in mine, I opened the door and stepped into my home, a place I never thought I would set foot in again.

The living room was minimally decorated, just as it had been when I'd left for Salem a few years back. A large, black sectional butted up against the left wall, and two matching recliners flanked the rectangular, cedar coffee table my dad had built. Our dusty, big-screen TV sat on the entertainment center against the opposite wall, remnants of my extensive movie collection stacked on either side.

With the exception of a few of my landscape drawings, there was no artwork on the walls, there were no family pictures. Although it had bothered me growing up, I understood now that it was probably a safety precaution taken by Dad, since he'd known why my mom had to leave…since he'd known about General Herodson's threats. It had been better—*safer*—if we weren't able to recognize her.

I shook my head at the husk of a life I'd lived, at the lies I'd thought were memories of my childhood—they *were* memories, but they were skewed and shadowed with more lies than I'd probably ever fully understand.

Dani was watching me, her face a careful, cautious mask that did little to hide the gentle waves of anticipation I could feel resonating around her. "It's weird, huh? Like it's the same, but different, too…"

Peering around the room, I realized that was exactly how it felt: everything was just as it had been when I'd left years ago, like absolutely nothing had changed. Only I saw things differently now, and the months I'd spent traversing the country with my friends had felt more like home than the dreary house I was standing in.

I headed toward the kitchen, poking my head through the doorway to find nothing out of place, except… "Someone's been here," I said with a mixture of dread and hope as I stared at the dirty plates in the sink.

"Jason and me—those are from the last time we were here."

My heart sank a little, but I shrugged and gave Dani a weak smile. Nudging her arm with mine, I turned and walked up the stairs toward my bedroom, each step bringing me closer to an impending clash of pre-Ending Zoe and new Zoe.

As I stepped into the hallway, I noticed my dad's bedroom door was closed, giving the hall an ominous feeling that made me slightly uncomfortable. I opened my mind completely, letting my feelers wander through the house in search of my dad's mind, but there was no one there but the four of us. I wasn't surprised. *He's gone, Zoe.*

Stopping in the hallway between Jason's room and mine, I stared through his open doorway. His room was a complete mess; clothes were strewn all around, the contents of his closet were spilling out onto the carpet, and his bedding was rumpled.

Recalling the dishes in the sink, I eyed Dani skeptically, hoping I wasn't looking at the aftermath of one of their sexcapades.

Dani rolled her eyes and raised her right hand. "On my honor as your best friend, I swear we've never done *anything* here. This is just the aftermath of hurricane Jason, when he was going through his stuff, figuring out what he wanted to take with him."

With a snort, I shook my head, ecstatic that I could easily block out those memories that I didn't want to see, and stepped into my bedroom. It seemed just as I'd left it; my queen-size bed was covered with my favorite purple and green comforter, a mountain of pillows were tossed messily at the head, and my cluttered desk seemed untouched against the wall across from it.

I vaguely registered Dani sitting down on my bed as I walked up to the corkboard hanging above my desk. I stared at the photos and drawings and notes I'd stuck to its surface over the years.

"There are so many memories," I thought aloud. "It's easy to forget about the good times." I wasn't sure which memories to hold onto…which keepsakes to take with me. Squinting, I stared at one particular picture, then pulled it from the board. It was the single photo I had of Jason and my dad, working in the woodshop.

I handed it to Dani. "Remember how upset my dad was when we took this?"

I heard the bedsprings creak as Dani stood. She drew closer to my side and linked her arm with mine. "I guess his aversion to having his picture taken sort of makes sense now…"

Nodding, I gently pulled my arm from Dani's and crouched

down to open the bottom drawer of my desk. I needed to get the items I wanted to take with me and get the hell out of the house. It felt too strange being there, too much like a bad dream.

The woodcarving kit I'd had since I was nine years old lay rolled up in the drawer, exactly where I'd left it. "This might come in handy," I said, setting it on the floor beside me. Prepared to close the drawer, I noticed the large, black canvas scrapbook I'd been putting together for Dani before she left for Washington, one that I'd obviously neglected in my rushed decision to move to Salem.

"I forgot about this," I said, pleasantly surprised, and handed it to Dani. "I'd meant it to be a project to work on when I came home to visit, since all my collage stuff is here. I guess I hadn't come back as often as I'd planned." I cringed, feeling a little guilty as I realized how absent a best friend I'd been over the past couple years.

Dani accepted it and stared at the photo framed in the window on the front cover—my favorite picture from our "boycott prom" camping trip, with our faces smooshed together, cheek to cheek, our hair concealed in beanies, and the ocean just barely visible behind us.

"What…" Seconds passed before Dani tore her eyes away from the photo. Blinking rapidly, she looked at me, her green eyes luminous. "What is this?"

Unsure why Dani's stunned reaction was affecting me so much, I bit at the side of my cheek and cleared my throat. "It's a scrapbook…of us." I opened it, so she could see the decorated pages inside. "I thought it would be nice if you had something in Washington, something that would remind you to come home every once in a while. But like a crappy friend, *I* ended up leaving, and I never finished it—obviously."

"Oh…well, I—" Dani shook her head, apparently at a loss for words. "I—none of that matters anymore." She shrugged. "Besides, I left first…" With an apologetic smile, she returned her attention to the scrapbook and slowly walked back to the bed. Lying on her stomach, she sprawled out on the comforter, scooting over to make room for me. "Come on. Let's see what kind of silliness you packed in this thing."

"I hardly remember," I said, crawling up next to her. I settled in, resting my cheek on my hand. When I glanced over at Dani, I grew equally as excited as she was. "This is going to be like Christmas for both of us…"

After Dani and I pilfered through my room a bit longer, I decided nothing I owned, save for the woodcarving kit and a whittled starfish figurine I'd made with my dad's help when I was twelve, was worth taking. Everything seemed frivolous and unnecessary or reminded me of a life I wasn't sure I needed to remember. Dani and I exited my room and plodded down the stairs, through the living room, and out the back sliding door to find the guys.

We stopped mid-step at the sight of Jason and Jake sitting in the cushioned deck chairs, smoking cigars. I glanced between them, amused. "Since when do you guys smoke cigars?" I asked with feigned admonishment.

Jason took a few quick pulls of his stogie and looked over at us. "Since we found Dad's stash in the woodshop."

"Dad had a cigar stash?" I was beginning to think I hadn't known my dad—the scatterbrained woodworker who spent more time in his shop than with his own kids—at all. *Who the hell were you, Tom Cartwright?* The fact that I didn't know stung a little.

I glanced at Dani, whose nose was wrinkled. "Now you're going to be stinky," she said, making a show of waving the smoke away from her with one arm while she hugged the scrapbook to her chest with the other.

Jason only chuckled and nodded to the scrapbook. "What's that?"

"Something Zo made for me," Dani said, a smile spreading her lips.

Jason made a funny face. "Were you doing arts and crafts up there, or—"

Dani walked by him and swatted his arm on the way toward the deck stairs. Jason responded by swatting her in return—on the butt—eliciting a high squeal and giggle from her.

"Come on," she said. "We've got a meeting to prep for. We need to get back to the ranch and wrangle in the others."

Jason heaved a sigh, but laid his head back against the cushioned chair instead of standing and closed his eyes against the glaring afternoon sun. "I just need a few more minutes," he groaned, reminding me of a little boy begging his mom for just a few more minutes of sleep.

"It might be faster to gather everyone over here; it doesn't look like he's moving anytime soon," I teased.

"That'd be great," Jason said, and he let a small smile tug at his lips. It was nice to see my brother so peaceful and…happy, a state I didn't think I'd ever see him in.

"That's all you're bringing back with you?" Jake asked, nodding to the whittling kit rolled up in my back pocket as he stood.

He'd been so quiet, sitting there, observing. *What's it like for him to be at my house, in my hometown…smoking a cigar with my brother?* I'd gleaned enough about Jake's past—seen the death of his mother and sister, seen Joe and knew how badly Jake missed him—but I thought I would've liked to spend a day with him and the old man in another life.

I shook my head. "This is it, there's nothing else I want to bring with me." I fingered the outline of the starfish in my front pocket, strangely content with the fact that my past life had boiled down to only two items that connected me to my dad.

Oblivious to my inner musings, Jake took a final puff of his cigar. It seemed strangely natural to see him with one in his hand.

Walking over to him, I linked my fingers with his. “What about you guys? Did you find anything besides cigars?”

Jake gave my hand a quick squeeze. “Some tools that’ll come in handy when we’re ready to settle. Jason and I were talking, and we’re partial to this area. Some of that farmland back around Petaluma was pretty ideal for what we’ve been discussing.”

“Yeah?” I was surprised to hear Jake say that, a sudden feeling of unease making my heartbeat quicken.

He eyed me for a moment. “That okay with you?”

With a slight smile, I nodded. “I guess I just figured we’d keep going, a little further north, maybe. Not so close to…everything.”

He gave me a quizzical look.

“There weren’t as many tools as I thought,” Jason interrupted. “Umph,” he grumbled as he peeled himself out of the padded chair. “Damn, I forgot how comfortable these things are.”

“Let’s take them,” I said, untying the cushions from the chair closest to me. “We can use them—”

“For?” Jason asked, curious.

“For extra padding on the cart and wagon benches…for sitting around the campfire…for your throne, your highness.” I snorted. “Consider it my wedding gift to you.”

Jason laughed as he walked down the stairs toward Dani. “I kinda like the sound of that: *Your Highness*.”

“I’m sure you do,” I muttered.

“Come on guys, we gotta go!” Dani called from atop Wings. “Aren’t you finished with those nasty cigars yet?”

Jason, Jake, and I chuckled in response.

As Jake and I finished untying all the cushions, I glanced around at my friends, at my family.

Jason leaned against Wings, fingering the fringe of her chocolate- and white-colored mane as he gazed up at my best friend, his new bride. There was no doubt in my mind that he was murmuring something inappropriate as he received a playful smack on his arm and a giggle from Dani. They truly loved each other, and although I wasn't sure *when* exactly they'd fallen in love, I was pretty ecstatic that they had.

"What are we doing with these?" Jake asked from beside me as he held up the cushions.

I looked up at him, unable to resist smiling at his beautifully rugged face and the warmth in his voice. "We can tie them to the saddles."

"Are they really necessary?" he asked. I could see the curiosity twinkling in his eyes.

I shrugged a shoulder and wrapped my arms more securely around the three overstuffed cushions I was holding. "They're not necessary at all, actually, but we came here to get some things, so why not?"

"I think you made your brother's day."

I gave him a mock bow. "It's the least I can do."

Jake leaned into me and pressed a soft kiss against my lips.

"We should get going," I said quietly and watched him as he walked down the steps.

Despite the craziness that had become our lives, for the first time in years, I felt content. I even ventured so far as to think that, if we all stayed together—even if we stayed around *here*—we could be happy.

26

DANI

MAY 24, 1AE

Bodega Bay, California

It was late afternoon, though the gray, misty cloud cover spreading from horizon to horizon and blocking out the sun made it feel more like evening. I stared up at the endless cloudy mass, trying to pick out the spot where the sun should've been.

"At least we don't have to deal with the fog," Zoe said.

"For once," I grumbled, and Jason emitted a noncommittal snort. It wasn't the "foggy season," but the fog didn't seem to care; it had been ever present since we'd arrived, lingering until only a few hours ago. By the time Jason, Zoe, Jake, and I had returned to the ranch from our excursion to the Casa di Cartwright, the dewy fog had finally dissipated.

As the only members of our group who were actually from Bodega Bay, Jason, Zoe, Grayson, and I were heading up our envoy to the "New Bodega" town meeting. Sitting atop our respective mounts, we rode along Westshore Road, past the turnoff to our home street, and followed it as it curved onto the peninsula. The bay was on our left, and our entourage of Gabe, Carlos, Jake, and Becca fanned out behind us. We'd selected which of us would attend the town meeting carefully, wanting people who could offer varying perspectives of the current state of the country.

Movement in the harbor caught my attention. “Look!” I pointed out at what I realized was the nearest of a handful of small vessels—both metal rowboats and inflatable dinghies—moving slowly as their oarsmen rowed them around the harbor.

Asking Wings to stop, I unbuckled my right horn bag and pulled out a small pair of binoculars, raising them to my eyes. The nearest boat stopped at a tiny buoy that was half red and half white. A quick scan of the water’s rippling surface around the boat revealed dozens of other buoys, all red and white.

The others drew to a halt around me to peer out at the activity in the harbor, and I glanced at Grayson. “Red and white buoy—that’s crab, right?”

“Yes,” Grayson said, squinting. “I count—”

“Seven boats, some with two people,” Jason said. “That’s a pretty big operation for a group of seventy.”

Grayson nodded. “Indeed, it is. We couldn’t have coordinated something like this before…”

I frowned. It made sense that others would have joined the Bodega Bay survivors, considering they had established the most stable—and sane—community we’d come across since all hell broke loose. And yet, I wasn’t overly excited about the prospect of leaping back into a settlement governed by anyone who wasn’t among my closest, most trusted companions. Sure, it helped that Grayson had been a member of the Town Council back when there were fewer than a hundred survivors, but he hadn’t been a part of the group for over four months. A lot could have changed in that amount of time, especially when the world as we knew it had ended in a matter of days.

“Look beyond them…to the harbor mouth,” Grayson said, pointing beyond the little boats. “A sail.”

Again, I brought the binoculars up to my eyes. “There are two more behind it a ways.” A thrill of excitement sizzled over my skin, and grinning, I handed the binoculars to Jason. I'd always loved watching the sailboats glide in and out of the harbor.

"Think they'll be interested in our proposition?" I asked Grayson, not taking my eyes from the tiny triangle of white that was slowly closing in on the marina's jetty. Though there were probably a few new faces on the Town Council, Grayson knew better than any of us if they would be interested in the plan we'd been hashing up since arriving in Tahoe. We wanted to settle somewhere we could be self-sufficient, but not completely isolated, and there was so much abandoned farmland in the nearby valleys, just a dozen or so miles inland. But if they didn't want us here, rivals for what limited supplies remained in the area…

"Setting up a satellite agricultural settlement would only be to their benefit," Grayson said. "I can't imagine why they wouldn't be interested in a mutually beneficial trade arrangement."

"Only one way to find out," Jason said, tugging his reins to the right and nudging his horse into motion.

Zoe, Grayson, and I followed suit, our horses falling into step beside each other while Jason led the way. I could hear the others' mounts clip-clopping behind us. Everyone was being exceptionally quiet, and I assumed it was because they were otherwise occupied, examining their surroundings.

I returned the binoculars to my horn bag, then shot Zoe a sideways glance and frowned when I saw her expression. Her eyes were narrowed as she focused on the road ahead.

I did the same. "What is it?"

"A wall."

It took me a moment—Zoe's vision had always been better than mine—but I could just make out a tall, gray wall. It stretched away from the road on either side, extending to the left a dozen or so yards, all the way across the shallow beach until it sank below the water's surface, and to the right, crawling uphill until it disappeared over the low crest. It was topped with an endless corkscrew of razor wire, and a chain-link gate crossed the road.

At my direction, Wings picked up the pace a little, carrying me ahead to ride beside Jason.

"What do you think?" I asked him. The wall was still at least a hundred yards ahead, but we were closing in quickly, and I could make out the shapes of a couple people standing on the other side of the gate. One was definitely carrying a gun…a big one.

"Smart," Jason said, nodding slowly. "If they did what I think they did, and this wall cuts across all the way to the ocean…" He stared at the place where the wall disappeared over the hilltop. "They isolated the whole peninsula…pretty fucking smart."

"It's got to be at least a mile from here to the other side," I said.

"We've been gone for almost five months, Red. That's plenty of time to build a mile-long wall."

As much as I agreed with his assessment—that building a wall and isolating the peninsula *had* been a smart move—I couldn't help the creepy feeling that bunched my shoulders and made my skin crawl. Walls were built for two reasons: to keep something out, or to keep something in. And sometimes, both. I shivered.

Zoe caught up to us, guiding Shadow in close on my other side. "What are you afraid of?" she asked, and I appreciated that she hadn't simply peeked into my mind to find which memories were floating closest to the surface.

I met her eyes for a moment. "Just déjà vu."

"Ahhh…I'm sure this won't be anything like the Colony." She offered me a supportive smile as our horses drew to a halt before the tall, chain-link gate, but I could see doubt shadow her eyes.

The two men on the other side of the gate watched us as we dismounted but didn't say anything until Jason, Zoe, Grayson, and I stepped up to the fencing.

"Which one of you is Daniel Grayson?" the man without a gun asked. He was the younger of the two, maybe in his late thirties, and was wearing khaki slacks and a light blue button-down shirt, giving him a clean, businessman vibe. In lieu of a weapon, he was holding a clipboard. The other man, dressed in dark attire more appropriate for guard duty, scanned our group with a cautious, watchful eye.

Grayson bowed his head for a moment. “I’m Daniel Grayson, envoy for the Bodega Bay Town Council to the Colony.”

The businessman nodded in greeting. “I’m Lance, the Town Council’s secretary. I was sent here to meet you and to give you a brief tour of New Bodega before the meeting.” His eyes moved from Grayson to me, Zoe, and Jason, then grazed over the others, who were still sitting in their saddles behind us. His attention returned to Grayson. “We weren’t expecting all of you to come.”

“This isn’t all of us,” Jason said.

Again, Lance’s attention shifted to Jason. “I’ll need to gather some information from each of you and go over some ground rules before you enter.”

Jason exchanged a look with Grayson. When the older man raised his graying, bushy eyebrows and shrugged, Jason nodded once. “Fair enough.”

Lance looked down at his clipboard. “I’ll need the name, place of origin, and type of mutation of every person who walks through these gates.”

“Type of mutation?” Gabe said from behind me. After a brief moment of creaking leather, I heard his footsteps on the asphalt as he approached. “That’s not quite accurate. Everyone here went through the same mutation—”

“—which you can tell Lance and the Town Council all about when we meet with them,” Grayson said, cutting Gabe off before he had the chance to launch into full-blown scientist mode. “You already know my name,” he said to Lance. “I’m from Bodega Bay, and my *mutation* has yet to be identified.”

I waved. “And I’m Danielle O’Connor. I’m from Bodega Bay, too, but I was living in Seattle when everything happened, and I’m a drifter—a two-way telepath, but only with animals.”

Lance scribbled down my information quickly, then turned his attention to Zoe.

"Zoe Cartwright, from Bodega Bay but was living in Salem, Massachusetts, and I'm an empath."

Getting the bizarre impression that we were introducing ourselves at some sort of an addicts support group meeting, I stifled a giggle. I always reacted inappropriately when I was anxious.

Lance stopped writing and glanced back up at Zoe. "Can you be more specific, please?"

Zoe bit the inside of her cheek. "I can, uh, sense other people's emotions and see their memories."

Nonplussed, Lance nodded while his pen moved across his page. When he once again raised his eyes, he looked at Jason.

"Jason Cartwright, Bodega Bay by way of Joint Base Lewis-McChord, and I can increase and decrease others' Abilities—er, mutations."

"Army?" Lance asked.

"Yes, sir—Green Beret."

Lance raised his eyebrows. "Colonel Marshall, the man in charge of the defenses around here, will be very interested in your service record."

"Colonel…is he Army?" Jason asked.

Maintaining eye contact, Lance shook his head. "Marine Corps."

Jason frowned thoughtfully, looking somewhat impressed. His eyes moved to the wall. "His idea, I take it."

Lance nodded. "It wasn't easy, but it's proved more than worth it."

"Has there been trouble? Zoe tells us the area's been clear for over a month—no sightings of the 'Lost Ones'—based on intel from *your* Town Council. If they misinformed us, and we've been operating under false pretenses…" Jason's voice contained the subtlest hint of warning.

"Ah, no," Lance said, glancing at Zoe. "What they told you was accurate. But when we first put up the wall, before Colonel

Marshall and his people managed to dedicate much effort to any sort of offensive strike on the Lost Ones, we had several attacks that likely would have resulted in fatalities had the wall not already been in place. But it *has* been over a month since we've seen any of the Lost Ones."

Apparently appeased, Jason nodded. "Glad to hear it."

The others dismounted and made their introductions and declarations.

"Very well," Lance said. "I just need each of you to answer one question, and I'll be able to tell if you're lying."

I raised my eyebrows. So Lance was a human lie detector, like Ben had been. It went a long way in explaining how he'd come by his current gig.

Lance looked at Grayson. "Do you have any intention of doing something that could cause any kind of harm to the people of New Bodega or to the settlement itself?"

"No," Grayson said, and one by one, the other seven of us echoed him.

Lance nodded. "Alright, the rules here are simple and few, but essential to ensure the safety of our people. Don't steal, and don't harm another person intentionally. If you end up becoming permanent citizens of New Bodega, certain things will be required of you—"

"Such as?" Jason said.

"Do your part—everyone has a role to fulfill here, and if you can't come up with something that benefits the settlement on your own, the Council will assign you a job—don't take more than you need, and never do anything that puts New Bodega at risk. When a transgression has occurred, the Town Council makes all final decisions regarding guilt. There is a single course of action on the rare occasions that the Council determines a party is guilty: banishment from New Bodega."

A low, humorless laugh rumbled in Jason's chest. "A little harsh as a one-size-fits-all punishment."

Lance met his eyes, cold smile for cold smile. "These are troubling times, and as I said, the rules are simple and few. But New Bodega is a good place, filled with good people, and *that* gives the threat of banishment almost more weight than capital punishment. There aren't many other places people can go."

I raised my hand, and when Lance looked at me, I said, "Can people come and go as they please?" Because, regardless of being on my home turf and sounding so idyllic compared to what lay on our side of the fence, not being able to leave New Bodega, being a prisoner in all but name, would be a deal-breaker for me.

Lance nodded. "You're free to leave at any time. Nobody will force you to stay." With a shrug, he added, "Organized society isn't for everyone."

I gave him a closemouthed smile and a no-further-questions nod.

Looking at the armed guard, Lance said, "Clark, if you'll let them in, please."

The guard lifted his rifle so the barrel rested on his shoulder and pointed up at the grayed-out sky, then stuck his hand into his pocket, retrieving a key. He unlocked the padlock securing the gate, rolling it to the side just enough for us lead our horses through in single file.

As Lance led us down the road, Jason and Grayson fell in step on either side of him, letting me take over guiding their horses. Zoe and I followed close behind them, with the others spreading out behind us.

"A lot's changed around here since I left in January," Grayson said to our guide.

Lance nodded slowly. "I can imagine. I've only been a part of the community since late February, but I know the stories—the massacre…" He shook his head, heaving a heavy sigh. "But at least something good came out of it."

I scoffed and gave Zoe a disbelieving look. *Something good?*

More than thirty survivors had been slaughtered, most of them people we *knew*.

But Lance remained oblivious to my reaction. "It gave the rest of the survivors a reason to pull together, something to work toward—the safety of the community. Which, as of Monday, consists of four hundred and thirty-seven people."

Grayson whistled appreciatively. "How do you feed everyone?"

"We have a few small garden-farms set up here, mostly in front and back yards." He pointed to a home coming up on the right side of the road.

A middle-aged woman and a teenage boy were working in the front yard, pulling weeds. Over a dozen rows of mounded dark, rich soil and a variety of plants, some barely sprouted, some well on their way to producing harvestable food, filled the mini-farm.

The woman paused with a snarly little weed in her hand and looked up as we passed. When her eyes moved from Lance and Jason to Zoe and me, I offered her a tentative smile. She returned it, nodding in silent greeting as well. *"Welcome,"* she said in my head, and my smile widened.

"Uh, D…" Zoe nudged my arm with her elbow. "What are you grinning at?"

"It's nothing, really." I pointed to the woman with my chin. "She's a telepath, and—" I was quiet for a moment while my thoughts floundered. "She just spoke to me telepathically." I met Zoe's eyes, biting my lip as I tried to explain why the brief telepathic greeting seemed like such a good sign to me. "She wasn't afraid to show me—a perfect stranger—her Ability. She feels safe here, safe enough to let her true self shine, and…well, she's a telepath, but she's not being forced to do telepathic things. She's *gardening*, not locked up in a room, forced to communicate with people, to lure them in." I lifted my shoulders. "It's just nice to see something that proves this place is different, better."

Smiling, Zoe nodded. "She felt content, too. Content, with a sense of purpose."

"You'll find a lot of that around here," Lance said, looking back at us. "Most of our people choose their assigned duty based not only on their skills, but also on what they enjoy." He pointed back at the woman, who'd returned to her weeding and was speaking quietly to the teenage boy. "Kathy and her nephew, Mikey, came here shortly after me. She was a teacher before, but gardening was her favorite hobby. The Council let her choose between taking up a teaching post at the New Bodega schoolhouse and running a home garden, taking on a couple apprentices so she could pass on her skills."

"The soil here isn't great," Grayson commented.

"It's not," Lance agreed. "And the weather's not ideal, the plots are too small, and it's too soon to have anything beyond the most minimal supplement to our main food source, but every little bit helps."

"The main food source being the ocean," Jason clarified.

Lance nodded. "Fish, crab, abalone, mussels, seaweed—we certainly don't lack adequate sustenance."

"We noticed that some of the houses around town still haven't been scavenged," Jason said, and I knew he was thinking of our family homes. "You aren't scavenging?"

"We are," Lance said, "but we focus on targets that promise a larger haul—wholesale stores, supermarkets, hardware stores, that kind of thing."

Jason glanced over his shoulder at the horses. "I'm assuming you have some better way to move what you find…?"

I patted Wings's heavily muscled shoulder. *"Don't pay any attention to him—you do a fabulous job of hauling our stuff around."*

Lance looked back as well. "We don't rely on horses for those trips, no, though we do have a herd of several dozen we keep on the Peninsula for shorter trips outside, and Colonel Marshall and the town guard use them when they head out on security sweeps." Shaking his head, Lance laughed softly. "We rely on something else entirely for the big trips."

Jason focused on Lance, giving me a good view of his profile. His expression was, as I would have expected, carefully blank. "Which is…?"

"We've, uh, requisitioned a few tanker trucks, as well as a few semis. Fuel wasn't hard to find at first—we even used it in the boats—but we burned through it so quickly that we've pretty much tapped every source of diesel in the area." He shook his head. "And regular gasoline is so touch-and-go now—half of what we come across is bad…" He shrugged. "We won't be able to rely on the trucks for much longer, but hopefully by the time they're no longer useful, we won't need them."

Zoe and I exchanged identical expressions—eyebrows raised and lips pressed together in little frowns.

We passed several more houses on the right side of the road, most with two or three people tending burgeoning gardens in the compact front and side yards, until we approached what had been, and still appeared to be, the boatyard. Dozens of people were hustling around, passing between and slipping under the hulls of at least ten sailboats sitting on boat stands.

"Keeping the boatyard stocked with competent workers…" Lance shot a sharp glance at Jason, then looked over his shoulder at the rest of us. "I don't suppose any of you happen to be sailboat mechanics…?" When he didn't receive any affirmatives, he sighed. "Well, you can't blame me for hoping." He returned his attention to the people cleaning and working on boats on either side of the road. "Since we rely on the ocean for most of our food, keeping the marine vessels in tip-top shape is a high priority, right up there with patrolling the wall and running sweeps through the area outside."

We spent several minutes just walking and taking in the hustle and bustle of such a well-oiled machine. As I looked around, I was struck by an odd observation—while there were a ton of sailboats, both on stands in the boatyard and in the marina up ahead, there were absolutely no cars, trucks, or SUVs. At first it seemed odd, but the more I considered it, the more I realized how logical it was. Driving land vehicles around the peninsula would be excessive and wasteful. It made much more sense to stockpile their fuel to use only for their big scavenging excursions.

As we neared the end of the boatyard, Lance stopped and turned around. The rest of us stopped as well, and most returned their attention to him. Jason, however, continued studying the way ahead, and I couldn't help but do the same. Small buildings lined the road on the right, and most of the slips in the marina on the left were occupied by sailboats or clusters of smaller, rowable vessels.

"This is the New Bodega town center," Lance said. He pointed his thumb over his right shoulder, indicating the marina's large boathouse; it was where we'd met with the Town Council and most of the townspeople back in January. "That's Town Hall, where the Council meeting will take place. There will be a reception with food and refreshments in the banquet room upstairs, where you'll have a chance to get to know us better in a more informal setting."

Lance switched hands, pointing over his left shoulder. "Here's the general store, grocer, hardware supply, and hunting and fishing supply shop. We operate on a simple barter system here, so if you want something, you'll have to trade for it. If you end up staying in New Bodega, you'll be provided daily rations, so you won't have to worry about bartering for food. And we have a steady supply of clean water, courtesy of a few of our people whose mutation enables them to desalinate and cleanse water of impurities."

That caused my eyebrows to raise. It sounded a lot like Tavis's Ability, though he'd never tried to do anything like remove salt from water—or, likely, freshwater from saltwater—but I didn't see any reason why he couldn't.

"Also," Lance said, once again raising his right hand to point over his shoulder at what lay on the marina side of the road, "the parking lot beyond Town Hall has become the marketplace, where people set up shop in a more temporary manner, selling surplus food and other supplies. We usually have a few outside traders there as well; currently there are two, one from another settlement down south, in the Monterey area, the other a roving trader. And beyond the market, we're in the process of developing several industrial shops—blacksmithing and metallurgy, woodworking, that sort of thing."

I watched Jason turn his full attention to Lance, a curious, considering expression on his face.

Turning, Lance continued down the road toward Town Hall. We passed the surprisingly crowded marketplace on our right. With only several seconds' examination, I noted that it looked just like a small run-of-the-mill farmer's market.

"You can tie up your horses here," Lance said, stopping by a bike rack partway up the cement path to the Town Hall's main entrance. "The Council will be ready for you at five." Lance peeked down at his watch. "That gives you a little over a half hour to explore. Feel free to wander around, just please don't keep the Council waiting."

We all nodded and said our thanks, and Lance quickly disappeared into the Town Hall, leaving us to tie our mounts to the bike rack. I felt giddy at the opportunity to explore this so familiar, yet so foreign place, and at the same time, I was bummed that I didn't —nor did any of my companions—have anything to barter with on hand.

"Hey," Zoe said, apparently picking up on my emotions. She linked her arm with mine and led me toward the jumble of folding tables and tents set up as mini-shops. "You could always offer your services as an animal whisperer..."

The eight of us gathered by the "hitching post" five minutes before the meeting was supposed to start, having spent the past half hour broken off into pairs as we wandered around the town center. I'd spent most of the time walking arm-in-arm with Zoe, looking at the various wares offered at each booth—from pots, pans, and cooking utensils to fabric and clothing to handmade net bags of fresh shellfish. With only a few minutes to spare, we'd met up with Jason and Jake, who'd passed the time walking around the far end of the parking lot, where the smithy and workshop were being erected, and the four of us had made our way back to the Town Hall together.

The Town Hall was a fairly large two-story structure with, as was to be expected of a boathouse, two indoor slips for small vessels on the harbor side. The rest of the ground floor was divided into rooms, including several small offices and a larger conference room. I was only familiar with the layout because one of my high school boyfriends had worked for the marina part time, and he'd snuck me into one of the lesser-used offices more than once for a clandestine rendezvous.

When we passed through the glass double doors and into a comfortable waiting room that had been redecorated in the months we'd been gone, Lance greeted us again. He led us down a hallway, past the closed doors to all of the smaller offices, and through the open doorway to the conference room at the end of the hall.

We shuffled through the doorway in singles and in pairs, spreading out along the wall on either side. Nine people were seated, facing us, at a long table that stretched nearly the entire length of the room. With Lance and the eight of us filling the other half of the room, the space was more than a little cramped.

The woman in the middle of the line of seated Council Members stood, extending her hand toward the chairs on our side of the table. "Please, sit." She was tall and slender, with brown hair streaked with gray, slightly lined features, and intelligent eyes. Her name was Bethany James, a former high school principal. I didn't know her well, but I remembered her from the last time we'd met with the Council. "Daniel, it's so good to see you again," she said to Grayson with a warm smile. "I hope you're well."

"I am," Grayson said as he sat in the center seat on our side of the table. "And you're looking quite well yourself, Beth."

I wasn't sure, but I thought Bethany James might have blushed. I eyed Grayson as I took my own seat between Jason and Zoe, then did a quick scan of the faces of the other Council Members. I recognized a few others besides Bethany, but at least five of them were new to the Council, or rather, new to *me*. One of the newcomers was a middle-aged man who, based on his fatigues, I guessed had to be Colonel Marshall.

Lance sat as well, claiming the only other chair, which was located at the far end of the table, his clipboard and a large, leather-bound journal resting on the table in front of him.

Bethany's eyes moved from face to face, examining each of us for several seconds, just long enough to make her gaze uncomfortable. Eventually, her focus returned to Grayson. "You and your people have been through quite a lot, Daniel. I can see it on your faces and feel it in your hearts." She smiled a warm, genuine smile. "We're glad you've made it back to us."

"As am I."

I looked from Grayson to Bethany and back, certain there were sparks floating between them. I held in a snicker. I was *totally* going to give Grayson a hard time about flirting with the leader of the New Bodega Town Council…later.

"Well," Bethany said, clearing her throat and sitting up just a tiny bit straighter, "we have an interesting proposal for you and your people, one we hope you'll be as excited about as we are—but first, we'd appreciate it if you could share with us some of what you've experienced." Her eyes shifted to Zoe. "From what you and the dreamwalker told us, some of you have come all the way from the East Coast, but you've all been as far as Colorado.

Most of our people are from the Northern California coast, and *none*, not even the traders who've passed through New Bodega, have been further than Oregon or Nevada. Not since the outbreak." Her gaze settled back on Grayson.

He held Bethany's stare, nodding slowly, thoughtfully. "Where would you like us to start?"

"How about the beginning," she said, the corner of her mouth curving upward.

"Hmmm…the beginning is different for each of us, but…" Grayson's focus shifted, and leaning forward, he looked at Gabe. "Your story might be the best place to start."

Shrugging, Gabe sat up straighter and rested his forearms on the table. "For me, it all started when the genetic engineering company I worked for received a DOD contract and moved to some facilities on Peterson Air Force Base in Colorado Springs. I—"

"That's the location of the Colony…run by this"—Bethany glanced down at a small notebook on the table in front of her, flipping back a few pages—"General Herodson?"

"Yes," Gabe said before launching into his personal story, which spanned a several-year period before the initial outbreak. He explained that he'd started working under Dr. Wesley on a program relating to heretofore untapped human potential, what we now knew of as "Abilities," and had quickly been initiated into the inner circle of those opposed to the program, *including* Dr. Wesley, *and* had been made aware of the General's Ability to control the minds of others.

He explained the moment when he first realized what Dr. Wesley had done, releasing the Virus on the general population and initiating what was essentially the end of human civilization—the moment he'd received a call from his best friend, Jake, claiming that his sister was sick and seemed to be losing her mind. Except Becca hadn't been losing her mind, she'd been developing an Ability.

He told them that the Virus was simply a mechanism to enable the mass spread of the gene therapy and explained the science behind the mutation every person who was infected went through. He told them everything he could about the Colony and the people there—the Re-gens, the T-Rs, the yellow- and black-bands, electrotherapy, Project Eden, my abduction, and how people with different Abilities were used as though they were *things*, not human beings—without hinting at Dr. Wesley's relation to Zoe and Jason, or at the fact that one or more of our people were likely working for the General.

"These 'Re-gens,'" Bethany started, skepticism written all over her face despite Lance not once having pointed out an untruth in Gabe's tale. "To reanimate a corpse—that's just…I don't see how such a thing could be possible."

"And yet, I am here," Becca said, speaking for the first time since we'd sat.

All nine sets of the Council Members' eyes snapped to her, and I had to hold back a grin. Even now, in a world so filled with wonder and the impossible made possible, people still wanted to hold on to their old, outdated view of reality. Humanity could be so stubborn; I was hoping *that* would be the one characteristic that might prevent us from dying out altogether.

"You're claiming to be one of these—these creatures?" Bethany said, her gaze flicking to Lance. When he nodded, she returned her attention to Becca, scrutinizing her face…her not-quite-right eyes. I knew what she was seeing—irises that were a little too dull, a little too gray, a little too dead. Camille and Mase's eyes had the same inhuman quality; it was the one external marker of their difference from non-Re-gens. Inside, well, that was another matter entirely.

Becca nodded. "I am."

"She's not a creature." Jake's voice was a low rumble. "She's my sister."

There was a prolonged, tense silence. A collective holding of breath.

Finally, Bethany shot another quick look to Lance, and when he confirmed what Becca and Jake had claimed with another nod, Bethany exhaled heavily. "Well…I must apologize. No insult was intended."

"Jake is the friend I mentioned earlier," Gabe said, earning raised eyebrows and opened mouths from some of the Council Members. "After Becca saw whatever she saw and killed herself, I did the only thing I could think of. I took her to Wes—Dr. Wesley—to see if she was a candidate for the Re-gen procedure. It was still very new then, but we managed."

"We would love to know more about this procedure," the man on Bethany's right said. "We have a few biotech people here who—"

"No," Becca said resolutely.

"Now, young lady, I understand that this may be a sensitive subject for you, but I don't see why you'd deny the rest of us the chance to eliminate death as a—"

"You do not *see*, because you do not know what *I* know." Becca turned her sharp, gray gaze to Gabe. "You cannot teach them this. You *must* not. It's imperative, Dr. McLau—Gabe."

I watched Becca and Gabe stare at each other for several heartbeats, until finally, Gabe nodded. "But I may be able to offer something else," he said to Bethany. "If you have any people with Abilities like Jason's, specifically the Ability to nullify others' Abilities completely, I can teach your biotech people how to make a 'neutralizer' that will protect whoever is injected from nearly *all* Abilities—including mind control—for up to a week. It wouldn't be something you'd want to use all the time, but it would be useful as a backup plan…just in case."

Again, Bethany exchanged a look with several other Council Members. "That's very generous of you." She tilted her head to the side. "What's the catch?"

Gabe offered her a chilly smile. "We'll do whatever we can to keep as many people as possible out of the hands of Herodson and the others like him."

"The *others* like him?" Bethany said, furrowing her brow.

A heavy silence descended over the room.

Carlos cleared his throat. "Yeah," he said, speaking for the first time since we entered the Town Hall. He rubbed the back of his neck as he started telling his own story, first captivating the Council with his tale of leaving Central Washington with his two siblings, then horrifying them with details of what happened when he arrived in South Lake Tahoe, of being forced to worship Mandy, a woman whose Ability stripped all around her of their will, leaving behind only mindless, adoring husks.

Bethany, as well as all but two of her peers—Colonel Marshall and the man on her right—were covering their mouths with their hands by the time Carlos finished. Most had unshed tears shining in their eyes as well, at least, those whose tears hadn't already escaped.

Bethany had to clear her throat several times before she could speak. "What happened to them, to Vanessa and Annie? Did you look for them after…once you were freed?"

When Carlos didn't show any sign of answering, simply stared down at his hands gripping his jeans, I jumped in. "We found them on our way back here. They're at the ranch right now."

"She's one of the Lost Ones." Colonel Marshall's voice was accusatory. "You can't keep her here. She should be put down."

Carlos didn't raise his head, but he did glare at the Colonel, and a faint crackling hum filled the air. The Council Members looked around the room, their eyes a little wild, and Zoe's breath hitched as emotions spiked.

I looked at Jason, alarm widening my eyes, but he only stared back at me, his expression placid. For whatever reason, apparently he wanted to let this play out.

Fine…that's just fine. But we couldn't let Carlos electrocute the rest of us in a dominance display, either. "Vanessa is one of us," I said. "We're a package deal."

I stared at Colonel Marshall, refusing to lower my eyes, and still the air tingled with electricity. The tiny hairs on my arm stood on end, and I could feel the flyaways floating around my head.

It was Bethany who interrupted what was turning into one hell of a staring contest. "In which case I think you'll find our offer very appealing."

The Colonel broke eye contact, shifting his gaze to Bethany, his features tense with irritation, or possibly anger, and the electric hum slowly faded away.

Bethany paused long enough to meet Colonel Marshall's stare, her own seeming to say "Yes? Did you want something?" before looking at Grayson. "The ocean is our main—and really, our *only* —source of food. Before your people made contact a few days ago, we were in the process of discussing what type of team might best be suited for establishing an agricultural satellite settlement nearby. We've been held up on trying to put together a group of people with the most effective combination of skills." She shrugged. "It would do us no good to set up an operation like this only to have it unable to defend itself, but the Colonel's ranks are stretched thin as it is—the more people we bring in, the more people we need on the town watch."

Grayson nodded slowly. "Interestingly enough, we came here intending to propose something very similar, so I think I speak for everyone when I say we're all ears."

Bethany smiled. "Based on everything you've told us"—she glanced at me—"and on your unwavering loyalty to each other, I can imagine no better group to take on the task." She scanned each of us quickly. "Do any of you have farming or gardening experience?"

I raised my hand partway. "Some. My grandma was a skilled gardener and herbalist, and I know a lot about animals…obviously." My eyes hardened. "I won't raise animals to be slaughtered, though. If you want someone to do that, you'll have to look elsewhere."

Bethany frowned, but didn't argue.

"I worked on a farm during my early adulthood," Grayson said. "I was a bit of a drifter." He tossed me a sideways glance. "Though not *that* kind."

Jason emitted a moderately interested grunt. "My dad was a carpenter—taught me most of what he knew—and Jake's good with anything mechanical. I think we can manage."

"It's settled then," Bethany said with a definitive nod. "You're the right people for the job, and I think you'll enjoy being autonomous, considering how long you've been out there, away from a society with hard-and-fast rules." She paused. "We're willing to provide you with the provisions you'll need to get up and running so you won't have to waste any time or energy procuring your own, so long as the majority of your crop, when ready, comes to New Bodega. You may, of course, reserve some for your own sustenance and trading purposes…"

"You've been thinking about this for some time, it would seem," Grayson said. "Do you already have a location picked out?"

The young woman sitting to the left of Bethany piped in with, "We actually have several possible spots: one in the Russian River Valley, near Healdsburg, one in the Carneros area, and one a few miles west of Petaluma."

Jason exchanged a look with Jake, then with Grayson. He was smiling.

"Petaluma sounds perfect," Grayson said.

"Wonderful." Bethany scanned each of us again. "And are there enough of you to run this new settlement, or do we need to provide additional workers?"

Grayson shook his head. "That won't be necessary. There are plenty of us, and we have more people waiting back in Tahoe who are hoping to join us eventually."

Bethany looked at Carlos. "These are the others who were controlled by that woman?"

Carlos nodded.

"I see." After a long moment, Bethany addressed the rest of the Council. "I propose that we move forward on the satellite settlement with Daniel and his people."

"I second," the woman on her right said.

Bethany nodded to her. "Any opposed?" she asked the rest of the Council.

Absolute silence filled the room.

"Motion passed." Bethany looked at Lance, who started writing furiously. "Let the record show that in exchange for…"

I tuned out Bethany's words as I realized that this was really happening. For the first time in a long time, we might actually have a place that was ours…a place we belonged. I almost couldn't believe how perfectly everything was falling into place.

It was almost too perfect.

27

JAKE

MAY 24, 1AE

Bodega Bay, California

Gabe, Becca, and Grayson chatted intently with Bethany as they left the conference room and headed toward the reception. Carlos and Dani trailed out behind them, animated and smiling with hope illuminating their eyes. Jake and Jason brought up the rear, already planning what sort of projects they could start when they arrived at their new settlement and discussing who would be best suited to do what.

"It would be great to have a shop where we can tear apart any old machines and repurpose the parts," Jason said. "I have so many ideas. I could keep you busy for months." He shook his head and let out a small chuckle. "There's going to be so much to do…I can see it already." When he glanced over his shoulder, he paused, and Jake followed suit.

Zoe still sat at the conference table, her gaze fixed on the sketched aerial map of New Bodega that covered the expanse of the wall behind the Council's table.

Jake turned to Jason. "We'll meet you up there."

Jason nodded, his features drawn in what Jake assumed was concern for his sister, but then he disappeared into the hallway.

Scanning the room, Jake realized that he and Zoe were the only two left.

Although he wasn't certain, he could imagine what was bothering her. Zoe was home, the place that for her held the most memories, the most secrets, and therefore the most heartache. While Jake found hope and comfort in the idea of having a home and the endless possibilities that accompanied starting over, Zoe might not share his sentiments, especially not when their new home would be so close to the one she so desperately wanted to leave behind.

Knowing her well enough to assume she needed a moment to collect her thoughts, Jake resisted the urge to reach out to comfort her. Instead, he did one of the things he was best at: he sat down and waited as she processed what she was feeling.

When the sun began to set, darkening the room, and the muffled voices coming from upstairs were all that filled the silence, Zoe finally faced him. Her eyes were burning with more emotion than he'd seen in them since *his* Zoe had come back to him a couple weeks ago.

"I'm not sure I can do this," she said quietly. "I thought I could—I mean, I wanted to—but…*so close*…?"

Jake turned to face her, needing Zoe to *feel* his resolve to stay, to *see* why he wanted this to work, for them. "It's a place to call home, Zoe."

"I just—" She lifted her shoulders, still shaking her head despondently. "It *was* home, Jake, but being here….the dreams are already worse. What happens if I stay?" She rose from her chair and began pacing. "What if I can't get over it? What if I lose myself like my dad did? You don't know what he was like." She continued to pace. "He was surrounded by memories, and it ruined him. I don't think I could handle it…"

Jake rose and closed the distance between them, reaching for her hand. "But the difference is you're not alone here," he said. "You have all of us…you have Jason and me and Dani."

Zoe seemed to calm momentarily, before her shimmering, turquoise-colored eyes widened with fear. "What if the General finds out we're alive, especially now that my mom knows? What if he comes looking for us? We're sitting ducks if we stay here. It'll be the first place he looks."

"We're not sitting ducks. Look at how far we've gotten, at what we can do now." He squeezed her hand in his. "You alone would know if he was coming a mile away." Indecision clouded her eyes, but Jake continued. "Zoe, I would never let anything happen to you, you know that. I would die a thousand times—"

She stiffened. "Why do you always have to do that?" Her voice was a hard whisper. For the first time—with her eyes so radiant, so piercing—Jake thought he saw the *real* Zoe, angry and unrepentant, with unbridled loyalty and determination that drove her to desperation. "Why do you always have to be the guy who saves everyone—saves me?"

He hadn't expected that reaction, but then again, he thought he probably should have. "You're upset with me because I want to protect you?"

With a quick, despondent exhale, Zoe closed her eyes and licked her lips before her palm gently cupped the side of his face. "Of course not." She said it so quietly that he barely heard her. "But do you think it's easy to watch you suffer?" she asked. "Burned beyond recognition or shot in the chest or stabbed in the back or so weak after a transfusion you can barely stand? Is it knowing you'll *eventually* heal supposed to make it easier?" She pulled away from him, a despairing sadness threading her words. "Do you have any idea how hard it is to watch that, to know you'd do anything for me? To see you so close to death that I can *feel* the abyss nearly swallowing you, the life draining from you, until you're almost nothing?"

Jake reached for her as a tear, too stubborn to be held at bay, slid down her cheek.

He hadn't ever thought of it that way. He tried to imagine lying at Zoe's bedside after she'd been shot and left for dead. He remembered the sting of misery he'd felt when Clara had poisoned her, when they'd all thought she was dead. He never wanted to relive that moment again.

"Your regeneration doesn't make it easier, Jake, it makes it worse. Every single time you get hurt, I ask myself, 'Is this finally it? Will I lose him forever? How will I be able to live with myself?'" She shook her head, and he could barely stand the hurt that made her voice hollow and distant. "I *can't* do that. I can't keep losing people—"

Her voice caught, and without hesitation, Jake wrapped his arms around her. "You're not going to lose me, Zoe."

Her head shook against his chest. "This place is cursed," she said. Slowly, Zoe wrapped her arms around him, clutching the back of his thermal shirt so tightly he thought she might never let go of him.

"I know it's hard to look beyond the past," he said, his cheek resting against her forehead. "But how can staying in a place that gives everyone so much hope be a bad decision? This will be good for us." Jake wanted her to see their future the way he did, to have something to look forward to instead of constantly being chased by what was behind them. "Now we can make this place *our* home," he added. "We can have our own memories…don't you want to live your own damn life?" His voice was soft and beseeching.

As if she finally *felt* his desperation, she said, "Of course I do."

Jake pulled her away from him and gazed down at her. "Then let's do this. You have your family now, your *real* family—that's what you've been waiting for. This is your second chance…*our* chance." He searched her eyes, the eyes he'd relied on to tell him what she wouldn't. He wanted everything they'd gone through to be worth something. He brushed the longer strands of hair behind her ear and dropped his voice to little more than a whisper. "I want you to smile because you're *actually* happy." He quirked the corner of his mouth up. "As obnoxious as it is sometimes, I want that determined glint in your eye back, your feistiness back…"

Zoe quickly glanced down, looking bashful, before gazing back up at him through her lashes.

"I love you, Zoe." Jake let his words, his heart, linger in the inch between them. "I want you to be able to start over…with me."

Licking her lips again, Zoe nodded, her eyes open wide and gleaming. "I love you, too," she said, and rose to tiptoes and wrapped her arms around his neck. "Okay."

28

ZOE

MAY 25, 1AE

Bodega Bay, California

The sound of a low, rumbling voice woke me from yet another haunting dream about my mom, and my eyes flew open. There was a featherlight pressure against the right side of my face. I stared up at the stars through the netted top of the tent, trying to steady my breath.

"Are you alright?" Jake asked.

As my desperation and fear subsided, I let out a deep breath. "Did I wake anyone?" I whispered, turning my head to look at him.

"It doesn't matter." It was his nice way of saying probably. He pulled me into his arms, somehow knowing it was exactly what I needed.

"You're becoming a pro at this," I tried to joke, but Jake said nothing. He simply stroked my exposed arm with his thumb, and I rested my head on his chest.

"Why is this happening?" I whispered. "I have the answers I wanted…I know the truth, but the dreams just keep changing. Why won't they go away?"

"Honestly," Jake said, "it's probably a test for me."

"Really? How so?" I craned my neck to look up at his shadowed profile, barely able to see the hint of a smile.

"Because every night you have your dreams, I get to pull you into my arms and hold you as close as I ever really get to, until you fall asleep."

I smiled. "And that's a test because..."

"My self-control is diminishing."

I could only chuckle softly. "You're trying to distract me..."

"Is it working?" He smiled against my ear.

Laughing, I tightened my hold around him, unsure what the hell I would do if he weren't there to comfort me. "Thank you," I whispered.

"For?"

I propped myself up on my elbows and gazed down at the contours of his face. "For your patience...for always knowing what to do and what to say to make me feel better...for being you." I leaned down to press a light kiss to his lips.

Jake reached his hand behind my head, his thumb gently brushing the side of my face as he kissed me a little deeper. Feeling the space between us charge to nearly unbearable levels, I knew what was to come. Us. Together. Our first time making love since my memory had returned.

It hadn't escaped my notice that, like last time, he was holding me after a dream. But this time, it was different. *I* was the Zoe he wanted, the one who occupied his thoughts. And knowing *that* made me want him all the more. I wanted his strength and love and protection to fill every fiber of my being, to fill up the emptiness that lingered in the days since my memories had returned. We were finally...*right.*

I kissed him deeper still.

"Zoe." The mere sound of him saying my name made my heart swell to near bursting. He pressed his lips against mine, giving me a slow, savoring kiss so intoxicating I thought I might die from withdrawal if he ever stopped.

Jake's warm hand found its way under the hem of my t-shirt, his fingers light as they trailed up my back. His body was hot, but mine was near burning. I needed air…needed to be rid of the confines of my clothes. I pulled my shirt over my head, flinging it into the corner of the tent.

"That was easier than I thought," he muttered, and I could feel the heat of his gaze as it raked over my body.

"Easy? So you planned this?" Jake shrugged, and I leaned into him, my lips brushing against his ear as I said, "You'd better be careful…or I'll have to punish you…"

"Punish me?" I could picture his broad grin curving his lips into a delectable smile. "You don't have it in you."

"No? Well, a lot's changed in the last month, and I have you right where I want you…"

Jake leaned his head back as much as his pillow would allow and let out a deep laugh. His chest rumbled, and I could feel the column of his throat move up and down as I pressed my lips against it.

"That was a bad move," I informed him. I nestled my face in the crook of his neck, lightly dragging the tip of my tongue against the scruffy, sensitive skin beneath his jaw. He smelled of leather and tasted of salt.

Groaning, Jake gripped my hips.

I tried to stifle a laugh as I straightened. "See what happens when you don't take me seriously?"

His hands splayed against my back, urging me back down to him. The moment his mouth, his tongue, found my collarbone and then the base of my throat, my eyes closed, and I let out a strangled whimper. He kissed an invisible line down to each of my breasts, each graze of his lips leaving behind an excruciatingly blissful throb that spiraled downward, making me desperate to cry out.

His grip on my torso tightened, and he rolled me over onto my back. I lost myself in a laugh of pure elation and to an overwhelming desire for more. I craved it. *Needed* it. I wasn't sure I could live another moment without it. Without him.

Fleetingly, I thought of the others, of the quietness that surrounded us, but then I realized my pants were gone, replaced by his hot, solid body on top of mine. By his insistent hands. By his devouring lips. And all else was completely forgotten.

After taking Shadow for a long stroll around the ranch, trying to come to terms with our decision to stay so close to home, I opened the pasture gate and led him through to graze with the other content horses. Unhooking his halter, I draped it over my shoulder.

"Thanks for being such a good boy," I said softly and brushed his scraggly, black forelock from his eyes. I would've trimmed it for him, but according to Dani, he preferred that I didn't. I gave Shadow's nose a gentle stroke with the back of my curled finger and patted the side of neck before pushing him away. He ambled toward Arrow and Brutus, gave them a little nicker, and lowered his head to the ground for a late morning snack.

It was our last day at Riders' Ranch, and I figured the horses might as well enjoy their final meal in the lush pasture before we headed for our new home in Petaluma. We'd never seen the farm, and aside from knowing it was big enough for all of us, we didn't really know what to expect.

Leaving the horses to their grazing, I walked back to the gate and closed it behind me.

Squeaking hinges and a hollow bang startled me, and I craned my neck in time to see Sarah storm out of the ranch house, wobble down the steps, and lumber around the side of the house and behind the shed as fast as her legs would carry her.

I waited for Biggs to run out after her, but instead, it was Mase who came to the screen door. He filled the wooden frame completely and peeked his head outside, a mixture of trepidation and fear twisting his features as he scanned the yard around the house. When he saw me standing in front of the pasture gate a couple dozen yards away, he shrugged.

Muffled sobbing and screaming reclaimed my attention, and I looked back over at the shed. Sarah walked a few steps away from it, her arms flailing emphatically, and she turned and disappeared behind the shed once more.

I gave Mase what I hoped was a reassuring nod then sprinted toward Sarah, more than a little concerned.

As I drew closer, I could barely make out what she was shrieking. "…not even real. It's not even real…" Coming up alongside the shed, I stopped, horrified by the images that were filling my head, by the feelings that were fogging my mind.

Sarah, scrawny and homeless with tattered clothes and more-wild-than-usual hair, walked into a cramped, nondescript building, where a man in a white lab coat stood with a clipboard in hand. Holding it out to her, the man pointed to the top paper. Sarah nodded, biting her lower lip as her eyes scoured the document. With a heavy exhale, she signed the bottom of the sheet, and the man smiled.

Like her memories were resurfacing from a long-buried past, another image emerged.

Sarah woke up in a hospital bed, IVs in her arms, tubes in her mouth, and electrodes attached to her head.

Stepping around the corner of the shed, my mind spinning, I watched her.

She was completely oblivious to my presence until she turned around again, stopping after taking a few awkward steps in my direction. Her eyes narrowed, then widened, and I could feel her inner battle—*see* her different selves fighting for space in her mind. It was like I was observing someone with multiple personality disorder carrying out several conversations with herself. Two images of Sarah flickered to life in my mind's eye, two different versions of her, screaming at each other about who was real, who was right…who should be in charge of *her*.

Sarah, strong and formidable, stood in the library of a grand home—what I'd thought was her *grand home. She looked like a completely different person, a determined, almost angry glare pinching her features. Her curly brown hair was pulled back into a tight knot atop her head, her clothes were black and form-fitting, and a handgun was gripped in her fingers.*

"There were no family photos," I said, remembering the walls adorned with original artwork, but nothing personal, no portraits of her wealthy parents or candid images from her childhood. We'd never even found her parents.

Sarah watched as men in fatigues removed a handful of bloodied bodies from the house, and a team of people hustled around her, removing photos and certificates from the walls, scouring through the hundreds of books lining the shelves, and tossing trophies into oversized garbage bags.

Sarah started pacing again. "I don't understand." She let out a whimper. "I don't understand. It's all a goddamn lie! What am I supposed to do? What am I—" When she glanced up again, it was like she was noticing me for the first time. She stopped in her tracks, tears pouring down her face as she wrapped her arms around her belly. "I don't know what's wrong with me, Zoe," she wailed and fell to her knees.

"Oh my God, Sarah, be careful!" I said, closing the distance between us and kneeling beside her. I wrapped my arms around her shoulders, trying to steady her shaking body. "What the hell happened?"

Completely despondent and unable to formulate a single coherent word, Sarah continued to sob. Unsure what I should do, I pulled her tighter against me, my love for my friend clouding the fear I should've been feeling in seeing her true past, in feeling the burning hatred she intermittently felt for me.

Purposefully, I watched a storm of jumbled images flash through her mind…images that made the hair on my arms and the back of my neck stand on end.

Sarah was walking beside a man in fatigues, her clothes changed into jeans and a cardigan, her hair down and bouncing with each leisurely step, and a softer expression on her face and a shimmer of innocence in her eyes.

I balked and stared down at my wailing, quivering friend. A torrent of emotions assaulted us both: resentment, terror, determination, eagerness mixed with affection, gratitude, guilt, and uncertainty.

"Sarah?" I said, recalling the night I'd dug around in her mind and had found *nothing* like the two lives I could now see commingling as one.

Sarah and I were in her bedroom back in St. Louis, jumping up and down and giggling so much that we could barely breathe. Biggs was there, standing in the doorway, and upon simply seeing him, adoration filled her entire being...

...Sarah, wearing her black pants and combat boots, was kneeling on the ground. A murderous look hardened her features as she dragged a blade across an old man's throat. His eyes were

wide with terror before his face, twisted in pain, slackened as he bled out in Sarah's arms. Her expression was blank, except for the victorious glint in her eyes.

I swallowed the dread nestled thick in my throat.

Sarah and Jordan walked in through the front door of my house in Salem, both smiling at me. Sarah proffered her hand in greeting, like she was a completely different person than the woman holding the knife...

The truth was glaring me in the face, suffocating, and I resisted the urge to scream.

I was sitting on my bed back at Fort Knox, Sarah brushing my hair...

...Sarah was watching over me while I slept, crying with concern as I lay in the hospital bed...

...Sarah was sitting at my kitchen table back in Salem, eating my food in my house, watching TV in my house, even when Jordan was out of town or at work.

I struggled to reconcile the two versions of the woman in my arms—trained, dangerous Sarah and bubbly, naive Sarah, who I'd grown to love almost like a sister. Having known it was possible, even likely, that she wasn't who we—who *she*—thought she was didn't make the realization any easier as I watched each memory of our experiences together fuse with those of a Sarah I didn't recognize, a Sarah I didn't trust, a Sarah who was frightening.

A Sarah who was trained to kill me.

"I'm so sorry," she sobbed, clutching onto me desperately. "I don't know what's happening to me, I don't understand—" She let out an agonizing cry and clutched her stomach. “Oh my God!” She struggled for breath. “The babies…something’s wrong with the babies…”

“Shit,” I hissed. As she knelt beside me, gasping in excruciating pain, I let the impending truth of her betrayal fall by the wayside, and my instincts took over. “Come on, Sarah. We’ve got to get you inside.”

She screamed again as I tried to lift her. “I can’t move, Zoe. I can’t—” Another piercing scream echoed through the late morning, and I hoped that by the time I could get her to her feet, the others would be there, ready to help.

“Hold on, Sarah. We’ve got to get you inside—”

“I can’t,” she breathed. “It hurts so bad, I—” She let out another bloodcurdling scream.

Squeezing her shoulders, I stared into her eyes. “Sarah, you can’t have your babies in the dirt. You would never forgive me. We have to get you up.”

Biggs and Harper barreled around the corner of the shed, horror filling Biggs’s eyes. They were still dressed in their gear from going into town to scavenge, but their jackets and gun holsters didn’t inhibit them—especially not Biggs. He fell to his knees on Sarah’s other side.

“Babe,” he gasped. “Are you alright…is it the babies?”

Sarah let out another wail in answer, and Harper helped Biggs lift her up to take her into the house.

“Sarah, you have to relax,” Harper said. “It’s just like we practiced—”

“I can’t relax!” she snarled.

“Deep inhale, Babe. Please,” Biggs begged, smoothing her hair back from her face.

She did as she was told, but the pain from the contractions made it difficult for her to concentrate for long.

“Zoe, we’ll need the blankets and towels from the trunk in the cart, and I need my medical bag. Hurry—we don’t have long.”

Harper's voice was controlled as he and Biggs made their way toward the house with Sarah propped between them.

I nodded, staring into Sarah's frightened eyes, before turning to run toward the barn.

"Zoe," Harper called. "Get Chris, too; we're gonna need her."

"Okay!" I said and picked up the pace.

"What can I do?" Dani asked as I sprinted past her and Annie.

"Get Chris, and we'll need water and soap for anyone doing any handling." Dani nodded and hustled away, leaving me to gather Harper's medical bag and the towels and blankets.

When I finally arrived back at the ranch house, out of breath, Chris and Biggs were helping Sarah settle on the makeshift delivery bed consisting of carefully arranged couch cushions on a small kitchen table. Dani straightened as she finished laying the sheet over it, and I nearly flung myself at her in gratitude. Her work at the ranch years ago, combined with her more recent, temporary use of it as a safe haven mere months ago, provided her a familiarity with the place the rest of us lacked.

Dani glanced from me to Sarah and back, her face scrunched in sympathy. I had to fight the urge to run to her, to cry into her arms and tell her what I'd seen—that I was finally certain Sarah was a Monitor. But Sarah's [illegible] diverted my attention, sobering my thoughts and bringing me back to the urgent task at hand.

Becca ran inside, the screen door slamming behind her and a wide-eyed look on her face. "Here are more pillows," she said.

I pointed to Dani, who grabbed the pillows, layering them behind Sarah's head to prop her up a bit more. Sarah offered Dani a brief, tight smile of thanks, and my stomach knotted. As harmless as Sarah appeared to be in the midst of giving birth, I couldn't ignore the unease I felt at seeing my best friend standing so close to someone so dangerous.

Sarah's eyes met mine, and I saw the roaring emotions and pain darkening them.

"Zoe?" Harper said, making me jump.

I shook my head and stepped closer, nearly stumbling on the tangle of clothes and gear that he and Biggs had shed in the chaos of moving Sarah. I handed Harper his medical bag and started gathering up the pile of gear from the floor and dumping it onto the seat of the antique armchair that had been pushed into one corner.

"Thanks, Baby Girl," Harper said, distracted as he opened his bag. "Biggs, get her breathing leveled out or she's going to hyperventilate."

Biggs and Chris were murmuring reassurances and instructions to Sarah, while Becca, Dani, and I stood by, dumbfounded and waiting for another command.

Becca glanced at me. "I'll be outside with Carlos," she whispered. "Let us know if you need anything else." The way she singled me out and squeezed my arm reassuringly made me wonder if somehow she knew my insides were riddled with fear and sadness—or if maybe she'd had a vision of what had happened to Sarah, that she knew a war had broken out in Sarah's mind. A war Sarah was losing.

I nodded and flashed Becca a grateful smile before moving closer to Harper.

Sarah shrieked in pain, her screams coming one after the other.

"Can you give her something for the pain?" Biggs asked, panicked.

Harper shook his head. "There's no way it'll kick in fast enough. It all happened too fast…"

"What now, H?" I asked, my voice sounding steadier than I felt.

"The babies are coming," he said, pulling on a clean pair of gloves. "Wash your hands and put on a pair"—he tossed the box of gloves to me—"because you're gonna help me deliver these poor kids. Otherwise they might be deaf by the time they get here." He winked at me, a Harper gesture of reassurance, but I could feel his fear building as he readied himself for the delivery.

Even though he hoped Sarah's twins would be okay, he knew

that her situation was so far beyond normal that there were no certainties…but then, there never were in childbirth.

Harper scrutinized me with his shrewd, green eyes. "Stop digging, Baby Girl, come on."

Steadying my nerves, I did as Harper said. I took a step closer to Sarah, and once again, her eyes flitted to mine. Her gaze was filled with pain and fear and hatred that she tried to quell. Her face was ruddy, her skin covered in a sheen of sweat. Wisps of hair were matted to the sides of her face, and her eyes squinted shut as she wailed.

Chris stood on one side of Sarah, Biggs on the other, each squeezing one of her hands while she faded in and out of bouts of pain. They were doing their best to soothe her, to shift her mood and mute her overwhelming pain, but their efforts only dulled it slightly.

I did what I could to help Harper, being another set of hands when he needed it and holding Sarah's legs down when she started to move around. After a few more minutes, Sarah's pain was almost more than I could bear; it resonated inside of me, bringing the sting of tears to my eyes.

And then, Sarah let out another agonized grunt, and Harper had a screaming baby in his arms.

He looked up at me, smiling.

"It's a boy," I said, an uncontainable smile engulfing my face.

"A healthy boy," Harper said more loudly.

There was relieved laughter and whispers as Harper cut the umbilical cord and moved to hand Sarah her baby boy.

She shook her head. "No, I—" She began screaming in pain again, her body tensing.

Quickly, Harper handed me the baby, refocusing his attention on Sarah. "Here comes the other…"

She screamed again, her eyes shut tightly as she tried to clench away the pain.

"I know it's hard, Sarah, but try to relax. This one should be quick."

There was more screaming and Sarah cursing at Harper, but as Harper predicted, the other baby arrived within minutes.

"It's a girl!" I said. "You have a baby boy and a baby girl, Sarah." I tried to hand her the amazingly precious little boy who had begun to fuss in my arms, but again, Sarah pushed him away.

Tears were streaming from her eyes as she tried to catch her breath. Uncertain what to do, I handed the baby to Chris instead, while Harper passed the baby girl to Biggs. He accepted the infant, but his gaze was fixed on Sarah, confusion and pain twisting his expression, nearly breaking my heart. When he tried to hand Sarah her baby girl, she pushed Biggs away.

"No," she snapped. "Get them away from me."

Biggs stood there, stunned.

"I said *take them away!*" The confusion, disgust, and shame she was feeling greatly outweighed her love and adoration for her new family.

The room quieted, everyone's eyes on Sarah.

"Just get out!" she yelled, and my heart nearly stopped, fear replacing my concern for her.

After exchanging glances with one another, Chris and Biggs filed hesitantly out of the room, a baby cradled in each of their arms. Dani looked up at me, worry filling her eyes, as she, too, followed them out of the room, leaving Harper and me alone with Sarah. I glanced over at her; her hands were covering her face, and her body was convulsing as she sobbed.

"Why don't you give us a minute, Baby Girl," Harper whispered.

"No," Sarah said, her head snapping up. "I want to talk to Zoe…alone. Please." She sounded as conflicted as I knew she felt.

Harper took a step toward Sarah. "We need to clean you up and—"

"Later," she said. "I *need* to talk to Zoe." She must've noticed my uncertainty. Her eyes flicked from me to Harper and back. "I just had twins. I'm not going to bite you."

I let out a dry laugh as Harper squeezed my arm reassuringly and walked out. Part of me wanted to call him back, but I didn't. I needed to talk to Sarah about what was happening to her, about the memories I'd seen. I needed to know how far gone she was before I told Jason, before he interrogated her or worse.

Once I could hear Harper outside, I took a step toward Sarah.

She took a deep breath and shook her head, more tears escaping down her cheeks. "I don't know what's going on," she croaked. "I feel like I'm losing my mind."

I stood a few feet from her, unable to relax no matter how adamantly I tried to convince myself that she could never bring herself to kill me. "I know you want to hurt me. I've seen—"

"But I *don't*," she said desperately. "At least, part of me doesn't…"

I could feel Sarah battling with her own emotions, using her children, her family, to ignore her building need to put a bullet in my head, to spill my blood. "I know what I'm supposed to do. Trying to deny my mission is like trying not to breathe." There was a sharpness to her voice I'd never heard before. Regardless of Sarah's determination to ignore the dangerous part of herself, she was failing, and we both knew it.

"You're my best friend," she said like she was trying to convince herself it was true. Despite her calmness, she was only holding on by a thread.

When Sarah looked up at me again, her brown eyes were bloodshot and filled with more unshed tears, but her mouth was tensed and anger pulsed inside her. "This is your fault," she bit out. "Your whole family's—your mom's…I wouldn't be in this situation if it wasn't for *you*." Her tone was scathing.

Almost immediately, Sarah clamped her hand over her mouth. "I'm so sorry, Zoe. I didn't mean that. I know it's not your fault, I

—" She stopped herself and shook her head. "I don't know anything anymore."

She was right, it was my fault that she'd become a tool in the General's "Great Transformation," and I thought, for the first time, that I might actually grow to hate my mom.

"I'm a murderer," she whispered.

"You're a mom now, too, Sarah," I said, knowing that if she hadn't been, I would probably already be dead. "I don't think he planned on that part. Giving birth changed you. I can feel it."

Sarah nodded. "Maybe, but my need to kill you isn't gone." Her body began to shake as she broke out in violent sobs again, and she tried to stifle her cries in the crook of her arm. "What am I going to do?"

Holding my breath to choke the emotion building up inside me, I blinked rapidly.

"You need to leave, Zoe," she said. Her hands clenched into fists. I could feel her mind swirling with hatred, her animosity and need for blood—*my* blood—building to a crescendo.

I took a step backward. "I have to tell Jason. I—"

Sarah nodded. "Just…get Biggs first…please."

Sobbing, I turned to leave, knowing this was the last time I was going to see my friend with any semblance of the Sarah I knew and loved; *that* Sarah was losing. She tried to stifle her crying as I walked away, and I had to fight the urge to fall to my knees. Her anguish, as well as mine, was so crushing that I tried to convince myself I didn't have to tell Jason. That she wouldn't act on it…

But I knew, deep down, that eventually she would attempt to complete her mission, and when she did, I would be dead. Sarah couldn't be trusted, no matter how badly I wished things were different.

I stepped into the sunshine and immediately headed toward the stable, where Jason and Jake stood with Harper. The moment my gaze met Jake's, tears blurred my vision once more, and I struggled to breathe. Another sob escaped from my throat as I stepped into

Jake's arms, and I nearly crumpled in his hold. "Where's Biggs?" I choked out. "Sarah wanted—"

A muffled gunshot came from inside the ranch house.

Devoid of thought and driven by my gut reaction, I spun, stumbling momentarily, and ran toward the house, wiping the tears from my eyes so I could see. I called out for Sarah, oblivious to any other cries or shouts around me as I flung open the screen door and flew into the house.

As my worst fear was confirmed, I fell to my knees in the entry. Sarah's body was crumpled on the floor by the antique chair in the corner.

Screaming her name, I scrambled over to her and pulled her lifeless body into my arms. "Sarah," I breathed, guilt and sadness making it too difficult to speak. As I readjusted my hold on her, my fingers splayed across a warm, wet opening in the back of her head, and I could only feel wetness and clumped hair against my hand.

Screaming, this time in horror, I let go, and her body fell limply back to the floor

Biggs and Harper were suddenly beside me, Harper pulling me away from Sarah's body and shoving me into someone else's arms —into Dani's.

I grabbed onto her, clasping her as tightly as I could, never wanting to let go. I refused to accept what was happening, unsure I ever *could*.

"I'm here, Zo," Dani said. "I'm here. It'll be okay."

I was shaking my head before I realized what I was saying. "No, it won't…it's my fault."

29

JAKE

MAY 25, 1AE

Bodega Bay, California

Jake walked toward the barn that seemed to glow in the dimming light, two bottles of warm formula in his hands. He couldn't believe how much had happened in the last few hours. There were two infant additions to the group, Sarah was dead, and Biggs was so despondent he'd become a completely different person. And for reasons Jake didn't entirely understand, Zoe had been inconsolable. Although Sarah had been Zoe's close friend, there was something else—something in the way that Jason looked at her, in the way that Dani consoled her, in the way that Gabe and Becca hovered nearby—that made him think Sarah's death was more than it seemed.

"—know we can't tell him the truth, Zo." Jake could barely hear Dani's voice over the crickets and evening breeze. "We can't tell *any* of them the truth. Not until we know who the other Monitor is."

Jake stopped in the doorway, curious but not wanting to intrude on Dani and Zoe's whispered conversation.

Dani peered over at him, her eyes widening with surprise.

"He already knows, sort of," Zoe said, shrugging Dani's concern away before her eyes quickly drifted back down to the baby girl in her arms.

For an instant, Dani seemed worried, but then she finally gave Jake a weak smile. Like Zoe, she gazed back down at the baby boy she was holding.

Remembering the bottles in his hands, Jake strode over to the picnic table where the two women were sitting and crouched between them. "Here," he said softly and handed them each a bottle. "Chris said you'd need these."

Dani accepted one before her gaze shifted to Zoe, expectant.

"He won't even look at them," Zoe said, her voice hoarse and distant. She continued to rock the infant cradled in the crook of her arm.

"Zo, Jake brought the babies' bottles. I don't know about that little princess, but this monster's getting hungry."

As if on cue, the baby girl began to fuss. Absently, Zoe reached for the bottle Jake was holding out to her. "They need names…"

Jake swallowed thickly. "Biggs said he wanted to talk to Sarah about naming them after his mother and father," he offered, finally getting Zoe's attention.

Her bloodshot eyes met his. "Really?"

Jake nodded. "Ellie and Everett."

Her eyes began to shimmer, and she returned her attention to the tiny little girl. "Sarah should be here…feeding them…naming them…"

"It's not your fault, Zo. Sarah wasn't herself; she wasn't *Sarah*."

As much as Jake wanted to know what exactly had happened, to know how much truth was intertwined with the story he'd put together in his mind, he couldn't bring himself to ask. Not when Zoe was so distraught.

Zoe shook her head and squeezed her eyes shut. "But she was, don't you see?" she said to Dani. "She killed herself so she wouldn't hurt me…it's *my* fault…"

"No," Dani said, her tone firm. "It's not."

Zoe craned her neck to look back at her friend.

"It's not *your* fault, Zo. It's Dr. Wesley's fault. It's the *General's* fault."

Zoe didn't say anything; instead she peered down at the infant in Dani's arms. "Everett and Ellie…I hope that's what he picks."

"Harper's talking to him now," Jake said as he stood. "Hopefully he'll come around soon."

"Is Biggs still keeping to the living room?" Dani asked as she gazed up at him.

Jake nodded. "He's not ready to leave yet."

"And what exactly is Harper going to say to him?" Zoe asked bitterly. "That it was postpartum depression? That Sarah was so depressed she took her own life?" She shook her head. "It's a lie."

"It's the only option we have right now, Zo, unless we want to put everyone else in danger."

"You mean put me and Jason in danger," Zoe corrected.

Dani took a deep, steadying breath. "And what makes you think that no one else will be caught up in this shit storm? We can't risk telling Biggs, for *everyone's* sake." She glanced down at Everett. "For *their* sake."

Approaching footsteps brought their attention to the barn door. Harper paused in the doorway before striding inside.

"How is he?" Zoe asked.

Harper shook his head. "He's angry," he said simply and sat down on the opposite side of the picnic table. "He doesn't understand that this happens sometimes…that it can be too much."

Jake could tell by the despondency in Harper's voice, the sadness, that he truly believed that was what had happened.

"We should give him more time," Dani said.

Harper rested his elbows on the table and rubbed his hands

over his face. "Jason and Ky are digging a grave. We'll bury her tonight and give Biggs some time to process before we move on."

Zoe held the bottle to Ellie's mouth as the infant began to gurgle and fuss more loudly. "Does he want to see them yet?"

Harper gazed down at the two swaddled newborns, then up at Zoe. "No, not yet. He's not thinking clearly right now, Baby Girl. He—"

"He blames them," she finished for him.

"They have us until he comes around. They'll be fine."

Zoe nodded, but she didn't seem to be listening, nor did she seem to notice as a tear rolled down her cheek.

Jake hated that this would become just one more unsettling memory to add to those that already haunted her.

30

DANI

MAY 26, 1AE

Petaluma, California

"Should be just up ahead," Jason said to me, pointing through a break in the trees lining the left side of the country road. We were on the floor of a shallow valley surrounded by a gently rolling sea of emerald—grasses, low shrubs, and a few clusters of wild oaks here and there, the largest of which spread out beyond a several-acre field beside the road. Jason glanced down at the map he'd folded to show this specific part of Sonoma County and added, "Just beyond that patch of woods."

He stopped his chestnut horse, and Wings drew to a halt beside the gelding without me having to ask. Turning in his saddle, Jason scanned the rest of our somber group, spread out in a loose column behind us. It jarred me every time I looked at the wagon and *didn't* see Sarah sitting on its high bench seat.

"Let's hold up here," Jason called out. "Let Dani, Zoe, and Ky do their thing."

Zoe and Ky guided their horses up to the head of the caravan, and the three of us took turns doing "our thing." Thankfully, neither Zoe nor Ky found anything of note in their mental examination of the valley.

We only continued our trek to the appointed farm once my animal scouts had scanned the area around each of the farm buildings, reporting that there were no signs of two-legs and that, according to a drake, there had been none since his hen's ducklings had hatched. He showed me an image of baby ducks that had to be at least a couple weeks old.

Several hundred yards later, there was a longer gap in the windbreak of trees lining the road, and I caught a glimpse of several large structures. They were the first buildings we'd seen since entering the secluded little valley, and each had weathered wooden siding and orangish roof shingles that, even from a distance, looked relatively new.

"That must be it," I said to nobody in particular, and a sudden thrill of excitement made me bounce a little in my saddle.

Jason was glancing at me sideways, a small smile playing on his lips.

I forced myself to be still and shrugged, feeling a little ashamed to be showing so much giddiness so soon after Sarah…after the chaos the group had been through the previous day. But the shame didn't decrease my giddiness, if anything, it only fanned it higher. This place—this cluster of farm buildings surrounded by fenced-in pastures and patches of oak trees and land just begging to be converted into vegetable gardens and fields of grains—this was our chance for a fresh start. This was our chance to settle down someplace new to all of us, leaving behind the horrors and sadness and disturbing memories of everything we'd experienced beyond these hills.

Wings picked up on my excitement and sped up, first to a fast walk, then to a trot, until she was cantering up the road. I laughed, unable to hold in the joy of running with Wings—a feeling I'd once allowed myself to feel *through* her, but now had to settle for experiencing from the saddle. I caught flashes of a large white building through the trees, glimpses of what I assumed was the farmhouse.

When Wings and I reached the gravel driveway flanked by two fenced-in pastures, my assumption was confirmed, and my mouth fell open. The house was huge. And gorgeous. And belonged in a museum.

As Wings drew to a stop in front of a wrought-iron gate set between two wide stone piers, I stared at the house at the end of the drive and waited for the others to catch up. Maybe I should've expected our new home to be this impressive. Maybe I should've assumed that the New Bodega Town Council would direct us toward the farm most able to hold us all in relative comfort. Maybe I should've let myself believe that, for once, something good would be coming our way. But I hadn't, and that alone made the sight so much more wondrous.

Fifty yards ahead, the gravel driveway gave way to a wide, two-story Victorian farmhouse that gleamed like a beacon shouting, "Welcome home! You're finally *home*!" It was painted a yellow so pale it could easily be mistaken as white, with white window trim as well as white columns and a white bannister wrapping around the front and sides, separating a wraparound porch from the lawn below. Whitewashed stairs led up to the porch and a dark-stained, screened-off front door, to the right of which were a couple of large, wooden rocking chairs.

The patch of dense woods we'd seen from the road crept up on the left side of the house. An old wooden cottage sat across from it, and beyond that, I could see a cluster of farm buildings surrounding a wide, gravel roundabout.

The whole scene was almost laughably idyllic. *Grams would've loved this place,* I thought, and for the first time in a long time, thinking of her didn't bring more sadness than fond remembrance.

At the sound of hooves and cart wheels on pavement, I looked over my shoulder to find Jason still hanging back in the lead of the caravan. He was watching me, smiling and shaking his head, as his horse—and behind him, the rest of our animals and people—slowly closed the distance between us.

I placed my hands on my hips and raised my eyebrows, feigning offense. "What?"

"I just love watching you ride, *really* ride…that's all," Jason said as his horse came to a halt on the left side of Wings. He reached for my hand and lifted it up to his lips, pressing a gentle kiss against the smooth wooden ring on my third finger.

Happiness flooded me, and I looked away, focusing on the gate, on the fields on either side of the driveway, on the gravel itself…on anything but Jason. It felt wrong to be happy, and self-loathing quickly replaced my joy.

Carlos, sitting atop Arrow, rode up to sit on my right side. The wagon, driven by Grayson, came to a halt on the gravel at the base of the driveway, the cart stopping behind it, and the rest of the horses, riderless and ridden, milling in the road.

"What's the holdup?" Chris asked as she guided Cookie in to squeeze between Carlos and the fence. "Oh, a gate. *Great.*"

Jason glanced over his shoulder. "Mase! We need your strength up here."

There was a loud thump, quickly followed by the crunching of gravel under boots as Mase jogged up to the front of the caravan, stopping behind our mounts. "What do you need me to do?"

Jason pointed to the center of the gate. "Can you force it open?"

After an unconcerned shrug, Mase made his way around Jason's horse to the gate, stopping in the dead center. He wrapped his hands around the second bar from the middle on either side, took a deep breath, and pushed. Groaning, the gate doors slowly moved inward, a few inches, then a foot.

I held my breath, waiting…waiting…waiting…

There was a metal *thwang*, and Mase stumbled forward as the gates opened with no further resistance.

"Thank you, Mase," Jason said with a nod. He nudged his horse forward, leading our people up the driveway. Looking back at me, he flashed one of his increasingly frequent, though no less devastating, smiles and uttered the same words I'd been thinking since the farmhouse first came into view.

"Welcome home."

Annie screamed, but it wasn't the squeal of joy we were all so used to hearing from her. It was a scream of outrage…of fear…of danger.

I froze in the middle of slipping Wings's saddle off and met Jason's eyes as he unsaddled his own horse. Without a word, I dropped the saddle on the gravel, turned on my heel, and sprinted in the direction of Annie's mind signature; it was just beyond the opposite side of the farmhouse. I didn't think I'd ever run so fast in my entire life.

Again, Annie screamed.

Jack raced past me as I sped across the overgrown lawn in front of the house and down the gentle slope on the other side. I pumped my arms harder, forced my legs to move even faster.

As a large pond came into view, half surrounded by wild oaks, I finally caught sight of Annie. Vanessa was struggling with her in the water. It looked like the small woman was trying to hold Annie *under* the water, but couldn't quite get a good enough grip on her.

"Vanessa!" I shouted. "Stop!"

The insane young woman paused and looked up at me just long enough for Annie to lash out. Her little fingernails dragged down Vanessa's neck, doing nearly as much damage as a small animal's claws would have done, and Vanessa shrieked. But she also released Annie.

The little girl floundered away, crawling toward the pond's edge.

Jack leapt into the water only a few seconds before me, snarling and snapping at Vanessa, but not actually striking. I aimed for Annie, yanking her up and out of the water and carrying her the rest of the way toward the edge of the pond.

She clung to me, sniffling and shaking and making pathetic whining noises. I didn't bother trying to disengage her surprisingly strong little arms from around my neck or her legs from around my waist, because Jason and Carlos were only a few strides from the pond, and pretty much everyone else wasn't far behind them.

Jason and Carlos had no trouble overpowering Vanessa. Jason dragged her up to the grass with Carlos right behind him, turned to mutter something to Carlos, then thrust Vanessa toward her younger brother. Reeling in his carefully restrained anger, Jason approached the spot where Annie and I were huddled in the unkempt grass, soaking wet and shaking and stinking of pond water.

He knelt on the ground and wrapped his arms around both of us. "Are you okay?"

I nodded, still breathing hard from the mad dash across the farm.

"But I *had* to," Vanessa shrieked, drawing both Jason's and my attention.

Jason pulled away just enough that he could watch Carlos attempt to reason with his not-so-harmless sister.

"You had to *what*, Nessa?" Carlos was crouched in front of Vanessa, who was sitting with her legs curled under her and rubbing her hands up and down her arms.

"Give her a bath. I had to wash her, don't you see? I *had* to!"

Carlos shook his head, the gesture giving off a sense of hopelessness. "No, I *don't* see. Why would you think—"

"I don't think. I *know*!" she shrieked. Standing up on her knees, she reached for Carlos, clawlike fingers latching onto his sleeves.

"Mom told me I'd lose her if I didn't do it. She doesn't love me anymore. I'm losing her, and Mom said I had to act more like *her*"—she threw her arm in the general direction of Jason, Annie, and me—"so Annie would love me like she's starting to love her. I *had* to!"

Chris approached the pair of siblings cautiously, holding out her hands. "Shhh..." she murmured when Vanessa turned wide, wild eyes on her. "Hush now, hon." Stopping behind Vanessa, she reached down and took hold of the smaller woman's arm to pull her to her feet. "Come on. Let's get you dried off and settled in."

After a silent exchange and a nod, Chris and Carlos each held onto one of Vanessa's arms while they led her back across the lawn toward the farm buildings.

Closing my eyes, I took a deep breath, hugged Annie tighter, and leaned my cheek on Jason's shoulder. "What are we going to do with her?" I asked softly.

With a heavy exhale, Jason shrugged.

I pulled away just enough that I could see his face. "Do you think—do you think that Colonel Marshall might have been right? That we should—that we'll have to, um, you know...*put her down?*" I said, mouthing the last part.

"No." There was a surprising amount of conviction in Jason's eyes.

"How can we be sure she won't try something like this again? She could've drowned Annie."

Jason hesitated, then said, "We'll keep her locked up—in a stable stall, like we did back at the ranch."

"Forever?" I said, my brow furrowed. "But she'll be miserable."

Again, Jason shrugged. "As miserable as Carlos would be if he lost her again?" He shook his head resolutely. "The kid's been through enough. I'm not putting him through that."

I sighed and pulled away further, uncrossing my legs in preparation to rise. "I suppose you're right."

About an hour later, after Annie and I had washed off in the creek that fed the pond and were dressed in cleaner, drier clothes, I walked the little girl back toward the farmhouse. We were just approaching the front steps leading up to the porch, me eager to get a peek inside, when Ky opened the front door.

"Let her air out a bit first, 'kay?" he said through the screen door.

Annie stepped onto the first stair and gave my hand a tug, but I didn't budge. "Bodies?" I asked.

Ky nodded. "Looks like a married couple."

I grimaced. "How bad is it?"

"Just a ruined mattress. Jason and Mase are taking it out back to burn with the bodies." He lifted his shoulders, offering me a slight smile. "But the good news is, they've been dead long enough that the smell's faded a bit. Should have the place aired out enough to be livable by tomorrow…if we keep every single door and window open."

I gave him a halfhearted thumbs-up. "Awesome."

"Don't worry, D, it'll be worth the wait. This place is *pretty* damn sweet."

"Awesome," I said, more genuine this time.

Ky's focus shifted to Annie. "I've got somethin' for you, kiddo," he said as he pushed the screen door open and walked out onto the porch, one hand held behind his back. I couldn't stifle the tiny twinge of fear caused by *not* knowing what was in that concealed hand.

Stop it, I told myself, forcing a smile. *We don't know anything for sure, and besides, he has no reason to hurt Annie or me.* But after Sarah…I couldn't *not* think about it.

Giggling, Annie tugged on my hand again, and this time, I let her go. "What?" she asked as she ran up the stairs. "Present?" We still hadn't moved beyond one-word sentences most of the time, but at least her spoken vocabulary was growing more varied.

Ky grinned down at the little girl practically bouncing with excitement right in front of him. "Does 'Mr. Potato Head' mean anything to you?"

Annie shook her head.

"Well, kid…you're in for a surprise."

I laughed softly as I watched Ky crouch down to Annie's level and present her with the way-too-big-to-be-a-potato toy and Annie examine the thing with serious intensity. "Can you keep an eye on her for a bit?" I asked Ky. "I want to check on Carlos…and Vanessa."

Ky nodded. "Harper's with them in the barn, cleaning up the damage caused by this little monster." He ruffled Annie's wet, blonde hair.

Annie swatted his hand away absentmindedly, frowning as she figured out how to open the latch on Mr. Potato Head's rear end to get to the goodies rattling around inside.

When Ky noticed me lingering, he made shooing motion. "Go. I got this."

Smiling my gratitude, I turned away from the porch steps and headed toward the cluster of farm buildings surrounding the roundabout. I'd yet to explore anything, only having come back to the roundabout—where we'd left the horses in all the Annie–Vanessa hubbub—to retrieve soap, towels, and clean clothes for Annie and myself before washing up in the creek.

The horses were all gone; a quick telepathic scan told me they were in the pasture on the far side of the driveway, along with the goats. The cart and wagon had been parked haphazardly between the cottage and a large, well-kept old barn. There was also a stable on the opposite side of the roundabout from the barn, and a long building, whose function I wasn't quite sure of, between the two.

Making a mental note to explore everything thoroughly later, I hurried toward the barn. Both of its double doors had been slid open, likely to let in as much daylight from the bright, spring sunshine as possible, but to my eyes, the interior looked completely dark aside from dozens of tiny lights glowing like stars near the ceiling. As I neared the doorway, I stared up at the criss-crossing strings of twinkly lights in confusion. Carlos had to be powering them, which made sense; what didn't make sense was why they were there in the first place.

Only when I stepped inside and lowered my eyes did I begin to understand. A handful of tables—maybe a dozen—were set up deeper in the barn, draped with pale tablecloths and set with centerpieces of withered flowers in shades of yellows, oranges, and browns. It took me a few seconds to realize that the farm must have rented out the barn as a wedding venue to make some extra money—and from the looks of it, there'd been a wedding right before the outbreak, and they'd never had a chance to clean up afterward. *Or the wedding never happened...*

The site was eerie, a haunting echo of the way the world used to be. For some reason, those tables and chairs, covered in a layer of dust and still set up for a celebration that may never have happened—a celebration whose attendants may very well all have died in the last six months—were far more unsettling than the idea of the dead couple being evicted from their farmhouse just a short ways behind me.

I heard a whistle, and snapped my head to the right, my heart beating double-time.

"Didn't want to startle you," Harper said with a casual wave.

He, Vanessa, and Chris were sitting at the right-most table, Harper's chair turned to face Vanessa, and Chris's right behind her. Carlos was leaning against the wall beyond the table.

With a smile, Harper returned his attention to Vanessa, wiping a cotton swab over the scratches on her neck. I was about to join them when I heard approaching footsteps crunching in the gravel behind me.

"There you are," Zoe said as I turned around. She had a swaddled infant in either arm and looked the picture of the quintessential exhausted new mom...except for the part where she *wasn't* a new mom, or a mom at all. "Here," she practically groaned in relief as she unloaded one of the slumbering babies into my arms. "I need a break from double-duty."

"Um...okay," I said, accepting the warm little bundle. "Which one is this?"

"Ellie...pink blanket," Zoe said. She readjusted Everett in her arms and, turning, started walking toward the corner of the barn, away from the driveway and farmhouse.

I watched her walk away for a few steps, then looked down at the tiny little person I was suddenly holding.

"D," Zoe said. "Are you coming?"

Only when I looked up again did I realize she'd stopped and was watching me, apparently waiting for me to accompany her. I caught up with her, moving slowly so I wouldn't wake the newborn, and we rounded the corner of the barn in silence.

"So...I've been thinking," she said. "I really think we should tell Biggs the truth."

"Zo—"

She skewered me with guilt-filled eyes. "He can't be a Monitor, right? So what's the harm in—"

"Dani!" Annie shrieked as she ran around the corner of the barn, just a short ways ahead. "Look!" She came to a skidding halt in front of me and held up Mr. Potato Head—the poor guy had arms for eyes, an ear for a mouth, and sunglasses and a mustache growing out of the right side of his body—just as Ellie stirred in my arms and started to emit a stuttering wail.

"Fabulous," I muttered.

31

ZOE

MAY 28, 1AE

The Farm, California

It was first thing in the morning and I'd already been awake for a few hours, tending to the needs of my demanding charges. I was in the kitchen, Annie and Sam eating their morning cereal while I made my third cup of coffee.

"Hey," Jake said as he walked into the kitchen and wrapped his arms around me.

"Howdy." I poured a generous cup of coffee for me, a little bit in a spare mug for Jake, and then more in mine, deciding I needed it more than he did. I'd learned to take advantage of every free moment I had without the twins, which meant eating, drinking coffee, and sleeping as much as I could were fair game.

Annie smiled at Jake, but soon a full-fledged grin engulfed her face. "Babies!"

"Babies?" Jake said.

After taking a much-needed sip of coffee, I turned around to find Camille walking away, leaving Jake with Everett in his arms.

Sam stifled a laugh, while Annie burst out in a bout of giggles that woke the infant Jake held awkwardly against his chest. Fussing and screaming ensued. Amused, I watched Jake as he stared down at Everett like he was wondering what the hell to do with something so tiny and loud.

Shifting Everett, Jake held him out away from his body. "Something's wrong with him."

I laughed. "Something's *always* wrong; he's a baby."

Jake stared at Everett a moment longer before tucking him into the crook of his arm. He glanced up at me, and I quickly looked away, pretending I was focused more on cleaning up my coffee mess than on Jake's discomfort.

Everett's face reddened and his screams grew louder by the moment.

"Maybe he's too hot," Jake said, and he began to unwrap Everett's blanket from around him.

"He doesn't like it when you remove his blanket," I said as I put the coffee grounds back in the cupboard. "I think it's a comfort thing."

Jake raised Everett up to his chest and began to pat his back.

"He doesn't like that either; it makes him gassy."

Jake frowned. "Well, what *does* he like?"

Annie and Sam were laughing at him again, no longer making any attempt to stifle their amusement.

"You two think this is funny?" Jake said with feigned irritation. When their laughter only grew more boisterous, Jake smiled. "Sabotage," he grumbled.

Taking pity on him, I set my coffee mug on the counter and took a step closer. "Here, I'll take him," I said.

With gratitude emanating from him, Jake unloaded the infant into my arms.

Like usual, I began rocking Everett in a steady swing, instantly taking his screams down to fussy gurgles and grunts. "You know, even though that was probably the most awkward interaction I've ever witnessed, it might've been the most precious thing I've ever seen, too."

"Really…" Jake said dryly.

I nodded and went back to the counter, simultaneously rocking Everett while I grabbed Jake's cup of coffee. "Here ya go," I said, handing it to him.

Collecting my own mug, I held it up to Jake's. "Bottoms up," I chirped. All I needed was a few moments to let the caffeine kick in and I'd be ready for another day of nannyhood.

Sitting in one of the rocking chairs on the farmhouse porch and holding a swaddled, contented Ellie, I basked in the early afternoon sunshine, trying not to fall asleep myself.

Abruptly, the front door was flung open, and Annie scurried out. Sam exited the farmhouse directly after her with a slam of the screen door. Ellie started, but thankfully she didn't start crying.

When Sam noticed us tucked away in the corner, his eyes widened. "Sorry, Zoe. I didn't know you were out here."

I nodded down at Ellie. "All the noise and voices inside were making her anxious."

Sam walked over, staring down at the baby. "Becca said they're important."

My eyebrows rose. "Did she?"

He nodded, and I knew Becca must've been alluding to more than the sentiment we all had for the babies already.

"I'm not sure why, but that's what she said." Sam gently brushed a wisp of silky, soft hair from Ellie's forehead, an image of his baby sister flashing through his mind, then he turned and headed back to the porch steps.

"Where are you two off to?" I asked as I resumed my rocking.

"We're gonna play!" Annie sang as she began jumping up and down, clapping her hands.

I couldn't help but smile at her enthusiasm. "I wish I could play," I said. "But I have Ellie duty."

Annie's face scrunched up, and she stopped jumping. "You look too tired to play."

The smile fell from my face. "Gee, thanks, Annie."

"You should take a nap," Sam called behind him as he jogged after Annie, who'd done a Tasmanian devil spin and sprinted toward the barn.

I *was* tired, but there was little I could do about it. I was still in a constant state of emotional exhaustion—but not physical exhaustion, which was what I missed. It had been three days, and Biggs was already doing better, his mind no longer the toxic mess it had been the first couple of days. But despite his improved mental state, it was still up to Auntie Zoe to tend to most of the twins' needs, and they didn't care if I was eating, had my hands in mud, or had just fallen asleep.

Regardless though, Biggs, Ellie, Everett, and I had found a temporary, affable routine that helped a little bit with my sanity. All it took were a few days of sink-or-swim, trial-and-error situations, and I was settling into my new job title surprisingly well. I understood the twins more—their quirks, their personalities—making it easier to be preemptive with their bottles and their naps and the noises they liked, disliked, and absolutely hated.

Ellie was the more even-tempered of the two, *but* whenever she did become fussy, rapidly blinking my eyes and talking to her like she was the cutest little baby in the world and I was going to eat her up seemed to forego complete tears and bloodcurdling screams.

Everett, on the other hand, was grumpy—a definite crier. He didn't like to be left alone, and he didn't like it when Tavis entered the same room as him. Everett also didn't like his diaper changed or the sound of his sister's crying or his bottle being too hot or too cold…he didn't like much of anything. So, as long as I remembered all of that *and* rocked them both while they were awake, they were content…mostly…sometimes.

Ellie cooed, and I looked down at her. Her wide blue eyes brightened with the golden glow of the sunset as she watched me, slobbering and mauling her incredibly soft, tiny hand. "We should make a date of this, you and I," I said, wiping a string of drool from her cheek. "You like sunsets just like your auntie, don't you?" Ellie's only response was a grunt and a spastic kick of her feet.

Hearing approaching footsteps from inside the house, I looked at the screen door just as it opened. Biggs stepped outside onto the whitewashed porch with a small smile on his drawn face as he peered down at Everett, who was nestled in his arms. "Hey, *Warden*," he said to me as he lowered himself into the rocking chair beside mine.

"Not the warden thing again," I grumbled.

Biggs shrugged. "Hey, it's not *my* nickname for you, it's your brother's. I asked him where you were, and he said the 'warden' was outside. Did you really kick them out of the dining room earlier?"

"Of course I did. I was in there with Ellie, minding my own business, and Jason and Harper sauntered in and asked me to draw up a diagram for them."

"What's wrong with that?" Biggs resituated Everett against his chest.

"Nothing, until they started bickering about projects that need to be done and who needs to do what, and then they woke up the baby."

"Oh."

"I asked them to leave, nicely," I added.

Biggs lifted his eyebrows and tilted his head a little to the left. "Yeah?"

I rolled my eyes. "Mostly."

Biggs smirked and leaned closer to gaze down at Ellie, whose eyes shifted to his lazily before she yawned, making me yawn in turn. "How's her sneezing today?"

"She's doing just fine," I said. "We soaked up some vitamin D this morning while I was drawing the farm layout for Grayson. If she's anything like her Auntie Zoe, she'll be better in no time. Sunshine'll fix anything." I offered Biggs a reassuring smile.

I was so relieved by the fatherly love he now felt for the twins. I was a good enough stand-in for a few days while he got his shit together, but the twins needed their father. He'd finally realized that they were all he had left of Sarah, and Sarah would've expected him to step up and love them the way they deserved to be loved.

"Thank you," he said quietly, staring out at the farm. Sam and Annie were playing with Jack and Cooper on the overgrown lawn beside the house. "I know you didn't ask for this role, and I honestly don't know what would've happened to my children if you hadn't stepped in." Biggs shook his head. "I'm so ashamed of myself for acting the way that I did. I can't believe I blamed them…"

Hearing his self-deprecating speech made me nauseous with guilt. He still had no idea what had *really* happened. He had no idea that all of this was my fault…mine and Jason's. "You were a wreck, Biggs. I don't blame you," I said. "I loved Sarah, too, and I wanted to help—I *want* to help you in any way that I can." I owed him that much.

Staring down at Ellie, I gave her a big smile and said, "Everything takes time, but we're getting there…we'll be just fine." Ellie's eyelids began to close, and as I tucked her blanket more tightly around her, I yawned again.

"You should go get some rest," Biggs said. "I'll take them for a bit."

I shook the sleepiness from my mind as I covered another

yawn with my hand. “I’m not sure why I’m suddenly so tired.” My stomach growled. “And hungry.” I looked at him. “When was the last time anyone ate?”

Biggs shrugged again, distracted as he bent down and scooped Ellie from my arms.

Taking my cue, I rose from the rocking chair, stretched, and then groaned, thinking how wonderful it sounded to crawl into bed for a couple hours. But then my stomach growled again. “I guess I’m going to make some lunch before I get any sleep.”

Biggs nodded. “It’s up to you…you get a free pass for the afternoon.”

“Thanks, Biggs.” Opening the screen, I padded into the house, hearing scraping and banging in most of the rooms as everyone was getting settled. At least we were finally moved into the farm-house and had a proper space to take care of the twins.

Walking into the enormous, bright kitchen, I stopped short. Other than the coffee I’d made sure to unpack and a few boxes of cereal, our food was still in boxes on the moss-green granite island in the center of the room. Without Sarah, it looked like any sort of cooking or culinary organization had completely ceased. *Where the hell is Becca?* She’d become Sarah’s helper over the months, and I’d expected to find her in the kitchen, organizing and cooking in Sarah’s place. But she wasn’t there, and now that I thought about it, I realized I hadn’t seen her all day.

If the Farm truly *was* our new home, we needed to settle in, and if we were going to do that, we needed to reestablish a routine. With so many of us, we needed some sort of schedule; otherwise we’d be so lost in our myriad of to-dos that nothing would ever get done. We needed group meal times and togetherness, and for that we needed a cook. While I was a miserable excuse for one, I was a better choice than some of the others. Hoping Becca would be willing to help me, I decided I would seek her out and *beg* for her help.

Searching the ranch, I found everyone busy, in the midst of

some chore or another. Mase was chopping firewood near the outdoor brick oven on the lawn area, while Camille stacked the pieces in the storage space beneath it, but there was no sign of Becca. I passed by an old shed, where Jake was wrenching on something, and poked my head inside.

He glanced up at me. "Hey."

I offered him a tired smile. "You hungry?"

"Always," he said. I leaned forward, and after he met me halfway, I gave him a peck on the lips. "I'll find your sister and make us all something to eat."

"Sounds good." He turned his attention back to the machine sitting on the table, and I continued on in my search for Becca.

I made my way through the stable and then into the storage barn, where I stumbled across Dani as she mucked out the goat pen. I couldn't help but smile at the sight of her curls escaping from her braid and the dirt smudged on her cheeks.

"Hey, Zo," she said, a grunt immediately following as she shoveled old food and manure and wet hay from the ground. "You look like crap."

I smiled at her. "Awe. You're so sweet."

Dani barked a laugh. "How are the twins? Are they finally asleep?"

I tilted my head to the side. "Nope, but I left them with Biggs." I suddenly remembered how low we were getting on formula. "Oh, I gotta remember to tell H to get more formula next time you guys head into town…we should be fine until then, I think…" My thoughts began to wander.

Dani stopped shoveling and straightened. Brushing a wisp of hair from her face, she leaned against the shovel she'd wedged into the dirt. "Everything'll be fine, Zo. You're doing a great job." She offered me a reassuring smile.

"Yeah…" I glanced around at all the clean animal pens. "It looks like you're making headway. Sorry I haven't been much help. I'm actually surprised you've been able to do so much with Annie running around like the crazy little banshee she is."

"Sam's a lifesaver," Dani said with an exhausted sigh. I was really proud of her for adapting to the survivor lifestyle as well as she had. I barely remembered the girly, dolled-up Dani I'd known growing up. Our little farm seemed to be giving her a sense of purpose, which I could understand, and I could tell by the revived glint in her eyes that she was happy here.

"Have you eaten at all?" I asked, wondering how long she'd been working without a break.

"Umm, no, not really. I sort of forgot."

I shook my head. "Tsk. Tsk. It's nearly noon."

Dani's eyes narrowed, and she cocked her head to the side. "Have *you* eaten?"

With a laugh that sounded almost like a sob, I rested my fists on my hips. "Touché, D, touché." I shook my head. "I'm actually planning on whipping something up for everyone right now. You seen Becca at all?"

"Nope, but then again, I've sorta been in my own world all morning."

"Animal chatting?"

Dani only gave me a guilty smile and wrinkled her nose. "But no drifting, I promise."

I nodded. "You're doing good, D." I gave her a small, approving smile and turned to go. "I'll let you know when it's ready—oh," I stopped mid-step and turned around again. "Harper set the infirmary up in the master bedroom, so you and Jason get the smaller room downstairs. Is that okay?"

"Is that the one with the ginormous walk-in closet?"

I nodded. "You worried you won't have room for the duffel bag containing the only clothes you own?"

She gave me a sassy smirk. "No, although it's past time for a little shopping spree…" Her eyes widened. "Anyway, I was thinking, since Carlos is sleeping in the stable with Vanessa, Annie can stay with me and Jason. I can make the closet into a little room for her."

"Sounds good." I gave her a quick goodbye wave. "I'll leave you to it."

"Thanks, Zo," she called, and I headed back to the farmhouse. Jogging up the porch steps, I nearly ran into Biggs as he hustled out the front door…without the babies.

"I thought it was 'dad time' with the twins," I said.

Biggs shrugged. "Jake needs my help. Harper and Chris took them into the house."

I shook my head as he walked toward the shed. "Bullet dodger," I grumbled.

Entering through the front door as quietly as I could so as not to disturb any sleeping babies, I walked down the hall to the living room and peeked my head inside. I grinned.

Chris was cooing at Everett, who gurgled and hiccupped in her arms as she rocked him. Harper was smiling down at Ellie, who was cradled in his lap. With Harper's dancing eyebrows and too-wide smiles, he was making the goofiest faces at her I'd ever seen on anyone.

"Have either of you seen Becca?" I whispered.

Chris glanced up at me and shook her head, a self-satisfied smile brightening her relaxed features. She was completely content. "Not since she moved her stuff up into her room."

Harper finally looked at me and shook his head. He was trying his damnedest to keep little Ellie in love with him like all the other ladies, but exhaustion filled his eyes, and I had to stifle a laugh. "She ensnared by your charm yet, H?"

He gave me a small, cocky smile. "We're getting there."

"Good." I nodded in the direction of the kitchen. "I'm going to make us something to eat. I'll let you know when it's ready."

Chris and Harper nodded in tandem and turned their attention back to their charges.

Assuming Becca was still in her room, I headed back toward

the front of the house and up the narrow staircase. The mahogany banister was cool beneath my hand as I ascended, and having grown up with a woodworker for a father, I could appreciate the carpentry that had gone into a house like this—the spindle baluster uprights and Grecian-esque crown molding that came into view as I reached the top of the stairs were just a few of the touches that gave the grand Victorian so much character.

The oak wood floors were polished, and I could see the pale pink and coffee-colored area rugs scattered purposefully throughout the second floor through the railing as I approached the landing. Black and white scenic photos of the property hung from the neutral-colored walls. Delicate lace and cream-colored curtains adorned the tall, skinny windows, letting in the early afternoon sunlight, and the minimal, blond wood furniture matched the floors, each piece strategically placed. It was hard to believe dead bodies had been in the house less than a day before we'd settled in, and I was grateful I didn't know which room had been their final resting place.

I headed down the hall toward the room I thought now belonged to Becca and the other Re-gens. I passed what I assumed was Chris's room, given the shotgun propped against the closet door on the far side and the pack that had been left on the bed, and stopped outside the door to Becca's room.

I knocked lightly and waited for an answer. Other than the sudden outburst of crying babies downstairs and the old house settling in the growing heat, I didn't hear anything on the other side of the door. I knocked again.

"I'll be out in a minute," Becca finally rasped from inside, a coughing fit immediately following.

"Becca, are you okay?"

Hearing sniffles and another cough, I began to worry. Without hesitation, I turned the handle and pushed the door open.

The room was mostly dark, the striped beige and chocolate-colored paper lining the walls only visible in the wash of sunlight that filtered in through the parted curtains. Becca sat on the edge of one of the twin beds, a sea of bloodied tissues on the floor and around her impression on the mattress.

"Becca?" My heart thudded, and I felt the color drain from my face as I rushed over to her. "What's wrong?" I searched her face for answers, her body for some indication of what was wrong, but I didn't know what to look for.

Her shoulders were slouched and her feet were dangling haplessly over the edge of the bed.

"Becca, what's wrong? Do you want me to get Harper?"

Slowly, she shook her head. "He can't help me."

I didn't like the sound of that. I scanned her body again. At some point over the past few weeks she'd grown thinner, and her eyes were rimmed with dark circles.

"Becca," I breathed. "What's going on?" I crouched on the floor beside her bed. When she didn't say anything, I reached for her hand, desperate for her to confide in me. "*Please*, tell me."

She cleared her throat, and I lifted my gaze to her heavy-lidded gray eyes as she looked down at me. "I'm dying."

My breath hitched, and I nearly choked. "You're *what*?" *First Sarah, and now Becca?* I didn't think I could handle losing her, too…I didn't think I could handle losing *anyone* else.

Becca's gaze seemed unfocused and distant. "The Re-gen process does not come without repercussions." She stared down at the bloodied tissue in her hand. "My organs are shutting down. It is only a matter of time."

"What?" I nearly screeched as I squeezed her hand. "No! You finally belong with us. Why…"

"You can't bring people back from the dead and expect them to go about life as though nothing has changed. It's not natural, and my body is failing."

I shook my head and rose to my feet. The space in the room wasn't nearly enough as I paced back and forth, my mind racing and my heart breaking. "And you know this because you've seen it?"

"Yes," she said easily, but I struggled to accept things as easily as she did.

"Then you must know of a cure," I said. "If you've seen this, if you understand, then you must see a way out…an alternative…" I straightened, realizing Jake had no clue. "You never said anything." *How can she do this to him again?* I suddenly felt desperate, angry but desperate. "Jake…"

In an unexpected display of emotion, Becca narrowed her eyes, apparently comprehending the directions my thoughts were going. "And why would I tell him? There is nothing *he* can do for me. He would just worry."

"Of course he would worry. Becca, you're dying. I—" I froze mid-step. I suddenly felt a flare of hope. "A transfusion. Jake could give you a blood transfusion. It'll be the first thing he thinks of, I know it will."

Becca shook her head. "That won't work. The process by which we're created—"

"Becca, we should at least—"

"Trust me," she said, her patience clearly thinning.

"And Mase…and Camille." Dani would be devastated; we *all* would be devastated. "We've already lost so many…" I stepped in front of her, searching her eyes for reassurance. "Please tell me there's a way to help you…to save you."

Her eyes softened, and she offered me a weak smile. "Mase and Camille are okay," she said so certainly I almost believed her. "They've both had so much electrotherapy that they should be fine…for a while."

Shaking my head, I tried to steady my voice and my breathing as I sat down beside her on the white down comforter. "Electrotherapy? Like what happened to Dani…or like what Carlos was doing to me?"

"Yes, both. But what Carlos was doing to you was only a fraction of the intensity that is needed to prolong our lives. It is similar to part of the process that creates us in the first place, and it seems to act as a sort of reset." Becca stared out the open bedroom door. "I have mentioned my degeneration to Mase and Camille, and they have no symptoms, not like me…and they will not for some time."

I gaped at her, completely speechless. Unable to take her silent contemplation, I stood and strode to one of the windows, peering out at our fresh start that seemed to be slipping away before it really even began. Like so many times in the past month, I felt useless. "Please, Becca. Please tell me there's a way." And just as I said the words, I turned to face her. "Carlos—"

"We cannot risk him burning his Ability out," she said. "You need him too much, and he is so young. I will not ask him."

I straightened, a jolt of anger shooting through me. "It's not your call," I said. "It's Carlos's. I don't want anything to happen to him, either, but he's been practicing on Mase and Camille; he's getting stronger. You don't know that he can't handle it…unless you do because you *saw* something."

Becca shook her head. "And you would risk him burning out? For me? Do you not see—" Becca began coughing again, this time lying back and curling into the fetal position, her features twisted in pain. "I shouldn't speak, it only makes it worse."

"Hold on, Becca. I'm gonna find Harper. We'll figure something out."

And before I knew it, I was running down the hallway toward the stairs. Gabe was the one who knew about this stuff, but he was with Sanchez back in New Bodega. Harper was a doctor, but not a Re-gen specialist, so I could only hope we would find a solution before it was too late. I rushed into the living room, where Harper and Chris were still sitting sleepily beside one another on the couch.

"H," I said, trying to get his attention without waking the twins. "H!"

Finally, Chris's eyes opened, and upon seeing the look of what

I assumed was horror on my face, she nudged Harper from his nodding state.

He immediately straightened, his eyes focused and alert on mine. "What is it, Baby Girl?"

"It's Becca," I croaked. "She's sick, and…I need your help."

As I took the babies from their arms, I explained what I knew in a rush of words I wasn't sure they fully understood, but they didn't waste any time. While Chris ran out to grab Carlos and Jake, Harper and I went upstairs.

Becca's coughing had momentarily subsided, but I could see the fear in Harper's eyes as he stood beside her bed, staring down at the bloodstained tissues surrounding her.

When Chris, Jake, and Carlos appeared in the doorway, I stepped aside, allowing them room to enter. The fear reflected in Jake's eyes, the grief, was nothing compared to the overwhelming sense of desperation that riddled every fiber of him. Worried I wouldn't be able to control my own emotions, not to mention everyone else's, I left the five of them alone and went out to the hallway to wait, a twin in each arm.

Aside from the bitterness I'd felt toward Becca during our initial meeting back in Cañon City, she'd become my friend. She'd been like a kindred spirit when I'd lost my memory, a sister of sorts. Jake might never recover from losing her again, and I couldn't bear the thought of it, either.

But it wasn't my choice, and it wasn't my life that would be in danger by trying to help her. It was a decision Becca and Carlos needed to make together. I just hoped it was the one I wished it would be.

After I paced for what felt like a half hour, Carlos walked out of the room. His eyes met mine instantly, and I wondered if that was a good or bad sign. He stopped in front of me and I held my breath, waiting.

"Of course I'll do it," he said on an exhale, and I let out an uneven sigh.

Harper and Chris filed out after, reclaiming the babies from me.

I steadied myself and moved to the doorway of Becca's room. The tension in my chest eased and tears pricked my eyes at the sight of Becca wrapped in Jake's arms.

32

DANI

MAY 28, 1AE

The Farm, California

"Hey, Carlos," I said as I walked into the stable.

I could see him through the open doorway of the first stall, Vanessa's room for the foreseeable future. He was seated on a wooden chair, his sister sitting on a sisal rug at his feet as he combed through her rat's nest of hair…or rather, *attempted* to comb through it. Carlos cringed more than his sister did as each stroke caught in the myriad of snarls, jerking her head back despite his obvious attempt to be gentle. Vanessa hardly seemed to notice, instead continuing to whisper to the empty space beside her.

I smiled at Carlos. "Can I borrow you for a bit?" I bit my lip, feeling guilty about stealing him away from Vanessa; his presence had an even more calming effect—if not a *saning* effect—on her than Chris's Ability, though Chris claimed she was making progress in working through the tangled synapses of Vanessa's mind.

Tossing the comb on a folding card table that was one of Vanessa's three pieces of furniture—the chair Carlos was sitting in, the card table, and a cot Jason and I had found while, *ahem*, "exploring" some of the barn's hidden recesses—Carlos sighed. "Yeah. Not like this is doing any good anyway."

"You could just cut it all off," I said with a shrug. "I'd offer to help, but I think she might bite me if I came near enough…"

Vanessa snorted and hissed, "Yesssss…" drawing out the sibilant word until she ended it with a harsh cackle.

"Nessa!" Carlos moved out of the chair and crouched in front of his sister so he could look her in the eyes. "If you don't have anything nice to say…" His tone was one a parent might use on an unruly child.

Rolling her eyes, Vanessa returned her attention to the air beside her. "I know, Rosie, you're right…she's trying to steal *him*, too. First Annie, now my little brother." There was a long moment where she said nothing, and then she giggled. "Like she wants to *be* me?" It was clear that Carlos and I were missing out on an integral part of the conversation.

"Nessa," Carlos said, reaching out to touch his sister's shoulder.

She brushed his hand away, flicking an irritated glance at him.

Again, Carlos sighed. "I love you," he whispered before he stood. "I'll be back in a bit, okay?"

But Vanessa didn't respond; she was too busy conversing with "Rosie."

Poor Carlos, I thought. I cleared my throat as he approached, backing out of the doorway so he could exit the stall.

"What do you need me to do?" he asked once the padlock keeping his sister locked safely in the stall was securely in place. He turned, looking at me, his eyes shining with frustration…and an immeasurable amount of loss.

"Carlos…" I shook my head. "It's okay. Stay with her. I can find some other way to—"

"Don't," he said. "Please." His face hardened, but his eyes still shimmered with all of the pain he was holding inside. "Don't pity me. I'm just lucky to have her back." He laughed cynically. "Even like this." And I knew he was thinking of Ky and Ben.

"Okay. Yeah, okay…sorry." Again, I shook my head, finding it impossible to shake off all of my pity for him. "I just…" I looked up at him. "I think it's really amazing what you're doing, you know, taking such good care of her." Reaching for his hand, I gave it a squeeze. "I'm so proud of you, and I'm sure your whole family would be, too. *She*"—I nodded toward the stall—"would be proud of you."

Carlos stared at me for a few seconds, then looked back at the stall door—more *away* from me than actually *at* the door—rubbed his hand over the several weeks of hair growing on his shaved head, and made a rough coughing noise. He sniffed once, twice, a third time, and wiped his hand over his face before returning his gaze to me. "You, uh, needed me for something?" he said, his voice a little hoarse.

"Oh, right. Yeah…" I smiled and pointed out the stable door, to the water tank a short ways up the hill behind the farmhouse. "It's empty. I need you to do your mojo and get the pump going so I can finish setting up the chicken coop." Eager, I rubbed my hands together and started bouncing on the balls of my feet. "I sensed a bunch of hens and a few roosters nearby—I'm going to bring 'em in once the coop's ready, and all that's left to do now is fill the watering thingies."

"Got it." With one final glance back at the stall door, Carlos strode outside, me at his side; I had to take three steps for every two of his. He stared out toward the raised water tank. "I just filled that thing this morning." He looked at me askance. "How'd we go through it so fast?"

I shrugged. "Just finishing getting the farm set up, I guess. I had to fill the troughs in all three pens and in the pasture, the water buckets in the goat house and all the stable stalls…" I glanced at Carlos. "Except for your sister's. And Mase and Camille converted part of the old barn into a washhouse—for clothes, not people"—I cocked my head to the side—"though that's not a bad idea. But anyway, Mase and Camille have been doing an epic load of laundry, and by the time I got around to the chickens, the tank was dry."

"Got it," Carlos repeated as we trudged uphill through overgrown grass and bobbing spheres of mostly white clover flowers and a few violet-tinged red clover flowers.

Without thinking, I picked one of the red clover spheres with a longer stem and started plucking off the tiny flowers to suck the nectar out. As far as I was concerned, it was never a bad time for something sweet. I held out the flowers to Carlos. "Want some?"

He shook his head.

I shrugged. "Did you know that when these get moldy, they act as a blood thinner?"

Carlos shot me a sideways glance that said "Why the hell would I know that?" more clearly than words could have. "That another one of the traditional medicine things your grandma taught you?"

I nodded slowly. "You know, I always thought she was so silly with all that stuff, but now I wish I'd paid more attention…remembered more of what she taught me. I think next time we make a trip to New Bodega, I'll stop by Grams's house and pick up her recipe book and some of her herbalism stuff."

"Stuff?"

"Yeah, you know, like a mortar and pestle, measuring cups, that kind of thing." I tossed the stripped clover stem onto the ground. "Could be useful," I said, thinking about Harper and his increasing hesitancy to give us antibiotics every time one of us injured ourselves enough to risk infection. According to him, the antibiotics might do more harm than good at this point.

"Seems like a good plan," Carlos said. "And hey, maybe there's some herbalism thing that can help with the Re-gens."

"Help with the Re-gens?"

"Yeah, you know, the degeneration thing that's making Becca sick…?"

I stared at him as we continued uphill. "Becca's sick?"

Carlos met my eyes, disbelief in his. "Zoe didn't tell you about what happened earlier?"

"I haven't seen her since this morning…when she was *looking* for Becca," I said, waving my hand in a keep-going gesture. "So what's going on? What hasn't she told me?"

"That the Re-gens…they're dying."

My stomach lurched. Stopping mid-step, I grabbed his arm and pulled him around to face me. "What?"

What he explained next horrified me. I felt like he'd punched me in the gut, then pulled the ground out from under me. If Becca was right, and the Re-gens were constantly on the cusp of degenerating back to their natural state—*dead*—then Camille and Mase were constantly in danger from what had been done to them at the Colony. They could die any day…unless Carlos, or someone like Carlos, was around to recharge their biological batteries every now and again.

"Are you sure you're up for that?" I asked, eyes wide with the horror his words had ignited. "I mean, maintaining Camille and Mase's health with daily doses of electrotherapy is one thing, but how much power is it going to take to revitalize Becca? Is it even possible?"

Carlos raised his shoulders. "Dunno, but there's only one way to find out." He continued walking, and I had to jog a few steps to catch up to him.

"Well, at least you won't have to do *this* much longer," I said, gesturing toward the water tank and tiny pump house several dozen yards ahead. "So you'll be able to save up all your juice for keeping them from devolving or degenerating or whatever you're calling it."

When Carlos's brow furrowed, I explained, "Jason's working on that old windmill down by the storage barn. He's pretty sure it's usable, so once he gets it working, we'll be able to use that instead. Should be a day or two…or three, but hopefully not more than that."

Carlos shrugged. "I'll do what needs to be done. Becca was stupid to wait this long to tell us. She's *really* sick, and even though I did a pretty intensive electrotherapy session with her earlier…" He shook his head. "I don't know if it'll work. She was just so stupid to—"

"You never know what she *saw*," I said as we reached the squat little pump house beside the water tank. "You know how she is…it could be that telling us would've meant we'd all die horrible deaths, or something like that." I leaned my hip against the edge of the roof of the pint-size building while Carlos crouched before the short door to open it.

Reaching inside, he touched the well pump's motor, and a few seconds later, it whirred to life. Touching whatever he was charging up was by no means necessary for Carlos, but it made the task a whole lot easier *and* it prevented the faint electric tingle that charged the air whenever he used his Ability from a distance.

I studied his youthful, handsome face. He was so freaking adorable. If only he'd been a little less attractive, maybe his first few months after the outbreak wouldn't have been so bad for him…except for everything that happened with his brother and sister…and Annie…

"What?" He was watching me watch him, his shoulders hunched.

"Nothing." I looked away, shifting my attention to the farm laid out below us. The barns and stable were set up in a "U" formation, with the gravel roundabout filling the empty space between them. The grand old farmhouse, its adorable little companion cottage, and the brick oven and flagstone patio took up the remaining side of the roundabout, and beyond them lay a large garden, a greenhouse, the root cellar, the orchards, and a creek feeding into the pond. It was our own little slice of homesteader heaven.

"Have you had a chance to explore this place much?" I asked Carlos.

He shook his head. "Been spending most of my time with Nessa and doing this…and now, helping the Re-gens."

"You should take a break, walk around…maybe stop by the windmill and see if Jason needs any help. Oh, and there are beehives over by the garden shed, too, just past the greenhouse. Those are pretty neat." I squinted, hoping to catch a glimpse of my other half between the end of the stable and the storage barn, where the windmill stood, but I couldn't see him. I sighed and focused instead on the garden. "Or you could find Grayson—help him with his surveying and whatnot," I suggested, thinking of our resident "farming" expert.

Carlos pulled out of the little mini-shed. He stood, took a step backward, and tripped.

I reached for him instinctively, and the moment my fingers closed around his wrist, I couldn't make them let go. Because I was suddenly on fire with electricity.

Wrenching himself free, Carlos stumbled backward.

My knees gave out, and I held myself up on hands and knees as I gasped for air.

"Jesus…look, Dani! Are you okay?"

Somehow, I managed to wave at him with one hand. "Yeah… yeah…I'm good."

Except for one thing: I couldn't feel a single mind. Electricity had knocked my Ability out…again.

As promised by the Council, a pair of New Bodega-ers made a delivery in the late afternoon. They'd spared some of their precious fuel supply to power up a hybrid SUV, bringing us not only three coolers filled with fresh seafood—rock cod, crab, shrimp, and abalone, as well as several types of seaweed—but also a solar-powered generator and a several-week supply of dry goods. The generator was meant to power the chest freezer in the farmhouse's enormous pantry so we could store the seafood longer and put more time between deliveries.

After the two of them left, Ky, Camille, and Becca built up the fire in the huge brick oven behind the farmhouse and started making dinner with the new supplies. The rest of us returned to our work around the farm—Harper putting the final touches on his infirmary in the ground-floor master bedroom, Tavis and Sam storing our spare weapons and ammo in the laundry-room-turned-armory, Carlos and Mase joining Jason to help with the windmill, Grayson appraising the fields across the road from the farm, Chris and Biggs scouting around the perimeter of the farm for the best path for a fence we could convert into a wall over time, and me mucking out the stables with Annie's help. Which consisted more of the little girl rolling around on the floor of the stable aisle with Jack, while Zoe, once again on baby duty, was watching me from a bench in the aisle, one little baby bundle in her arms and the other in a carrier on the bench beside her.

"I am not sure I'm cut out for this, D," she said, her voice barely above a whisper.

I paused, turning just enough that I could see her through the stall door. "You volunteered to take care of them…"

"You would've done the same thing in my place." She gave me a sidelong glance before she peered down at the baby she was holding; I assumed it was Ellie, given the pink blanket the infant was swaddled in.

"I suppose…" I continued shoveling. "So, I forgot to ask you about this earlier—I heard you screaming in your sleep again last night. Are those dreams about your mom still bothering you?"

"I don't know…yeah." Zoe was quiet for a moment, then she added, "It's just, all of this stuff about her creating the Virus and having this other family…it just seems so crazy, you know? I mean, my *mom* is the fucking doctor responsible for it all." She leaned against one of the stable doors and let out a slow, deep breath. "It's a lot to take in, I guess."

As though she were responding to a cue, our resident Crazy squealed, the high-pitched noise trailing off with a girlish giggle.

Which Ellie didn't like at all. There was a brief windup period, filled with cute little noises, but soon she was wailing away, and bringing Everett right along with her.

"Uh-oh," Annie remarked wisely from the aisle floor. Jack, who'd been enjoying the belly rub of all belly rubs, rolled onto his feet and, hackles rising, started to growl in Vanessa's direction.

"Stop that," I told him, and he sat, quieting immediately, though not taking his eyes from the locked stall at the end.

And all the while, the babies cried like their lives depended on it.

"Damn it!" Standing, Zoe crossed the aisle and entered the stall, thrusting the distraught infant at me.

I held out my shovel. "What am I—"

"Just for a sec, D, please?" Zoe said, barely giving me time to set the shovel against the wall and peel off my work gloves before leaving me with Ellie and rushing out of the stall to pick up Everett. "Shhh…shhh…shhh, baby boy. Please, Everett…please go back to sleep." She walked around in circles with the baby, cooing and shushing and rocking him gently. "Shhh…shhh…shhh…"

Unfortunately, Everett didn't seem to understand.

Frowning, I looked down at Ellie. Remarkably, *she'd* stopped crying. She stared up at me with enormous blue eyes and started making bubbles with her mouth, and I couldn't help but smile.

"Hey there, little girl…you're not so scary, are you?" I said as I walked through the open stall door leading out to the pasture to bask in the afternoon sunlight. "You're just a little snuggle bug, huh?"

Ellie blinked.

"Yes you are," I cooed. "You're just the cutest little princess there ever was."

I heard Zoe's low, soft chuckle from behind me and froze, caught in the act of being a total softy. Slowly, I turned around.

Zoe stood in the exterior stall door, Everett in her arms, soothed into silent sleep. She was shaking her head and clicking her tongue at me in disbelief. "First Annie, now Ellie…it's only a matter of time, D." Her rueful smile broadened.

"A matter of time for what?"

"Babies," she mouthed, her brow dancing excitedly as she sidled up next to me and nudged my arm with her elbow.

I readjusted my hold on Ellie, shifting her head higher, and sighed. "A matter of time?" I wanted my own family with Jason… someday. But not yet. *Definitely* not yet. Our world was just too unstable. Plus, we already had two infants, a little girl, and an adolescent boy to take care of on the farm. Any more kids might break us.

"I can see the gleam in your eyes, D. I know you want to see what it would be like to have your own…" Her teasing ceased and suddenly her eyes turned pleading. "Just for a little while, as least?"

I rolled my eyes, nearly snorting. "I knew there was an ulterior motive in there somewhere…" I flashed her my most innocent smile and batted my eyelashes. "Sure, if you want to muck out the stable that badly, I'll take the twins for a while. You can shovel, and I'll watch the munchkins."

Zoe's smile withered under the threat of yards of moldy hay and manure. She glanced down at Everett. "I think I've had my share of poop for a *long* time."

"Ahem," someone said from the stable aisle behind Zoe.

We both jumped a little, Zoe spinning while she did.

Ky lounged against the stall's doorframe. "Dinner's ready, and Jason and Grayson want everyone up there so they can do one of their patented dinner–team meeting things. They're waiting up at the tables now."

I forced a scowl to hide a smile. He'd surprised us on purpose, I knew it. "Did Jason finish the windmill?" It had looked a lot more like a multiday project than a one-afternooner, so I doubted it.

Ky shrugged and started for the stable's backdoor. "I'll be up in a bit…gotta track down the others," he said over his shoulder.

"Alrighty…Jason summons, we come." I walked back into the stable to retrieve Annie and my dog while Zoe started gathering the twins' things into a baby bag one-handed. I paused in the stable doorway to wait for her and Everett.

Zoe waved a hand at me. "You guys go on up. I'll be right behind you."

"Okeydokey." With Annie and Jack in tow and Ellie sleeping soundly in my arms, I emerged from the stable and headed straight for the three round tables we'd moved from the barn to the flagstone patio surrounding the behemoth of a brick oven. Jason, Carlos, Mase, and Grayson were sitting at one of the tables, Jason deep in conversation with Grayson while simultaneously taking notes. Camille was standing in front of the oven's arched mouth, using spatulas to flip what looked like some sort of biscuit or flat-bread cooking in cast-iron skillets. The rest of the group had yet to arrive.

When we were about halfway between the stable and the patio, Carlos spotted my little entourage and nudged Jason, leaning in to murmur something, and Jason looked our way. He'd been writing in his notebook, but his pen stilled almost as soon as his eyes landed on me. The corners of his mouth curved upward the barest amount, and his expression, filled with yearning more than desire, seared through my heart. Beside him, Carlos was grinning from ear to ear. Jason said something to Grayson and, pushing back his chair, stood and started striding toward us.

"Jason!" Annie squealed. She ran ahead, throwing herself into his waiting arms.

He lifted her up by the armpits, spinning her around in a circle and earning a second, prolonged squeal. When he finally set her down again, he was laughing, and Annie's face was flushed with excitement.

"We scooped poop!" she told him, pride emanating from her.

"Did you?" He held onto one of her hands, leading her back the way she'd come. "You're turning into quite the farmer. We'll have to start calling you Farmer Annie, soon."

Annie nodded enthusiastically, but Jason didn't see it because his eyes were locked on me.

"I think Camille needs your help," Jason said to the little girl, and she skipped away. When he reached me, Jason raised one hand to clasp the back of my neck and leaned in, brushing his lips against my cheek. "Well, hello there."

Hiding a smile, I pulled back and peered up into his jewel-blue eyes. "What's put you in such a good mood?"

"You."

Skeptical, I frowned; I smelled like horse manure and sweat, and I was fairly certain I had clown hair, so it definitely wasn't my present state that was inspiring such happiness. My eyes narrowed and I peeked around him at Carlos. "What'd Carlos say to you?" Because whatever the teenager had said had to be the spark.

Placing his palms on either side of my face, his fingers forming a gentle cage around my head, Jason leaned in again, this time brushing his lips against mine. He lingered, giving me the sweetest, most tender kiss possible. Pulling away, he smiled. "I believe it was…'Check it out.'"

"'Check it out?' *That* made you all…uber-happy?" I pulled back and studied his face. "*Why?*"

"If you'd seen you, with the baby and Annie and Jack, you'd be smiling, too," he said as his focus shifted to a spot behind me. He raised his voice. "How're the twins today?"

I glanced over my shoulder to see Zoe approaching, Everett nestled peacefully in her arms. "See for yourself," she said as she neared. She paused just long enough to say, "Consider it practice," barely containing a smile as she handed Everett to Jason, then continued on her way up to the tables.

I rolled my eyes. Why she suddenly wanted to add more screaming babies to the mix was beyond me.

Jason stared down at the baby that had suddenly appeared in his hands, then looked at me, eyebrows raised in curiosity. "What was that all about?"

I smiled wryly. "Let's just say she's not beyond using any means necessary to finagle some help with the babies. As it turns out, motherhood is hard, having twins is harder, and raising someone *else's* twins is turning out to be the hardest of all."

An hour later, we were all seated at the tables on the patio, empty bowls in front of us and only a few stray biscuits remaining in the baskets set in the center of each table. Zoe'd retreated into the farmhouse with the twins to put them to bed as soon as Jason and I had handed them back over to her, and she'd yet to reemerge.

Harper reached for another biscuit and glanced at Jason, who was sitting on my left. "So, what's the plan for tomorrow? Infirmary's good to go, or as good as it can be with the supplies we've got right now."

Jason brushed biscuit crumbs off his hands while he chewed his final bite. He nodded slowly as he swallowed. "We've got to head into town, stock up on what we need to get this place running."

"I'd like to come along," Harper said before tearing off a quarter of the biscuit and popping it into his mouth.

Again, Jason nodded, the motion slow and contemplative. "That works." He shifted his eyes to me. "You up for a day trip?"

I smiled but shook my head. For some reason I couldn't explain, I felt like if I left the farm, I might never return. And beyond that, I wasn't the right person for the job, not while my Ability was burned out. "Much as I'd like to go with you, I think I'm more useful here, with the animals." When Jason didn't respond, only blinked, I continued, "Ky's just as good at scouting, anyway"—I looked at Ky, who raised a shoulder—"and *way* better in a sticky situation. You three boys go…scout stuff…do manly things."

Meeting Jason's eyes, I stared into their unfathomable depths until he shifted his attention to Ky and Harper.

Out of the corner of my eye, I caught Ky watching us with a strange intensity, but when I looked at him fully, whatever I'd seen was gone, and he wore his usual lazy smile.

"Right, so here's the deal," Jason said. "We've got four objectives tomorrow: assess Petaluma for any present or future dangers to the farm, load up on the seeds on this list…" He paused to tear a piece of paper out of the notebook he'd been writing in when he'd been talking to Grayson, handing it to Harper. "I know there are a few seed banks in town. They were big on sustainability and that grow-your-own-food shit here, before…"

"Good for us," Harper commented.

"That it is," Jason said with a nod. "We'll also load up on medical supplies, and search any bookstores, libraries, or anywhere else we can think of for books on"—he looked down at his open notebook—"managing an orchard, gardening, sanitation, irrigation, food preservation, composting, beekeeping…"

"I'm glad you're staying tomorrow," Grayson said from across the table, and it took me a moment to realize he'd been speaking to me. "I know you have some knowledge about herbs and such, and I thought you might be interested in converting the vegetable garden, or at least part of it, into an herbal garden."

"Oh…yeah. That would be great, actually." His timing was perfect, uncanny even, considering what Carlos and I had talked about briefly during our walk up to the well pump.

Grayson smiled, excitement lighting his eyes.

Jason gave my shoulder a squeeze and leaned in to press a kiss against my cheek. "Are you done? Because I am…"

Harper and Ky reached for another biscuit at the same time, and as their fingers brushed, Harper jumped to his feet, knocking his chair backward, and pulled his pistol. He leveled it at Ky's chest.

Ky did the same, only he aimed his gun at Jason.

The rest of us froze.

The backdoor to the farmhouse slammed open, and Zoe yelled, "Jason! Ky's one of them!"

"Don't do it, man." Harper's voice was a low warning.

"You don't get it. I *have* to do it," Ky said, right before he pulled the trigger.

CRACK.

Jason's body jerked, and I screamed.

CRACK.

CRACK.

Ky stumbled, knocking his chair backward.

I didn't understand what the hell was happening. I pulled my own handgun, but I didn't have anywhere to aim it.

Ky slumped on the ground, his arms hanging uselessly at his sides, his legs sprawled in front of him akimbo, and his chest rising and falling rapidly as he gasped for breath. Blood stained his lips as well as the front of his t-shirt, turning fabric that had once been faded green almost entirely crimson. He was staring past me, at Jason.

I glanced over my shoulder as horror knotted in my gut, a writhing, visceral feeling. Blood streaked down Jason's sleeve, and my stunned brain finally processed Zoe's words. Ky was *one of them*—a Monitor. And something had triggered him, and he'd attempted to carry out his mission…to *kill* Jason.

If Harper hadn't *seen*, if he hadn't been ready…

I shook my head, unable to believe what was happening.

Ky was a Monitor. Ky tried to kill Jason. Ky…my friend.

"Sorry…man," Ky managed to say between gasping breaths.

"I know, Ky. I know," Jason said. "Fuck!" There was so much hurt and rage and desperation in his voice that it shredded my heart.

"Do it," Ky whispered. "Kill…me." He let out a ragged breath, and blood bubbled on his lips. "I won't…stop…"

"Damn it, Ky!" Jason shouted, finally losing the battle with his emotions. "God…"

"Oh, God," Zoe groaned and met my eyes. "It was me, in the stable, when I mentioned my mom…he was listening…" Her eyes closed, and tears broke free, glistening on her cheeks. "*I* triggered him." She slumped lower in her chair, hanging her head in her hands. "It was me…"

"Zo…" I wanted to go to her. I *yearned* to go to her, just like I yearned to go to Ky. But I couldn't. Not yet.

"Alright, this is what's going to happen," Jason said, raising his unsteady voice. "We're going to remain nice and calm while I explain how this extremely fucked-up situation isn't what it looks like. Harper didn't just shoot Ky in cold blood." He looked at Harper. "Please, see if there's anything you can do for him."

I watched as Harper made his way to Ky while the others exchanged nervous, confused glances.

Beside me, Jason took a deep breath. "Here's the truth. My *mother*"—he practically spat the word—"is Anna Wesley, the General's pet doctor."

I watched the others' faces as he spoke, shock and horror widening their eyes, twisting their familiar features into masks of outrage and disgust.

"The General keeps her on a leash by dangling the constant

threat of death—mine and my sister's—in front of her. He placed Monitors close to us, people with hidden commands to eliminate us if she ever tried to contact us." He paused, letting his words sink in. "Well, she contacted us, Ky found out, and he just tried to kill me."

"It's…true," Ky wheezed, and I risked glancing down at him. He was staring at Jason, his eyes both empty and imploring. "It's true."

There was a long moment where nobody said anything. Crickets sang. Frogs croaked. An owl hooted. But nobody said anything.

"And if any of the rest of you are like him," Jason said, "if any of you come after my sister or me, I *will* kill you." His threat hung in the air until the others lowered their guns, and I did the same.

My eyes drifted to Ky and Harper, and I finally got my first up-close look at Ky's wounds. My throat constricted, and my eyes burned with the need to shed more tears than I already was. Ky wasn't going to make it. I didn't think even a transfusion of Jake's blood could fix him…he was just too damaged.

I felt a hand grasp mine, and I looked to my right to see Zoe standing beside me, her face a mask of grief that mirrored mine. I gave her hand a squeeze, then reached for Jason's with my left and threaded my fingers through his.

But he didn't look at me, didn't tear his eyes away from Ky. His Monitor. His best friend. Who was dying.

Ky coughed, drawing my attention to him. His lips curved into a sorry attempt at a smile that lasted about a second and was driven away by a grimace. When his features relaxed once more, he stared up at Jason. "Not…your…fault…"

And then he exhaled for the final time.

33

ZOE

MAY 28, 1AE

The Farm, California

"It *is* our fault…it's *all* our fault," I breathed. Seeing Ky lying there, another friend bloody and lifeless, was too much. "Sarah…" I closed my eyes, the image of her lifeless body still fresh in my mind. "And now Ky…"

"What about Sarah?" Biggs said.

I spun around to find him standing behind me, shocked and confused, with a crying Everett in his arms. "I heard gunshots…" As he registered the horror on my face, my regret, his grip on Everett tightened, like he knew to steady himself for another blow.

I lost what final shred of composure I had left, and my silent tears turned to violent sobs. "Biggs, I wanted to tell you—"

His eyes darted around the group; everyone was quiet, shocked and waiting. "Tell me what?"

Fists clenched and my heart pounding emphatically, I took a step toward him. "Sarah was one of them, a Monitor. I'm so sorry. I saw everything right before…"

His brow furrowed. "A what?"

"She was going to kill me—she was trying not to—right before she went into labor, but she—she couldn't." I took a shaky breath. "She sent you away because she knew what she had to do." My chest felt so heavy, so tight, I struggled to breath.

"What the hell are you saying, Zoe?"

I tried to swallow back my cowardice. He needed to know, Biggs *deserved* to know. "Sarah killed herself to protect me."

His eyes hardened with understanding. The burn of guilt only intensified as I watched his features twist with anger and felt his mounting sadness all over again.

I closed my eyes and took a deep breath, bracing myself for what might come next. As I exhaled, I opened my eyes and said, "It wasn't depression, I—"

Biggs glared at Harper. "You lied to me?"

"He didn't know," I croaked. "No one did but me and Jason." Although that wasn't exactly true, there was no reason to share the blame. Our friends were dead because of *us*.

For a fleeting moment, Biggs's features softened, and I knew he was thinking about Sarah, relieved she hadn't taken her life because of the babies, because she'd regretted having them. But then his eyes found mine, and I held my breath. "I blamed myself…I blamed *them*, and it was *your* fault. You allowed me to think—"

I let out a choked sob and took another step closer. "I wanted to tell you, Biggs." I let the tears fall freely, let his anguish fill me the way it was filling him. "I wanted to, but I couldn't. I—"

"You could've," he growled. "You could've, but you didn't." And before I knew what was happening, Biggs was storming back toward the house, Everett's fussing turning to bloodcurdling screams.

Body numb and clumsy, I ran after him. "Biggs, please don't—"

"Leave me alone, Zoe!" He stomped up the stairs and flung open the screen door. "Stay away from my children."

I froze. "Biggs, please…"

The screen slammed in my face. *What's he going to do?* When I heard him march up the stairs, when I felt his resolve and disgust and hatred for me, I knew. Sadness flooded through me.

Flinging open the screen, I ran in after him. "You can't leave, please don't leave. We can help you."

Biggs ignored me as he strode into his room, placed Everett in his crib, and pulled out his duffel.

"Please don't do this. Please don't leave. I want to help, I want to—"

"Get. Out." He stopped and glared at me. "I said, *get out.*"

My presence was only making him more despondent, more outraged, so I reluctantly straightened and backed out of his room. I wished he would listen, wished he would stay. "I *am* sorry," I warbled. "I am so, so sorry." Biggs was going to leave, to take the twins, and there was nothing I could do to change his mind.

"You'll never come near my children again," he said so evenly I knew it was true, and I sobbed harder as he slammed the door in my face.

JUNE 1 AE

34

DANI

JUNE 16, 1AE

The Farm, California

"I can see why the dream freaked you out so much," Zoe said. She was kneeling beside me in the overgrown grass surrounding the mound of dark earth over Ky's still-fresh grave. A simple wooden headstone with his name and dates marked the head of the grave. Jason was working on gathering the tools and materials needed to create a more permanent, granite gravestone, but it would still be a while.

A couple of blessedly quiet weeks had passed since Ky's death and Biggs's retreat to New Bodega with the twins. We felt the loss of all of them deeply, but we couldn't afford to dwell on what was gone; we had to focus on what we still had. We had to keep going. We were slipping into a routine of long hours and hard work that felt a little more natural every day. The Farm wasn't quite a *well-oiled* machine, but it was getting there.

Thinking about the nightmare that had left me clammy and breathing hard early this morning—a vivid replay of me shooting the child-Crazy a few months back—I nodded to Zoe. "I mean, I know the little girl was a Crazy and was pretty much about to rip your face off, but…I just…" I groaned in frustration, reaching out to rearrange our daily offering of wildflowers over Ky's grave for the third time. "She was barely older than Annie…and I killed her."

Zoe took a deep breath, exhaling slowly. I could see that it was practically painful for her not to take over my meager efforts to create a visually pleasing pattern, but I appreciated that she restrained herself. I needed to do this, but I was grateful that she made time to visit Ky's grave with me every day.

"Personally, I like having my face," Zoe said. "You did what you had to do to protect me when I couldn't protect myself." She grabbed my wrist and squeezed. "Thank you for doing that, D."

I bit my lip, then squeezed my eyelids shut and nodded once. "You're welcome, Zo. I don't know what I'd do if—if—"

"I know, D. Me too."

I opened my eyes and stared into hers; they were so startlingly blue, so wonderfully familiar. "I love you, Zo." I loved Jason with all of my heart, but in so many ways, Zoe really was the other half that fit perfectly with my soul.

Zoe's arms were suddenly around me, and we were both stifling convulsive sobs. "God, D…I couldn't do this without you. I really couldn't."

I pulled away and wiped my cheeks, not the least bit embarrassed at my impromptu display of soppy affection. After all, what was the point of surviving the apocalypse if I couldn't tell my best friend how much I loved her every once in a while?

My eyes drifted to Ky's temporary grave marker. We'd erected one for Ben, too, right beside Ky's, though we didn't actually have Ben's body; we had his memory. At least it was a way for the brothers to be together. They deserve that.

Zoe grabbed my hands. "D…"

I leaned away a little and eyed her.

"D!" she repeated, practically bouncing on her knees.

"What?" I shook my head, totally confused.

"You just spoke in my head!"

I continued to shake my head. My latest period of electricity-induced Ability burnout had proved to be the longest yet, lasting well over two weeks. It had only just ended a few days ago, and it had been fluctuating unpredictably since it had come back online.

Zoe squeezed my hands. "You said, 'At least it's a way for them to be together, they deserve that'—but you said it *in my head!*"

As I continued to shake my head, I realized that something inside me *had* changed—I could feel her mind. I felt an enormous, wondrous grin spread across my face. I could sense people again. For the first time in months, I could speak to them telepathically. My Ability was fixed. *I* was fixed!

I searched the farm for one specific mind and found it within seconds. *"Guess what, Jason? I'm back..."*

35

JAKE

JUNE 17, 1AE

Bodega Bay, California

After giving their names at the heavily guarded wall, Jake and Jason rode their horses into New Bodega, construction plans and "shopping" lists rolled up and strapped to their saddles.

"They should have one of those serpentine belts somewhere, right?" Jason asked.

Jake nodded, leaning down and patting Brutus's shoulder. "Yeah, but the question is whether or not they'd let me use one…or three."

"We have plenty to barter with, I'm sure."

Jake shrugged as a thought occurred to him. "I guess if they don't have any quarter-inch belts, I can look for a different-sized chain," he said. "Although I'm not sure a chain would be as efficient."

"I've got to stop in the hardware store, too. I need a few more clamps if I'm going to get that additional shed up before the first wave gets here from Tahoe. I just hope the shop has some."

Jake tried to imagine making room for another group of people on the Farm. "When's that happening?"

Jason squinted out at the harbor as it came into view. "A couple weeks. They're just passing through. When Dani checked in with Lance last night, he told her there's another farm a few miles past ours that's ready to be worked if there are willing, capable bodies. And Holly and Hunter said they have a few group members who are more than willing."

Jake stretched in his saddle. "That's good. It'll be nice to have another farm close by." He scanned the mostly abandoned street.

Fog still hung low, but Jake had grown used to living near the coast and knew it would burn off by midday. The clip-clopping sound of horse hooves on the pavement echoed in the morning fog as they rode toward the town center. Beyond the boathouse, Jake could barely make out the tents compiling the marketplace.

The two of them meandered in silence, taking in their surroundings as they rode further down the winding road.

Jason pointed to the bike rack–hitching post in front of Town Hall. "Let's see what they have in the way of materials, then we'll worry about the crab."

Jake nodded. "Dani's gonna love you for that."

A broad smile engulfed Jason's scarred face. "I know."

Jake chuckled as they secured their horses to the bike rack. After unstrapping his backpack, he turned toward the morning market and bustling merchants readying their tents and tables for the day. There was a fresh produce stand with eggs and veggies, a seafood tent, another displaying jewelry and gemstones, and others with leather bags and crocheted blankets, jams, and jellies…the tents and stands went on and on.

After Jason patted his horse's withers and pulled his pack up onto his shoulder, he headed across the street to the hardware store.

"I'll meet you in there," Jake said and walked beside Jason. He broke away, heading toward the hunting and fishing supply shop. "I need to get some more arrows for Zoe and the boys."

Jason nodded and continued on toward the store a few doors down.

Jake entered the first shop in the row, greeting the older woman at the counter before he began to sort through what few options the shop owner had in the way of arrows. Zoe had been spending a lot of time practicing archery, meaning she was getting better and breaking less arrows, but she was still going through them pretty quickly. Although Jake hadn't told Zoe about it, Jason had agreed to teach him a thing or two about woodworking so he could make custom arrows for her…eventually. He wanted it to be a surprise.

"Sorry, it's not much," the woman said, her eyes not leaving the weathered paperback book in her hand. She pushed her reading glasses higher on the bridge of her nose. "I should have more stock in within the next few weeks. Just waiting for the next big scavenging trip to the city."

Jake made a noncommittal noise before picking a set of arrows he thought would suffice and trading a quart of goat's milk for them.

"Thank you," he said, giving her a slight wave as he pushed open the door.

"Have a good day."

Jake headed out the door and toward the hardware store a couple doors down. When he stepped into the tiny shop, he expected to find Jason poring over the new chisel sets and the sharpeners that lined the shelves, but Jake didn't see Jason at all. The portly shopkeeper, with his long hair and even longer beard, was the only occupant. He strolled up to the counter from the workshop in back.

When he looked up, he flashed Jake a welcoming smile. "Morning."

With a nod, Jake approached the counter. "Morning. I'm looking for my friend, Jason. I was supposed to meet him in here."

The shopkeeper shrugged. "I've only had a few people in this morning. What's he look like?"

"He's a big guy, dark hair?"

The man chuckled. "I've lived here for years…seen a lot of visitors by that description."

"Perfect. You might know his family, actually—the Cartwrights?"

Although the shopkeeper's expression never wavered, Jake could have sworn some of the color drained from the man's face.

Jake took a step closer to the counter. "Everything okay?"

The man seemed to blink himself back to the present and nodded. "I *did* just open up. Your friend might've come up when the door was locked." He busied himself behind the counter, and Jake got the distinct impression the man was avoiding his gaze.

"Did you know the family?" Jake asked as he glanced around the shop, wondering if Tom had been a regular back in the day.

"I did, actually." He cleared his throat. "I was a friend of their father's." He stilled for a moment and met Jake's eyes. "Honestly, I thought they were all dead."

Jake shook his head. "Not all of them." Jake stood there a moment, contemplating. "Alright, well, thanks anyway." He turned to leave just as the door opened, and Jason walked in.

"Morning," he said to the shopkeeper, who offered him a tight-lipped smile in return.

"Good morning."

Jason scanned the store. "I need three twelve-inch hand-screw clamps, if you have any." He laughed softly and shook his head. "Zoe'd love the smell of this place."

Jake watched the shopkeeper, waiting for him to check his inventory, but he just stood there, watching Jason intently. Jason didn't seem to notice the man's scrutiny.

"Did you have those clamps?" Jake prompted, and Jason turned his attention back to the counter.

"If you don't," Jason said, "I'll take three of the closest thing you've got."

The shopkeeper gave him a curt nod. "I've got 'em," he said. "Just a moment." He headed into the attached workshop.

When he returned, he set the clamps out on the counter.

"These will be great, thanks," Jason said.

As the shopkeeper wrapped up the clamps, his eyes narrowed slightly on Jason, then on Jake. "What are you boys building?" he asked.

"A new shed." Jason pulled his pack off his shoulder and set it up on the counter, preparing to barter with the shopkeeper, but the shopkeeper waved him away.

"It's on the house," he said and slid the wrapped clamps over to Jason.

Jason looked thoroughly confused.

"He knew your father," Jake explained when the shopkeeper said nothing. Jake watched the owner's placid expression.

Jason's head tilted to the side. "Really?" He outstretched his hand. "I'm Jason. I'm afraid I don't remember you."

The shopkeeper extended his hand, as well. "Charles, and don't worry. I wouldn't expect you to."

"Zoe, can you get me the diagrams you're working on for the farm?" Jason asked as he walked up the porch steps. "I'm trying to figure out where we need to focus our attention."

Zoe nodded. "I guess I'll practice later." She winked at Jake as she set her bow and new set of arrows on the porch railing and headed inside for the diagrams she'd been sketching. It had been a few weeks since Biggs had left with the twins, and Jake was glad to see Zoe was finally getting some of her pep back and finding her groove again.

"You planning on finishing the shed in one day?" Jake asked. "I know you like projects, but…" He smiled.

"Just trying to keep everyone busy. Between you and me, I'm hoping the shed'll be done in the next couple of days. If Harper and Tavis can have enough of the field dug up, we can—"

The crunch-crunch of hooves on gravel came from the end of the long driveway. Jake turned his head to watch a gray horse and rider pass through the open gate. When he noticed the shaggy-faced, portly man from the hardware store, he frowned.

"What's he doing here?" Jason asked, looking at Jake.

"I don't know," Jake said. "He was acting strange at the shop…"

"Really?" Jason eyed Jake. "I thought he seemed like a nice enough guy. You don't trust him?"

"Not completely, no."

Exhaling heavily and scratching the back of his head, Jason said, "And now he's here…*why* is he here?"

Jake didn't like the unease that settled inside him, but all he could do was shrug, and together, he and Jason walked out toward the approaching horse. Warily, they watched Charles dismount.

Jake heard the screen door swing closed behind him, but he didn't turn back; instead he kept his eyes fixed on Charles.

A hollow thunk shifted everyone's attention, and Jake turned around to see Zoe standing in the driveway behind him, a notebook sprawled on the ground at her feet, her eyes wider than he'd ever seen them and her mouth gaping open. She was silent for a moment, until she finally blinked and took a reluctant step forward.

"Dad?" The word was barely a whisper.

Jake's brow furrowed, and when he turned back toward Charles, he no longer saw *Charles*; a taller man, with a medium build and graying, light brown hair stood in his place. Shaking his head, Jake stared at the man who seemed to have morphed into a completely different person, apparently into Zoe and Jason's dead father—Tom? Jake had never seen a picture of him, and the resemblance to either Zoe or Jason was minimal, but Jake had heard enough about Tom—both the relationship he'd had with his kids and the fact that he was supposedly dead—to give him pause. But the way Zoe's eyes brightened, the way they filled with a storm of emotions so turbulent that they began to shimmer, was all the proof he needed that this man was, indeed, Tom Cartwright.

In stunned silence, Jason watched Tom, and neither he nor his father seemed able to move. Neither of them even seemed able to speak.

But not Zoe; she moved toward the newcomer, stopping close enough to reach her hand out and touch his face. "You're alive. You're really standing here," she said. Her eyes scoured the length of his body, as if she thought she might be staring at a ghost. "I thought you were dead. Grams said you were dead…"

"Because that's what I wanted her to believe," Tom said, his calm, smooth voice seeming to fit this version of himself more than it had fit his portly counterpart.

"Why would you…" She shook her head. "You're alive," she said again, and with a sob, wrapped her arms around him.

Tom embraced his daughter, closing his eyes and letting her cry on his shoulder.

"You're alive." Her sobbed words were muffled by his well-worn, checkered flannel shirt.

Although Jake wanted to give Zoe privacy during her reunion with her apparent father, he was too wary of the man's Ability to alter perception to leave her alone with him.

Jake heard the screen door open and looked over his shoulder to see Dani emerge, Annie at her side. Hand in hand, they walked toward the commotion. Dani's features were scrunched in confusion.

Until Tom lifted his face away from Zoe's hair.

Dani gawked. "Mr. Cartwright?"

"Why?" Zoe asked, pulling away from her father and wiping the tears from her face. "Why would Grams think you were dead? Why would you *want* her to think that?"

He gave her an apologetic shake of his head. "I couldn't risk

Herodson finding out I was alive and using it to somehow hurt you kids…or your mom. I'm so sorry, sweetheart."

"But all this time…we thought you were dead." Zoe's features hardened. "You knew about all of this, about mom…"

"Yes, sweetheart, I knew." A pained expression softened his features. "I've known all along. Not the details, but…enough. I knew enough."

Zoe's eyes narrowed.

Tom looked at Jason, whose expression was blank, then back at Zoe. "I wanted to tell both of you—so many times—but I couldn't." Gently, he touched Zoe's temple with his fingertips. "I can see that you know about the Monitors…and that yours are gone." He sighed and shook his head. "Now that you know the danger, I hope you'll understand."

Zoe's hands clenched into fists at her sides, and she took another step back.

Her father let his hand fall down to hang at his side.

"Is there anything else?" she said, her voice cold.

Tom frowned. "Anything else?"

"Anything else we should know about? Now that we know about Mom and her role in all of this…and that you're alive. Is there anything else?"

Her father started to shake his head.

"And, please, don't lie." She closed her eyes, drawing in and then exhaling a steadying breath. "We can't take any more lies."

When she finally looked at him, he shook his head the barest amount. "Other than my Ability, no, there's nothing else. Not that I can think of."

For the first time, Zoe seemed to notice Jason standing there, staring at their father. "Jason, you were just staring at him. When I came out here…how could you not see it was Dad?"

Her brother looked at her, a hard, cold glint in his eyes. "He didn't look like *him*."

"You must've been able to see through the 'glamour' because your Ability's so much like his, Zo," Dani said from beside Jason. She gave Zoe's father a timid wave. "Hey, Mr. Cartwright."

He inclined his head. "Dani. It's good to see you're still alive and with the family."

She shrugged and gave him a weak smile. "I'm sort of a hard person to get rid of, I guess."

He chuckled softly. "I'm glad to hear it."

"Why didn't you tell Jason who you were this morning?" Jake asked, his arms folded over his chest. "Why ride here, pretending to be someone you're not?"

The man's gaze leveled on Jake before it shifted back to his kids. "I wanted to make sure this place was safe, that you kids were safe and not here under some sort of manipulation." When both Jason and Zoe remained quiet, he continued. "When I saw you this morning, Jason, I was so shocked, I wasn't sure what to do. Everything I've done has been to keep you safe, in the hope that, one day, I'd find you again. I had to stay hidden—to live in disguise—if I wanted the chance to meet up with you again. I wanted to stay in Bodega Bay, in case you returned, but I couldn't stay there looking like *me*."

Jason started clenching and unclenching his jaw. "We thought you were dead," he said, his voice hollow as he repeated Zoe's earlier words.

"I know, son, and I'm sorry. But it was the only way. You're not the only one Herodson put Monitors on."

After a hesitant moment, Jason seemed to accept the explanation, because he wrapped his arms around his father so suddenly that even he looked a little stunned.

The older man closed his eyes as a relieved smile tugged at the corner of his mouth, and he returned Jason's hug.

Jake looked at Zoe, whose eyes were gleaming with surprise and confusion, with relief and uncertainty as she watched her brother and father embrace. Focused solely on Zoe, Jake closed the distance between them, intent on making sure she was alright.

Her shimmering eyes met his. "I…I can hardly believe anything that happens anymore…"

Jake remained quiet and wrapped his arms around her. "Neither can I."

36

ZOE

JUNE 17, 1AE

The Farm, California

"I've seen Mom," I blurted, unable to suppress my curiosity. "Did you know she was still alive?"

My dad's face brightened at the mention of my mom, but only minimally. Like her, he'd clearly become well-adjusted to masking his emotions. "I hoped," he said. His gaze shifted between Jason and me. "I hoped she was, but more than anything, I hoped that her hard work had paid off, that you had Abilities…that you'd survived and were able to start over."

"Her hard work?" I glanced at Jason before my eyes narrowed again on my dad. "She killed *everyone*."

"It's complicated, Zoe. You don't understand."

"I don't understand?" I wasn't sure if I should vomit or scream. "You have *no* idea what we've been through over the past six months, all because of her…what our friends—the people we love—have gone through. You've been hiding in Bodega Bay while we've been literally fighting to survive. Our friends are dead. *Grams* is dead. All because of Mom."

"Zoe, please don't—"

"No." I held up my hand. "Let's, just for a minute, pretend she didn't wipe out all of humanity. I've had friends die in my arms. I can *see* and *feel* things no one should ever have to." I flung my arm to the side, pointing in Jake's general direction. "Jake's sister has to have daily electrotherapy sessions just to stay alive. Jason has to null Dani's Ability every night to prevent her from turning into a wild animal. My memories—"

I felt a hand on my shoulder and looked back. Jason was standing behind me, a grave expression on his face. "Zoe, you can't blame him for being happy we're still alive."

My dad took a few steps toward me, and the closer he drew, the more my volatile emotions consumed me.

I looked at Jason. "Of course not," I said softly. "But, Jason, we're alive at the expense of everyone else." I turned to meet my dad's pale gaze. I'd wanted a real family all my life, to learn the truth and discover what it was that had always been left unsaid, but not at the cost of everyone else. "You talk about it like everything that's happened is just a casualty of war, something that needed to be done."

My dad took another step toward me. "I'm sorry," he said and offered me a weak smile. "I guess I've just been in this so long that I forget how new it is, how hurtful…I know it's hard to understand." He reached out to me. "But no matter what you think, know that your mom really does love you. She wanted what was best for you, no matter how horrible you think she is."

Tears were hot on my cheeks. I knew her intentions had been good, that in her own way she loved us, but it wasn't enough to overshadow the truth of what she'd done anymore. "Then why isn't she here? Why won't she leave him? Why won't she leave Peter? She won't even bring him with her. She wouldn't even consider it—"

"Peter?" The confusion in my dad's voice sobered me. He didn't know. "Who's Peter?"

"Shit," Jason muttered. He stepped up beside me and rubbed

his hand over his hair. “There are some things we need to tell you, Dad.”

Dad didn’t know... Part of me guessed it made sense. *When was the last time he’d seen Mom? Does he know the extent of all she’d done, the things she’s created?*

“What the hell?” I heard Jake say as he started down the driveway. I followed his line of sight, my feet moving toward him of their own accord. I squinted at movement on the road, my gaze landing on a figure in white—a person. Soon, more figures appeared, what looked like dozens of them, maybe more.

Dread thickened in my throat and my blood ran cold. I heard shouting and hurried footsteps behind me, but I barely registered them as fear and curiosity paralyzed me.

I was preparing to open my mind to them when Dani said, “They’re Re-gens.” I hadn’t even noticed that she was beside me. “They’re *all* Re-gens.” This time her voice was only a whisper.

In my periphery, I saw Jason and Dani draw their pistols, and I briefly wondered if we even stood a chance against the approaching throng of Re-gens.

“It’s Becca,” Jake breathed as soon as the figure in white drew close enough to make out clearly.

“Becca!” My mouth was suddenly dry.

The Re-gens behind her stopped, and Becca exchanged words with a bald, gangly man directly behind her before turning back to face us.

Slowly, she alone began to walk toward us, her pale gaze shifting from me to Jake.

“What’s going on, Becca?” Jake asked as she drew closer.

Hearing the accusation in his voice, I looked at his profile; his confusion was written plainly on his face.

“We need your help,” Becca said, stopping just out of arm’s reach. “And one day soon, you will need ours.”

The End

Keep reading for a preview of
BEFORE THE DAWN
book four in The Ending Series

CAN'T GET ENOUGH OF THE ENDING SERIES?

Website: www.theendingseries.com
Facebook: After The Ending

BEFORE THE DAWN

THE ENDING SERIES BOOK FOUR

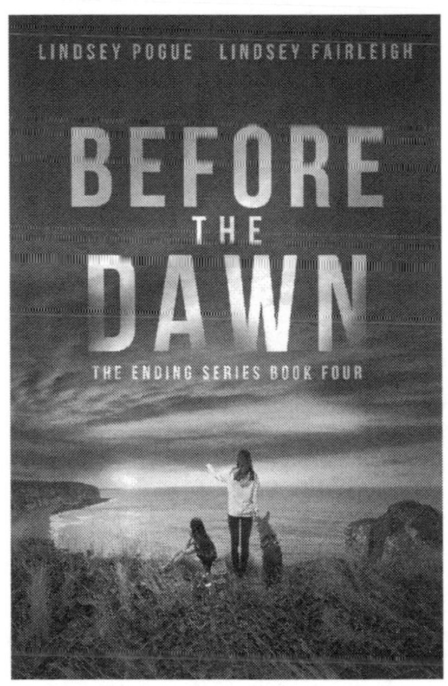

NOVEMBER 1 AE

PROLOGUE

ANNA

NOVEMBER 23, 1AE - The Colony, Colorado

Anna brushed her son's bangs off his forehead as he settled back in the reclining chair. She would have to trim his hair again soon; it was growing so fast now. "Just close your eyes," she said, ending the softly spoken words with an even softer sigh. She hated the pain Peter had to endure every day simply to stay alive, but such was the cost of a second chance at life. Such was the cost of being a Re-gen. "It'll be over soon."

John, the former coroner who'd been in charge of electrotherapy since the treatment's inception, turned away from the small switchboard controlling the electrical current flowing through Peter just enough to toss Anna a weak smile over his shoulder. "A word outside while his, uh, treatment is going?"

Anna clenched her jaw, closed her eyes, and took a deep breath. Despite his irritatingly hesitant and uncertain demeanor, Dr. John Maxwell was valuable. He was short in stature, shrewd of mind, and as far as Anna was concerned, more knowledgeable about the anatomy and physiology of the human brain than any other living person. She just had to remind herself of that sometimes. If she lost sight of that—of the help he, and as far as she knew, *only* he, could offer her son—she might "slip up" and remove him from her inner circle.

And nobody survived to talk about Anna's inner circle once their membership was revoked. Her life—her child's life—depended on absolute secrecy, and dead men couldn't talk. Unless they were brought back as Re-gens, but still...*they* had limited memories.

Anna shook her head, disgusted with the direction her thoughts had gone. She was thinking like Gregory, something that seemed to be happening to her more and more with each passing day. What would Tom, her first husband—her *true* husband—say if he could see her thoughts now? Nothing good, she imagined, and definitely nothing flattering.

Peter gave his mom's hand a squeeze, drawing her back to the here and now. The heavy glove Anna wore protected her from the worst of the electrical current humming through his body, but she still felt a slight buzz. "It's fine, Mom. Go with Dr. Maxwell." Peter offered her a slightly strained smile. "I'll live, promise."

Anna clenched her jaw harder, then forced herself to relax and release her son's hand. Standing, she removed the rubber-lined glove and tossed it on the wheely chair she'd just vacated. She paused at the door John was holding open and met her son's eyes. If it had been her in the chair, hosting an electrical current as strong as the one flowing through Peter, she would have been seizing, her brain sizzling and turning to relative mush.

But not Peter. Because Peter wasn't like her. Peter wasn't really like anyone...not anymore. How much longer could this go on? How many more experimental treatments could a sixteen-year-old boy's body endure? How much higher could they crank up the electrical current without it harming even someone like Peter?

Peter flashed Anna another tense smile, and her heart twisted. How long did she have until Gregory lost patience with their son's stop-and-go—mostly stop—recovery?

Holding her breath, Anna left the room and shut the door. "What is it?" she said on her exhale. "You're very"—she scanned John from sneakered toes to balding head—"twitchy, today." Or, at least, twitchier than usual. "What's changed?"

John hunched his shoulders. "You know that Peter is…he's…"

Anna crossed her arms and raised her right eyebrow. "Peter is *what*?"

"He's, uh, different…fr—from the others, I mean." John scuffed his shoe against the linoleum floor. "Because of the chemo and radiation, not to mention all of the experim—treatments we've performed on him and…" He met Anna's eyes and blanched. "Which were very successful. Excellent ideas, all of them. Wouldn't have done any differently myself, had it been my kid who—"

"Cut the bullshit, John." Anna leaned in toward the pointy-featured man, planting a hand on the wall just behind him. He seemed to cringe into himself. There were *some* perks to being Gregory's wife, however unpleasant the drawbacks. It wasn't a fair trade, not even close. But it was something. "Tell me," she demanded gently.

John took a deep breath and held it for several seconds. "He—he's dying."

Anna shut her eyes. Breathed. Again. And again. When she reopened her eyes, she said, "I'm sorry." Deep breath. "I must have misheard you."

"The treatments aren't as effective as they used to be for Peter…and certainly not as effective as they are for the others." John wrung his hands. "The degeneration is progressing more quickly in him…not that it's not to be expected, considering that he's older in Re-gen terms than the few others left after the rebelli—"

John must've caught the dangerous glint in Anna's glare, because he shrank back even further. "It's as though I can't target the parts of his mind that are breaking down, like his synapses are firing too intensely, um, burning themselves out before I can reset the connection. And the less effective the treatments become, well, the more quickly the degeneration will progress." Quickly, he added, "And I'm sure it's not just him, or at least it won't be. Soon, the others will reach the same point." He nodded frantically. "I'm certain of it."

Anna narrowed her eyes. "I don't care what you have to do. Find. A. Way. To. Save. Him." She eased away from the wall—and the terrified doctor—and carefully straightened her lab coat. Purposefully, Anna raised her gaze to lock on his. "Find a way, or you'll be of no further use to me." And there it was again, disgusting proof that Anna was, deep down, just like Gregory.

John blinked several times. A deer in headlights held nothing on him. "I—I'll see what I can come up with."

Anna nodded and bared her teeth in a self-disgusted smile. "You do that."

Quick footsteps drew Anna's attention to the stretch of hallway behind her, and she turned around to see Howard, one of Gregory's favorite lackeys, approaching. At least, he was one of Gregory's favorites amongst the lackeys he still had after the uprising, and one of the few who'd remained *by choice* in the chaos and instability that had followed. The Re-gens had exacted a high toll with their unexpected rebellion, and it was one her son paid for every day with his increasingly rapid descent into illness. She needed more Re-gens…more subjects to run her tests on…more scientists to brainstorm possible solutions.

She needed Gabriel McLaughlin.

John tipped the scales in terms of intelligence, but he was an inside-the-box thinker. Gabriel, on the other hand, somehow managed to turn scientific experimentation into an art, constantly redefining the concept of "the box" with his intellectual creativity. Where John was an unquestionably smart man, Gabriel was a true scientific savant. If anyone could find a solution to the degeneration plaguing the Re-gens, Gabriel could.

But Anna hadn't had so much as a glimpse of him in her dreams for months. Not that it was his fault. These were dangerous times in the Colony, and only when Anna was feeling exceptionally desperate or bold would she dare to let her guard down, just for a brief window, while she slept, hoping Gabriel might be trying to contact her in her dreams. It had yet to bear fruit. Each time Anna woke from such an attempt, she had only disappointment to warm her bed—disappointment and the megalomaniac who'd long ago claimed her as his property…as his "wife."

Howard stopped just a little too close to Anna. But she was used to his intimidation techniques. Keeping her feet firmly planted, Anna squared her shoulders and met Howard's eyes. "Did you want something?"

"General Herodson needs you." Howard held her gaze, challenged it. "Come with me." And without another word, he turned and strode back up the hallway.

Anna forced herself to unball her fists. After several slow, even breaths, she looked at John, who was still trembling against the wall. "What do you need to increase the effectiveness of the treatments?" She spoke the words low and rushed. Much as she might find pleasure in making Gregory wait, she knew the repercussions; the anger he would take out on her and the pleasure he would gain from her pain would be far from worth it.

"More Re-gens. More assistants." John paused, squinting. "A more intense electrical current."

Anna blew out a breath. "Alright," she said as she turned away from him to follow after Howard. "I'll see what I can do." Gregory would have to see reason, especially when that reason came in the form of releasing the interred rebel Re-gens into her custody so she could use them to hone the treatment process—and, if she and John were able to make enough progress, save Peter's life.

Her spark of hope dwindled when she realized Howard wasn't leading her to Gregory's office on the other side of the Colony, but to the underground holding cells two buildings away from the electrotherapy lab. Doubt sprouted in her chest, spreading like a noxious weed. Gregory had been keeping his distance from the makeshift prison and its ailing Re-gen occupants. She feared his presence there now could mean only one thing—he'd finally settled on their punishment for rebelling. And when Gregory came to a decision, he acted on it quickly and without mercy. It was one of his few qualities that Anna actually admired. Except for right now.

Anna had no doubt of the severity of the punishment the uncooperative Re-gens would suffer, had no doubt that she was walking toward a mass execution. And she had no doubt that by extinguishing the rebel Re-gens' second lives, Gregory would be all but killing their son.

A livewire of tension and frustration, Anna descended the stairwell leading down to the long, underground hallway and its intermittent holding cells beneath one of the former college buildings. She couldn't allow Gregory to kill the few remaining Re-gens, not when she needed them so badly. Her mind was awhirl with thoughts…possibilities…logic…arguments…excuses…pleas… none of which would be good enough if Gregory's mind was already made up.

The first door on the right, a heavy, metal barrier set in the reinforced cement wall, stood ajar, and Anna could hear Gregory's disinterested voice floating through the doorway.

"—but some mistakes are just too great to make amends for, MT-01. I can no longer trust you. Your words are now meaningless to me."

Howard passed the doorway and took up a guard stance on the far side of the opening. Anna stopped opposite him and hung her head. Now that she knew which Re-gen Gregory was addressing in the cell, she recognized the emotionless quality of his voice for what it really was—a mask to cover the betrayal he felt, to hide his utter heartbreak.

Mikey—MT-01, in Re-gen terms—had been Gregory's favorite. He'd been loyal to "the General" before his death and had trusted Gregory implicitly, to the point of volunteering for the Re-gen program when it was still in the experimental phase. He was the only Re-gen that Gregory didn't address using a Re-gen identifier. Or, rather, he had been…before the uprising.

And while Mikey hadn't actually participated in the rebellion —in the massive slaughter that had taken place during those few, terrifying minutes that the General's people had been immobilized by Camille's metal-controlling Ability—he'd admitted to knowing about it before it happened. How could he not have when the oracle and orchestrator of the rebellion, RV-01—Becca—had been the closest thing he'd had to a best friend?

"Pl—please, Father." Mikey was sobbing, the sound sloppy and gut-wrenching. It was rare for a Re-gen to feel intense emotions, let alone express what they were feeling, and it yanked on the tangled wad of stored-up heartbreak that Anna kept tightly wound inside herself. She couldn't imagine what it would take to summon such an intense emotional response in her own son. "I kn—knew you w—would be safe," Mikey said between gasping breaths. "I—I would have w—warned you if I thought you—"

His words cut off with the sound of flesh hitting flesh, but his sobs continued.

"There are few things I enjoy less than the bitter taste of disappointment," Gregory said quietly, "and I could count on one hand the number of times I've felt such intense disappointment as I do now."

"Pl—please, Father—"

There was another fleshy smack, closely followed by a wet crunch that brought to mind a sickening image of the Re-gen's skull cracking against the cement wall.

"You were my favorite," Gregory said in the silence that hung in the absence of Mikey's sobs, thick to the point of choking. "I loved you like a son," he whispered.

Anna couldn't bring herself to step through the doorway, to enter the holding cell that she knew now contained only one living thing. At that moment, she refused to think of Gregory as a person —he was so much less.

Anna squeezed her eyes shut. Gregory truly had loved Mikey like a son; she knew it, had seen it with her own eyes. And he'd killed him anyway.

She just hoped he wouldn't inadvertently do the same to his actual flesh and blood.

1

ZOE

NOVEMBER 24, 1AE

The Farm, California

Hurrying through the mud and drizzle toward the stable proved detrimental to both staying clean and staying dry. Wet earth squished beneath each footstep, and I couldn't help but wonder why we hadn't moved our excess canning supplies out of the house sooner. Only a few steps from the sliding stable door, my right foot slipped in the mud, and it was all I could do not to face plant in the muddy gravel with an armful of empty jars. "Shit," I mumbled, letting out my held breath in relief as I regained my balance.

"That's a bad word," Annie observed behind me. "We're not supposed to say bad words."

I glanced back to find her half lost in concentration with each careful step, her little red rain boots spattered with mud. Muddy boots were better than muddy clothes, which Dani had made me promise to keep clean. Sam only shook his head.

"I know, no bad words," I said, straining as I used my foot to slide the stable door open wide enough for the three of us to scramble through and out of the rain. "I'm sorry. I didn't mean to say it." With an oomph, I managed to push the door open, and Annie shuffled inside, Sam and me following behind her.

Although it was chilly inside the stable, it smelled of leather and hay, a pleasant surprise since many of the horses had opted to remain cooped up in their stalls most of the week.

"Why are we bringing the jars in here?" Annie asked, her tiny voice taut as she crept inside. I passed her in search of a place to store our armfuls.

"Over here," I said, using my chin to point at the table stacked with Vanessa's tattered and soiled clothes—the few items she'd allowed us to remove from her to be cleaned and mended. It was the table Chris and Carlos had put in Vanessa's makeshift room during their daily visits to the last stall on the left.

Hearing Annie grunt, I looked down at her and smiled. Each of her steps was strategic and determined as she drew closer to the table, holding the four jars she'd insisted on carrying, like boulders too big for her tiny arms. As always seemed to be the case when I was around cute little *crazy* Annie, my heart melted a little.

"Why are we putting them in here?" she asked again.

"Because," Sam grumbled, "we all have to eat inside again." He set his case of jars on top of mine. "We need the kitchen table for dinner tonight because of the stupid rain."

"It'll stop soon," I said, but I wasn't sure that was true. We'd been mostly indoors for a couple of days, and none of us were sure when the weather would let up or for how long the break would last once it came, not even Tavis.

"But why aren't we putting them in the shed," Annie rattled on, "with the jellies and the pickles and the—"

Sam cut her off. "We're just storing them in here until Jason and Grandpa Tom can fix the roof on the shed," he said, sounding bored. "They have to wait for the rain to stop again."

"Oh, Sam," I said, nudging him with my elbow. "It's just a little rain…okay, maybe a *lot* of rain. But it'll let up soon."

With a grunt, Annie finally stopped in front of the table, squeezing the jars so tightly I could hear glass grinding against glass. I held my breath, waiting for them to crash onto the hay-scattered cement floor but hoping they wouldn't. Vanessa was chatting happily away to herself in her stall, and I didn't want to send her into a spiraling fit.

Naturally, Sam reached out to help Annie unload her jars, but she turned away from him, her wild blonde hair bouncing despite its damp tendrils. "I can do it," she said primly.

Sam's palms flew up, and he stepped away from Annie's accusatory glare. "Sorry."

Carefully, Annie placed one jar on the table, her brow furrowed in concentration. She set down another. "They're all wet and slippery," she grumbled, smearing a water drop on one with her fingertip.

"That's what happens when it's raining," Sam retorted, ever the older brother he'd seemed to become. "I told you I'd carry them." Although Sam often feigned annoyance with Annie, I knew she amused him, and like with the rest of us, she often made him smile despite his grumpy mood. She was contagious that way.

With a derisive sound, Annie scrunched her face. "I don't like the rain anymore," she said, sounding like Sam, but I knew it wasn't necessarily true. Annie didn't like that she had to stay indoors when it rained, but she thoroughly enjoyed the overabundance of puddles that popped up all over the property. More mud meant more fun, at least where Annie was concerned.

Wishing I'd been in less of a hurry and grabbed my jacket, I ignored the visible puff of breath I exhaled as my fingertips felt for the small cubes protruding from my back pocket.

"Tavis should make the rain go away," Annie said, adamant as she placed the last canning jar expertly on the table. She grinned, triumphant.

"Tavis can't send the rain away just because we don't like it, Annie," I tried to explain.

She looked at Sam, scrunched up her face again, then looked at me. Her bright blue eyes narrowed, but she listened without argument.

"Don't you like curling up on the couch, reading your animal stories with Mr. Grayson?" Despite how much Annie groaned about having to stay indoors, I knew she loved story time almost as much as she enjoyed romping around with Cooper and Jack in the dirt. And Mr. Grayson, *old* Bodega Bay's infamous history teacher and captivating orator—or Daniel, as some called him—was the best man for the job.

Annie huffed, an exaggerated, impatient sound. "Yeah, but—"

"But what? We need the water in the wells and to fill the pond, munchkin. And we need it for our winter garden," I explained. As if on cue, the encroaching storm above us worsened. Raindrops fell harder, echoing on the stable roof, and a gale of wind made the structure shudder and groan.

Shadow stirred in his stall a few doors down, and when Annie noticed my hand was in my back pocket, she grinned from ear to ear.

"I thought we weren't supposed to give sugar to the horses," Sam said wryly. Though he was going for disapproving, I knew he enjoyed our clandestine snack times with the horses as much as I did.

I brought my index finger to my lips. "Dani just said in moderation." I walked over to Shadow, deciding he might like the company since he was cooped up indoors like the rest of us. Little pattering feet followed, and Annie giggled.

When Shadow's head bobbed up and he anxiously approached the opened stall window, my grin widened. He looked like an oversized mountain pony with his shaggy, onyx coat, longer from the cool winter weather, and his unruly mane.

"Hey, boy," I said softly as he stuck his head through the window. Shadow's eyes were opened wide and bright, and I knew that meant he was growing anxious and ready for exercise. "Sorry, buddy, not today." A notion suddenly dawned on me. I looked back at Annie. "He's going to roll in the mud the first chance he gets, isn't he?"

She simply giggled.

"I knew it." Patting the side of his face, I put one of the sugar cubes out on my flattened palm for Shadow's greedy lips to find and gave the rest to Sam and Annie. "It'll be our little secret." I winked and pointed toward the other stalls. "Just be careful of the last one," I said. Annie and Sam both looked at Vanessa's stall. They nodded, familiar with the drill.

Unfazed to have a Crazy living in our stable—one who'd "cared" for Annie to the best of her mentally unstable ability before Dani had stumbled across them back in Tahoe—Annie giggled and pranced from stall to stall as she and Sam visited each of the horses. Just as they were finishing petting Brutus, Sam squinted beyond me, toward the tack room. I knew that look.

I glanced behind me and saw nothing, though I wasn't surprised. I'd grown used to Sam hearing things the rest of us couldn't.

"Kitty!" Annie sang, then she trotted past me to the corner of the stable, where one of the three two-month-old kittens meowed to life and stretched in the doorway of the tack room.

All of us smiled, unable to resist the brown kitten's sweet mewing while she traipsed toward us in want of attention; her brown fur, blue eyes, and bobbed, fluffy tail looked like—to Annie at least—the Mr. Potato Head doll Ky had given her right before *the incident.* "Ky liked Mr. Potato Head, and he would've liked this name," Annie had said when she'd named the little kitten Miss Potato. No one had argued with the determined little fireball, even if it was a painful memory. It didn't matter that Jason had been forced to shoot his best friend in self-defense, to *kill* Ky—the Monitor the General had placed on him. It was a day we all wished we could forget.

"She's getting bigger," Sam said, smiling as he watched Miss

Potato spastically frolicking and squeaking as she played in the straw.

Unlike Sam and Annie, my mind was shadowed by darker times. Thinking of Ky made my heart ache, then burn with guilt and regret as my thoughts jumped to memories of Sarah's suicide. I thought about Biggs and the twins, whom we hadn't seen in almost six months. They were all gone because of me, because of the tangled, messy web of lies my life consisted of.

Annie giggled and gently stroked Miss Potato's tawny belly as the kitten flopped and played at her feet.

"Where are the others?" Sam asked, peering back at the tack room, the cats' secluded safe haven during our coastal storm.

"Bubbles is coming," Annie explained. "But Doodle is getting a bath."

With hands in his front pockets, Sam leaned back on his heels and let out a deep exhale, one that exuded incredulity, like he might never be able to completely wrap his mind around Dani and Annie's animal-speaking Abilities.

"Look who I found crying outside the door," Tavis said, striding into the barn. His dirty blond hair was matted, and water dripped from his nose as he held out a nearly drowned, squeaky black kitten.

"Bubbles!" Annie exclaimed.

Sam chuffed. "I thought you said she was inside?"

Annie ran over to Tavis and the drenched kitten. "No, I said she was coming."

"What was she doing outside?" I asked. I made my way over to Tavis and the kitten. "She could've gotten washed away."

Annie greedily snatched Bubbles from Tavis's hold. He grinned at me and stepped aside to let Annie fawn all over the kitten. "She was exploring, and then it started raining," Annie explained. "She got scared."

"Well, I'm glad Tavis found her then," I said, and crouched down to pet the matted black mess.

I saw a flicker of something in Tavis's mind, a memory of the past that sent a wave of longing through him—not lustful longing, but something lonelier. He glanced at me.

"Zoe," Annie said.

I looked down to find her holding Bubbles close to her chest.

She glanced from the crying kitten to me, a mischievous look on her face. "Your hair is the same as Bubble's is." She smiled widely, a gaping hole where her right front tooth would've been.

"Yeah?" I eyed the kitten's soggy black fur, dabbled with streaks of white and gray. "I hope not *exactly* like hers," I muttered.

I barely heard Sam's amused grunt over the sound of the dinner triangle clanking and ringing outside. Annie jumped up, startling the kittens when she shouted, "Food!"

"I'm going to eat it all before you get there," Tavis taunted with a wink in my direction, then he rushed back out into the rain, egging Annie on in their daily bout of catch-me-if-you-can.

"You better hurry," I goaded her, "or there'll be nothing left for dinner!" With peals of laughter, Annie handed me the kitten and ran out into the rain, toward the farmhouse. "Stay out of the puddles!" I called after them, hoping the amusement in my voice didn't drown out my authoritative tone completely.

I set Bubbles and Miss Potato back in the tack room with Mama and Doodle, then stalked toward the slightly opened stable door, anxious to get out of the cold and back into the warm house.

The moment I stepped outside, rain pelted me mercilessly, or at least it felt that way as it soaked what seemed like every inch of me. Quickly I pulled the sliding door shut, squinting through wet lashes toward the house. Apparently my authoritative tone needed some work, because, as I'd expected, Annie seized every opportunity to jump in the puddles on her way to the porch. Tavis smiled at me, winked, and ushered the kids inside, and all I could do was hope that Dani didn't kill me when she saw how muddy Annie had gotten, despite my best efforts.

After latching the stable door shut, I jogged toward the house.

Heavy, quick footsteps squished behind me, and I couldn't help the knowing grin that parted my lips. It was Jake. We were connected on so many levels now; I could sense his presence and his mind better than anyone else's. He was no longer the mystery he'd once been, with walls and armor that kept him distant and apprehensive. Now, he was the warmth to my cold, the strong to my weak. He was the second half of me I had never realized was missing until I'd known what it felt like to lose him—to lose *myself* and become someone who had no memories at all. At least Gabe, genius that he was, was able to help me get my mind back, the memories that made me *me*.

"Evening stroll?" Jake asked as he jogged up beside me, squinting into the rain. He lifted part of his flannel jacket to shield me from the downpour.

"Yeah, it's been such a beautiful day." I wrapped my arm around his waist, and together we hurried to the shelter of the porch. His heat steadied my cold, trembling bones. He'd become a protective cocoon; I would never grow tired of the warmth and vitality he exuded, always making me feel loved…making me feel safe. With him, I could lose my inhibitions and my fears and, on my favorite occasions, let loose my desires.

"What are *you* doing out here?" I asked, letting go of him when we reached the porch steps. The wood creaked beneath our urgent footsteps. I stared down at my dirt-splattered jeans and mud-caked boots. "Shit." Using the edge of the step, I tried to scrape the chunks of mud off the bottom of my right boot. I could picture Annie now, running around the house and rolling all over the furniture, covered in far more mud than I was.

"I was checking the leaks in the shed," Jake said as he shook out his hair. "The tarp's holding well enough for now." A gust of wind picked up, and I shivered. As I scraped the mud from the bottom of my other boot, Jake shrugged off his jacket.

Laughter, dishes clanking, and amiable chatter emanated from inside as everyone no doubt gathered around the dinner table, just as we'd done most nights since the winter weather had worsened. It was a tight fit to have all fifteen of us together—seventeen when Mase and Camille were around, visiting us from the Re-gen homesteads in Hope Valley—but we made it work. We were growing used to it. In the darkening gloom, I could make out bustling silhouettes illuminated behind the thin, drawn curtains.

"Not that meteorologists were right very often," I said, "but it would be nice to know when the rain is coming and how long it's planning to stay. A little preparation time would be appreciated."

"Are you sure the storm wasn't summoned?" Jake muttered.

I ran my fingers through my damp hair, the shorter strands no longer a shock as they'd grown out a little. "What?" I precariously wiped the water from under my eyes. "Why?" I momentarily opened my mind up to his, wondering his meaning and hoping to catch a glimpse, but then he glanced down at my chest, my gaze following his, and I didn't need to know what he was thinking; it was written clearly on his face.

Jake handed me his jacket. The front of my white, long-sleeved shirt was wet, leaving to the imagination only what was hidden behind my peach colored bra.

I glowered at him as I donned his jacket, my head tilted in a silent scold for insinuating that Tavis had brought the rain. "I'm pretty sure he had nothing to do with it," I said dryly.

Jake's left eyebrow rose, mirroring my expression, and his mouth quirked at the corner. "Lucky me then," he said. He stepped closer, and although I'd planned on a reproachful response, the intensity of the base desire that burned somewhere deep in my belly whenever he was around, prevented the chiding remarks from forming on my tongue.

"I think this is the first time I've gotten you alone all week," he said, his voice quiet while his mind swirled with tantalizing thoughts that made me forget about cold and hunger and our waiting friends inside the house. He wrapped his arms around me, his heat enveloping me, and he pulled me into him. Chills raked through me, making me shiver with pure anticipation.

"What about this morning?" I whispered, vaguely remembering the feel of his lips on my temple when he woke me before the sun was even awake. My eyelids flitted closed as his lips softly brushed against mine. I couldn't remember the last time we'd been together. Everything had been so crazy, and we'd been so exhausted, it had become a rarity when we were able to lie in bed and lose ourselves in each other's arms.

Despite the plip-plop of rain on the porch awning and the cacophony of voices inside, I began to give in to my desperation to be alone with him. *Just for a little while.* His hands were rough but gentle, his lips firm but pliant against mine. His stubble tickled and teased my mouth and cheeks, the sensitive nerve endings tingling to life. A small moan escaped me as his arms tightened around my waist.

"Zo," Dani's voice whispered in my mind. *"Your dad just asked me where you are. Please don't make me tell him you're making out with Jake on the porch...assuming he doesn't already know."*

With a groan, I leaned my forehead against Jake's shoulder. "We'd better get inside," I said and let out a thwarted breath. "Apparently they're waiting for us."

Reticent, I pulled away from him and opened my eyes to find Jake's silhouette washed in a crimson haze. I blinked a few times, encouraging the desirous fog to dissipate, until I could finally refocus. I grinned. He was staring at me with lust-filled eyes, and images of us, upstairs together…alone…filled his mind.

Anxious for what was to come later, I leaned in for a final, promise-filled kiss and entwined my fingers with his before leading him into the house to join the others.

My bedroom was bright and open, the sunshine pouring through the window illuminating my toy-cluttered floor. Hunger rumbled inside my belly. Setting my doll down on my princess comforter, I climbed off my bed, humming as my tummy rumbled again.

Tugging down the hem of my sundress, I walked into the hall and plodded down the stairs on little legs, heading for the kitchen. The carpet tickled the bottoms of my bare feet, making me smile. I didn't hear the usual clanking of pots and pans that I usually did whenever Daddy was in the kitchen.

"Daddy?" I stopped in the kitchen doorway, expecting to find him fumbling around inside. But he wasn't there. Still humming, I turned and walked into the living room. He wasn't in his recliner in front of the television either. "Daddy?" I wondered if he'd gone to pick up Jason. Fear flittered through me, and I wondered if Daddy left me home all alone.

Then I heard angry voices coming from the back porch.

Noticing that the sliding glass door was slightly open, I walked over and peered outside. My humming ceased, and I froze. Daddy was standing on the porch with a pretty woman. Her hair was long and black, like mine. Her face was pink, and she rushed around like she was scared or upset.

Suddenly, I was standing outside with them. The woman was staring at me and looked like she might cry as she reached for me. "Come here, Zoe," she said.

I tried not to flinch away from her touch, but I couldn't help it. Scared and confused, I looked up at Daddy. He looked sad, too.

"You look so pretty in your dress," the woman said. She tried to smile, and I found myself hesitantly smiling back at her. I liked her eyes. They were special and seemed familiar.

"I knew you'd come back here," a man said. I jumped when I heard his voice, but the woman didn't seem surprised. Her hands flew to her stomach, and I wondered if she was hurt.

I blinked, and then the man was standing next to me, like he appeared out of nowhere. He had a mustache and a smile that didn't seem happy.

Daddy looked angry and afraid. Something didn't feel right, and I wanted to disappear.

"They didn't know I was coming here, Gregory," the woman started to say. "I just needed to—"

But the man with the mustache held up the palm of his hand. "Shhh," he said, staring only at me. I wasn't sure why I felt scared, but I was trying not to cry. "Look how big you've grown," he said and crouched down before me. He smiled a big smile, his slightly crooked teeth evoking a sudden panic that made my throat tighten. "And you're beautiful, just like your mommy." He looked back at the woman gripping the patio table. Her eyes were shimmering, and I noticed her holding Daddy's arm tightly with her other hand, like she was holding him back.

"Don't you dare touch her," Daddy said, and the smile on the man's face fell a little. I saw something in his eyes that unleashed the tears I'd been trying not to shed. Something bad was happening, I could feel it.

"Daddy..." I began to sob. But it wasn't Daddy who picked me up, it was the scary man.

"There, there, little Zoe. It's okay." He patted my leg and smiled at Daddy and the woman. They said something to him, but I was too stunned to listen. For the first time, I noticed men lining the fence of our backyard. They appeared out of nowhere, like the scary man had. There were a lot of them, but only a few had big guns. Their faces were mad and mean.

I cried louder. I wished Jason was home.

"I told you what would happen if you ever left, Anna. Did you think I was bluffing? That I wouldn't notice...again?"

Through a veil of tears, I peered back over at Daddy and the woman. Daddy was frowning, angrier than I'd ever seen him. I called for him again, but the man's grip on me tightened. I shrieked in pain.

"I will kill your son if you hurt her," the woman growled, and she pointed to her tummy. "I will end your legacy."

The man's fingers dug into my leg, and I hit at his hand without thought, trying to get him to let me go. When he finally set me back on the ground, I ran to Daddy.

"You will not harm them, Gregory. Or I won't hesitate to kill this child. I promise you that." I stared at her belly. I didn't see a baby, but her tummy was big.

"You won't kill an innocent child, Anna," the man said. "Me, on the other hand…" He stared at me again and smiled. "And then there's the boy, too."

"You leave him out of this!" Daddy shouted, and I could feel his body shaking.

The scary man's face hardened, and I noticed his body stiffen. "Watch yourself, Sergeant. My compassion only goes so far."

The woman pulled a needle like they used at the doctor's office from behind her. It was the kind that always poked my skin and pinched me, but just for a minute. "So help me God, Gregory. If you hurt my family, I will *kill yours."*

The scary man looked at all of us, and his voice was angrier than before. "Then there's not much of a reason for me to keep any of you around, is there?"

"I'll come back with you," the woman said, reaching for him. "If you'll just leave my family alone."

The man pounded his fist on the patio table. "I'm *your family!"*

"Not if you hurt them," she said. The woman looked angry, but she still sounded scared.

Daddy bent down to me. "Go inside, sweetheart." He leaned in for a hug and whispered, "Hide. Until I can make it go away…hide."

I nodded, not understanding what he meant, but wanting to hide all the same.

I didn't know why the scary man wanted to hurt us. I didn't understand why the woman wanted to kill the baby I couldn't see either. But I knew the man with the mustache was evil, and I was afraid that if I looked away, Daddy would be gone, and I would never see him again.

The scary man shook his head. "I thought we agreed last time that your family was as good as dead if you ever came back. Yet here you are, again." He clenched his fist. "I trusted you. I thought your word was worth your freedom. Apparently I was wrong."

The sad woman took a step toward him. "I was just scared, Gregory," she said, rubbing her belly. "You don't understand how dangerous this is for me. I just needed to see them, needed to say goodbye." She wiped the tears from her eyes. She didn't look scared anymore. "I promise, once I leave, I will never *come back."*

The scary man's eyes narrowed, and he glanced from her swollen cheeks down to her belly. "You have one more chance, darling. If you even try to leave again, if you do anything *to undermine me and my mission, or our family..." He glared over at me.*

"Go inside, Zoe!" Daddy yelled.

I ran toward the house, but stopped inside the door and listened, waiting. I didn't want to leave Daddy.

"Regardless of what you do in the future, measures will be taken now," the scary man said, and when I peeked around the doorframe, the woman looked relieved. "Monitors, in fact. And if you do misstep, even in the most minimal way, I will hurt your children and make Tom, here, watch, and you might never even know it. That, my dear, is my *promise to you."*

When my eyes met Daddy's, wide and sad, everything suddenly faded away. I was in my room, crying in his arms. His familiar eyes were empty as he stared at me. Gently, he brushed a tear from my cheek, and then everything changed again. The memory of the scary man faded away. Then the sad woman started to change. Her special eyes disappeared, her features vanishing one by one until she was faceless and frightening...until she was completely gone, too.

There were no men in the backyard, and Daddy wasn't upset. There was no reason I could think of for why I'd been crying or why Daddy would look so sad.

2

DANI

NOVEMBER 25, 1AE

The Farm, California

With a grunt, I adjusted my hold on the box I was carrying and attempted to reach for the doorknob on the cottage's front door. The glassware in the box, an amalgam of random glasses, mugs, vases, and bowls I'd collected from the massive—and dusty—storage room in the barn, shifted and clanked in warning.

"Crap," I hissed. *"Jason?"* I called telepathically. Having my Ability firing on all cylinders was useful in so many ways, not the least of which was being able to request aid from pretty much anyone, anywhere, at any time. *"Come get the door?"*

"Give me a second." He was inside the cottage, in what was slowly transforming into our bedroom in the back corner of the small house. I could sense his mind signature there. Stationary. Not rushing toward the door to let me in.

I pressed my lips together and exhaled with a huff. Clearly, being able to request help telepathically and receiving said help were two entirely different matters.

Gritting my teeth, I raised my right leg and used my thigh to shift my increasingly precarious hold on the box once more. It certainly didn't help that the cardboard was damp from the drizzling rain or that, thanks to the chill in the air, I could barely feel my fingers. At least the porch's shallow eave protected me from getting rained on further. *"Unless you want a mountain of broken glass on the stoop, it'd be great if you could come get the door now..."*

I could sense Jason's movement instantaneously, and seconds later, the door swung open and he plucked a box that had been just shy of way too heavy out of my arms with annoying ease. I flexed my fingers, cringing at the uncomfortable mixture of numbness and sharp, stinging pain.

"You shouldn't have tried to carry this in the first place." Jason gave me a reproachful look—eyebrows raised, chiseled jaw flexed, jagged scar intensifying *everything* about him—before turning and heading through the cozy living room with the box. He set it on the single free corner of the rustic farm table that separated the "kitchen" from the rest of the living area. We'd found the table in the storage room—which, in all reality, put most old attics to shame with all the treasures it contained—and had relocated it to the cottage almost a week ago, during our last "moving day."

Days off were rare on our little communal farm, and Jason and I had been setting up the cottage to be our small family's own comfy, compact, and moderately private home for over a month now. I was more than ready to move out of the farmhouse and settle in here with Jason and Annie and my beloved German shepherd, Jack. To have my own space...to not always be stepping on the toes of every other living person I knew...to make a home with Jason...

I sighed, and after scanning the combined living room and kitchen and beautiful river-stone hearth, after taking in the columns of boxes and piles of clutter that still needed to be moved out, arranged, or put away, I felt my shoulders slump. It looked like I wouldn't be settling in to my little piece of domestic paradise on this rainy November day. *Maybe next week…*

"Red." Jason planted himself in front of me and rested his work-roughened hands on my shoulders. "Look at me."

Unable to resist an order from him, especially one delivered in such a low, silky rumble, I raised my gaze to his and fell in love with him just a little bit more. His sapphire eyes were filled with such warmth, such light and heat and wonder, that I couldn't help but lose myself in them. Lose myself to him.

"What did I tell you last night?" he asked, face placid.

My cheeks flushed and my whole body heated as I remembered things whispered in the cover of darkness. Secret things. Things I was almost certain I couldn't repeat while it was daylight or while I was staring into his eyes…or *ever*. "Um…" I drew my bottom lip between my teeth and lowered my eyes and blushed even more. "Well…"

Jason chuckled, his thumbs tracing the underside of my jaw. "While I think it's pretty fucking fantastic that your mind went *there* automatically, I was actually talking about the promise I made about moving. Into the cottage. Today…"

"Oh!" My eyes flashed up to his, and I smiled shyly. My face and neck were still on fire.

"Unless you're planning on spending the rest of the day digging around in that room"—his focus shifted to my hair, and he pulled a clumpy cobweb from my ponytail's unruly curls—"we'll have plenty of time to finish up in here."

I assessed the chaotic space once again and puckered my lips, attempting to imagine everything arranged just so. And failed. "But—"

"The bedrooms are all that really matter, anyway." Jason shrugged a shoulder and looked down the short hallway to both ours and Annie's future bedrooms. "And those are done."

Narrowing my eyes, I scrutinized Jason's face. He hadn't shaved today—not yesterday, either, I'd have wagered—and the slightly unkempt cowboy look made his already minimally expressive features harder to read. "What do you mean 'they're done'?" I tilted my head to the side. I hadn't been in either bedroom for days, having spent all of my time working around the farm and most of the morning "shopping" in the storage room in the barn. "Annie's room still needs furniture, especially a bed, and—"

Jason shook his head. "She doesn't want a bed; you know that."

I frowned. "She's just a kid. Don't you think she needs—"

"Yeah, she's a kid, and about as unusual as they get."

It was my turn to shake my head. "But still…she needs a bed, Jason. Where's she going to sleep—er, drift?" My voice rose in pitch. "With us?"

Again, Jason chuckled. "No way in hell. At night, you belong to me and *only* me."

A splash of my earlier flush returned. "So…?"

Jason smiled, just a little. "Becca's been helping her set up her room." Almost on cue, Annie's pure, crystalline giggle came from her bedroom.

Capturing my hand, Jason led me into the short hallway and toward Annie's room. Another peal of laughter came from within before he opened the door, swinging it inward with a creak

Jason glanced at the door, then back at me, and mumbled, "I'll have to fix that."

My gaze was pulled away from his and into the bedroom. In the dim late morning light coming in through the room's two small windows, the space resembled a forest clearing as much as a bedroom—a cozy forest clearing, but a forest clearing nonetheless. All four walls were covered with painted trees, some a dark, ashy brown and others fading to smoky gray in the "distance," but each wall was vastly different, as each represented one of the four seasons. There were silhouetted animals in the shrubbery painted near the floor and birds resting on branches here and there.

"What—*how*?" Eyes wide, I stepped into the room and turned

in a slow circle, taking in everything. A rough-hewn wooden chest and matching dresser—both looking almost as though they'd simply grown into their current shape—had been placed against one wall. In one corner, what I could only identify as a nest of pillows and blankets spilled out, filling nearly half of the room. I pointed to the furniture, then to the walls and the nest. "How'd this—I don't understand."

Annie giggled, finally drawing my attention to where she sat with Becca and Jack, nestled in her bed-nest-thing and lazily scratching the dog's side. She threw herself onto her back and pointed to the ceiling.

I held my breath. I'd yet to look up. And when I did, I exhaled a long, slow, "Whoa…" The moon, larger than life and surrounded by a choir of stars, practically glowed overhead.

"Did—did Zo do this?" I couldn't imagine how she could have; she was easily as busy as me with farm work. Everyone was.

Standing behind me, Jason wrapped his arms around my shoulders and pulled me flush against him. His body heat practically seared through my cool, damp clothing. I hadn't realized how deeply the chill had settled in from being out in the barn all morning with only a hooded sweatshirt for warmth.

Slowly, Becca stood and brushed off the front of her jeans. After a moment, she looked at me. "It was not only Zoe," she said in that careful way of hers, her voice as raspy as ever. "I helped her paint the room. She wished to surprise you by doing something special to make your home as perfect as possible, but she didn't have the time to do it all herself."

Eyebrows raised, I stared at Becca. "Zo…and you?"

She clasped her hands together in front of herself and nodded demurely. "My brother tells me I was an artist of a sort, similar to Zoe, but different in that I preferred three-dimensional art. Though I do find the act of painting quite soothing." I frowned as she glanced around at the walls. I hadn't realized she'd been an artist, too. "Zoe is an excellent teacher, wouldn't you say?"

I blew out my breath, once again taking in the masterful work she and Zoe had done. "Yeah. You guys did an amazing job." I looked at her. "It's beautiful." Glancing from her to Annie and back, I gave her a warm smile. "Thank you for doing this."

Becca nodded, eyes downcast, and walked to the dresser. Placing her hand on the surface, she returned my smile. "This and the chest were Tom's work."

I blinked several times, then turned around in Jason's arms. "Your dad made them? But when?"

"He—" Jason took a deep breath, and tension filled him. "His intentions were good, and he swears he only altered perception around him a few times to keep it a surprise for us."

I felt some of Jason's tension seep into me. After everything that had happened at the Colony, I *really* hated the idea of someone —anyone—messing with my mind. Again.

"He showed me the pieces once he was finished making them." Jason paused for a moment. "We got into a big fu—" Catching himself, he glanced at Annie, then returned his focus to me. "A big argument. He won't admit it, but I think it's hard for him to just live—not changing what those around him perceive to fit his needs. He's been doing it for so long now that it's become second nature."

"Still...I don't like it, Jason." I gave him a meaningful look. *"I don't want anyone messing with my mind."*

A low grunt hummed in Jason's throat. *"I know."* He gave my shoulder a gentle squeeze. *"He wasn't fully aware of what the General did to you, but he knows now. He really just wanted to surprise us, that's all, and he's taking every precaution to make sure he doesn't slip back into old habits. It won't happen again."*

Awash with relief, I smiled. *"Well, that's something."* Forcing the smile to remain, I approached the dresser and examined the odd combination of gnarled and elegant decorations carved into its surfaces. "Well, kiddo?" I peeked back at Annie, who was still staring up at the painted moon. "What do you think of your new bedroom?"

Annie flung her arms out akimbo and sighed dramatically. "I love it *so* much. It's the best bedroom ever!"

I grinned at her. "Like, *ever* ever?"

She nodded enthusiastically. "*Ever* ever." Abruptly, she sat up and stared at me, her face serious and her blonde curls a wild tangle. "But I like yours, too."

"You do?" Curious, I turned around to look at Jason. His face was a mask of bland innocence. "You've been busy." As I considered all that had been accomplished right under my nose—without me suspecting a thing—I realized just how much time and effort I'd been putting into working around the farm. Maybe a smidge too much…

Jason stuck his hands into his jeans pockets and shrugged.

I crossed the room to him and smacked him on the arm. "I don't like it when you keep secrets from me," I said with mock severity.

The faintest smirk touched Jason's lips. "But you like my surprises."

"Yeah, but—"

"You can't have it both ways, Red."

I tried to keep my face stern, but I couldn't hold back my eager grin. "Grams used to say that surprises always leave behind a trail of secrets; good or bad, if you look hard enough, you'll find 'em." My grin faded along with the fond memory, but when I once again focused on Jason's face, it returned at full force. "Well, are you going to show me, or what?"

Jason laughed, low and soft, and turned toward the doorway. Annie was up and running before I'd taken my first step to follow. Somehow, the lithe little sprite managed to make it through the doorway before Jason. I watched him follow her out.

"You love him very much," Becca said from right behind me.

I yelped and spun around, my hand pressed against my chest in a vain attempt to slow my suddenly racing heart. "Jesus, Becca. You startled me."

"I'm sorry," she said, her voice barely more than a whisper. Her eyes, however, shone with a feverish intensity. They'd changed since Carlos had started administering electrotherapy on her, as had the eyes of the other Re-gens; they were no longer that dull gray I'd come to expect of their kind, but hers a violet-gray that was somehow both eerie and entrancing. The returning vibrancy to the Re-gens' eyes seemed to mirror their reemerging personalities and emotions, as though their eyes really were windows to their souls.

Quietly, Becca asked, "What is it like to be in love?"

Taking a step backward, I frowned. "Um…it's great. Why?"

"You and Jason love each other very much." She took a step toward me, her focus intent on my face. "But doesn't it scare you?"

I shook my head, taking another step backward. Sometimes Re-gens could be funny with how they treated personal boundaries—or ignored them. "I don't understand."

Becca took a deep breath, and I had the impression she was struggling with how to voice her thoughts. "It makes you happy, that is obvious, but…if one of you was suddenly gone, the other would be devastated. Love like that seems like a terrible gamble, and I just wanted to know if it's worth it."

Unease took root in my stomach. Was Becca curious because she was interested in someone romantically, or was this something else…something more? "Is it worth what, exactly?"

She licked her lips. Her eyes were haunted, but intent on me. "The pain it causes. The potential for unimaginable loss. The possibility that one day it might be gone. There's something…" She shook her head. "I just need to know if the good balances the bad. I need to know if love is worth the fear and the pain." She swallowed roughly. "Even with my visions, tomorrow is never certain. I just need to know if it's worth it."

Unease was quickly morphing into dread…anxiety. This

strange, totally out-of-the-blue behavior was exactly why I never felt completely comfortable around Becca. She was different from the other Re-gens in that she could see the future, or snippets of it, and she was different from the only other person I knew who had a similar Ability—Harper—because she didn't possess a lifetime's worth of practice interacting with people and delivering life-changing, potentially devastating news. It made her really hard to relate to and all but impossible to understand, at least for me.

But part of me could understand her question. We were living in pretty damn uncertain times, even for one with the Ability to see some of what was to come. Whatever she'd seen in her murky view of the future, whatever she'd felt, it seemed to me that she needed reassurance that there was something worth living for, something worth fighting for, something worth hanging onto, no matter what.

"Yeah," I said roughly. "I think it's worth it." Shaking my head, I amended my answer. "It *is* worth it. I mean, just look at Jason and Zo's mom—she's torn the world apart because she loved them too much to let them go. If that's not evidence proving that love is more valuable than almost anything else, I don't know what is."

Slowly, Becca's entire demeanor changed and she was, once again, the slightly withdrawn, awkward Re-gen just trying to find her place in the world. "Thank you for that…for being so honest." Her gaze sank to the floor. "Sometimes it's hard to relate. Sometimes we feel so strongly, like you, but other times it seems more like a memory of a feeling. I just needed to know."

I cleared my throat. "Sure." I wanted to know if she was telling the whole truth. I wanted to know if her questions about love were rooted in a deeper motivation, if they stemmed from some secret vision she'd seen. I wanted to know—and I *never* wanted to find out. Flashing Becca a pathetic excuse for a smile, I added, "Any time."

Annie was suddenly in the room, skipping circles around us. "Dani! Dani! Dani! Dani! Dani! Dan—"

"Alright, little one," Becca said, expertly capturing Annie's tiny arm and stopping her whirlwind progress around us. I was always amazed with her ability to handle my adopted wild child with such ease. "Let's give Dani and Jason some time to explore their new bedroom." Meeting my eyes briefly, she winked.

I gaped at her as she led Annie out of the room. *Becca winked at me? Becca* could *wink?* Moments later, I heard the sound of the front door opening and shutting.

"Red," Jason called from the room opposite Annie's.

Bewildered, I made my way down the short hallway, past the compact bathroom, and through the doorway into our bedroom. I felt like a zombie, as if Becca and her odder-than-usual behavior and our unsettling conversation had drained the life out of me. Until I actually saw the bedroom—Jason's and my bedroom. My mouth fell open.

The bed appeared to be made of repurposed wood, and it was absolutely stunning. But I'd known about it, as well as the matching armoire, dresser, and simple bedside tables. What I hadn't known about was the quilt Jason must have snuck onto the farm after a visit to Grams's house just outside New Bodega's walls. It was the quilt from Grams's guest room, made up of interlocking circles of blues and purples, and though it really was a beautiful quilt, it was the fact that Grams had made it that tugged at my heartstrings.

"Oh, Jason…" I stepped into the bedroom and ran my fingertips over the quilt. Having it in the room made the space smell like Grams's house in the subtlest ways, hinting at candle wax and at herbs used daily to make teas and tinctures.

Tears welled in my eyes, and without thinking, I turned and flung myself into Jason's arms. My mouth sought his, my hands tugging at his clothes to bring him closer to me. And for a little while, I forgot about the knot of anxiety spooling inside me. For a little while, I let Jason remind me why love—our love—was worth it.

I hummed to myself as Jack and I strolled out to the stable to gather the horses' evening snack. They received plenty of sustenance from grazing out in our abundant pastures, but I still enjoyed the special spike of pleasure they felt when they took a nibble of an apple or a carrot from my hand.

"I already told you, talk to Mase or Becca," I heard Carlos say, his voice raised. "If you've got a problem with their system, take it up with them." His voice was filled with frustration, or maybe with exasperation, and when I rounded the corner of the stable and caught my first glimpse of him through the open door, I wasn't surprised by his tense, almost aggressive stance. He was facing two male Re-gens, one shorter and plumper than him, the other taller and thinner.

I recognized them both as residents of the farm just north of ours. With the Re-gens and the Tahoe folks now residing in our little valley, we'd managed to get two more farms up and running and were putting the physical structures of another two through renovations while we began to cultivate the adjacent land. Our short string of self-sufficient homesteads had come to be known as Hope Valley among our people as well as among the residents of New Bodega, and with each passing week, it seemed more and more likely that our hopes for a better, safer, and more stable future would become a reality.

I didn't know the two Re-gens' names, but they'd both seemed kindly enough the previous times I'd crossed paths with them. Now, not so much; now, they were demonstrating just how much the regular electrotherapy sessions had expanded their emotional ranges. The tall one was pointing his finger at Carlos's chest, nearly poking him, and the short one had his fists clenched and held at his sides and was practically vibrating with pent-up aggression.

"Everything okay, guys?" I asked as I approached.

Jack, who'd been walking at my side, trotted forward a few paces, hackles raised and lips retracted. He considered Carlos a part of his pack, and he was more than ready to fight for the teen if and when necessary.

Carlos swatted the taller Re-gen's hand away. "Yeah. They were just leaving." He turned his back to the Re-gens and retreated further into the stable, no doubt heading for his sister's stall at the end.

The Re-gens stared after him but didn't follow.

"You should go," I said as I passed them. When they still showed no signs of leaving, I asked Jack to gently—and none-too-gently, if the kinder approach failed—escort them away.

A slight smile touched my lips as I listened to his warning growls and the snap of his teeth clacking together as he nipped at his temporary charges. When I heard the approaching click-clack-click of dog claws on cement, I peeked over my shoulder. The Re-gens were gone, and Jack was returning to me.

"Thanks, Sweet Boy."

He wagged his tail happily and let out a single yip.

Ahead, Carlos stood before the sliding door to his sister's stall, his forehead resting against the barred-off window, his hands gripping two of the bars tightly. I stopped a few feet away and crossed my arms over my chest. Jack, however, continued forward, sitting as close to Carlos as was physically possible without actually sitting on his feet. Inside the stall, Vanessa, Carlos's eighteen-year-old sister and our resident Crazy, was experiencing a blessed—and rare—moment of quiet.

"So…what was that all about?" I asked.

Carlos exhaled heavily. "They were here because Jimmy, Dan, and Lawrence—" Seeing my blank stare, he clarified, "They're Re-gen sparklers, but they're not as good as me at electrotherapy." I knew *sparklers* was his slang for people who could handle electricity like he could.

I coughed a laugh. "So humble…"

Carlos shrugged with minimal effort. "It's true. They're not as good at controlling the currents. And they're weaker…and that makes the electrotherapy they give weaker. Maybe in time, after they've strengthened their own Abilities by electrotherapizing the shit out of each other, they'll be way better than me, but now…?" Again, he shrugged.

"So what? You're like name-brand electrotherapy and the others are knockoffs?" I glanced back up the empty stable aisle. "And not everybody's getting Carlos-brand electrotherapy, are they?" I stuck out my bottom lip, just a little.

Carlos turned his head to look at me, his temple resting against one of the metal bars. "Yeah, and Mase and Becca and Camille have been really cutting down on who I work on—just them and the other sparklers, mostly. Everyone else gets one session with me per month."

I was undeniably grateful to Mase, Camille, and Becca for their innate ability to more or less rule over the other Re-gens, as well as for their foresight where Carlos was concerned. Six months ago, when the Re-gens first arrived en masse, seeking our help to stave off their slow death by degeneration, Carlos had tried to help everyone, which had led to overexertion in less than a day and a period of burnout that had lasted for three full days. And when his Ability came back online, had Mase, Camille, and Becca not stepped up and reined in the Re-gen horde, they'd have begged and whined and pleaded and bullied Carlos into doing it all over again.

"It's raining…it's pourrrrring," Vanessa sang from within her stall. "The old man is snorrrrring."

I eyed the shadows through the bars, uncomfortably grateful that I couldn't see Carlos's sister in the dimness. The intermittent rain and cloud cover was making all hours of daylight feel like dusk.

"He went to bed," Vanessa continued, "and bumped his head and couldn't get up in the morrrrning."

I shivered, and without a word, Carlos slipped his leather coat off and tucked it around my shoulders. "You know, soon it'll be too cold for her to stay out here all the time," Carlos said, and I didn't need Zoe's Ability to know that having his sister locked up because she was a danger to herself and others was killing him inside.

We'd loaded Vanessa's space with all sorts of blankets, but without the electric heat the stable had been designed with, I knew he was right. We all did. What we didn't know was what the hell to do with her. Could we get by with letting her stay in the house, simply keeping a guard on her day and night? It was a thought…

"It's raining…it's pourrrrring." Vanessa's voice was growing shriller with each word.

"We'll figure something out," I told Carlos, giving him a side hug.

"The brother thief is snorrrring…"

I exchanged a look with Carlos. *Brother thief* was Vanessa's name for me, we both knew it. We also both knew that whatever was going to come next in her revised version of the old song wouldn't be overly pleasant.

"You should go," Carlos said quickly.

"You'll go to bed," Vanessa sang. "Rosie'll bash in your head, and you won't ever get up *again*!"

I shivered, and this time it had nothing to do with the damp cold. Deep down, I hoped we never let her out of that stall again.

OTHER BOOKS BY LINDSEY POGUE

THE ENDING SERIES

The Ending Beginnings: Omnibus Edition

After The Ending

Into The Fire

Out Of The Ashes

Before The Dawn

World Before: A Collection of Stories

NOVELS BY LINDSEY POGUE

A SARATOGA FALLS LOVE STORY

Whatever It Takes

Nothing But Trouble

Told You So

FORGOTTEN LANDS

Dust And Shadow

Borne of Sand and Scorn

Wither and Ruin (TBR)

Borne of Earth and Ember (TBR)

NOVELS BY LINDSEY FAIRLEIGH

<u>ECHO TRILOGY</u>

Echo in time

Resonance

Time Anomaly

Dissonance

Ricochet Through Time

<u>KAT DUBOIS CHRONICLES</u>

Ink Witch

Outcast

Underground

Soul Eater

Judgement

Afterlife

<u>ATLANTIS LEGACY</u>

Sacrifice of the Sinners

Legacy of the Lost

ABOUT AUTHOR LINDSEY POGUE

Lindsey Pogue has always been a sucker for a good love story. She completed her first new adult manuscript in high school and has been writing tales of love and friendship, history and adventure ever since. When she's not chatting with readers, plotting her next storyline, or dreaming up new, brooding characters, Lindsey's generally wrapped in blankets watching her favorite action flicks with her own leading man. They live in the Napa Valley with their rescue cat, Beast. You can follow Lindsey's writing shenanigans on social media and online at www.lindseypogue.com.

ABOUT AUTHOR LINDSEY FAIRLEIGH

Lindsey Fairleigh lives her life with one foot in a book—as long as that book transports her to a magical world or bends the rules of science. Her novels, from post-apocalyptic to time travel and historical fantasy, always offer up a hearty dose of unreality, along with plenty of adventure and romance. When she's not working on her next novel, Lindsey spends her time trying out new recipes in the kitchen, walking through the woods, or planning her future farm. She lives in the Pacific Northwest with her two rather confused cats. You can find out more at www.lindseyfairleigh.com.

33401476R00281

Made in the USA
Middletown, DE
15 January 2019